FIC
GILES

Miss Willie

Miss Willie

Janice Holt Giles

Foreword by Wade Hall

THE UNIVERSITY PRESS OF KENTUCKY

Published in 1994 by The University Press of Kentucky
Foreword copyright © 1994 by The University Press of Kentucky

Scholarly publisher for the Commonwealth,
serving Bellarmine College, Berea College, Centre
College of Kentucky, Eastern Kentucky University,
The Filson Club, Georgetown College, Kentucky
Historical Society, Kentucky State University,
Morehead State University, Murray State University,
Northern Kentucky University, Transylvania University,
University of Kentucky, University of Louisville,
and Western Kentucky University.

Editorial and Sales Offices: Lexington, Kentucky 40508-4008

Library of Congress Cataloging-in-Publication Data

Giles, Janice Holt.
  Miss Willie / Janice Holt Giles ; with a foreword by Wade Hall.
    p. cm.
  ISBN 0-8131-1885-9 —ISBN 0-8131-0831-4 (pbk.)
  1. Women teachers—Kentucky—Fiction. 2. Mountain life—Kentucky—
Fiction. I. Title.
PS3513.I4628M5 1994
813'.54—dc20   94-12223

This book is printed on acid-free recycled paper meeting
the requirements of the American National Standard
for Permanence of Paper for Printed Library Materials.
⊗ ⊛

To
my mother, Lucy M. Holt,
and to the memory of
my father, John A. Holt,
who spent their lives together
in the schoolroom

Acknowledgment

Once again I want, publicly, to acknowl-
edge the help of my husband, Henry E.
Giles. I have not written anything, and I
doubt if I ever shall, in which he does not
have his part. In its deepest meaning, he is
a faithful collaborator.

FOREWORD

KENTUCKY authors have written two of the most engrossing and inspiring books about teachers in American literature. Jesse Stuart's *The Thread That Runs So True* (1949) is an autobiographical novel about the trials and triumphs of a male teacher in Eastern Kentucky in the 1920s and 1930s. Janice Holt Giles's *Miss Willie* (1951) is a fact-based story of a female teacher set in the ridge country of South Central Kentucky shortly after World War II. Both Stuart and Giles were describing a profession they greatly admired and a part of the state they knew intimately. Stuart was a native of Greenup County, the setting for most of his fiction and nonfiction, and for many years served as a teacher and a school administrator. Arkansas native Giles was working in Louisville during the war when, on a bus near Bowling Green, she met Henry Giles, a soldier who became her husband. After the war the couple moved to Adair County, which Mrs. Giles made the setting for most of her books. Indeed, two of the characters in *Miss Willie*, Hod and Mary Pierce, are modeled on Janice Holt and Henry Giles. Unlike Stuart, however, Giles was never a classroom teacher, although in *Miss Willie* she pays tribute to her mother, who taught for forty years in the public schools of Arkansas and Oklahoma.

The story is focused on Miss Willie Payne, a second grade teacher in El Paso, Texas, who is bored with her life and her career. As a young woman she had wanted to become a missionary and go to China, but family responsibilities killed that dream. After more than twenty years as a teacher, she feels unfulfilled. "Something's missing," she confides to herself. "I get up in the morning moody and depressed, and I teach all day feeling as if I were getting nowhere and accomplishing nothing." Her life is a monotonous treadmill.

Her niece Mary, whom she reared after her parents died, is also a teacher, but she has recently left her position to marry Hod Pierce, whose home is in a remote community in rural Kentucky called Piney Ridge. Mary writes her aunt joyful letters about her new life. One day Miss Willie receives a letter that awakens her missionary impulses: "Do you remember what the Macedonians wrote to Paul? 'Come over into Macedonia and help us.' Miss Willie, come over to Piney Ridge and help us!" The school she would take over, Mary tells her, is a one-teacher, one-room log building with eight grades and forty students ranging in age from six to sixteen. The school term runs seven months, from July to January. It is a desperately poor community, with people living "only a little above the margin of necessity." Tobacco is their main cash crop, and even that provides but a meager income. Most families have a cow, a few chickens, and a small garden and live in a hovel with a leaky roof and a sagging floor. "They make out, and that's about the best you can say for the way folks live on the ridge," Mary summarizes.

It's a challenge that seems to Miss Willie like an answer to prayer. The forty-five-year-old spinster takes stock of herself: "I am a thin, dried-up old-maid schoolteacher. I am brittle and barren and plain. But they need me!" She has heard the Macedonian call and takes the leap of faith that will transform her life. She will go to what seems like a foreign mission field in the wilds of Kentucky and, like a true missionary, convert the natives to her ways of life. She may not be able to save the world, but she can at least save a little Kentucky corner of it. That will be her mission—and her problem—because eventually she will learn from these backward Kentuckians more about life and love than she teaches.

When Miss Willie arrives at Piney Ridge to take over the Big Springs School, she is overwhelmed by the natural beauty of the landscape. She is also delighted to be moving near her beloved niece, now a woman who has found happiness as a wife and mother-to-be. But Miss Willie soon discovers that there are many serpents in this beautiful new Eden. The people appear to be poorer and more ignorant, backward, and complacent than Mary had described. Nevertheless, with the zeal of generations of Presbyterian true believers in her blood, she accepts the challenge gladly. "Nothing is hopeless," she asserts, and rolls up her sleeves to become carpenter and janitor as well as teacher at Big Springs.

Alas, Miss Willie begins her tenure on the wrong foot when she attempts to establish her authority by holding classes the first day of school and seating her scholars by her rules rather than by local custom. Her autocratic style begins to seem strange and overbearing to the community, but most of the people accept her "quare" ways, even when she goes so far as to begin a community-wide campaign "to wake these people up." Her improvement program is designed to get the people to eat less fried food, become more sanitation conscious, and be more aggressive about reducing ignorance and disease. Furthermore, she announces, something must be done to modernize the open spring that provides drinking water for the school.

Soon she has gained a reputation as a well intentioned busybody with advice for everyone. In the health class she starts for women, she instructs them in how to rid their children of itch and head lice and how to improve their living conditions generally. Indeed, Miss Willie's reform movement has vast implications for the ridge people and their habits and traditions. The women listen respectfully, eat her refreshments approvingly, and go home nodding affirmatively. And nothing happens: "But the children's lunch buckets continued to hold cold biscuits and fat meat, the children continued to come to school with the itch, with colds, and even with whooping cough." Even the reformer herself has caught the seven-year itch and must undergo an embarrassing treatment of sulphur and lard. After one especially difficult day that included encounters with a wild man and a wild animal, she is on the verge of despair: "This is the ridge for you! Start the day with a mad man, and end it with a polecat!"

But Miss Willie is hardly a quitter. She is a tough old bird for whom endurance is a guiding light. For two years she teaches her motley pupils, gradually learning to accept the local customs that cannot be—or need not be—changed. She endures an outbreak of typhoid fever at her school, several violent deaths, including an axe-murder, as well as numerous practical jokes calculated to embarrass and ridicule her.

Except for one boy, Miss Willie is generally respected or at least tolerated by everyone in the school and the community. The exception is thirteen-year-old Rufe Pierce, "the golden boy" to whom she is strangely attracted, despite his active dislike for her. Rufe roams the woods with his dog, digs ginseng, and believes that only he can hear the birds sing. He also takes every opportunity to disobey and humiliate Miss Willie, whom he calls "that mealy-mouthed, pussyfooted, dried-up old maid!" Their relationship reaches a critical point after she becomes romantically involved with his father, a middle-aged widower with four children. The climax occurs when the teacher becomes the student and vice versa. Rufe finally tells Miss Willie frankly why he despises her so much. It is, he says, her superior, patronizing attitude and her refusal to recognize "the mess of living" that exists everywhere, not just in Piney Ridge, Kentucky. Miss Willie has been agonizing for two years about her "calling" to Piney Ridge. Now her epiphany is made possible by the very boy who has been her nemesis. Through the agency of this bad boy with the golden hair, she has learned that this poor and backward community has a thing or two to teach her. In fact, the people she has come to save have saved *her*. Moreover, they have given her a husband, a family, and a new life. The barren spinster from Texas has become a wife with children in her new Kentucky home.

Indeed, Giles portrays Piney Ridge as a community rich in history and tradition. There are citizens slovenly enough to sit at the same table with Erskine Caldwell's poor white trash in rural Georgia, but there are also hardworking, intelligent people whose lives are filled with beauty and joy. There is the handsome, swaggering moonshiner who dies in a shoot-out with the revenuers, but there is also the well mannered, decent Wells Pierce, who woos and wins the teacher from Texas. In fact, he helps her to learn and finally accept the folkways of her new home. It is a way of life in which even the religious services are foreign to her, as she discovers when she attends an all-day meeting at Bear Hollow Chapel and hears the whiny, nasal shaped-note singing for the first time. She learns, however, that this community has been around much longer than she has. She learns that if she is to be a part of it, she must respect its ceremonies and customs—from possum-hunting to moonshining to tent revivals and river baptizings. Even with reservations, she must fit somehow into this male-dominated society, where women wear themselves out with childbearing and child rearing, water toting, food growing and cooking, housecleaning, and husband tending.

Indeed, in *Miss Willie* Mrs. Giles has documented the mid-twentieth century life of an isolated Kentucky community better than a library of government statistics or sociological surveys. She has rendered its hill dialect accurately and sensibly. She has described in lyrical language the landscape in its seasonal variety, and she has set the people in their proper relationship to the natural world. The birth of Mary Pierce's baby elicits this hallelujah to life: "The rhythm of the earth turning around the sun, of corn greening and then ripening, of dayspring and nightfall, and of a woman's time come in the night. It was a rhythm of pain and ecstasy, mingled and blended until there was no knowing the beginning or the end of either. It was a rhythm that was timeless and spaceless—the rhythm of creation."

Miss Willie is ultimately Janice Holt Giles's love song to the land of her husband and his people, a people who, despite their sometimes backward ways, know how to live vital, fulfilled lives. It is a novel of optimism and hope and inspiration, a story that says life will be worthwhile for people who work hard and love each other and the land that sustains them. Mrs. Giles learned the ways of her husband's country like a native. She observed them with the objectivity and freshness of a newcomer. And she recorded them with the sensitivity of a talented writer. *Miss Willie*, the second novel in the author's Piney Ridge trilogy that included *The Enduring Hills* (1950) and *Tara's Healing* (1952), is a reminder of the remarkable ability of Janice Holt Giles to bring a world to life and populate it with believable people we can care about.

WADE HALL

PREFACE
TO THE SECOND EDITION

In 1948, my mother, Lucy McGraw Holt, had to retire from forty years of teaching. This was compulsory retirement. She could easily have taught another ten years and taught well. But in Arkansas all teachers had to retire at 65 and no exceptions could be made.

My mother chose not to do substitute teaching. She decided instead to indulge her love of travel, confined all those summers to brief trips. She had the maximum teacher's retirement pension, a small private income from some rent property, and she was quite independent financially.

In September of that year she came to spend a few months with me before going to spend Christmas with her brother in Florida. We lived in Louisville, Kentucky, where I was secretarial-assistant to the Dean of the Louisville Presbyterian Seminary and where my husband, Henry Giles, worked at International Harvester.

I had written one book, *The Enduring Hills*, at night after my day in the office. It seemed certain of publication although there was no firm contract yet. With my mother visiting and taking over most of the housework for me, I began another book, again writing at night.

Perhaps the fact that my mother was present, that I saw her daily, studied her, thought what a good teacher she had been all those years, gave me the idea of writing a book about a good teacher, much younger than my mother, but experienced and tired of city teaching.

I thought of what a really good teacher could do in one of these foothill Appalachian one-room schools, so I had Miss Willie invited by her niece to "come over into Macedonia" and help out on the ridge about which I had written in *The Enduring Hills*.

I used several of the same characters as those in *The Enduring Hills,* Mary Hogan, Hod Pierce and the Pierce family clan. But this book was much more inventive, based on no facts given me of ridge life. It was all mine and entirely fictionalized. My mother's character formed the basis for the good teacher Miss Willie, but in no other way was she like my mother. And none of the experiences that happened to Miss Willie ever happened to my mother.

The book went easily and smoothly and it was about two-thirds finished when my mother left to spend the rest of the winter in Florida, about mid-December. Shortly afterward I had a telegram saying that *The Enduring Hills* was definitely accepted for publication and that a contract was on the way.

I laid *Miss Willie* aside. We had been planning and hoping to buy a small farm in Adair County, Kentucky, where my husband grew up. The $500 advance which came with the contract, plus most of our savings, was enough to pay cash for the little rocky, woodsy forty-acre farm we wanted (we paid $1100.00 for it!). In May of 1949 we made the move, giving up our jobs and certain income.

Miss Willie was finished that summer "sort of inbetweenst" as one of my neighbors said, for there was much work to be done on that little farm. Henry told me about a strange and oddly sweet experience of his own, that when he was a small boy, that until he was about eleven years old in fact, he believed he could hear things nobody else could hear. He could hear the birds singing. Never in his life had he heard anybody, not his father, his mother, any of his family or neighbors, mention the birds singing. He never mentioned it because he thought he was perhaps an "oddling."

The only change I made in *Miss Willie,* therefore, was to create the new character, Rufus, the little boy who heard the birds singing. He gave me a natural conflict because I made Miss Willie young enough to marry. She married the boy's father, and the boy did not like her. The conflict was beautifully resolved at the end of the book when quite casually one evening Miss Willie mentioned the sweet song of the wood thrush and the boy realized he was not an "oddling" at all.

This is probably the most genuinely creative book I ever wrote and certainly I was happier writing it than with any other book. Not a word had to be rewritten. It was accepted immediately. It was a Doubleday Book Club selection and for many years it was used as supplemental reading in teacher training courses on "The School and the Community."

The book is dedicated to my mother and my father. Not until she read the published book did my mother know that Miss Willie was at least partly herself.

I am glad that Houghton Mifflin is reissuing the book. I hope it has success again and that its emphasis upon good teaching, upon love, upon the open heart, is as timeless as ever.

JANICE HOLT GILES

Spout Springs
Knifley, Kentucky
June 18, 1970

Miss Willie

CHAPTER

❧ 1 ❧

THE BOY AND THE DOG FOLLOWED A COW PATH through the woods, the boy's eyes taking in the slick, shiny green of gum and sassafras bushes, the red spray of sumac, the heavy veins of dogwood seedlings. Morning dew hung sparkly and brilliant on every leaf and blade, showering a small rain across the path where the dog brushed against the bushes.

When the path cleared the woods and penciled off through a pasture, the boy and the dog angled on down the ridge. "Ain't no use lookin' fer sang hereabouts," the boy said. "Wait'll we git down in the holler."

The north face of the ridge swelled gently, easily, shouldering itself toward the deep ravine which gashed it midway. Suddenly the easy slope sheered off sharply and plunged downward. Steep and abrupt it fell straight down into the hollow, its sides patched with thick rugs of moss under the trees. The boy dug in his heels and slid from one bed of moss to another, sinking his feet deep in the soft mat, letting its plush brake him against the downhill pull. The dog scampered ahead, waiting in the easy places.

The floor of the hollow was narrow, boxing in a shallow stream which raced rapidly between its walls. White water foamed around the rocks and chattered a noisy song. The boy and the dog drank deeply and then followed the stream up the hollow, branching off into a deeper ravine on the right. Here the floor widened, and was bedded with a heavy leaf mold through which a rank growth of small sprouts and plants pushed themselves.

"Now, this is it," the boy said. "Here's where the sang grows best. I takened notice o' this place last year."

Across a log a bed of ginseng lay dark and green, slender stems spiking proudly upward, pronging at the top to bear the soft, ivy-green leaves. "All of 'em three prongs," the boy exulted. "No! There's one of 'em's a four-prong un. See that there big un next the log, Jupe! Oh, hit's untellin' whenever we've found a four-prong un!"

Jupiter sniffed the log. "You, Jupe!" the boy yelled and the dog fled, tail drooped between his legs.

Gently the boy dug the plants from their beds, and breaking off the tops, he slid the roots into his overalls pockets. "Hit won't take many like these to weigh heavy," he said. "We'll have us three-four ounces 'fore you know it. Bet hit'll bring anyways three-four dollars."

When they had cleaned that bed, he and the dog wandered on, always looking for the dark-veined sang, whose roots, when dried, were good medicine for so many ailments, and which brought sixty cents an ounce when sold to the country store-keeper at the Gap. The boy's pockets filled until they bulged, and the dark hollows grew bright with the noon-riding sun. The dog no longer raced ahead. He lay in the shade waiting, his tongue lolling and his sides heaving. The boy's shirt turned dark with sweat. He squinted up into the sun. "Reckon hit's about time to go home," he said, and he led the dog up the steep flank of the ridge.

They came out of the hollow into a clearing in a grove of beeches. Abruptly the boy stopped. He stood rigid and his hand reached out to hold his dog to heel. The noon sun shafted white columns through the interstices of the trees and turned the boy and the dog into tawny, golden statues.

The boy lifted his head, turned it a little to one side, and listened. An April thrush, up near the sun, was pouring out its song, and the notes fell, fountainlike, down through the trees. Note by liquid note descended, pure and clear and sweet. The song rose rapturously, mounted lyrically, ecstatically, flung sun-ward in joyous abandon. And the boy's face, lifted to the sun and the song, stilled and quivered under the wash of golden sound.

Suddenly the song broke off. The boy sighed and moved restlessly. "Hit's flew away," he said. He waited a moment more and then shook his head. "No, hit's flew away. They ain't no use o' waitin'. C'mon, Jupe."

They moved off, dwarfed by the giant overshadowing of the trees. The boy whistled a few notes and then stopped. "Cain't nobody go like that there old thrush," he told the dog, "even if they could hear him. Hit's a quare thing, but on this whole endurin' ridge ain't nobody but me hears the birds asingin' an' atalkin'. Hit appears they'd leastways be another'n, but they ain't e'er 'nother soul has ever named it."

His bare toe kicked idly at a fallen log lying across the way, and a small, scared rabbit ran for the thicket. The dog yelped sharply and bounded after the rabbit. "Git him, Jupe," yelled the boy, taking after the dog. "Git him!"

His heels flew across the ground and the hole in the seat of his overalls gleamed whitely as the sun spotted the bare skin. The bushes of the thicket shook violently as the skeltering race of dog and boy parted them.

Down in the hollow Mary Pierce stood for a moment in her back door. Hearing the yelping of the dog, she shaded her eyes against the sun to look up the side of the ridge. She caught a brief glimpse of the dog and the boy tearing across an opening in the brush. She chuckled. "Rufe and his dog have jumped another rabbit."

She turned back to the kitchen stove and stirred the big pot of beans simmering there. She lifted a spoonful and tasted. They were done. They ought to be, she thought. She'd soaked them overnight and first thing this morning had put them on to boil in the old iron kettle that had belonged to Hod's grandmother. Hod said white beans ought never to be cooked in anything but an iron kettle, and they ought to simmer slow and long over a low wood fire with a big piece of fat meat gradually melting into soft white sweetness. These beans were just right — tender, the skins peeling delicately, but not mushy. Beans, Hod said again, ought not to lose their individuality when cooked. They should remain whole, every bean apart, unto itself, but communing one

11

with the other in the rich juicy soup with its thick blobs of fat meat.

She glanced at the short ray of sunlight lying across the floor. She must hurry. When it touched that crack by the door, it would be noon and she must call the men to dinner. Quickly and lightly she stepped around the room, placing plates and silver on the table, dishing up corn and tomatoes from her own cans in the cellar, setting the white bowl of beans in the center of the table, heaping the squares of golden bread in a gay basket and covering it over with a red-checked napkin, pouring tall glasses of buttermilk from the blue pitcher, and setting it near at hand.

She stripped her apron from her and stopped for a second in front of the wash shelf as she went toward the door. She glanced quickly at her reflection in the small mirror that hung there and brushed her hair back. Then she wiped a smudge off her nose and went through the door into the back yard.

A dinner bell was mounted on a short pole at the corner of the house, and she gave its rope a swift tug. When Hod was working near the house, a call would bring him; but when he was down in the hollow, in one of the lower fields, he would listen for the bell.

It was a deep-throated bell, with a friendly, urgent tone. And the hills that rose steeply on either side of the hollow walled in the sound so that it went bounding and echoing against the rocks, chased by its own reverberations into the bottleneck which was the upper end of the hollow. Mary tugged the rope once more, and then stood passively in the warm April sun and let the shower of bronze sound drench her where she stood.

She looked down the long meadow of deep grass where the cows moved indolently, lazily switching their tails, and on beyond to the hills that had been split to form this hollow. Wishful Creek began somewhere up in those hills in a bright, bubbling spring, and followed the cleft in the ridge down to the floor of the valley.

This was Wishful Hollow, a narrow, fertile valley, stretching some three or four miles between the ridges. In the two years she had been living here, Mary Pierce had not grown weary of the soft mists that settled over the curves of the creek; or of the long stretch of meadows and fields down the valley; or of the high wall of the hills on either side. Nor had she grown tired of this house to which Hod had brought her, which had been his great-great-grandfather's homestead. The original log cabin was still the main room of the house, and the chimney which Hod's great-great-grandmother had built herself when Jeems was off to the wars still warmed the log room adequately. Hod's grandfather, Dow Pierce, had added two rooms when he lived in the cabin, and Mary and Hod had added two more. The house stood now, low and rambling, weathered by rain and sun, a monument to the hearts of a man and woman who had believed in this land.

To Mary Pierce it stood for clan continuity, for roots probing deep into the land and welding generations of Pierces to it with a passionate love for its ways. It stood for the women of the family — Amelia, Abigail, Annie, Hattie, and now Mary. For their courage and strength, and their loyalty to their men. It stood most of all for her own immortality. Such a family was as ongoing as the surge of the sea, as unending as time, as deathless as truth. And Mary, rooted in that past rich with strength, felt free of mortality in a future that would inherit the past.

Here, now, she was caught in that strong-flowing stream of life. For her own child would soon be born. The sixth generation Pierce on Piney Ridge. She laughed aloud and she felt full of never-ending life. She was glad her child was to be born in this house, and she was glad his feet would tread the land that belonged to him.

Mary was a tall woman, a little past first youth. She was high-bosomed and long-legged, with narrow hips and broad shoulders. There was an easy grace about her which Hod had always compared to that of a young colt. There was the same hint of awkwardness in her movements, overlaid with a swift co-ordination. Her brown hair had the clean, shiny look of a chestnut colt's satin coat, and she had a way of flinging up her head in alarm occasionally when she was startled. Her skin was already tanned by the spring sun, and her eyes crinkled like brown water in the

13

deep pools of their sockets. Her mouth was wide and full — sweet and big and compelling — and her chin underlaid it with a square, firm foundation. Mary had a good face, and a fine figure. In a quiet way she knew these things. There was no vanity in her, but there was a proud sense of worth.

Hod and Wells were turning in the back lot now. Hod was tall and broad-shouldered, fair as a Norseman, with heavy straw-colored hair rumpled over his head. Even from here she could see that his face was ruddy from his work in the sun, and his blue jeans hung lankly on his thin hips. As she watched his slow plunging walk, she felt the bubbling of excitement that seeing him at a distance always brought to her throat, and she laughed as she remembered the ways in which he was tender and good and sweet. She yearned toward him in love, and she felt her throat tighten as she watched him moving toward her.

Oh, her friends had said when she married this Kentucky farmer, what does Mary Hogan see in him! How can she give up the lovely life she has worked so hard for . . . her beautiful apartment, her position in the schools, her music, all her friends! They haven't a thing in common. What can she find in him!

They wouldn't know, of course. And you couldn't tell them. Their scale of values didn't go far enough. They only knew that two and two make four. They would never understand that sometimes it makes six or ten or twenty. No. They wouldn't know, and you could never tell them of the quick, flashing togetherness that made speech unnecessary between them . . . the startling unity of their minds . . . the intimate knowledge, shared across a room, across a gathering of people, so perfect that like darting, sunlit sails their minds had met and gone over the horizon together. No. That was something one learned for oneself, and only in company with the other half of that perfect whole.

You couldn't tell them of the poignant, puissant tenderness in this man. Of the quality of gentleness and fineness that was almost maternal in its shy and awkward solicitousness. It threw a veil of safety around one — this knowledge of being so greatly loved, so deeply cared for.

You couldn't tell them, either, about the naïve idealism that

14

had made it impossible for him to live in the city. He was forever being hurt, forever being crucified by the harshness and
bitterness of people massed together. That horrible, anonymous
massing that drained people of their personalities, their personal
dignity, and even of their humanity. He had valued himself too
highly to allow himself to sink into that anonymity.

She drew a deep breath and gave thanks that this man was
hers. Thanks for their possession of each other, and for the child
that was on its way.

Hod's cousin, Little Wells, who was helping him fence the
lower field today, looked short and stocky as he strode along by
him. He was a solid, squatty man, swarthy of skin. He was older
than Hod by some ten or twelve years, but they had always been
good friends. Wells was a merry person, quick to laugh, and with
a ready quip on his lips. He had deep-set, twinkling eyes which
wrinkled at the corners. Mary had come to like him and to trust
him. "Hi, Wells," she called and flung up an arm in greeting.

"Howdy, Mary," he answered. "Got anything a couple o' starv-
ing men kin fill up on?"

"Got plenty," she said, laughing. "It's on the table. Wash up,
now, and hurry."

"See," Hod said, nudging Wells, "what'd I tell you? Just got me
a plumb dominatin' woman. Always orderin' you around! Never
any peace!"

Wells dipped his head in the big tub of water sitting on the
wash bench by the stoop. He snorted and blew water at Hod.
"I'll trade fer her e'er day you say. I could use me a smart
woman."

Hod handed him the towel and ducked his own head. Wells
flicked him on the back of the neck. "He's agittin' too big fer his
britches these days. Must be on account he's goin' to be a papa
purty soon. Wait'll he's got seven or eight runnin' around. He
won't act so prideful then. He'll be scratchin' an' diggin' too hard
tryin' to feed 'em to take much pride in 'em."

"I've never heard you complaining of your four," Mary put in.

"No," Wells said, and his eyes went past Mary down the
meadow. His voice softened. "No, I ain't complainin'. They're all
I got left of Matildy."

15

He straightened up and threw the towel at Hod. "Well, let's git in there an' git them beans eat. This ain't fencin' that pasture of your'n."

Quickly they put away a sizable meal and left the bowls and platters empty. Mary kept the breadbasket filled, and the milk pitcher overflowed constantly into their glasses. When they had finished, the two men pushed their chairs back and tilted them against the wall. "That shore was good eatin', Mary," Wells said, around the toothpick in the corner of his mouth.

Mary made a mock bow. "I thought maybe Rufe would come in for dinner, I saw him and his dog up on the ridge a while ago, chasing a rabbit from the way they were going."

Wells laughed. "Him an' that dog's allus out wanderin' the woods. I don't know where he's at half the time. I'd ort to git more work outen him. He'll soon turn fourteen, but he's slippery as a eel. Out an' gone 'fore you know it."

Mary turned a little in her chair and eased her legs under the table. "I ought to get up there oftener than I do," she said, "but climbing the ridge is pretty hard for me, and it seems like I have more than I can get done here at home."

"Don't you fret none 'bout it, Mary. Rose does right well fer a sixteen-year-old, an' Abby's gittin' up big enough to he'p a right smart. Manthy's got Veeny over at the Gap, an' we make out jist fine." He poured a little more milk into his glass and drained it with a swallow.

Mary leaned her elbows on the table and cushioned her chin in her palms. "How'd the trustees' meeting come out, Wells?"

"Hit never come out. Whichever way you turn, we're up agin the same old thing. We need a good teacher. Big Springs ain't had a good teacher in too long a time. But we ain't got the money to pay nobody to come here an' teach. Cain't pay 'em but seven months outen the year the way it is. Who's gonna come way back here in the hills an' teach a ridge school fer seven months' pay? Nobody in their right mind, I kin tell you that!"

"It's a pity," Mary said. "These children need a good school the worst in the world. If the Skipper wasn't on the way, I'd be tempted to try it myself."

Wells sighed. "I hate fer my young'uns to grow up like I done,

16

no more learnin' than I got. Seems like a man owes it to his kids to give 'em a better chancet than he got. But I swear back here in these hills might as well be the other side the waters. Looks like the best we kin do is that Owens boy agin. My kids says he don't do much more'n keep books, an' e'er one o' the oldest ones kin outsmart him."

"What does Lem say about it?" Hod asked.

Lem was Hod's uncle who lived down on the pike. He was another of the school trustees.

"Oh, he hates it bad as anybody. But he ain't got no more idee what to do than the rest of us. Lem's been puttin' in his share an' more on the teacher's pay fer a right smart while. Hit ain't fair fer him to do no more. You've give all you kin, an' several others as well. But ifen you cain't raise but so much, that's all they is to it. We'll jist have to make out."

Mary drummed the table with her fingers. "I wish . . ." she said, and stopped. She flicked a crumb to the floor with her thumb. The men waited.

"You wish what?" Hod prompted.

"Oh, nothing." She rubbed at a spot on the tablecloth. "Yes, it was. I was wishing Miss Willie would come out here and teach the school!"

Hod stared at her. "You mean give up her good job teachin' in El Paso and come out here to *this* school?"

"Oh, it was just an idea."

"Who's Miss Willie?" Wells wanted to know.

Mary pushed her chair back from the table and stood up. "She's my aunt. The one I lived with after my father and mother died. She teaches in El Paso. But it wouldn't be fair . . ." she stacked the plates and folded the napkins. "Only I was just remembering. Hod, you know Grandfather was a preacher, and Miss Willie always wanted to be a missionary. Even when she was a little girl she wanted to be a missionary, and she always planned to go to China. Then just when she finished college and was about ready to go before the Board of Missions, Grandfather died, and Miss Willie had to take care of Grandmother. Now that Grandmother's gone, Miss Willie is free, of course, but it's too late for her to be a missionary. She must be in her middle forties by now."

17

"Was you thinkin' she might be interested in comin' here to the ridge?" Wells asked.

"I was just wishing she would, Wells. She's a wonderful teacher. My goodness, what she would do for those children!"

"She's used to gittin' good pay, I reckon."

"Yes. She makes a good salary, as far as teachers' salaries go. But she has a little income of her own besides. She doesn't have to depend on her salary entirely. Grandfather left some land and there's a big oil boom out in West Texas just now, so she gets a pretty good income from her oil leases. You know, Hod," and Mary's voice quivered with excitement, "the more I think about it, the more I think maybe we've got something here. This is just the sort of thing that might appeal to Miss Willie. You know how interested she's been in this country ever since we came down here. . . . Maybe she'd like a change from city teaching. Maybe she would . . ."

"Maybe she'd what?" he asked.

"Maybe she'd like to do a little missionary work on the ridge."

The three were quiet for a moment, thinking it over. "What do you think, Wells?" Hod wanted to know.

"Boy, ifen she'd come," Wells said, "I'd say we'd be beholden forever to her. She'd be doin' us a favor we couldn't never repay!" His voice was warm and thick with feeling. "Why, jist me by myself would welcome her an' uphold her on account o' my own kids. An' they's half a dozen others'd feel the same way!"

"Why don't you write her then, Mary?"

"Just like that? Just write her and ask her to come teach the Big Springs school? Doesn't someone have to act officially?"

"Well, I'm actin' officially," Wells snorted indignantly. "What you reckon I'm a trustee fer? Go ahead an' write her! I'll guarantee the rest'll back her!"

CHAPTER

❧ 2 ❧

I T WAS FIFTEEN MINUTES YET before the second grade would be dismissed, and the children were restless in the sticky, unseasonable heat of the April afternoon. That was the worst of this crowded condition. The afternoon group were not at their best, especially as the spring came on and the days grew hot and long. Miss Willie sighed and pushed her glasses up on her nose. It was a thin nose, and her glasses were constantly slipping down. The habit of pushing them back in place was so old as to be automatic, and it had become a part of Miss Willie's personality. Hundreds of second-grade children would remember this mannerism. They would remember too the clear, lustrous blue of her eyes behind the glasses; the slight slender figure that stood so uncompromisingly erect; the heavy coil of fine, soft hair which had never been cut and which lay in a thick figure of eight atop her head; the wide, generous mouth which could smile so approvingly.

Thirty small heads were bent over drawings on the two long tables by the wall. Thirty little bodies wiggled and squirmed. It was a sign of fatigue that Miss Willie had set them to an aimless task for the last thirty minutes of the day. Weakly she had set out fresh paper and allowed Marie and Salvador to get out the colors. She had told them to draw what they pleased . . . anything at all. It was sheer busy work and Miss Willie despised busy work. She was convinced that only a poor teacher ever resorted to it. But this had been a long day . . . and the April heat had been close.

She glanced around the familiar room. At the gray-green walls and the sprigged yellow curtains. At her low rocker near the front of the room and the hooked rug before it. At the border of drawings pinned along one side of the room, and the small chairs and tables before the windows. She felt an objective distaste for the plants growing in pots on the window sills. They seemed suddenly to be silly substitutes for gardens and lawns and widestretching spaces. She had always taken pride in the comfortable,

19

homelike atmosphere of her schoolroom, believing ardently that for small children, venturing so insecurely into the wider world, the schoolroom should offer a measure of the feeling of home. So she had brought her little rocker and her hooked rug and her pots and green plants to school to give it a warmer and a snugger look, to draw in the horizons of the new world to a safer, more enfolding circle. She brought her knitting also, and many times when she sat in her little rocker, knitting, she watched a feeling of contentment, security, safeness, spread over the room, the purring, satisfied contentment of a child who can sprawl happily over his work because his mother sits nearby with her sewing. She believed all this was good. Where, then, had her satisfaction in it gone?

She straightened her thin, bony shoulders and rubbed the place in the small of her back that ached so dully and so persistently. Somehow, somewhere along the twenty years she had been teaching in this room the spring had gone loose in her. Had come unwound. There was a bitter taste in her mouth, as if she had breathed too much chalk dust. She ran her tongue over her dry lips and swallowed. Soon, now, the bell would ring, and these thirty restless small bodies would be released.

Out of the corner of her eye she noticed that Billy Norton was edging over near Donny Brown. She ought to nip that in the bud right now. Donny must have a crayon Billy wanted. If she didn't stop him, there would be trouble. But she didn't move. Maybe the bell would save Donny's crayon.

But it didn't. And in one fleeting second she saw Billy snatch quickly, saw Donny grab futilely, and then there was a wail as Billy made off with the crayon, scuttling crabwise down the room. "He got my color, Miss Willie!" Donny cried, waving his hand wildly at Billy. "He got my purple color. It's my color, and I was making a purple tree. I just laid it down a minute and he grabbed it!"

Miss Willie pushed her glasses up her nose. "Billy, give Donny his purple crayon," she said sternly. "You know you mustn't take another person's things."

Billy was sullen. "It's not his color! The colors don't belong to anybody. You said so yourself. You said they belong to the school

20

and we could all use 'em. I can have any color I want!" His lower lip stuck out ominously.

"Donny was using the purple crayon, and while he was using it, it belonged to him, Billy. Give it back to him immediately." Miss Willie started toward the table. The rest of the children had stopped and were watching warily.

Billy looked at the crayon in his hand and then looked at Miss Willie moving relentlessly toward him. He clutched the crayon tightly for a moment, and then, his defiance melting before the inevitable approach of authority, he flung the offending crayon blindly at Donny and collapsed weeping in his chair. "I wanted to make a purple tree too," he sobbed. "I like purple trees best too, and Donny gets the purple color every time. He always makes purple trees, and you always let him. You like Donny best!" The small voice was accusing.

Something quivered inside Miss Willie and came achingly alive. She reacted always to this inconsolable yearning of all small children. This uncertain need for love and affection. This outreaching, hungering longing for the security of adult approbation. "I don't like Donny best," she said, reaching for Billy's bent head. "I like all of you best. You and Donny and all the others. All of you. I couldn't get along without any of you. But see what happens when you quarrel? You are unhappy, Donny is unhappy, and all of us are unhappy. It hurts every one of us. Now, hush, and pick up the crayon and give it back to Donny. He didn't know you wanted to draw a purple tree. Perhaps if you had told him he would have been glad to give you the purple color."

Billy sniffed and rubbed the back of his hand across the end of his nose. He caught his breath in a sob and walked across the room to pick up the crayon. At the sight of the envied purple color his grief mounted in him again and his eyes filled and overflowed. His lips puckered and trembled. But he held out the crayon to Donny. "Here," he said, bluntly.

Donny took the crayon and cut his eyes at Miss Willie. And then he thrust it back at Billy. "You can have it," he said, "I'll make me a pink tree."

The bell rang and Miss Willie let a limp and thankful sigh escape her. "May Billy have the purple crayon at drawing time tomorrow, Donny?" she asked.

"Oh, sure," Donny said nonchalantly, sticking his hands in his pockets. "If he wants to make a tree like mine, I'll help him."

"Well, we'll see. Maybe he'd rather make his own kind of tree. Pick up the papers and put the colors away now. You can finish the drawings tomorrow." She guessed weakly that there would be a drawing time the rest of the spring.

The second grade swarmed to the cupboards with their unfinished drawings and put the crayons neatly away in their boxes. And then they hovered briefly around Miss Willie.

"Good-by, Miss Willie."

"Good-by, Marie. Good-by, Sanchez. Good-by, Katherine. Don't forget to bring your kitten tomorrow so we can see her. Good-by, Donny. It was nice of you to give Billy the purple color."

Beaming, Donny ducked his head. "Aw, I didn't want to make another old purple tree, anyhow. He can have it every day if he wants it."

Miss Willie laughed. "Well, it was nice of you anyhow."

She was setting the room to rights when her friend Louise Wright came to the door. "Come on in, Louise," she said. "How was your day?"

Louise taught the third grade. She was a tall, rangy woman with big shoulders and broad hips. Her voice was deep and heavy like a man's. She crossed the room slowly and stood before the windows, playing with the pull on one of the shades. "Just like every other day this year. I'm a little tireder than usual. Guess it's the heat."

Miss Willie opened the top drawer of her desk and dumped an assortment of odds and ends, pencils, erasers, paper clips, and two or three broken crayons, inside. She closed the drawer with an unnecessarily hard shove. "I don't know what's wrong with me, but all at once I am horribly bored with everything . . . El Paso, my home, the children, school, everything. I get up in the morning moody and depressed, and I teach all day feeling as if I were getting nowhere and accomplishing nothing."

Louise shrugged her shoulders. "Oh, all teachers have that feeling occasionally. Along toward the end of the year, mostly. It wears off with vacation, and you come back at the beginning of the year ready to go again."

"Yes, I know. I've had it before . . . but only for brief periods of time. I always had down underneath a conviction that what I was doing was important, and as long as I felt that, I knew my lethargy was only physical and that a rest or a change of scenery for a few months would take care of it. This is different. Ever since Mamma died . . . no, since before then, since Mary left, I've been restless. And the last three or four years I've had to take myself in hand to keep from being indifferent about things."

"Partly your age, don't you think?" Louise suggested.

"Yes, partly," Miss Willie admitted. "I do get tired quicker than I used to. But that's just rationalizing. Something's missing. Something vital has gone."

Louise laughed her strong, deep laugh. "You need somebody to take care of, Willie. These children here don't really need you, and you know it. Any good teacher can do what you're doing here. You can't get over having to be a missionary. That's all that's wrong with you. Me, I'm very glad not to be concerned about anyone but myself. It suits me just fine not to be needed."

Miss Willie pinned her hat to the bun coiled on top of her head. She smiled at her friend in the mirror. Then she let her arms fall limply and stood looking out the window. The days ahead of her. The long days stretching ahead. A woman alone is so terribly alone, she thought. However she might fill these days of hers she could never quite get them full. Always there was a last thin edge of emptiness. She shrugged. "Come go home with me for dinner."

Louise shook her head. "Term paper to do on that course I'm taking. I'll drive you home, though, if you like."

"No," Miss Willie answered, gathering her purse and a couple of books off the desk. "No. I like to walk. I'll go on."

She walked down the street slowly, a slender little figure bordering on thinness. Usually she walked with short, rapid steps . . . purposeful steps that knew exactly where they were going. But today she moved slowly. The street was lined with

23

thick-walled adobe houses. Miss Willie liked the adobe houses. They sat so solidly against the ground, so thick and squatty, looking as if they had grown up out of the ground itself. There was no meeting place between them and the earth. They seemed all of a part with it.

The sky was a brilliant blue bowl cupped over the earth, and its brilliance hit hard against the white and cream houses. Miss Willie squinted in its glare. The heat bit down between her shoulders, and she felt a trickle of perspiration run tantalizingly down her back. A heavy haze hung over the mountains across the river in old Mexico and turned them purple with distance. If this heat keeps on, Miss Willie thought, everything will soon be sun-baked and dry and Constancia will be wanting to go home to her people.

Constancia was her maid of all work, and each year when the summer season came on she became enamored of the greenness of her father's irrigated farm down in the valley. Miss Willie had long since resigned herself to doing without help during the summer months. She might have replaced Constancia, but in her own way the woman was faithful and when the heat had passed she turned up on the doorstep like a good dog come home again.

Her slow steps brought Miss Willie to a small adobe house set back from the street in a walled garden. The house was a smooth, creamy white, with a bright-blue door. Miss Willie smiled every time she saw her blue door. There was a saying that long ago among the Spanish-speaking people a blue door signified the presence of a marriageable daughter in the house. It amused Miss Willie to paint her door blue in spite of the legend . . . or perhaps because of it! For certainly she had been a marriageable daughter for a good many years! Inside, the house was always cool and dim, and it was with relief that she pushed open the blue door and stepped within.

There was a little entrance hall, and to the left and one step down was the living room. Its walls were whitewashed and almost empty of ornaments. Miss Willie liked their virginal cleanness. There is something about a clean, white wall, she said. Something which gives a feeling of depth and space. It takes you out of yourself into a third dimension . . . a dimension of quiet-

24

ness and calmness. A flat surface is peaceful, drawn out, refined. She always came into this room with a feeling of gratitude for its pool of quiet. With its white walls, its few pieces of fine furniture, and its absence of clutter, it was sanctuary to her.

Constancia appeared in the doorway, her head bound with a red bandanna and her hands floury. "A letter," she said, nodding toward the table under the window. "It come today."

"Yes, thank you, Constancia," Miss Willie answered, taking it up. "Oh, it's from Mary! How nice! You remember Mary, Constancia?"

"Sí," Constancia beamed. "She the nice lady come three, four years ago."

"That's the one."

"Sí. The phone all the time ring when she here. The soldier all the time call up. ¡Hijo! We do not have such an excitement in this house before!"

No, Miss Willie thought. We do not have such an excitement in this house before. Not in this house. She smiled as she remembered that time. Mary, arriving tired and worn-out from the long bus trip, but radiant with some strange inner glow. Mary, with a romantic, exciting story of a soldier she had met on the trip. Mary, warm and happy, answering the phone which seemed always to be ringing. Long distance from Camp Swift, night after night. The romance had brought fresh life to the house, and to Miss Willie. She had captured something of its radiance for herself during the brief time it had been housed beneath this roof. Such an excitement in this house!

"She marry the soldier, no?" Constancia was saying.

"She marry the soldier, sí. And now she lives on a farm in Kentucky and she doesn't teach school any more. Are you making cookies today, Constancia?"

"Sí. I make the seedcakes. They be done soon."

"Well, don't hurry supper. It's too hot. Let's wait until the sun is down and have it in the patio. I want to bathe and lie down awhile before eating."

Constancia nodded. "You read your letter. I finish the seedcakes."

Like a child wanting to save the best for the last, Miss Willie

laid aside her niece's letter until she had bathed. Then, in a cool, thin wrapper, she stretched out in her big long chair and gave herself up to reading what Mary had written. It was a thick letter. "Miss Willie, love," it began.

<h1 style="text-align:center">CHAPTER</h1>

❧ 3 ❧

M<small>ISS</small> W<small>ILLIE</small> <small>SMILED</small>. "Miss Willie, love," the letter said. "This leaves me fine and hoping you're the same. My book of ridge etiquette tells me all proper letters begin with that formula. I should never want to be improper or impolite in a letter to you.

"Truly, I *am* well, and I have never been so happy in my life. I am overwhelmed and overflowing with happiness. No one ever told me that I'd literally walk on clouds during this whole nine months! I needn't tell you that we can hardly wait till fall to welcome the young man.

"Our spring planting is going on apace. Hod has been fencing a new field which he intends to put in corn this year. The tobacco beds are exquisitely beautiful just now. The plants are a pale, delicate green like mint ice cream. Oh, you really should see a tobacco bed when the plants are only a few inches high! They look as if they had been dipped in moonlight!

"And now, Miss Willie, I come to the point of this letter. Do you remember what the Macedonians wrote to Paul? 'Come over into Macedonia, and help us.'

"Miss Willie, come over to Piney Ridge and help us! There is a little school here . . . the only one for miles around. There are about forty children enrolled, and they range in age from six to sixteen, and from the first grade through the eighth. The school term is only seven months long. It can't begin until July because the children are needed in the fields in the spring and early summer, and it closes in January because the weather gets so bad that the roads can't be traveled later than that.

"The children attend very irregularly, and I suppose it's very rare that any one child gets as much as a full five months' schooling. Almost any excuse is good enough for them to stay at home,

26

or for their parents to keep them out.

"I don't know what the physical facilities are, for I haven't been inside the building. Hod tells me there are desks, of a sort, and that when he went to school, there was at least one blackboard and a map. Heat is provided by a huge wood stove, which sits in the middle of the room.

"The water comes from a big spring situated about a hundred yards up the side of a hill, from which the school gets its name . . . Big Springs School. You cannot imagine anything more primitive. And yet it *is* a school, after a fashion!

"The problem, of course, is to find teachers. The pay is meager, a little better than a hundred dollars a month, and when you think that the term is only seven months long, and when you think further of the physical limitations of the school itself, you can understand easily enough why no one wants to teach at Big Springs. In all conscience we here on the ridge cannot blame them.

"This year the trustees are up against the same old problem. Of course there are ramifications which they do not see. They believe if they had money enough to pay a good teacher, somehow, miraculously, they would have a good school. Actually they are pretty blind about the physical conditions of the school. Here on Piney Ridge what was good enough for 'Grampa' is good enough for the kids. That, generally, is the opinion of the trustees, with the possible exception of Hod's cousin, Wells Pierce. I believe he truly has a greater sense of responsibility. But at least a start would be made if we could just get a good teacher. And I cannot get it out of my mind, Miss Willie, that you are that teacher!

"First, of course, you are an excellent teacher. You would do wonders for the school. Second, the salary would not have to be a major consideration for you, although that shouldn't excuse the school from paying the most it can. But at least you would not have to depend entirely upon the tiny salary. And last, but by no means least, it would be good to have you near me. There are so very many Pierces here on the ridge! Sometimes I get mighty hungry for my own kith and kin!

"When I think of what I am asking you to do, the enormity of

27

it stuns me. You have a good position, well-paid, with the honor and prestige due you as a reward. You have a lovely little home and your life is well ordered, comfortable, and full of beautiful things. In one sense of the word you have earned the right to spend the rest of your days as easily and comfortably as possible. And here I am asking you to give it up!

"I won't minimize the hardships you would know here. You would live sixteen miles from the nearest town. There is not a musical instrument on the ridge except my piano and the various guitars and banjos scattered here and there. There are no books and there is no library. There are a few cars up and down the ridge, but by and large the principal means of travel is still a wagon and a team of mules. It's the only thing that will get through these roads. There is no electricity. We all burn kerosene lamps here. There is no plumbing, except the 'necessary' out back. Every drop of water must be drawn from a well, or dipped from a spring. There are no furnaces or central heating. In the winter you will shiver and shake until the wood stove is hot enough to warm the room. There is literally nothing here . . . except the people and the country!

"I shan't plead with you, because you must decide for yourself. I must say just one thing more. We *need* you! This is April, and the school term starts in July. Could you face it, do you think?"

Miss Willie let the letter drop into her lap. She leaned her head against the back of the chair and closed her eyes. This niece was very dear to her and almost the only family she had left. When her sister, Mary's mother, and her husband had died within a few short months of each other, Mary had been a young girl, yet in high school. She was the youngest of four children, the others already married and established in homes of their own. Miss Willie had watched her thin, tearless face at the second funeral, and had known that the girl was suffering an anguish that only the tightest hold on herself could control.

What is to become of the child, she had thought. It would be more natural for her to go with the sister than with one of the sisters-in-law. But there was a span of twelve years between the two, and Miss Willie knew that to Mary the older sister, who had been married and gone from home almost as long as she could remember, would seem like a stranger. It was in her face during those days, the fear and the dread of this arranging of her life.

Miss Willie had seen her shrinking helplessness before the situation, and had watched the frightened, lost, small-animal look grow to terror in her eyes. She could not bear it! So, suddenly, warmly, generously, she had said, "Mary, would you like to come home with me?"

Mary had flung her a startled look, and her eyes had widened darkly. She drew in her breath sharply, and bit down upon her lower lip. "For a visit, Miss Willie?" she had asked, "or to stay?"

"To stay."

Mary had curled her long legs under her and leaned her head against the back of the chair. Miss Willie remembered how dark her hair had looked against the pale blue of the chair, and how white and lustrous the skin had been drawn over the high-modeled cheekbones. She remembered, too, how nervously the child's hands had worked in her lap. She had lifted one hand and gnawed worriedly at a knuckle. "Will they let me?" she asked.

"I think they will." She had not hurried the girl. "It will be strange, dear, and it may not be easy at first. There's Grandmother to remember, and she's an invalid. But at least we shall be all women in the house together, with a more or less common point of view."

Mary had brought her eyes back from distance and fixed them upon Miss Willie. They were dry and strained, with dark circles lying shadowy underneath. Miss Willie went on. "This is a cruel thing to happen, Mary. To lose father and mother almost at once, and to be thrown helplessly into a new life. But we have no control over such things, and the only thing we can do is to pick ourselves up and go on as best we can. Your brothers, and Beth, have their own families and their own homes, and any one of them will make a place for you with them."

Mary's mouth had quivered. And Miss Willie had hastened on. "But they have small children, and their lives are busy and full . . ."

Mary had interrupted. Passionately she had cried: "I don't

want to live with any of them! I don't want to be taken in and given a home! I don't want to be a burden to anyone. I want . . ." and she had bent her head in her hands.

Miss Willie's voice had been soft and warm, then. "You want to be loved and wanted, as you have been, so tenderly and so deeply, all your life. Of course, dear. That's why I think you would be happier with Grandmother and me. We can't take your father's and your mother's place. Bitter as it is, you have to accept their going. But we *can* love you in our own way, and you *can* know that you are loved and wanted, and, even more, that you are needed. For we *do* need a young person in our house." Miss Willie had smiled wryly then. She herself was only twenty-eight, but she felt as old as time. "We're in a rut, Grandmother and I, and we're drying up. We need your youth and vitality and your fresh interests. This isn't entirely an unselfish offer, Mary."

So Mary had come to live a few brief years here in the little adobe house. She had come, and, at whatever costs to herself, had made the adjustments necessary to that house, dominated and controlled by a sick old woman. Miss Willie had ached over the quiet, poised little figure, and had loved her and protected her as much as possible from the autocratic old invalid.

She had seen to it that there were gay new clothes, gracious meals together, just the two of them, and shared hours before the corner fireplace listening to her vast collection of records, or reading, each in her own place on either side of the flickering fire. Little by little Mary had let down, and Miss Willie had watched her stretch and grow in the security of love and home again.

Near the end of the first year Miss Willie's mother had died, and then out of the blossom of Miss Willie's love for the girl had come the full fruit. She lifted the letter and looked again at the free, flowing handwriting.

The next two years with Mary had been so perfect, so beautiful, so completely happy for them both. The tight-closed bud that had been Mary the first year had opened out full and generous. The quiet, withdrawn child had bloomed quickly into a beautiful, gay, winsome girl. Miss Willie remembered — oh, so well she remembered! — those years. When the house was overflowing

30

with Mary's belongings left carelessly helter-skelter; when the record cabinet became stacked with Glenn Miller and Benny Goodman records; when the refrigerator was never full enough to satisfy the hunger of the raiding gangs of boys and girls that gathered so often; when the ring of the phone had brought Mary flying swiftly and eagerly to answer it; when Mary had become at last so rightly and so safely a normal, happy girl. Those two years had been a flawless gem to Miss Willie, to be taken out and polished and looked at again and again.

And then Mary had gone away to college . . . four long years at the university. There had been her letters, frequent and long and full of her activities. There had been her times at home, summers and during holidays. And when Mary had majored in education, Miss Willie had hoped she would teach here in the city and their life together might go on for a time. Selfishly she had hoped it, for Mary filled her heart and her days with an overflowing interest.

But that was not to be. For almost upon the heels of her graduation Mary had gone to Kentucky. They had talked of it one night. Mary had sat there, on the edge of the bed, her arm braced behind her and one foot swinging idly as she talked. "I want to be on my own, Miss Willie," she had said. "I could teach here, of course, but I should always be Miss Willie Payne's niece. I would always be following in your footsteps . . . nothing but your shadow. I want to see what I can do on my own!"

Miss Willie had felt her heart plunge in a sickening downward motion. She had wanted to plead with the girl. But what of me, Mary? she had wanted to ask. What about me? She wanted to tie the girl to her and hold her and keep her close. What of me, now? The years have been so dear . . . so short . . . so sweet. How can I go on alone, after filling myself so full of you? How can you expect me to cut myself loose from you?

But she had said nothing of that. She had cried the tears she had to shed, alone, and had said to Mary: "Of course, Mary. You must do what you think best." She had freed the girl of her own close-drawn love and let her go, unfettered, to make her own destiny. She, who had never been free, knew its glory so well.

31

So Mary had gone to Louisville, and the years had passed. There were still her letters, and always her vacation months spent with Miss Willie. Miss Willie had expected her to marry soon, but somehow the time had gone, and although there were always a few men in her life, Mary hadn't married early. She seemed, instead, to be testing, and searching, and questioning life.

And then had come the war, and the summer Mary had come home full of the soldier she had met on the bus; and at war's end had come the marriage to the soldier, and the end of Mary's teaching and the beginning of her life on Piney Ridge. Now, here was her letter.

A fine thread of excitement ran through Miss Willie . . . a fine silver thread which began deep inside her and fled in narrow, tingling chills out to her finger tips. Well . . . she thought. Well! This is April, and the school term starts in July! How wonderful!

Abruptly she rose from her chair and walked with her quick, rapid steps over to the long mirror that hung over her dressing table. She looked at herself a long time, stripping herself down to find the last small ounce of her strength. Objectively she looked at the small, slender body reflected there. At the soft, fine, mouse-colored hair piled on top of her head. At the calm, blue eyes, and thin, narrow nose. Automatically she pushed her glasses back in place, and let her hand drop slowly to her side. I am forty-five, she thought. I am a thin, dried-up, old-maid schoolteacher. I am brittle and barren and plain. But they need me!

The fine silver thread spread to her legs and her toes. They need me! She looked around at her lovely room . . . at the wide, soft bed, and the pale walls . . . at the exquisite porcelain of her Chinese lamps . . . at the wall of books, and the glint of her mahogany radio. And in one all-rejecting moment she denied them. They need me!

She hurried to the kitchen. "Constancia," she called, "Constancia! I am going to Kentucky to live!"

CHAPTER
❦ 4 ❦

THE REST OF THE SCHOOL TERM sped by so rapidly that almost before she was aware of it her last days in El Paso were upon Miss Willie. She went about the city attending to the last details of leaving, with no regrets and with a fine excitement mounting within her.

She debated selling her house, but decided against it, renting it instead, furnished, except for the few personal things she felt she wanted about her wherever she was. These, and her books, she packed carefully and shipped ahead of her to Piney Ridge.

She was amazed at how easy the parting came. After all these years she had supposed it would wrench her to break the ties. But she was already projecting herself into the future, onto the ridge which she knew so well from Mary's letters. She looked ahead with gladness, feeling wanted again, feeling needed. The days took on a new shine, and she felt welling up in her a vigor and strength that had lessened these last years.

She had followed Mary's instructions and made application to the county school board, and had in due time received their approval. Now it was the middle of June and time for her to be going. She went by train to Louisville, and then by bus to Columbia, the county seat, where Hod and Mary did all their business.

Hod met her at the bus station. Miss Willie had met him only once before, when he and Mary had visited her in El Paso one summer, but she remembered his lean longness, his sun-browned face, his straw-covered head on which he never wore a hat. When she saw him through the bus window she thought, He'll always look like that. If he lives to be a hundred he'll just add a few wrinkles, and maybe a few pounds, but out of his eyes he'll always look the same. As if hills and hollows and cornfields and tobacco patches were mirrored in them, at home in them. Like any man who knows where he belongs and is contented there.

"Where's Mary?" she asked him.

"She decided not to come." He laughed. "You'd ought to remember that Mary doesn't like to say hello or good-by to people in public! Said she'd rather see you the first time at home. Anyway, she gets tired pretty easy these days, and ridin' over the kind of roads we've got back here in the hills is not too easy on her."

"Ah, I was forgetting," Miss Willie said. "But she's well?"

"Fit as a fiddle." And Hod loaded her bags in the back of a rickety old car. "Got to go to the bank a minute, Miss Willie, if you don't mind. I meant to get that done before the bus got in, but I was runnin' a little late."

"That's all right, Hod."

Up on the square, Miss Willie looked around at the quaint old town. Columbia was built, as are so many old Kentucky towns, around the courthouse, which housed a huge clock in its tower. In most towns built in a square, the streets enter at the corners. But here, Miss Willie smiled to notice, they entered directly in the middle of each of the four sides of the square. These sealed corners snugged the square around the courthouse, like a hen's wings covering her brood.

On the courthouse steps loafed a crowd of men, talking and spitting, and around the four sides of the square people walked, unhurried, stopping to talk with passing friends, or looking in the store windows. The town had a sleepy, lazy look in the sun-drenched afternoon; a quiet, villagey look which the slow glossing of time had given it. Miss Willie felt that life would keep step with the slow movements of time here. That it would not rush at one, and strike one down. Instead, it would hold back its keen edges and, paced by the heavy hands of the courthouse clock, lead one graciously through the years.

She sighed and let the tiredness of the trip have its way with her body. It was good to be nearing the end of her journey. She wanted to see Mary. She hoped Hod would hurry. And then she smiled at the incongruity of her thought. Hadn't it just occurred to her that hurry was a word that would have little meaning here?

Hod was back then. He crawled into the car and stepped on the starter. He nodded at the bank. "That's the bank Jesse James

34

robbed one time," he said.

Miss Willie peered at the building. "Bank of Columbia," it said across the windows. "Why, I didn't know Jesse James ever got over into Kentucky!"

"He did, though. Must have been pretty exciting too. Old Mr. Martin was killed during the robbery. The bank keeps a picture of the old fellow hanging in the front to this day."

So, Miss Willie thought. Life wouldn't strike out at one here! How ridiculous! Life strikes out wherever it pleases, and a sun-drenched, lazy little town couldn't hide one from its suddenness.

Miss Willie was prepared for the narrow, winding, dirt road out to the ridge, but even so its deeply gouged ruts and the bouncing of the car from one side to the other made her clutch her hat and hope fervently that her partial plate would stay put. Hod grinned at her and yelled, "Hold tight, Miss Willie!" She grinned back and held tight. She was glad Mary hadn't come.

Much of what she saw along the way was already familiar to her through Mary's letters. The beautiful, rolling countryside, with its green, swelling hills, wide-stretching valleys, and little, rushing creeks. It was so green, so lush, so softly lovely, after the wide, dry reaches of Texas.

She was prepared too for the evidences of poverty she saw when the road took them deep into the hills. "This is a poor country," Mary had said. "People scratch the barest sort of living out of the thin soil, and exist only a little above the margin of necessity. They depend on one crop, tobacco, for cash. Most of them have a cow, a little flock of chickens, and a garden patch. They live in two- or three-room houses, with a leaky roof over their heads, and a sagging floor under their feet. They make out, one way or another, from one year to the next, mostly on what the women put up from their gardens, and the milk and butter and eggs they sell. They make out, and that's about the best you can say for the way folks live on the ridge. Beauty, graciousness, even comfort, are things ridge folks have no conception of."

When she saw with her own eyes what Mary had written, she knew there had been no exaggeration. She saw too that it was what economists had been writing about Southern farmers for years. But to most people it remained forever academic, textbook material. She drew in her breath deeply. Well, she was going to open the textbook, now, and make it come alive. She was going to *do* something about the things she had only heretofore read about! This was what she had come for. She was needed here.

Piney Ridge was a part of a chain of hills called the Tennessee Hills. This chain laid itself ponderously across southern Kentucky, and northern and eastern Tennessee. After it entered Tennessee, it humped itself higher to become part of the Cumberland range. But here in Kentucky the hills were long, saw-toothed, and sharp, bending and folding over themselves with countless steep ravines and hollows between them. A little to the north, between this range of sharp, edgy hills and the narrow band of peculiarly conical hills known as the Knobs, lay a fertile and fruitful plateau called the Pennyroyal Plains. Actually the Tennessee Hills were geologically in that section. But there was little either of fertility or fruitfulness atop their shallow, spiny furrows.

Miss Willie knew that one of Hod's remote ancestors had settled this country on a Revolutionary War grant, and she knew also that up and down the straggling ridge backs lived innumerable Pierces, descendants of that old soldier. If she wondered why they, and Hod, continued to live, precariously and poorly, on these ledgy slopes, she said nothing. A man's reasons for calling one place home are innumerable, and they are usually voiceless, coming as they do from the heart and not the head.

The sun was banding the hills with streaks of gold, and purple shadows were creeping across the sky, when they turned off the road up the hollow, leaving the ridge humped solidly to their left. Miss Willie knew that up on that ridge was where Hod had been born and reared, but he and Mary had chosen his grandfather's old home down here in the hollow.

The car crept cautiously down a narrow trail which opened up in a heavily wooded section. Although it was little more than a path, the floor of the trail was smooth . . . smoother than the road, and it wound in and out under the tall, dark trees. The last of the sunlight was gone here, and the shadows hung ghost-like around the trees.

"What a beautiful place!" said Miss Willie. "This is like a forest straight out of Hans Christian Andersen! Gnomes and dwarfs and elves should dwell here!"

"Maybe they do," Hod chuckled. "Mary loves this piece of woods too. She comes here a lot."

"I don't wonder. Does it belong to you?"

Hod nodded. "All my land is down in the hollow and on the other ridge."

They threaded their way through the woods for about half a mile, and then the road slanted down an easy slope into the open. The next ridge had edged over into this one, folding itself gently against it, and almost at once they were in the cup of the hollow.

"You can see our house down there now," Hod said, pointing straight ahead. "This is the head of the hollow, and that's Wishful Creek there."

Miss Willie looked down the hollow and saw the weathered gray house held there in the curve of the creek, as if in a loving embrace, the hills rising steeply on either side. The supper smoke was curling gently upward, and the trees around the house bent softly toward it. Wishful Hollow! No wonder Mary loved it! Here in this beautiful valley, bounded by the hills, she must have found a whole new world. Living here must be like living in the hollow of God's hand, borne ever aloft in beauty and in loveliness. The gray-green picture blurred, and Miss Willie dabbed impatiently at her eyes. She wasn't going to meet Mary with tears in her eyes!

"We come up to the back of the house this way," Hod said. "It fronts down the hollow. There's Mary now!" And he sounded the horn.

Miss Willie felt a knot in her throat, as she strained to see Mary. Ah, there she was, waving from the back gate. She hasn't changed, thought Miss Willie. She hasn't changed at all! And then she checked herself. Why did I think she would have changed? And how did I think she would have changed? What a snob I am after all! I know better than anyone else what she has gained by marrying this man and coming to this place to live! Better than most I know how little she had before, because that's all I ever had. How convention betrays one! Of course she hasn't changed, except for the better!

When the car stopped, Miss Willie was out the door in a flash, and into Mary's arms. "Mary, Mary," she cried, straining the dear figure to her.

"Now, Miss Willie," Mary laughed — "now, Miss Willie, you're not going to cry, are you?"

"Oh, let me cry if I want to! Let me! Be still and let me look at you! Oh, you're beautiful, beautiful! Isn't she beautiful, Hod?"

"Well, I wouldn't go so far as to say that. But she's a right nice-looking woman to be as long-legged as she is."

"Oh, shut up and go get my bags! Mary, I'm here! Now it's real! I'm here! The last three days have had a dreamlike quality as if I were still back home and only my thoughts were projected into the journey. But this makes it real. To be here with you!"

"Miss Willie, Miss Willie! I've had a thousand doubts since I wrote that letter! I shouldn't have asked you to leave all you had to come here to the ridge."

Miss Willie drew away from her and looked at her. "Why, Mary! What did I have? What did I have, Mary? What did I leave? Surely you know how little it was!"

Mary's mouth trembled. "That makes it all right, then. That's all I wanted to know. You'll not be sorry if you feel like that."

"No. I'll not be sorry. No matter what happens now, I'll never be sorry, Mary. I'm glad I'm here."

Hod interrupted them. "You all go on in the house and I'll bring these things in."

"Come on, Miss Willie," Mary said, "I want to show you my house."

They moved around the corner of the house, by the old stone chimney. Mary laid her hand on it as they passed. "Hod's great-grandmother Abigail built this chimney herself, with stones from the creek bed there. I've written you about it. And the yellow rose here she planted. The family say that Amelia Pierce brought a cutting of this rose from her home in Virginia when she came to Kentucky. Abigail brought this one, cut from that plant, and now there's always a yellow rose in every Pierce yard. Those old apple trees were set out by Great-grampa Jeems. See how gnarled and ancient they are?"

"And these logs were cut and shaped by him, weren't they?" Miss Willie touched a corner of the log house.

"Yes. He felled and squared these logs and raised a one-room cabin. This part of the house is over a hundred years old."

Across the front of the house was a wide, screened porch. When they stepped through the door, Miss Willie saw that it was comfortable, with chairs and tables grouped at one end.

"Hod makes those," Mary said. "You know he has a workshop out in the old woodshed where his grandfather made chairs."

"Yes, you told me," Miss Willie answered.

And then they were inside the big log room. A lamp was lighted, and in its flickering light the logs were burnished copper. Miss Willie stood and let the feel of the room creep over her. The floors were wide and darkly gleaming, with ovals of braided rugs scattered across them. Mary's piano filled one corner of the room, and the huge fireplace took up the opposite wall. An old pine dresser stood against another, and a deep couch covered with a quilted pattern sat beneath the windows. Big easy chairs were grouped before the hearth, and a low, polished table stood between them. The roof lifted high overhead and the great, smoked beams stretched from wall to wall. It was a lovely, gracious room, and Miss Willie let its charm flow over her.

"And here is your room," Mary said, opening a door. Here was the same ancient charm . . . a high wooden bed, softly shining in the lamplight . . . a tall mirror over a marble-topped chest of drawers . . . a deep pine blanket chest at the foot of the bed . . . a low rocker with a quilted cushion, and the same gay, braided rugs on the floor.

Miss Willie turned to Mary. "You have a lovely home, my dear. Another person might have ruined it, but you've kept it beautiful."

"So much of this was already here, Miss Willie. I've just tried to restore it. This bed belonged to Abigail . . . this little rocker too. This blanket chest was Gramma's . . . Grampa Dow made it for her. There aren't many things in the house that have been 'fotched on.' I've only had to put them together again."

"Even so, you've done a lovely thing here. You've given Hod the heritage of his forefathers. It might so easily have been lost."

39

"Someday it will be the Skipper's, Miss Willie. Besides what it means to Hod and me, I want our son to know his past, how rooted it is in this place. And I want him to grow up loving it. You know what my life was like . . . always moving . . . never putting down roots. Not once in my life until I married Hod had I slept under a roof I could call my own. Not once had I walked on land that belonged to me. O Miss Willie, I've learned that the most fundamental pride in the world is the pride you have in owning a little piece of land! You've got to live on your own land, walk on it, work in its dirt, to know the final pride of being free. And I want my son to know that, always. I want him never to know what it is to be rootless and insecure. I want him always to know where he belongs."

Terribly moved, Miss Willie felt her throat knot. "You're a big woman, Mary Pierce. And Hod and the Skipper are mighty fortunate men!"

Mary laughed. "Here we stand talking! And you're hungry and tired! I'm forgetting the very first rule of Piney Ridge hospitality! There's fresh water in the pitcher there, and when you've freshened up a bit, supper will be ready."

After supper they sat on the wide screened porch and talked of the thousand and one things two women can find to talk about when they haven't been together for a long time. Talked of Texas and Miss Willie's friends; of this acquaintance Mary would remember and that one; of Miss Willie's trip and her anxiety over the ribbony, black-topped road down from Louisville; of Mary's first days here on the ridge; how she and Hod worked so hard remodeling the house. And inevitably again to the long history of his family here on Piney Ridge. "Tell her, Hod," Mary said.

And Hod tilted his chair against the wall, drooped his eyes, and lifted his voice in Grampa's endless tale. "Old Tom Pierce, he come here from Virginny, back in the olden days. He was a soljer in the Revolution, an' they paid him off with some land in Kentucky. He brung his woman an' their young'uns, an' house plunder through the Gap in a wagon, an' settled this land an' raised his kids. His name was Tom Pierce. An' he fit the Injuns an' plowed his land an' lived an' died right here on this ridge.

Give it the name o' Piney Ridge . . ."

His voice droned on and Miss Willie smiled. All Hod's love for his old Grampa Dow sang richly through his voice. But more than that, all his love for this land and these people was in it. In every word, every tone, every slow, drawling inflection. She had expected to love this man for Mary's sake, but in that moment she began to love him for himself.

The June night rested softly on the hills, and the stars arched the sky from ridge to ridge with a spangled bridge. Under the trees a white mist curled slowly from the creek, and fireflies pricked the shifting veils with dimmed and softened lanterns. An owl hooted up on the hillside, and in some dark, quiet pool a frog grumbled deep in his throat. A late thrush sent a fluting trill across the meadow, and on the very rim of the ridge, high and far away, a thin, silver moon cut a crescent out of the sky.

Miss Willie felt an ineffable peace within her. This is going to be all right, she thought. This is going to be fine!

CHAPTER
❧ 5 ❧

MISS WILLIE WAS AWAKE EARLY the next morning. She knew it was early although the sun was streaming in her window. The air had the texture and the feel and the smell of something new and unused. Like a freshly minted coin, bright and shining. There was a crisp vigor in it and an energy waiting to be put to work . . . a lightness and a strong excitement. It lifted and bore one aloft. Only in the very early morning was this so. Later the air would take on the burdens of the day. It would be heavy and tired.

Early as she knew it was, Miss Willie heard the sounds of breakfast stirring out in the kitchen. The smell of coffee came drifting into her room and she sniffed eagerly. Coffee, she thought, smells brown . . . like it looks. Rich and heavy and brown. Suddenly she was hungry . . . ravenously hungry, and she threw the blanket back and rose and dressed quickly.

When she went into the kitchen, Mary looked up from the

dough board where she was cutting biscuits. "You were supposed to rest this morning," she scolded.

"Too excited," Miss Willie confessed. "I'm like a child on a visit . . . eager to be up and around. Are you making hot bread this morning, Mary?"

Mary laughed. "I make hot bread *every* morning, lady! My husband comes from a long line of biscuit-for-breakfast people!"

She whirled quickly toward the stove. Taking the lid from a deep skillet, she frowned anxiously over the chicken which was frying, turning first one piece then another, setting the lid back in place finally and shoving the skillet toward the back of the stove. "Chicken's almost done," she said. "Miss Willie, you want to run down to the creek and get the fruit juice and cream? Down by the tall sycamore you'll find a little springhouse built over the creek, and the cream is in a blue crock and the orange juice is in a fruit jar."

When Miss Willie returned, Mary was piling fried chicken on a deep platter. She set it in the warming oven when it was full. "Now you can set the table if you like. The dishes are in that corner cupboard."

"Where's Hod?" Miss Willie asked.

"He's milking and feeding. He'll be in pretty soon, though. He ought to be through by now." As she talked, she opened the oven door and glanced in. "Biscuits are nearly done." She went to the back door and looked out. "He's turning the cows out." And then she was back at the stove again.

"Mary, is this corner cupboard cherry?"

"Yes. Grampa Dow made that. And this dough table here. All these things were Hod's grandmother's."

Miss Willie clucked softly to herself. "Your house is full of museum pieces, isn't it?"

"And right here's where they'll stay." Mary was stirring gravy at the stove.

Hod came in with the foaming buckets of milk. "You're up bright and early, Miss Willie. Hardly an hour past sunup! Sleep good?"

"I slept fine, Hod. I thought I was going to be so stiff I couldn't move from all that bumping yesterday, but, strangely

42

enough, I'm not! And I feel as though I had enough energy for a dozen people."

"Breakfast is ready," Mary called, pouring coffee into the big, ironstone cups.

Miss Willie looked at the table. Mary's love of beauty was evident in the bright blue cloth, and the pot of flowers in the center of the table, but Hod's needs were evident in the hot biscuits piled in the basket, the platter of fried chicken, the deep bowl of cream gravy, and the jars of jam and jelly clustered about the butter dish. Miss Willie thought of her own breakfasts in the little adobe house. Fruit juice, toast, and coffee, and she frequently only nibbled at the toast. On Sundays she sometimes broiled a bit of bacon and added a spot of jelly. Year in and year out her breakfasts had been the same. Drawing a good breath, she opened a biscuit as she saw Hod doing, and floated it in the thick white gravy. Then she took a piece of chicken and bit into it. Heavenly! At this hour of the morning too.

"Well, what you two goin' to do today?" Hod asked.

"I thought we'd walk down to the schoolhouse this afternoon. Unless Miss Willie needs to rest. I imagine she's anxious to see it and to begin to get her bearings."

"Oh, no. I'm not tired at all," Miss Willie said. "I'd like that. When does school start?"

"July twelfth."

"I'd better see the schoolhouse, then. And we had also better begin to think of where I'm going to live."

"Why, you're going to live right here," Hod said.

"Oh, no, I'm not."

"But, Miss Willie, that's what we've planned all along. That's your room that we've got ready for you," Mary protested.

"Well, you'll just have to unplan then. I have no intention of staying here with you and Hod. If this were a visit, I should love to stay here. But I have come to Piney Ridge to stay awhile, and I want a place of my own while I'm here."

Hod pushed his chair back from the table. "Miss Willie, this ain't El Paso. There's water to draw, and fires to build, and lamps to keep cleaned and filled, and wood to chop. A woman can't live by herself in this country. It'd be too hard on her."

43

"Oh, I didn't mean a house of my own. I know that isn't possible. I meant a room somewhere."

"Is this idea of yours for our sake or for your own?" Mary wanted to know.

"Both. You and Hod don't need anyone else around just now. And I like to be alone at times. We are too much alike for you not to understand that, Mary."

Mary looked across the room at Hod and smiled. Hod pulled at his nose. "O.K., Miss Willie. Mary said that's what you'd say. But we'd have liked to have you."

"I know you would. But it will be best the other way. Now, do we do the dishes, Mary?"

That afternoon Mary and Miss Willie set off down the hollow for the schoolhouse. "Should you be walking, Mary?" Miss Willie asked.

"Oh, yes. I puff and pant a little when I climb the ridge, and I don't do some of the heavier work as I used to. But otherwise I follow my own inclinations. It's only about a mile to the schoolhouse, and it's a pretty walk."

They were following an old road which tunneled a shady path under the close-hanging trees. And the creek rolled and tumbled along beside them. There was a scent of clover and dry, sun-baked soil, intermingled with the damp smell of leaves close-packed under the trees. It was a soft blending of odors overlaid with the lazy heat of the afternoon. When they walked near the stream, Miss Willie could see the minnows darting here and there in their abrupt, swift way. Their movements were broken into flashing forays from dark to light pools, behind rocks, over ripples, and under roots tangling the water.

"This is going to look pretty bad to you," Mary warned. "Nothing I wrote can give you any idea of what it's really like!"

"I'm not expecting much," Miss Willie said. "I shouldn't have been interested in coming if it had been a good school. I was in a fine school where I was, remember?"

The road came out in a widening meadow which was lush and deep in grass. Out of the opposite woods came a man and a

44

woman, with three small children straggling behind. The woman was carrying a fourth child too small to walk.

"Oh, heavens!" Mary exclaimed, "there's Matt Jasper and his brood. Of all people for you to meet the very first day you're here!"

As they came nearer, Miss Willie thought of the characters in *Tobacco Road* or *Grapes of Wrath*. She had the amazed feeling that she was watching them come to life. They don't live outside of books, she thought.

The man was slight and bony, his overalls hanging sacklike over his thin frame. His scant beard was a week old, and his shirt collar buttoned loosely around his gaunt, stringy neck. His mouth worked constantly around a cud of tobacco, and spit drooled from the corners onto his chin. His battered old felt hat was pushed down around his ears, and his long, shaggy hair curled up all around the edges. He had a flat, vacant look on his face.

The woman was filthy, emaciated, and stupid-looking. Her mouth was packed with snuff, and she spat sloppily at her feet when they stopped. The child in her arms was covered with sores, mewling and crying fretfully as it turned its head restlessly from side to side. Its skin had a blue tinge, and its legs hung thin and spidery from its swollen stomach. Miss Willie felt her own stomach heave uneasily. She swallowed hard.

The children drew up behind their parents. The oldest one, a boy, had a large head — too large for the rest of his body — covered with a thatch of coarse red hair. His face had a sly, foxlike look. He stood scratching his chest, running a grimy finger inside his shirt front.

The other two were girls, less repellent than the boy but obviously stupid and simple. They were skinny little things, with sharp, whetted features. All of them were unwashed and uncombed and clothed in filthy rags.

Mary had stopped. "Why, hello, Matt . . . Lutie, how are you? Have you all been to the store?"

"Howdy, Miss Mary," the man spoke, after shooting a thin stream of tobacco juice to one side of the road. "No, we wouldn't have nothin' to go to the store fer. We're goin' sang diggin' up the holler, if it's all right with Hod. Hod, he said they was some

45

up on that fur hillside. Told me oncet I could allus have what I found on his land. But I reckoned to ast him, jist the same."

"I'm sure he won't mind," Mary said. Turning to Miss Willie, she went on. "This is my aunt, Miss Willie Payne. She's come to teach the Big Springs School this year."

"How do you do?" said Miss Willie, although her voice was thick with effort.

"Howdy," said the man. The woman didn't speak. She simply stared. And the children drew up in a tight huddle behind the man and woman. Miss Willie felt all their eyes fixed on her. All the eyes, blank, expressionless, unmoving, simply lying on her, heavy and solid. Their look was thick with substance, and she shivered with a chilling omniscience of evil. She moved closer to Mary and touched her arm.

"We'd best be gittin' on," the man finally said, and they shuffled on up the road.

"Dear Lord, Mary," Miss Willie sighed, when they had passed on. "Are there many like that here on the ridge? They made me feel positively unclean!" She groped for her handkerchief and wiped her face and hands.

Mary shook her head. "I know. I know. The first time I saw them I was so nauseated I almost disgraced Hod. I had to get away from them where I could be sick. No. There aren't many like Matt and Lutie, thank goodness. Matt is simple-minded and epileptic."

"And the woman! What about her? She was as repulsive to me as the man!"

"Lutie? Lutie is normal, as far as anyone knows. She has just been dragged down by hard work and forever bearing children. I don't know how many she's had, but these are all that are living. Most of them die either when they're born or soon after. That one she's carrying is about two, and she lost one last year. Oh, something ought to be done about things like that! I tell Hod, and I tell him. And he says what can you do? And I don't know what you can do! Matt ought to be institutionalized! But someone would have to go through the legal process of having him committed, and no one is willing. Not even Hod. He says Matt isn't crazy, and that he would die if he were put away somewhere. He says Matt lives in fear of that happening. He has a brother who was sent to Danville, and he has a horror of it. He hides away in the hills when he feels the convulsions coming on. Hides back in a cave somewhere and stays for two or three days at a time, to keep people from knowing. But to keep on bringing children into the world of parents like that! If we were a more civilized people, it wouldn't be allowed! They could never have married!"

"Why did she marry him, do you suppose? If she's normal, surely she wouldn't have married him!"

"Miss Willie, do you know how old Lutie Jasper is?"

"She looked about forty to me."

"She's twenty-five! And she married Matt when she was fourteen! How much sense has a fourteen-year-old girl got? Besides, Matt didn't start having these seizures until he was grown. They had been married several years when he had the first one. Hod says he can remember when Matt Jasper wasn't a bad-looking boy. He was sixteen when they married."

"How can children that age get a marriage license? Aren't there any state laws here?"

"Oh, yes. But fourteen is the minimum age, with parents' consent. And the kids forge their parents' signatures, and that's all there is to it."

"Don't the parents ever do anything about it?"

"No. Not on the ridge. No one wants to get mixed up with the law. Once it's done, it's done. Oh, I'm sorry we had to run into them today. I wish you could have seen some of the good things about the ridge, first. And I wish you could have met some of the good folks. Because there's more good than bad here, even with the bad as awful as it is."

"It'll balance in the long run, Mary. I'll see the good too. These folks leave a bad taste, but after all they're people, and we shouldn't draw away from them."

They had come to the wide mouth of the hollow, and in a flat open space at the foot of the ridge the schoolhouse hugged the hill. Back of it the trees climbed the steep slope in serried ranks, and formed a solid green backdrop against which the great square logs were painted in bleached gray. Those logs had soaked up

47

a hundred years of sun and wind and rain, and from them had been drawn the strong yellow of the pines and the poplars and the fine white cleanness of the oaks. Little by little they had been washed and dried and sunned into the present ancient silver and were beyond further saturation.

A lofty elm, majestic, kingly, and august, allowed its lower branches to sweep delicately over the shingled roof, and in its intense shade the curled boards had put on a covering of moss — rich, vivid velvet, green against the gray.

The schoolyard had been tramped down by generations of running feet, and the bare ground looked white and beaten under the trees which still enclosed the space. These were nearly all giant elms — ancient trees — with a few tall maples and half a dozen beeches.

"There," said Mary, pointing. "There it is, and you may rue the day you ever saw it!"

They had stopped at the edge of the grove, and Miss Willie had been still, taking all this into her. Nothing could be too bad, she thought, that was so quietly beautiful. I should have lived a hundred years ago, her thoughts went on. I should have been a little girl going to school here. I should have heard the wind and the rain crying through these trees. I should have had a young love to carve twined hearts on that great elm. Is there something in all of us, she mused, that keeps one longing heartbeat in the past? Is that the only way we can bear the present? Do we all of us belong in another age with some part of ourselves?

Mary was walking through the grove and around the building. "Here," she said, "is the family tree." And she pointed to a gray-beard beech. "See, there are Grampa Dow's initials on that side. And here, a little lower down are Lem's and Gault's and Mr. Tom's. And here, still young and clean, are Hod's. Someday the Skipper will cut his just below his father's." She stood looking at the tree, and then she turned. "Miss Willie, is there always something selfish, something inevitably personal, in our desire for goodness? It's because of the Skipper that I want a better school, isn't it? If it weren't for him, would I have bothered?"

"If it weren't for him," Miss Willie answered, "you would have bothered so much you wouldn't have sent for me! You would have

48

done it yourself. Of course the pattern of goodness is centered in some personal want, Mary. It has always been so. All conceptions of goodness have had their beginnings in the minds of people . . . people who found their happiness in thinking good, or doing good, or being good, or wanting good. Goodness can't be abstracted from the personal. But it isn't any the less good for being personal! Let's go in. I want to see the worst of this at once."

Inside, the building was long and dim, its windows high and on one side. The desks were very old and battered, and many of them were broken. They were all of the same height, and Miss Willie saw that the short legs of the younger children would swing painfully from them.

In the front of the room was a pine table, which was evidently the teacher's desk. On the wall back of it was one small blackboard, cracked and gray with age. In the center of the room was a round, drum stove, rusty and sagging, the door missing from the front.

"Isn't it horrible?" said Mary.

Miss Willie didn't answer. She was wandering around the room, trying the seats and running her hand over the desks, looking at the inevitable carved initials marking their tops. "Here is Hod's place," she said, "he must have sat here once."

Mary hurried over to stand by Miss Willie, looking down at the carved name. "Well, at least I don't see Mr. Tom's or Grampa Dow's. The desks must be newer than their time!"

Miss Willie laughed. "Isn't it unbelievable? When I think of the equipment we have in the cities! A quarter of it would seem like riches here!" She shook her head, and repeated, "It's unbelievable!"

They went outside again. "And where is the spring?" Miss Willie asked.

"Here," Mary said, "on the hillside."

A wooden washtub had been embedded in the slope of the hill, and a tiny stream of water ran constantly into it over the pebbly soil. It came from farther up the hill and it had channeled a narrow furrow in the shaly earth. It ran clear and sparkling over the moss and rocks, and dripped in an invariable and

49

regular stream. It ran off down the hill in a ditch which had been dug for that purpose. Even so the ground was wet and muddy around the tub.

Miss Willie looked up the hillside at the narrow stream of water. "This is dangerous, Mary."

"Of course it's dangerous! The spring is a hundred feet up the hill. It may be pure . . . it probably is. But it runs in an unguarded stream over the ground, and people or animals passing can wade right through it, to say nothing of any other sort of pollution. But this is one of the blind spots I mentioned. We have not been able to get anything done about it. But it *must* be changed! I only hope we don't have to have an epidemic of some sort to get it changed!"

"Changing it is part of my job?"

Mary laughed. "Your conscience wouldn't let you leave it unchanged, would it?"

"No. I'm afraid not." Miss Willie squared her shoulders. "Well. It's pretty bad. Worse than I imagined. But nothing is hopeless. We'll just have to see."

Mary moved toward the road. "We'd better start. I thought we'd go by the ridge road and stop at the folks' for a while."

Miss Willie followed, turning once or twice to look back at the ancient trees and the weathered old log building. As a schoolhouse it was pretty terrible. As a beautiful old structure it had the grace that time lends all old things, and the charm of faded and blended colors. She liked it. She thought she was going to be very happy in it. And there was real challenge in this place.

They followed the road back down the hollow until they came to a path which crossed the creek on a foot log. Here they stopped for Mary to rest. The shade was very heavy, and the air was cooled by the creek. They sat on the foot log and swung their feet over the swift running water. Miss Willie bent over to watch. "Makes me dizzy," she said, straightening.

"Oh, there's Rufe," Mary said suddenly, and she waved across the creek. A boy, about twelve, maybe fourteen, and a dog were standing there under a tall tree. The boy waved, and then he and the dog disappeared. "That's Wells Pierce's boy," Mary explained. "I wrote you about Wells. You'll have Rufe in school."

Miss Willie was watching the woods where the boy had disappeared. "Why did he run away?" she asked.

"Oh, that's just Rufe," Mary said. "He and his dog roam the woods all summer. He digs ginseng, I suppose, and the dog jumps rabbits. You're likely to see them 'most any time you're out."

"Wells is one of the school trustees, isn't he?"

"Yes. He's Hod's cousin. We're very fond of him. His wife's dead. He lives on up the ridge past the folks'. He's kept his home going somehow, though with four children to look after I don't know how he's done it. Well, three. His sister took the youngest when Matildy died. Fortunately the oldest is a girl, Rose, and although she's just sixteen, she does a pretty good job of taking care of things."

"Four children?"

"Yes. Rose, and Rufe — Rufe's about thirteen, I guess — and Abby. Let's see, Abby must be nearly eleven. And Veeny, the baby. I imagine she's six or seven now. But Manthy has had her since she was less than a year old."

"Was his wife nice?"

"I never knew her. She died before Hod and I were married. While he was overseas. But Hod says she was a fine woman. Short and dark and sort of plump, and a happy, easygoing sort of person. From what I've heard she and Wells must have been very happy. Hod says they always seemed to have such a good time together."

"How did she die?"

"Of pneumonia. Took a cold and didn't take care of herself. And before they realized she was seriously ill, she was gone."

Miss Willie was quiet. Everything she had heard about Wells Pierce was good. He had had more to do with her coming to the ridge than the other trustees, because he was a man interested in a better school for his children. He was also a man who had somehow held his home together after the death of his wife. And he was a man of whom Mary and Hod were very fond. Yes, she looked forward to meeting him.

"We'd better go on," Mary said, and they crossed the log and pushed on up the steep and rocky path.

They came out at the silver birch just below Gault Pierce's place. Becky was sitting on the front porch. "Hi, Becky," Mary called. "Can we have a drink of water? We've been down to the schoolhouse and have just climbed that hill from the hollow. I'm as thirsty as old Buck when he's been plowing all day."

"Why, shore," Becky answered, rising from the slat-backed chair drawn to the edge of the porch. "Jist git you a cheer, an' I'll go git the bucket. I jist went to the spring not more'n fifteen minnits ago, so I know the water's still cold."

Mary and Miss Willie sat on the edge of the porch, Mary leaning back against a post. Becky returned with the bucket of water and offered them the gourd dipper which hung from a rafter. The water was as cold as ice, and there was a faintly sweet taste to it from the gourd.

"This is my aunt, Miss Willie," said Mary. "And Becky is Hod's Uncle Gault's wife."

"Pleased to make yer acquaintance," murmured Becky, offering a limp hand. She was a small woman, even smaller than Miss Willie, and frail-looking. Her black dress hung on her in folds, hardly touching her body anywhere. Over it was tied a crisp white apron, its ruffles fluted into frilly stiffness. Her head was no larger than a child's, and the hair was skinned back from her face so tight that her eyebrows seemed to be drawn up at the ends. Her face was wrinkled and brown, and her mouth was bunched with a dip of snuff. She spat over the edge of the porch when it overflowed.

"You've come to teach the school, ain't you?" she asked.

"Yes," said Miss Willie. "We've been down looking over the building. There's lots needs to be done."

"They is that, fer a fact. Hit's a sight the way things gits run down when they ain't used. In jist five months that schoolhouse kin git so spider-webby an' dusty hit takes three, four days to red it up. I'll be glad to he'p ifen yer a mind to git at it soon."

Miss Willie looked at Mary. It hadn't occurred to her that she would be expected to clean up the building before school began. She made a wry face. Of course there would be no janitor here. If it was to be bright and shining for the opening of school, she would have to do it, with the help of anyone who offered.

Mary spoke up hastily. "That's good of you, Becky. But I think we'll get some of the men to do most of the work this year."

Becky sniffed and squirted a thin, brown stream expertly into the grass. "Never seen a man yit could red up a place like it ort to be! Takes a woman to scrub an' clean. Best count on me'n Hattie he'pin' out."

"We'll let you know," said Miss Willie pacifically. "I want someone to help me make some curtains for the windows, and I'd like to have two or three bright braided rugs. Do you know where I could get them?"

"Braided rugs? Well, upon my word an' honor! What you want with them in the schoolhouse?"

"I think they will brighten up the room. I want some pretty yellow curtains too."

Becky shook her head. "Kids go to school to larn, don't they? Cain't see why you need rugs an' curtains."

"They learn a lot more than what's in books, Becky," put in Mary. "Anyhow, you just leave this up to Miss Willie. Do you know who's got some braided rugs or where we could get some made?"

Becky folded her hands in her lap. "I've sorta caught up on my work lately, an' ifen you think they're good enough, I could whip you up a couple I reckon."

"I was hoping you would say that," laughed Mary. "Becky makes the prettiest and the best rugs on the ridge. Everybody will tell you that!"

Becky's face glowed with pleasure, but she disclaimed such credit immediately. "They's a heap kin make 'em purtier'n mine," she said. "Mine is jist hit-er-miss. I don't never foller no pattern like some does."

"That's what makes them so pretty! Well, there, Miss Willie! There are your rugs practically made!"

"An' I'll he'p with them curtains if yer set on 'em," Becky offered.

"I do thank you, Becky," said Miss Willie. "You'll see what a difference they make."

"Doubtless they will. Hit's a unknown sight what a splash o' color will do. Air you all goin' to the singin' Sunday, Mary?"

"What singing?"

"Over at Bear Holler. Brent an' Dude Johnson's goin' to hold a all-day singin' . . . dinner on the ground. I allowed you'd be goin' on account of Hod lovin' to sing so good."

"I didn't know anything about it, and if Hod knows, he hasn't mentioned it. Are the rest of the family going?"

"Hattie an' Tom is. Me'n Gault is goin' with 'em. Hattie's already abakin'. Said if you all went, they wasn't no use o' yer havin' to bake. She'd jist bake up enough fer all."

Mary rose and shook the skirt of her dress and hitched her stockings up. "Hod'll want to go I'm sure. And I'd love for Miss Willie to go to an all-day singing. I imagine we'll be there. If we go, we'll see you over there and we'll all have dinner together."

"Oh, hit's a spread. Ever'body jist puts their stuff together."

"All right," said Mary. "Come on, Miss Willie. The sun's almost down. We're not going to have time to go on to the folks' now. I'm going to have a hungry husband in about half an hour. We better go back to the hollow."

On up the ridge Matt Jasper stumbled down the road, Lutie, sagging under the weight of the child in her arms, following him. The children were strung out in a long and straggling row behind. Matt was muttering under his breath. "Old Hod don't like me no more. Old Hod's gittin' mean to me. Don't like me. His woman don't like me, neither. Looked funny outen her eyes too. Don't nobody like me no more. Ever'body looks funny at me outen their eyes."

He swung around suddenly, facing Lutie. She stopped abruptly, and her hooded eyes narrowed. "*You* look funny outen yer eyes too," he accused. "You don't like me no more neither!"

Lutie shifted the toothbrush in her mouth. "Le's git on home, Matt. Hit's gittin' late. Don't git none o' yer idees."

"Idees come an' idees go," he mumbled and started on, lurching from one side of the road to the other. His breath was foul with whisky. "You better not look funny at me," he warned. "You better not go tellin' the law to git me." He stopped again, his frail body shaking. His voice rose and he screeched at her, a trembling

54

finger pointing. "You better not! I'm atellin' you! I ain't goin' to no 'sylum. I'll kill anybody turns me in. I'll kill 'em dead! You better be keerful an' not git no idees yerself!"

Lutie changed the child from her right arm to the left. "C'mon, Matt," she said. "Ain't nobody got no idees but you. This kid's powerful heavy, an' I'm tard. Le's git on home."

CHAPTER

❦ 6 ❦

SUNDAY MORNING THE SUN CAME UP over the ridge into a cloudless sky. Miss Willie was aware of a tingling anticipation. This was the day of the all-day singing. She had been so afraid it would rain and spoil everything. But the blue dome rounding over the hills promised a blessing on the summer day.

All day yesterday she and Mary had been busy preparing for the dinner — dressing chickens, boiling potatoes for salad, baking beans, and a double quantity of Mary's snowy, light loaves of bread. Miss Willie had churned again, although they had churned only the day before. Mary wanted to take extra butter along. They had visited the cellar, prying about in the dimness among the jars for pickles and spiced peaches and corn catsup.

"Surely you needn't take so much, Mary," Miss Willie protested.

"There'll be those who can't bring enough, Miss Willie," Mary had answered. "The Jaspers, if they come, and Old Man Clark's family."

And as she dressed now, Miss Willie could hear Mary out in the kitchen and could smell the heady odor of frying chicken. The singing would start at ten o'clock, Hod had said, and you wanted to be there for the beginning.

Miss Willie was terribly excited. Her thin face was flushed and her eyes sparkled. She hummed a gay tune as she pulled on a crisply ironed wash dress. She laughed as she recognized "Turkey in the Straw." They had had some music last night, Mary at the piano and Hod with his guitar, and Hod had tried to teach her the words to that song. It fitted her mood today. It was a sort

55

of prancing tune, and prancing a little herself, she went out to help Mary.

After breakfast they packed four huge baskets with food and gave them to Hod to store in the back of the car. Miss Willie was thoughtful as she watched him carry them out the door. In those baskets was nothing that had not been grown here on this farm. Nothing except flour and salt and sugar. Hod had only a meager thirty acres all told, and yet from it he produced all the food the household needed; raised his nine tenths of an acre of tobacco and fifteen acres of corn. There was no want here, and yet she remembered the gray, rubbling shacks that hugged the hollows down by the pike, the leaning walls of Old Man Clark's house, the tenant place on Gault's farm, and the shambling, prideless beggary of Matt Jasper. It was true, then, wasn't it, that men were not created equal, even if they were offered equal opportunities. Matt Jasper had once had a farm as large as Hod's . . . and Old Man Clark had once owned one twice as large. He had sold off small chunks of it until there was none left to sell; then he had thrown himself on the mercy of the neighborhood and had accepted the charity of Gault's tenant house.

Must society always carry on its back the old man of the sea? Were there inevitably those too inert to labor, too shiftless to toil? And were they therefore a responsibility of all those who did? Was it better to take along enough lunch to feed them too, or was there hope of their ever being able to feed themselves? And was it loving your neighbor more to feed him or to instruct him? She wondered.

In that moment she felt a reinforcement of her conviction that she was here with a sense of mission. There was something she had to do here on Piney Ridge. She, Willie Payne. She was too good a Presbyterian to doubt that she had been led to this place, even as she chuckled at the conceit that lay back of her conviction. "The Lord's been running Piney Ridge a mighty long time without you, Willie," she cautioned. And then she giggled. "Maybe that's why He sent for you!"

Bear Hollow Chapel was set in a grove of trees at the head of the second hollow over from Wishful Creek. When they drove up, a crowd had already gathered. The grove was thick with vehicles

56

of every sort — wagons, buggies, carts, and ancient and broken-down automobiles. Hod's car, which was at least ten years old, was the best-looking of the lot. Mules and horses were hitched to the fence and to the wagon and cart wheels. People were milling around, talking in groups which were constantly being broken as those on the fringe moved on.

Miss Willie looked eagerly at the restless throng. She saw that the oldest women were dressed in their shapeless dark cottons, tied about with spotless aprons, Sunday sunbonnets knotted firmly under their chins. The dark dress, the starched apron, the slatted bonnet were apparently their uniform.

Women of Hattie's age ventured timidly into a discreet gaiety with their colored cottons. They were restrained to pale blues, pinks, yellows, and greens, with infinitely varied patterns of tiny flowers. It was as if at forty and fifty one might delicately own to the last fading moment of youth and indulge it cautiously in the pastels of the rainbow. Not yet must these shy women of middle age put on the black and brown of age. The aprons too were left off, a further mark of the still present energy to work. The white apron represented the time of sitting in the corner. Only Becky had put on voluntarily the garb of her elders. Miss Willie wondered about that. Neither did this middle group wear bonnets. On their heads were perched the flowering straws of Montgomery Ward and Sears, Roebuck.

It was among the girls that color rioted boldly. In cheap rayon and jersey dresses they flaunted their young loveliness, letting the brazen stripes and gaudy floral arrangements of the manufacturers wrap themselves lovingly around their slender curves. Their permanented heads, frizzy with curls, daringly took the sun and the wind, and their tanned young legs were innocent of stockings. They gathered in groups, chattering shrilly and laughing loudly, conscious of the boys gathered in similar groups on the other side of the yard. In a single, lucid moment Miss Willie knew the aching excitement they were feeling, and her mouth trembled into a smile when one girl's laugh rang high above the others. It was so important to be noticed!

The men, Miss Willie noted, were not so sharply delineated as the women. Most of them were in faded but clean overalls and denim shirts. A few, like Hod, had on fresh white shirts and slacks, but none had on coats or ties.

The boys, like the girls, bloomed colorfully. Their shirts were gay checked and plaid sports shirts, and a few had even braved the heat in loud blue, green, or brown coats.

A battered old Ford drove up and two men got out, reaching into the back of the car for their guitars. "That's the Johnson brothers," Mary whispered. "They're to lead the singing today."

They greeted people with loud howdies, circling around the crowd. Then there was a general movement toward the doors, and a breaking up of the smaller groups. Hod came back from taking the baskets to the picnic grove and helped Mary from the car. "About time to start," he said. "We might as well go inside."

At the door they stopped a moment, and Miss Willie saw that the men were all seating themselves on one side of the room, the women on the other. She looked questioningly at Mary, whose eyes were twinkling. "That's the way it's done down here," she said, putting her hand under Miss Willie's elbow and urging her gently toward the women's side. She spoke over her shoulder at Hod. "See you at noon."

He nodded. "Try to save me some of your things," he said.

Mary smiled and motioned him away. He joined the men across the wide aisle, and Mary and Miss Willie seated themselves beside Hattie and Becky.

Miss Willie looked around. The chapel was small, but it was light and airy and pleasantly clean. The walls were pine, painted white, cut by long, narrow windows which let in broad beams of sunlight. At the front of the room a platform was built up about a foot higher than the floor. A lectern made of stained pine boards sat near the front of the platform. The benches upon which they sat were sawed, ten-inch white pine planks, and one rail had been nailed to uprights at intervals to form a back. For an all-day singing this was going to be powerfully hard, thought Miss Willie.

There was some milling and stirring on the platform, and almost immediately the Johnson men, who were tall, lanky, and rawboned, were passing out songbooks. Miss Willie took one and passed the stack on down the row. She looked at it curiously. It was a pink, paper-backed book with *Gospel Tide* written across the front in tall letters. Inside the cover, the title page carried the legend "Stamps-Baxter Music and Printing Co., Inc. Price, 35 cents a copy. Shaped notes." She opened the book to the first song. Shaped notes. She had heard her father talk of the old hymnbooks when he was a boy. They had shaped notes. But this was the first time she had ever seen one. The notes were really shaped, then. Some were full diamonds, some half diamonds. Some were full squares, others were triangles. Some were full circles, others were half circles. But what did they mean? She nudged Mary and pointed to the notes.

Mary whispered behind her hand. "Each shape represents a tone. Do, re, mi, fa, sol, la, ti, do."

Miss Willie scanned the hymn. She shook her head. "I never would get it straight. Why aren't the notes of the scale just as simple to learn?"

"Because they're fixed tones. This way, 'do' is always the keynote of the song. In whatever key the song is written . . . here, I'll show you. Here's one written in B-flat. B is 'do' in that song."

Miss Willie puzzled over it a moment, then she giggled. "That doesn't make it any simpler."

The tallest and lankest of the Johnson brothers stepped to the front of the platform, announced the song, made a little pep talk, and lifted his arm for the down beat. The guitar-playing brother threw his head back and swallowed his Adam's apple and plucked a rich chord from the instrument. A thrill of anticipation ran over Miss Willie. Now she would hear some real old country singing!

The volume of sound was terrific! Everybody knew the song and there wasn't a silent soul in the house. The full impact of a hundred voices raised in unison, each to its loudest pitch, struck Miss Willie without warning. Involuntarily she shrank from it, and in spite of herself her hands lifted toward her ears. She glanced sidewise at Mary, and felt Mary's tremble of laughter, then she set herself to endure it. Singing? Well, that was one name for it!

The leader's brassy baritone brayed out over the heads of the people. Apparently he must be heard over the other ninety-nine! But they must make the effort to drown him out! Loudly, stridently, nasally, the voices filled the house, the women's with a high, whiny whang; the men's with a bellowing, grating harshness. The rhythm was broken into short, choppy phrases, and there was never the slightest degree of feeling for the words, nor the slightest shading of tones. There was perfect time, perfect harmony, on a dull, flat, monotonous plane.

To Miss Willie's ear, trained to Bach, Handel, Haydn, and Mozart in church, this was a travesty of all sacred music. She had listened too long to exquisite and singing blending of tones, to high, exulting sweeps of emotion, to perfect poetry of feeling, to accept this as music. These people knew shaped notes, it was true. Most could read them and carry a tune. They had a sense of rhythm. But they could neither sing nor make real music. She felt flattened by the force of the noise, and by the end of the first song she knew that the day would be torture for her. Four verses of that high nasal whanging told her that. When the brassy, harsh voices came to the end of the song and held the last flat note dully, Miss Willie shuddered. She would have Hod teach her this do, re, mi business, and they would see about some singing in the schoolroom! At least her pupils were going to know the difference between good singing and bad singing!

Only once after that was Miss Willie really stirred, and her Calvinistic soul denounced that as a sort of sacrilegious stirring. The Johnson brothers announced they were going to do a special number. "Hit's real easy-like. You've heared it over the radio, likely. Hit's called the 'Golden Boogie.'"

Dude Johnson tuned the guitar, twanging the strings noisily; then he bent low over the instrument and, cuddling it close, picked a chord from its bosom — a chord so infinitely soft that it floated into the air and brushed the ear like a butterfly wing resting on a honeysuckle bloom. Then he straightened and sent his fingers solemnly walking up the neck of the guitar in a slow boogie rhythm that was purposefully solid and sweet. He grinned at the crowd.

Brent was twitching his hips and shuffling his feet. He bent over and clapped his hands together. Straightening, he flung his arms wide, and the guitar-playing brother broke his walking fingers into a run:

60

"When the bells are ringin' all the folks start flockin',
When the bells are ringin' all the folks start rockin',
Flockin' and arockin', rockin' and aflockin',
    To the golden, gospel bells.

"When the bells are ringin' sinners all start shoutin',
When the bells are ringin' Satan, he starts routin',
Shoutin' and aroutin', routin' and ashoutin',
    To the golden, gospel bells."

"C'mon, ever'body!" the man shouted, "you know the tune by now, c'mon an' join in!"

Laughing, the crowd picked up the solid beat and began chanting the words, their bodies swaying. Somewhere in the back hands began to clap softly. The sound spread and swelled and was like the beat of a drum, sharp and regular. Miss Willie was horrified! Boogie! "Golden Boogie"! The idea! But the rhythm was so contagious, the beat so solid, the glory so infectious, that she found herself swinging along with the crowd, her foot tapping in time, her hands clapping along with the rest. It reminded her of the old-time Negro camp meetings. All it needed was old fat Angeline cutting a buck and wing!

And then it was noon and time for the picnic dinner.

The picnic ground was a grassy plot to one side of the yard. The trees formed an arch over it so that it was heavy with shade. In this shade and on the grass the women had spread white cloths in a long streamer, and then the food from all the baskets had been set out upon them. The folks gathered around, children greedily eying everything, plotting, while they waited for the blessing, what pieces of chicken and what big chunks of cake they were going to get. The older people lined up on both sides and stood quietly. Brent Johnson lifted his hand. "I'm goin' to ask Gault Pierce to say grace."

Gault's deep voice rumbled forth unhesitatingly. Miss Willie knew that the ease with which he prayed came from long experience. So had her father prayed at the table. No doubt Gault's voice was lifted in thanks to his Maker at every meal in his house, and so comfortable was he in conversation with Him that the presence of others did not dismay him.

61

At the end of the brief prayer Brent Johnson took charge again. "Now ever'body eat hearty. They's aplenty fer all. Pitch in an' fill yerselves up, an' then we'll call intermission until two o'clock to let it settle. Don't nobody stand back an' be bashful. Ever'body he'p theirselves."

No one needed urging. Mary took two of the paper plates she had brought and filled them, giving them to Hod and Miss Willie. She laughed as she handed his to Hod. "All of that's mine," she said. "Isn't it flattering, Miss Willie, to have your husband like your cooking so well he won't eat anyone else's?"

"You like it," Hod grunted, gnawing on a chicken leg.

"There's Wells," Mary said, and, standing, she waved across the crowd. "Come on over, Wells."

Miss Willie watched him as he made his way around the end of the table, laughing and joking with the men as he passed. Like the other men, he had on faded, patched overalls. Patched, more than likely, by his own hands, Miss Willie thought, as she noticed the long, uneven stitches. His shirt was a blue denim, open at the throat and laid back from his strong, short neck. The shirt had been smoothed by an iron not too hot, for it was still wrinkled, but it was clean and the man himself looked soaped and scrubbed. His powerful, broad shoulders stretched the stuff of his shirt tight at the seams, and where his sleeves were rolled back, his arms emerged thick, heavy, and muscular. They were matted with a mesh of sun-bleached hair, wiry and golden against his brown skin.

As he came up to them he shoved his hat back on his head and ran his hand over his face. "Howdy, folks," he greeted them. "Ain't seen you all in some time. Didn't know whether you'd git over here today or not. This yer aunt, Mary?"

Miss Willie winced at his grammar.

"Yes, this is Miss Willie, Wells. Wells is Hod's cousin, Miss Willie, and he's a very important man to you. He's one of the school trustees, so you'd better do a little bowing and scraping."

Wells laughed and held out his hand. "I don't reckon she's goin' to be able to do much bowin' an' scrapin' with that plate full o' stuff in her hands. Howdy, ma'am. I'm powerful glad yer here. I been aimin' to git over to make you welcome, but I been

62

right busy lately. We're bankin' a lot on you this year down at the school."

Miss Willie set her plate down and took his hand. It was a square, brown hand, with a horny palm which felt rough and hard to her own. She liked the firm clasp of it. It seemed friendly and solid, somehow. She liked, too, his brown, sunny face, open and merry and genial. Don't be an arrogant fool, she chided herself. Of course he talks like the rest of the ridge folks. How else would you expect him to talk! Here is a good man, her thoughts went on. Good like Hod is good. Honorable, gentle, and kindly. She noticed his eyes, warm, brown eyes set far apart, frank and sweet. Yes, here was a good man.

"Don't look for too much, Mr. Pierce," she said, wanting honestly that he should know she admitted of human frailty. "I'm afraid Mary has led you to think too highly of me. This will be a new experience for me, and I am very likely to make many mistakes."

"Why, shore," he said cordially, "ain't nobody but makes mistakes. More'n likely you'll make yore share. But the main thing is yer a good teacher, an' a good teacher is a good teacher wherever you put her. What I had in mind to say, though, was to tell you to call on me fer e'er thing you need. I ain't so wearied about you makin' mistakes as I am you'll git so disgusted with us you won't stay. If e'er thing comes up to weary you, jist holler, an' I'll come arunnin'. Mary an' me, we cooked up this scheme, an' we feel honor bound to stand back of you. Bein's you was good enough to come when we ast you. My kids, some of 'em, will be in yer school, an' I'd like to say right now I don't want none of 'em givin' you no trouble. If they do, jist light into 'em an' frail the dickens outen 'em. They's some you cain't. Folks is tetchy. But I'm aimin' fer mine to respect the teacher. An' I ain't goin' to stand fer no foolishment from 'em."

"I hope that won't be necessary," said Miss Willie, who had never frailed the dickens out of one of her pupils in her life.

"Did the children come with you, Wells?" asked Mary.

"No. They went over to Manthy's yesterday. She was aimin' to take 'em to the county seat to git their school clothes, an' she allowed she'd keep 'em the night. Hod, gimme some o' that food 'fore you eat it all up!"

"Nobody's holding you back," Hod said, making way for him by his side. "You heard what Brent said. Plenty for all."

"They'll be aplenty gone 'fore long, too," Wells laughed. He filled a plate and moved over to squat by Hod.

Miss Willie looked at the short, solid figure squatting there, and she felt a great tenderness for him and a deep respect. Four — well, three — motherless children to care for, and he could keep a placid poise that turned a laughing face to the world. Whatever his own sense of loss, and whatever his deepest confusion, he had not allowed them to shadow his life.

She felt again her own restlessness, and she wondered if there were times when he felt completely alone and unanchored. He was not an insensitive man, she knew, so his hurt must have bitten deep. But he had laid it over with the necessities of fatherhood, and had not allowed its acid to etch into the core of his being. Or perhaps the sweetness of his memories was enough for him. After all, wasn't most of life remembering?

The women had begun to gather up the scraps of food, repacking baskets and piling the refuse in heaps. Mary moved over to help. "I must get my things," she said. "I'm going to pack all this stuff in one big basket and make Wells take it home with him. The children will enjoy it."

Becky came up just then, and Miss Willie stayed to talk with her. "Have you started my rugs yet, Becky?" she asked.

"Oh, I got one about done," Becky said, smoothing her apron. "Hit don't take me no time to whip up a braided rug. How big you want 'em?"

Miss Willie thought for a moment. "About four by six, I guess. If I put one in the front of the room and one by the stove, that ought to do."

Becky nodded. "That's jist about what I figgered. I'll have 'em done fer you 'fore school starts. How're you likin' the singin'?"

"I'm liking it a lot," Miss Willie answered.

"This ain't a really good singin'," Becky said, apologetically. "Them Johnson boys cain't lead near so good as Ferdy Jones over on the ridge, or Wells or Hod, neither. I jist wisht they'd let Wells an' Hod git up there . . . they'd show 'em up in no time."

"Why, I didn't know Hod could lead singing!"

"Yes," Becky said, and her mouth was prim with pride. "Yes, he's follered leadin' singin' sincet he was jist a boy. Hit comes natural with him. All the Pierces is good at it."

"And Wells too?"

"Wells is actual better'n Hod. But then he's older — he'd ort to be. Ifen you kin git Wells an' Hod an' Ferdy Jones, an' Matt Jasper fer the tenor, I've heared folks say they ain't no better singin' anywheres in the world."

"Matt Jasper!"

Becky nodded vigorously. "He's got about the truest tenor in these parts. Used to sing a heap. But you cain't hardly git him to no more. Hit's worth listenin' to when you kin."

The therapy of music! Where had it failed with Matt Jasper? Or had it been drowned in the faithlessness of life for him? What fears had he known that kept him from standing before his friends in pride, winsomely lifting the sweetness of his voice before the altar of their approval? Hod had said Matt Jasper had once been a good-looking man . . . and now Becky said he had the truest tenor in these parts. How much the iron of degradation must have seared his soul! Like a leper he was scarred by his disease, and like a leper he must walk before the world crying: "Unclean! Unclean!"

Miss Willie turned her thoughts from him with an effort. "Becky," she said, "I must find a place to live. Do you know of a family on the ridge who has room for me?"

"Why, ain't you goin' to live with Hod an' Mary?" Becky asked.

"No. I may be here several years, and it wouldn't be right to stay with them that long. Besides, I'm more comfortable in my own place."

Becky was silent for a time. She fingered the frill of her apron and eyed Miss Willie askance. She cleared her throat several times, and finally, ducking her head, she said: "You kin stay with me, ifen yer a mind to. I'd like it a heap myself."

"Why, Becky, how wonderful! I was thinking it might take me several weeks to find a place, and here you make room for me the very first thing! I'd like it a heap myself, Becky. When can I come?"

"E'er time you say. Ain't no reason I know of you cain't come on over tomorrer."

"No, not tomorrow," Miss Willie said. "I have to get Hod to take me to town first, and pick up my boxes and trunks and things. But when we've done that, I'll move right in. How good you are to let me stay with you!"

Becky's eyes were fixed on her feet. "Hit ain't good," she blurted out. "I liked you the first time I laid eyes on you. I was awishin' you'd be clost enough I could see you ever' day. Hit's me I'm a thinkin' of. They's other places you'd maybe ruther stay, an' maybe like better. But I've sich a likin' fer yer company, I made bold to offer you to stay with me. Hit'll be sich a mort o' pleasure fer me."

Miss Willie was touched. "It'll be company for me too, Becky. And I thank you for wanting me. Now I'd better help Mary before she gets everything done."

There wasn't much difference, after all, Miss Willie thought, between Billy Norton, who grabbed at crayons, and Becky, who grabbed at friendship. The same essential loneliness moved them both. That loneliness which pervaded all mankind, which was inherent at the partition of birth and was never assuaged until death sent the spirit back into the darkness of time from which it had come.

Again Miss Willie had the feeling of being led. There was something she and Becky could give each other.

CHAPTER

❧ 7 ❧

M ISS WILLIE, YOU CAN'T STAY with Becky." Mary was vehement in her protest. "Becky has only two rooms. It's physically impossible!"

"But, Mary, why should she offer to let me have a room! I just don't understand." Things had taken a bewildering turn. Miss Willie had been so pleased to have this arrangement with Becky. She had spoken of it to Mary confidently, happy to have it settled, and feeling certain that, since Gault was Hod's uncle, he and Mary would approve. Mary had been dismayed.

"Becky didn't tell you she had a spare room, did she?" she wanted to know.

"No," Miss Willie admitted, "not actually. Not in so many words. But surely she would know I meant . . . why, she wouldn't possibly think of having me in her own room!"

Mary laughed. "In hers and Gault's, you mean. That's just what she did mean, though. It wouldn't occur to Becky that there was anything improper in your sleeping in the extra bed in her front room. That's her sitting room, parlor, and bedroom. Here on the ridge, when people come to spend the night, they occupy whatever beds are available. It doesn't matter if there are two or even three in one room. Neither does it matter if men occupy one bed and women and children the others. Darkness is their privacy."

Miss Willie was aghast, and she pushed her glasses up on her nose in agitation. "What in the world shall I do? I might spend *one* night like that, but I can't spend months in such a situation. My goodness, Mary, it's positively uncivilized! Oh, I should have let you and Hod make some arrangement for me! I had no business to go barging ahead like that!"

They were sitting on the screened porch where Mary had brought her churning, and Miss Willie was sorting over Hod's socks in the big darning basket. She pushed the needle unhappily through a huge hole. "What are we going to do about Becky?"

Mary lifted the churn lid to peer inside. "It's nowhere near come," and she replaced the lid and started the dasher going again. It made a comfortable slushing noise, cavernous and full. "One of us will just have to tell her it's impossible. Because you simply can't do it. I'm afraid her feelings may be hurt too. She's such a queer little person. I don't even pretend to understand her. She's so withdrawn and remote . . . always wears those black dresses. Goes around so quietly."

"Wonder why."

"I don't know. Nobody knows a lot about Becky, to tell the truth. Hod's mother says Gault brought her home one day and said they were married. None of them had ever seen her or heard of her before. She came from over near Elkhorn somewhere in

67

those hills. And the only folks she seems to have is a sister over there she goes back to see occasionally. I've always felt there's a mystery somewhere about Becky. But if there is, it belongs to her. And she's a good, dear soul in her own way."

Miss Willie was silent. The morning was soft and still. Down the hollow an amethyst haze hung over the wrinkling hills. The sun was lazy getting up over the ridge, and the grass and bushes were still sparkling with the heavy dew. Hod's dog, old Duke, came around the corner of the house and dropped his fat, ancient body heavily to the ground.

They were quiet for a time, Mary shoving the churn dasher up and down, Miss Willie pushing her needle back and forth. Then she let the darning drop in her lap. "We're not going to hurt Becky's feelings, Mary," she said. "I'll move up there and something will happen. I can manage for several nights and then we'll see. But whatever else I do, I am not going to disappoint Becky. Her face positively beamed when I was talking to her. It would be like punishing a child to take her pleasure away from her."

"Miss Willie, really you can't do it. Hod will be able to tell her so that she'll understand."

Miss Willie shook her head. "Oh, I'm sure she could be made to understand. But all the understanding in the world wouldn't keep her from being disappointed. By now she has it all planned and she's probably been cleaning and polishing that room until it shines. No. I got myself into this and I'll get myself out of it. How, I don't know. I think I'll leave that to the Lord. He should have been watching me a little closer anyhow!"

Mary got up and moved toward the door. "I've got to get some water to make that butter come," she said. "That's a pretty large order for the Lord, Miss Willie. You don't know what you're getting into!"

Hod added his word to Mary's that night. "I aimed to speak to Ma, Miss Willie," he said. "They've got an extra room now that Irma and I are both married and Gramma's gone. You would be comfortable there, and you'd have a place for your books and things. Becky meant well, but she'll understand. I can tell her you have to have a place to read and study. I don't believe she'd be the least bit hurt."

Miss Willie shook her head. "No," she said. "I spoke impulsively to Becky, but the more I think of it, the more I believe there is a reason for my going there. I don't see it clearly just yet, and I don't know how I'll manage, but it will work out. Things usually do, if you give them time."

Mary was near tears. "Miss Willie, you have no idea . . . you just don't know . . ."

Miss Willie laughed. "Then I'll find out. Now don't fret over it any more. I'm going to pack tonight, and Hod can drive me up there tomorrow. I want to get settled before school starts."

When she went to her room, Hod puffed on his pipe and scratched at old Duke's ears. The dog thumped his tail gently against the floor. "Kinda hardheaded, isn't she?"

Mary gathered up her sewing and crammed it into the basket. "No," she said slowly, "not really. She just has a strong sense of duty."

"Becky's part of her duty now?"

"Yes. I talked too much today."

It was left that way, and the next afternoon when he came in from the fields, Hod drove Miss Willie and her luggage and her boxes of books up the ridge. "Well, it's just a whoop and a holler down to our place, Miss Willie," he assured her; "you can run down to see Mary any time you like, and she can come up to visit you. But I hope you get something better worked out before long."

Becky was on the porch, and she rose to greet them. "Come in," she called heartily, "come in. Hod, I'll fetch ye a cheer."

"Not for me," Hod said, "I've got to get on back. I just came to bring your new boarder. I'll unload these things and then I've got to get along home."

"I was lookin' fer you," Becky said to Miss Willie. "I allowed you'd be along this evenin'. I've got the place redded up an' supper's a waitin'."

"That's nice, Becky," Miss Willie answered. "Where shall Hod put my things?"

Hod had set two large bags on the porch and he was dragging out the cartons of books. "Is all them your'n?" Becky wanted to know. "Law, I knowed in reason you'd have a suitcase, but I never thought on you havin' sich a passel o' stuff as that! We'll make room fer 'em, though. Jist set 'em here on the porch, Hod. Miss Willie kin figger out where she wants to put 'em inside."

Miss Willie thought of her trunk, which was still at Mary's, and the packing boxes of small articles she had brought from home — an Italian print she especially loved; a quaint old wine flask which she used to hold flowers; a cloisonné box; a piece of tapestry; an India shawl that she had liked; and a jade figurine. Small things which she had thought would help make a room into a home. Well, they could stay where they were until she could see her way more clearly. This was enough for now.

When Hod left, Becky led the way inside. It was a sparsely furnished room that Miss Willie saw, the two beds standing in opposite corners. A few chairs and a dresser and an old tin trunk were the extent of its furnishings. Becky's braided rugs were scattered about, and the stone of the huge fireplace had been freshly whitewashed. An old clock ticked peacefully on the mantel, and above it hung a framed sampler, its faded red stitches praying, "God bless our home."

"This here bed's your'n," Becky said, pointing to the farthest one from the fireplace. "Gault, he allus likes to sleep clost to the fire. I cleaned out the bottom drawer of the bureau fer you, but I don't reckon hit'll be enough fer all them things you got. Mebbe we kin clean out that there trunk tomorrer. I keep my rags fer my rugs in it, but I kin put them somewheres else."

"Don't worry about it, Becky," Miss Willie said, "I'll keep my things in my bags until we decide about something. I'll just bring them in and slide them under my bed. And the boxes are full of books. They can stay in the boxes for a while. We'll just shove them back on the porch for tonight."

"Well. Hit don't look like rain, an' they ain't e'er thing to bother 'em. Ifen you don't need 'em, we'll jist leave 'em be till mornin'. Now, supper's a waitin'. I'll go call Gault, an' then we'll eat. The wash place is right by the door here in the kitchen," she called back, "reckon you'll be wantin' to wash up."

Miss Willie followed her to the kitchen and dabbled her fingers in the cool water Becky poured for her. "Ain't you goin' to wash yer face?" she asked when Miss Willie reached for the towel.

Obediently Miss Willie bent her face over the basin. Dear Lord, she thought, just help me get through these next few days . . . and let something turn up mighty quick!

When Gault came in, he and Miss Willie sat down to the table. He was a tall man and thin, but there was no stoop in his broad shoulders. His frame was big without being massive, and was as flat as a strap. He had a shock of iron-gray hair, which he had dampened and combed at the wash bench before coming in, but Miss Willie knew by its look that it was coarse and unruly and that usually it sprang up like bleached straw over his head. His face was thin, deeply tanned, and seamed with lines. There was a kindly look in his eyes, and his full underlip kept his mouth from being severe. Here was a man of conviction, she thought, poised in his assurance of himself, and quiet in his unquestioning faith.

Gault bent his head and quietly blessed the Lord for his care of them and asked him to use them in his service. Miss Willie liked his voice and the way he spoke. There was no unctuous holiness in his prayer; it was a friendly, manly thank-you, and a recognition of his obligation in return. When they lifted their heads, Gault turned to her. "Now, jist fall to an' he'p yerself, Miss Willie. I reckon Becky's got plenty, an' if she ain't, we'll git it."

The table was burdened with food — fried chicken, green beans, creamed corn, pickles, stewed tomatoes, half a dozen jars of jelly and preserves, fruit pies stacked twelve inches high, and a tall four-layer cake. There were two kinds of bread, corn bread and biscuits, and Becky diffidently offered boughten bread in addition. "Knowin' you was used to it, I thought to git some from the huckster yesterday," she explained.

"Now, don't buy special things for me," Miss Willie said. And then, noticing that Becky was standing to one side of the table, she asked, "Aren't you going to eat now?"

"I'll wait on you all," Becky said.

"We can wait on ourselves," Miss Willie protested, "come on and sit down with us."

Becky looked at Gault out of the corner of her eye. Gault was taking out generous helpings of food on his plate. Without pausing, he said quietly: "Hit's a woman's place to wait on her menfolks. Becky'll eat when we git done."

Miss Willie choked and coughed.

"Git Miss Willie a glass o' water, Becky," Gault directed. "She's got somethin' down her Sunday throat."

When the meal was finished, Gault went outside to finish up the chores. The evening light was fading and the kitchen was dim and pleasant. Miss Willie sat on at the table. Becky fussed around the stove and took up the remainder of the food. "Now you go on inside," she said, "an' set down. I'll jist eat a bite an' red up in here."

"No," answered Miss Willie. "I'll sit here with you. It's nicer. And then I'll help you wash the dishes."

"Oh, I didn't aim to set down. I mostly eat comin' an' goin'. I jist nibble on somethin' while I'm doin' up the work."

"Well, you're not going to nibble on something tonight! You sit right down at this table. I'm going to wait on you!"

Becky's mouth dropped, and then she laughed. "Law, Miss Willie, you've got the quarest idees. Why, they ain't nobody waited on me sincet I was a young'un."

"It's time they started, then. Now sit down. What do you want to drink?"

Becky sat down and filled her plate. "I reckon I'll take buttermilk." She sighed. "Ain't this nice? To be asettin' here with someone to talk to? I knowed in reason you was goin' to be a pleasure to me, but you ain't called to wait on me. I don't know as Gault'd like it."

"What Gault doesn't know won't hurt him," snapped Miss Willie. "A woman's place to wait on her menfolks, my eye!"

"Don't you go gittin' Gault's back up, Miss Willie," Becky warned. "He's easygoin' mostly, but he's got some strong idees about wimmin."

"I've got some strong ideas about men too. But I'll not anger
72

him if I can help it."

When Becky had finished, she took the two water buckets from the wash shelf. "I've got to git up the night water," she said, "down at the spring. You jist git you a cheer an' rest yerself."

"I'll go with you."

"Now, they ain't no call in you doin' that. Hit's jist a steep old pull back up that hill from the spring. Hit'll jist git you all winded."

"No, I want to go. I can carry one bucket."

Becky gave in and handed Miss Willie a bucket. They crossed the yard and followed a winding path through the back pasture to the edge of the hill. They came then to a barbed-wire fence, and Becky set her bucket down and rolled expertly under the fence. "Keerful," she warned Miss Willie. "Don't git yer dress caught an' rip it. I been after Gault hit's untellin' the times to make me a gate in this here fence, but jist looks like it goes in one ear an' out the other'n. I don't rightly mind packin' water from the spring. Hit's good water, an' cold, an' not too fur to be unhandy. But I shore git almighty tard o' rollin' under that there bob-war fence!"

Miss Willie scrambled under the wire and looked back at the fence. "How long have you been carrying water from the spring, Becky?"

Becky's face showed her surprise. "How long? Why, ever sincet me an' Gault was married. Twenty-five year, I reckon."

Miss Willie started to speak, but she thought better of it. She was too new yet on the ridge to speak her mind plainly.

When they were back at the house Miss Willie was winded and her arm was aching from the long climb with a heavy water bucket. They lighted a lamp and washed the dishes in its soft yellow glow. There was a contentment in the familiar task, and the big room enfolded them gently. Miss Willie hummed as she put the plates and bowls in the corner cupboard, and she smiled when she caught Becky's eye. "You're going to be a pleasure to me too, Becky," she said warmly. And Becky ducked her head and scrubbed a knife vigorously.

When Gault came in, they went in the other room, and Becky lighted another lamp. "I kin see to read by this 'un," Gault said,

73

"no need wastin' coal oil."

"I jist thought mebbe Miss Willie'd like more light," Becky answered.

Gault looked at Miss Willie across the room inquiringly. She shook her head. "No. You needn't light another lamp for me, Becky."

Becky turned the lamp down and blew the small flame out. The room was dimmed and muted around them. Gault took a large book from the mantel and went back to his chair. He opened the book and thumbed through it, and then, finding his place, cleared his throat. "We allus foller readin' the Scriptures 'fore goin' to bed," he explained.

"I'd like to listen," Miss Willie assured him.

He put on a pair of glasses and settled them on his nose. Involuntarily Miss Willie pushed her own in place more firmly.

"I'm a readin' from The Book of Isaiah, the sixth, seventh, and eighth chapters. We read straight through the Bible ever' year. Three chapters on weekdays, an' five on Sundays." He cleared his throat again and began. " 'In the year that king Uzziah died I saw also the Lord sitting upon a throne, high and lifted up, and his train filled the temple.' "

The vision of Isaiah! Gault's voice was unusually beautiful . . . deep, slow, and rich. He never stumbled over the words, and he gave them a cadence properly belonging to their poetry. " 'I heard the voice of the Lord, saying, Whom shall I send, and who will go for us? Then said I, Here am I; send me.' "

That's for me, Miss Willie thought. She remembered hearing the words when she was a child. A visiting missionary was preaching in her father's pulpit. He had talked of his field in China, speaking with passion of the people and their needs . . . pleading for help for them. "Here am I; send me." Miss Willie had sat tensely in the front row, echoing the words in her heart. That had been her moment of dedication. "Here am I; send me" . . . and she had consecrated her life from that time to the high purpose of ministering to the Chinese. That she had been thwarted she felt was the Lord's will. He had other work for her to do. And now, after all those years, she felt again a moment of dedication. This might not be China, but the needs of these people were just as great.

When Gault finished the reading, she leaned forward in her chair. "That was beautiful, Gault. Thank you for reading that portion of Isaiah tonight. It has always been one of my favorite passages."

"The Scriptures is all good readin'," he reminded her, putting his glasses away. "You kin turn out the light now, Becky."

Becky looked at Miss Willie. "Is they e'er thing you want outen them bags, Miss Willie?"

Miss Willie was startled. "Are you going to bed now?" she asked.

Gault was already slipping off his shoes. "They ain't no reason to stay up, fur as I kin tell. The beasts an' the fowls is a sleepin', an' man had best be gittin' his rest too."

Miss Willie drew a deep breath. "Just let me get a few things, Becky," she said. "It won't take me a minute."

She took a nightgown from her bag, and looked wildly at her toothbrush. Better let my teeth go tonight, she thought. It would be just like that old coot to turn the light out on me while I was brushing them. Becky waited patiently.

"All right, Becky."

"Ain't you goin' to take yer hair down?"

"Oh, yes, I forgot." She looked over at Gault's corner, but he was winding the clock. She slipped the pins out and let the long loops fall over her shoulders.

"Ain't it purty," Becky said, reaching out her hand and touching it. "I jist knowed it would be soft an' fine like that. Jist like a little girl's. I was hopin' you'd take it down where I could see."

Gault was fidgeting and Miss Willie hastily braided it. "I'll not brush it tonight," she said. "Now you can turn the light out, Becky."

"Let me git me a chaw o' terbaccer," Becky said to Gault. She glanced apologetically at Miss Willie. "I allus have to have a leetle piece to go to bed on."

O Lord, Miss Willie thought. Just get me out of this in a hurry! Just get me out of here!

75

In the darkness Miss Willie took off her outer clothes and slipped the nightgown over her head. Under its cover she timidly removed her underwear. Her hands shook, and she hurried to crawl into bed. She had trouble finding the sheets, and then she realized that there was only one sheet and it was on the bottom. A light quilt was the covering.

What *is* this mattress made of, she thought, as it rustled and gave beneath her. It must be hay, or straw, she decided. Over in the other corner she could hear Gault and Becky settling themselves. This is indecent, she thought. Positively indecent! Even in China perfect strangers don't sleep in the same room! Or do they? If Louise Wright could see me now! And suddenly she giggled. Indecent or not, it certainly would make a wonderful story to tell.

I'll never go to sleep, her mind wandered on. It's far too early. She turned on her side. Her bed was drawn up under the window and the night sky leaned intimately down. The thin crescent moon of last week had swelled to adolescence, and it hung naïvely over the far-flung stars. The air was clean-smelling and fresh. She listened to the night sounds, thinking how little they disturbed the tranquil peace. From a pasture down the ridge came the muffled tones of a bell, swinging in staccato rhythm. Near at hand there was the sweet, sleepy twittering of birds and the drowsy monotone of cicadas. Miss Willie tucked one hand under her cheek like a tired little girl, and slept.

CHAPTER
❦ 8 ❦

SEVERAL DAYS PASSED in the slow cadence of summer. The mornings were light and unburdened. Dawn came quickly up here on top the ridge, the sun heaving itself powerfully up over the eastern rim of trees. Miss Willie stood on the porch watching its round, disklike edges cut through the thin pink sky, waited for the pale pastel streaks to deepen and darken, and felt the sweeping climax of the morning as the full red ball lifted itself clear of the hills, majestically diminishing the heavens. The pale greens

76

and pinks and smoky grays were washed out by its radiance, and only the blue of space sustained its brilliant gold. Far down in the valleys the mists smoked hazily, curling under the increasing light toward the tops of the hills. Each morning was a new delight to Miss Willie. And each morning she claimed this time as her own, while Becky and Gault were busy with chores.

Later, the air became somnolent and sluggish, and they moved lazily about the tasks of the day. Gault came in for dinner and slept through the heat, rising in late afternoon to go back to the fields. Becky moved like a shadow about the house.

The evenings were another miracle of quiet, blued by dusk and the darkening sky. Then the hills seemed ancient and tired, resting tranquilly in a hushed stillness, waiting for the transmuting of night. In that brief time between twilight and dark, before the sounds of night began, Miss Willie felt caught up in the transcendent moment, lifted above and beyond time and space. She had a feeling of absolute stillness within herself . . . an absence of all unrest and conflict. Always one thought came to her at this time: "Be still, and know that I am God."

That moment broke with the stirring of the leaves in a lifting air, for with the breeze came the first notes of the evening nocturne — the call of a mourning dove; the high, descending lyrics of the whippoorwill; the low, insistent drone of the insects; and the deep bass drum of the frogs.

Later, there was the ordeal of going to bed in the same room with Gault and Becky. But Miss Willie had lessened it by staying outside long past their bedtime, thus gaining for herself a measure of privacy. And, she said to herself honestly, one gets used to anything.

It was the first of July when she said to Becky one morning that she was going to walk down into the hollow back of the house. She had wandered down the road in both directions, and across the fields to each side of the house, but down the steep hill past the spring lay an unexplored land.

"They ain't nothin' down there but rubble an' weeds," objected Becky. "You'll jist git yerself het up fer nothin'."

"Well, I want to see," Miss Willie answered. "I like to know what's all around me."

77

She borrowed one of Becky's bonnets and crawled through the fence of the back lot and made her way down the steep slope. She was disappointed in what she found, for, as Becky had said, there was nothing to be seen but gravelly ledges and waist-high growths of weeds.

Turning back, she climbed the hill, arriving at the top breathless and hot. She went through the barnyard again, and under the shade of a big walnut tree stood fanning herself with the bonnet. That's funny, she thought. I haven't seen that little log house there before. And then she noticed that the woodshed stood between it and the house. She walked over to it, curious as to its purpose. It was small, not more than twelve feet square, but it was complete with roof and chimney. Its high windows were empty and open, and the door sagged on rusty hinges. Except for a few places the chinking was still good, and along one wall an ancient and untidy rosebush climbed sturdily.

She peered in through the gaping door and saw that it was filled with odds and ends of junk — old broken furniture, pieces of rusted farm equipment, harnesses, stacks of feed, and so forth. Gault must use this for a storeroom, she thought. She was turning to go when the idea struck her: Why couldn't this little cabin be made into a home for her! She could still take her meals with Becky. And maybe Gault would let her use wood from his woodpile this winter. She could learn to build a fire. It would be worth cold mornings to have her own place! If Gault just had some other place he could put all that stuff!

Excitedly she squeezed past the sagging door and picked her way over the piles of feed and other things. The floor was still good. A board or two missing and several places that needed repairing. But it would do. She looked at the walls and quickly decided that wallboard would be the quickest and best way to take care of them. Painted white, she thought. Leave those beams too, but ceil the inside of the roof. The fireplace was filled with heaps of rubbish, but it looked all right. Paint the stones white, ruffle that old mantel with unbleached muslin, tie muslin curtains at the windows. Two of Becky's rugs on the floor. The idea was fast taking hold of her.

Gingerly she poked and prodded at the furniture. There was

78

an old wooden bed leaning against one wall. She pinched her lip between her fingers and studied it. Wash it down with soap and water and give it a coat of shellac, new springs and mattress. There was a table in the corner. She ran her finger over it, then hastily picked up a feed sack and cleaned the dust off the top surface. "Why, it's cherry," she said. It's a beautiful drop-leaf cherry table! Her excitement mounted. There was a rocker too, with the springs sagging and the cushion frayed. A spoke or two was gone in the back, but it would sit there by the fire on long winter evenings and gently rock the hours away. Oh, this was perfect! This was the answer. This would make a lovely home.

Everyone on the ridge helped get Miss Willie's house ready for her. The womenfolks came with scrub brushes and strong lye soap and soft, clean rags. They scoured and mopped and cleaned until the little cabin was spotless. Then Wells Pierce came, and Hod, with saws and hammers and nails, and soon the floor was whole, new windows were in place, the roof mended, and the clean white wallboards nailed over the old logs.

Miss Willie worked on the furniture with paint remover out under the big walnut tree, and was filled with joy when the soft patina of old cherry emerged, not only on the table, but also on the old bed. She exclaimed over its rich depth, and ran her hands lovingly down the sweetly curving posts. "Oh, it's beautiful!" she cried. "See how lovely it is!"

The table was mended and rubbed down with wax, and it took on a rich, glossy sheen. Wells put new spokes in the back of the rocker and Gault tied the sagging springs in place. Miss Willie then took a square of pieced quilt work and tacked it over the cushion.

There were trips to town for muslin and curtain rods and paint, and finally Hod brought the big packing box up from the hollow.

The day came when it was finished. Miss Willie stood in the door and drank it in, spreading out full and wide with contentment. The windows were softly draped with the muslin, and a frill of it banded the dark old mantel. Over the mantel hung the

India shawl, its fringe drooping gracefully around the Seth Thomas clock Becky had found for her in the loft room. On either side of the whitewashed stones stretched the bookshelves Hod had put up, and the blue and red and green bindings of her books blended in the dark tones of an old masterpiece.

In one corner stood the bed, the new mattress bulking high and comfortably under the woven coverlid Mary had brought. The cherry table was against another wall, the Italian print hanging over it, and the exquisite gray-green figurine reflected in its shining surface. From Hod's mother had come the chest of drawers in which even now Miss Willie's clothes were neatly put away, and Becky had massed a huge armful of her beautiful peonies in a tall, creamy pitcher on its marble top.

And finally there was the floor — Miss Willie loved the floor. She had painted it a dull, berry red, varnished it, and waxed it, and it now was a glistening pool of color, against which two of Becky's rag rugs lay softly.

Miss Willie drooped with tiredness. It had been hard work. Terribly hard work. But when she slipped between the sheets of her own bed that night, she was happy. I am in my own home, she thought. Tonight I shall listen to the heartbeat of the ridge in my own home.

CHAPTER
❧ 9 ❧

School started the second Monday in July, and Miss Willie left for the hollow bright and early. As she picked her way down the path, she felt a bright glow of anticipation — a keen tingling of joy at the task that lay ahead of her.

It was a beautiful morning, sharply clean and shining. Beads of dew hung in great, glistening drops on the bushes along the way, and the cobwebs that barred the path were frames of intricate lacework, hung with colors borrowed from the rainbow where the sun touched them gently. She went around them to keep from breaking them. They were too perfect and too fragile to touch.

80

Down in the hollow the shade was deep and sweet with clover smell, and Wishful Creek ran swiftly and noisily over its white stones. The fog was low here, and her hair clung damply to her forehead. This walk would be too long when winter came, she knew. She would have to have a horse to ride, and she would have to go down the ridge and around the road. But as long as she could she would walk the mile and a half, both morning and evening.

When she came within sight of the schoolhouse, she looked at it with pride. It had become hers now. This was her place, and here was her work. In the past week she had placed her stamp upon it, and in the next years it would hold her influence and her personality. The school ground had been freshly raked and cleaned. Hod and Wells had done that, and they had also brought from town, at her command, several dozen tin cups for use at the spring. She intended that each child should have his own cup, at least.

Inside, the room had been swept and scrubbed. Hattie and Becky and Mary and other women from the ridge had worked with her two days cleaning and scouring. Becky had helped her make the yellow curtains that hung at the windows, and there were two bright splashes of color on the floor — one in the center of the room by the stove, and one by her desk. She had decided two were enough. Hod had built her a row of shelves under one of the windows, and she had stacked dozens of books there. She had selected those books carefully, hoping they might open doors of adventure to eager minds. She wouldn't press that now, but the books would be there and the day would come when young hands would reach for them.

On her desk she placed a bowl of Becky's marigolds, letting their fringed green leaves frame the brilliant yellow. She looked around her, taking in the room. Everything was ready. Hod and Wells had cut off the legs of several of the benches in front, so that the smallest children could sit more comfortably. On a table at the back of the room she had placed stacks of paper and boxes of crayons. The one square of blackboard had been freshly painted and there was a new box of chalk. A roll of maps had been hung. Beside her desk were the cartons of textbooks, delivered last week from town. At least the state furnished free textbooks to these almost forgotten children!

There were voices outside, and she glanced at her watch. Seven thirty. Half an hour yet before time to ring the big dinner bell there on the corner of her desk. She smiled when she looked at it. How many years had that bell, vigorously rung, called these Piney Ridge children to their books? The handle was smooth and shiny, and there was a small crack in the rim of the bell. She had lifted it one day last week and let the clapper fall gently against the cup. The tone had been richly mellow and vibrant, in spite of the crack. It would ring out strongly in this hill-rimmed hollow, and send its deep-voiced summons to every nook and ledge.

Miss Willie went over the outline of her program for the day. Names and classification first. Then the distribution of books and assignments to the older pupils. While they were studying, she would work with the smallest ones. Then they could go outside with an older girl while she heard the first of the classes. She wondered how she could have eight grades in one room. How she could pack that much into each day. But others had done it, after a fashion, and she must do it too.

There would be a handful of small children, just starting to school. These would require time and patience. There would be another handful just beginning to read and write; a few more who could read a little better and write a little more legibly and who would be struggling with elementary number work. And then there would be at least three full grades with geography, history, reading, arithmetic, spelling, language, to say nothing of writing, music, and any science and art she could wedge in. She felt the same sense of frustration she had felt when she first looked at the hodgepodge of textbooks. How can you be expected to do it! Well, she would have to find some way to overlap things, to give less emphasis to some subjects — and here her mind chortled, What things are less important than others? — and perhaps she could work out some system whereby the older and obviously good students could help her. At least she didn't have to do everything today. Today she must make a start, and that was all.

82

At eight o'clock she stepped to the door and rang the bell. She had been conscious of the confusion of many voices as she studied her program, but as she looked out over the schoolyard, she felt suddenly afraid, and her heart sank dismally. There were so many of them! Forty, Wells had said. There seemed to be twice that many!

They lined up in front of the steps, the girls in one line and the boys in the other, the smallest in front and the tallest in back, making twin stairsteps ascending from her feet to the level of her eyes, slanting back into the yard. She had been on the point of turning back into the building, expecting them to come trooping in after her. But this was an orderly and expectant double file of freshly combed, cleanly washed children. But what did they expect? Heavens, she thought. What I am supposed to do now? Why hadn't she asked Mary or Hod or even Becky or Gault more about the procedure? Hod had warned her to do things the way they had always been done, until she had the confidence of the people.

But no one had told her these youngsters would line up the first thing in the morning and stand stiffly straight with their eyes glued on her, waiting for something, she knew not what. Maybe I'm supposed to make a speech, she thought wildly. But she dismissed that immediately. They might have clustered around the doorway if that were true, but they would hardly have lined up in this precise and orderly fashion. Maybe they sing before going inside was her next guess. But that didn't seem plausible either.

And then a middle-sized boy waved his hand. "Kin I beat the time?" he asked, when she nodded at him. Of course, she sighed. They lined up and marched in. "Yes," she answered and stood aside. The boy went to the big tree at the corner of the building and picked up a piece of iron leaning against it. He pounded a warning note on a broken wagon spring which hung from the lower limb. The lines straightened as if by magic, and then the boy slowly beat out a rhythmic one, two, three, four, to which the lines moved forward, up the steps, and through the door, keeping time to the clanging iron.

Inside, the boys seated themselves automatically on the left side of the building and the girls took the seats to the right. Miss

83

Willie's mouth quirked at the corner. "Male and female created he them." Even to the six-year-olds!

Once seated, the boys and girls looked around the room curiously. There was some whispering and snickering and pointing to the curtains and rugs and flowers, but she ignored it and went directly to the business at hand. "The seats in front," she said, "have been shortened for the little folks. Will those of you who are older and larger move to the rear and make room for them?"

There was a general scuffling and shifting, and some hesitation on the part of the least ones to leave older sisters and brothers. But Miss Willie waited, her attitude plainly saying she expected no difficulty. One small redheaded girl whimpered as her sister led her up front, and hid her face and clung to her sister's hand when she tried to leave her. Miss Willie reached out and patted the red curls. "She's skeered," the older sister explained.

"She'll be all right," Miss Willie promised. "You go on back to your seat."

The little redhead hitched herself around on the seat and watched her sister go back to the rear of the room, and the tears flowed steadily down her cheeks. Miss Willie kept her hand on the bright curls, occasionally patting them, but otherwise she made no attempt to comfort the child. So far and no farther, she knew, could one go into the unknown with another. This child was having her first experience in venturing beyond the walls of home, and she must do her venturing for herself. As she turned loose from the old and familiar, she must have something warm and real in the new, but it could only be a touch, a quiet hand and a steady voice. Tomorrow that hand and voice would be a part of her, and her enlarged horizons would take in the new personality and add it to the family.

When all the little folks were up front Miss Willie collected them and took them to the table at the back of the room. "Here are colors and paper," she told them. "I want you to make something for me. Think of something you saw on the way to school this morning — something lovely, like a flower or a bird. Draw it for me and paint it some beautiful color, like red or blue or purple or orange."

When she turned back to her desk, Miss Willie pondered the

situation. It would be best to have them seated by grades. Then she could move from one class to another easily. She pushed her glasses up. Yes. That would be best. She faced the group, smiling. "Today," she said, "today we shall start by getting acquainted and by enrolling. All of you know each other well. You have known each other all your lives. And I suspect you also know that I am Miss Willie Payne, Mary Pierce's aunt. But I shall have to learn who you are. Suppose I ask all who are in the eighth grade to stand in the back of the room for a moment."

Perhaps a dozen moved from their seats. "Now give me your names, please. One at a time."

A tall, thin girl with bleached blond hair was first. She kept her eyes on the floor.

"Your name," Miss Willie prompted.

"Pearly Simpson," the girl giggled and slewed an oblique glance across the room at the boys' section.

"Your parents' names?"

"Jodie an' Quilla."

"And how old are you?"

"Sixteen."

Sixteen, and in the eighth grade. Was that usual here, or was the girl just slow?

A couple of boys were next. Bill Johnston. Joe Sanderson. And then a plump, round, berry-brown girl gave her name as Rose Pierce. Ah, Wells's Rose, who kept house for her father and mothered the younger children. Miss Willie looked at her sharply. She was short and stocky, like her father, and she had her father's merry brown eyes. They crinkled now under Miss Willie's look, and her small, red, full-lipped mouth widened in a smile. "We're might' nigh kin to you," she laughed, "seein' we're Pierces too."

The girl was pretty in a wholesome, healthy way. She looked like a plump little brown wren, Miss Willie decided, and she laughed too as she answered, "Yes, that's true." Rose was sixteen also.

Miss Willie had the eighth grade sit down in the rear of the room, and then she took the seventh grade. Here was Sarah Pierce, Hod's little sister. The baby born so late in his mother's

85

life, whose coming he had so bitterly resented. Miss Willie had heard from Mary the story of this baby sister whom Hod had called "the tomato" once, but whom he now adored as if she were his own child. She was a shy, beautiful girl, and Miss Willie smiled at her gently.

Then came the sixth grade — a huge, milling group of children. There were Hickses, Squireses, another Simpson, two of Old Man Clark's boys, and Ewell and Sewell and Bewell Jones, Ferdy's triplets. There was also Sylvie Clark, a slender, silvery-haired child with an elfin face pointed with tiny, perfect features. Miss Willie felt a quiver of joy when she looked on this beauty. How could the child be a Clark, she wondered. She thought of a lily with its roots mired in mud.

A thin, overalled boy was next.

"Name?"

"Rufe Pierce."

Miss Willie looked up sharply. He was lean and brown, as were all the boys, with a shock of yellow, tousled hair. His face was honed down and hollowed, and over the cheeks the fine bones looked as if they had been rounded by firm thumbs. His jaw line was sharp and lean, and the chin squared off under the mouth decisively. There was a deep cleft in the chin, as if a probing finger had left its mark, and Miss Willie remembered that Hod had the same sunken spot in his chin.

The boy's eyes met hers boldly. Eyes that were so clear a blue that they blazed with light. At Miss Willie's quiet look they dropped, and the lashes lay tenderly and girlishly long on his cheeks. With that moment of dropping his lids, Miss Willie drew her breath quickly. His whole face changed. When the blue blaze of his eyes was quenched, the face softened and the straw-colored curls and the tawny lashes and the sun-drenched, tight-drawn skin were merged in a golden suffusion. Somewhere in Italy she had seen a head like that. A boy's head painted in those same warm sun tones, the flesh overlaid with deep gold so that it ran into the edges of the hair, the lashes dusty with gold laid gently against the chiseled bones of the cheek. The effect had been that of warmth and richness. The feel of the earth and the sun and winds and rain. Yes, now she remembered. It was in that

86

little church in Taranto. She had stood there in the dim light, on a gray day, while the weary rain fell outside and blotted out the sun, and she had felt the warmth of the sun steal through her chilled body from that golden head. She remembered thinking that the artist must have loved that child very much to have painted him so warmly. Putting all of the sun into his hair and eyes and skin . . . making of him a young golden god. This golden boy now . . . this Rufe Pierce!

Suddenly she was conscious of the passing of time. "Your father's name?" she asked.

"Ever'body on the ridge knows Wells Pierce is my pa," he said.

"But I'm new on the ridge," she smiled at him. "I wouldn't know."

The lashes dropped again and he said nothing. Miss Willie felt rebuked. She had known, of course. The question had been automatic.

On and on the enrolling went. How many children there were! In the fifth grade there was another of Wells's children. Abby, little, thin, and blue-eyed, looking not even remotely related to Rose and Rufe. But finally it was done. The textbooks were distributed then, and Miss Willie went through the weary business of making assignments.

"We don't never go to school the first day," volunteered one of the older boys.

"What do you do?" Miss Willie asked.

"Well, the teacher jist gits us all enrolled; then he ginerally goes to git the books. We don't actual start till the next day."

"Well, we already have the books. I think we might as well go ahead with school today." Miss Willie was pleasant as she dismissed the question.

She turned then with relief to the youngest children. They were like old friends to her. These little ones she understood. Quietly she moved among them, learning that this one was Jimmy Clark, that one Jewel Simpson, this one Clarissa Jones, and here was Hod's sister's little boy, Johnnie Walton. He held up a stork-legged bird with brilliant plumage for her to see. She nodded seriously. "That must have been a beautiful bird you saw this morning, Johnnie."

87

He ducked his head and grinned, showing four wide spaces where he had lost his teeth. "I think hit was a blue jay," he said. "He was flyin' so fast I couldn't make out fer shore, but that's what I think he was."

"Blue jays don't have all them colors," snorted another boy.

"This un did," stoutly insisted Johnnie.

"Of course," said Miss Willie. "Let's get your books now, and then you may go out to play."

When she turned around, Rufe, who was far to the middle of the room, raised his hand. "Are we goin' to set in these seats all the time?" he wanted to know.

"Not necessarily," Miss Willie answered. "As soon as we get things straightened out, you may be assigned permanent seats. But I think it will be best if each grade sits together."

"We ain't never done it that-a-way before," he insisted. "I've allus set next the window there. Hit's been my seat ever sincet I started to school."

"We'll see," Miss Willie promised.

The boy bent his head. Cranky old maid, he whispered under his breath. Cranky, ugly, old maid teacher. Allus have set by the winder. A feller kin look out an' see the woods, an' watch the wind apassin' through the leaves, an' see old Jupe settin' out there under the tree waitin'. An' hear that leetle ole mockerbird that's got a nest clost by. I cain't noways stand to stay all penned in here in the middle, he muttered. Hit ain't right. Only way I kin stand to go to school is to set by the winder. He laid his head in his arms and wished he hadn't come today.

It was ten o'clock, then, and Miss Willie dismissed the entire group for the midmorning recess. She handed some of the older girls the stacks of cups and asked them to see that they were distributed at the spring. "Make sure each person has a cup," she said. "Here are black crayons. Mark each one's name on a cup for him."

The girls giggled, took the cups, and went outside. Miss Willie went to the door and watched the yelling, milling crowd of children for a moment, and then she turned back. She would start with the reading classes, she decided.

She was busy the entire thirty minutes and was hardly conscious of the noise outside. After this she must get out too, but today there was too much to do. Before she realized it, the time had sped by and she must ring the bell for "books" again. She stepped to the door. It was only then that she noticed how unnaturally quiet it was. She looked around the schoolyard and saw the girls huddled in small groups, watching the door, giggling and whispering among themselves. Not a boy was in sight except the very smallest ones. Well, perhaps they played somewhere on farther down the hollow by themselves. She rang the bell and the girls came slowly toward her. They didn't line up this time, but passed her in the doorway, eying her solemnly, and moving slowly to their seats.

She waited for a moment and then went to her desk. I shall not ask them where the boys have gone, she decided. She felt the tension in the air and knew that something serious had happened. Her heart beat fast and a frightened feeling settled in her stomach. I shall not be disconcerted, she said to herself. Whatever has happened, I shall not be humiliated before these girls. Her mind was whirling with her thoughts, and a deep feeling of dismay spread over her. But she stood calmly behind her desk, and deliberately pushed her glasses into place.

"We shall have the third- and fourth-grade reading classes now," she said quietly. "And while I am hearing these classes, the sixth, seventh, and eighth grades will work the problems assigned this morning."

The room was so still that not a breath was heard. Pearly Simpson and Rose Pierce looked at each other, and then bent over their books. As if that were a signal, the other girls opened their books, and Miss Willie took a deep breath. At least the girls were not going to rebel!

Somehow the day moved on. Through the morning, the noon hour, and the early afternoon. Through arithmetic, geography, and history. And still there were no boys. Miss Willie began to suspect that they were not going to come back, and there was a heavy weight in her chest. On my first day, she thought. It will be all over the ridge! What did I do that was wrong? And how do you handle an open revolt? What sort of big stick were these boys waving over her, and what did they want? What were they

89

trying to do? She had heard tales of how new teachers in country schools were deliberately tried to see if they could handle the school. Was this what lay back of it?

Just before four o'clock, as she was getting ready to dismiss the group, the boys filed in through the door, one at a time, Rufe Pierce leading them. When she looked up and saw them, Miss Willie's anger flared. The little tramps, she said to herself. The little ruffians! And that beautiful, brazen, golden boy! He must be the ringleader!

The boys had stopped just inside the door. Rufe looked at her boldly. "We don't never go to school on the first day," he said. "An' we want our old seats back."

Miss Willie's head went up, and her anger spread so rapidly and so thickly over her body that she trembled with the effort to control it. She had to try twice before she could speak. "You are not going to sit anywhere," she said, and her voice sounded harsh even in her own ears. "You are not even coming back to school until you bring me written excuses for your absence to-day. You left school without permission, and you can't come back without permission. Do you understand that?"

She whirled quickly and spoke to the entire group, rapidly and sharply, the words dropping like pellets from her mouth. "Listen to me, all of you. I may be a new teacher on the ridge, and I am a woman. But I will *not* have rebellion in this school. I don't want to be a dictator. But if we have to have authority in this school, I want every one of you to understand that *I* am that authority. If I *have* to issue orders, I certainly shall! And please understand another thing. I am not easily frightened. You *cannot* force me to do anything, either by threats or by action. Now you boys get out of here, and either bring written excuses for your absences to-morrow, or don't come back!"

Her knees were weak and shaking, but her voice remained calm and icy. Each word had been spoken precisely and without tremor. But she was thinking, Now I've done it. Now I shall probably have all the parents on the ridge on my neck, and shall have to leave here in disgrace, and Hod and Mary will be shamed before their relatives and friends. But she could not check the angry flow of words. She was madder than she had ever remem-

90

bered being in her life, and she was determined that these boys should *not* get by with this sort of threat.

"School is dismissed," she said curtly, and she began stacking the papers on her desk. I shall have to see Lem Pierce at once, she thought. He was the chairman of the trustees. And Wells, and Hod. Hod wasn't a trustee, but she wanted him there. I shall have to tell them what has happened and what I have done. If they don't stand behind me, then I shall have to leave. And Jodie Simpson. He was a trustee. But no teacher can be bullied and retain the respect of her pupils, she told herself. This had to be faced, and I've done the best I could.

She felt a certain peace then, and turned to the smallest children with a smile. They had not understood her words, but the tone of her voice had left them wide-eyed. She made her voice warm and friendly to them as she said good-by, and she spoke gently to the girls gathering around her. Rufe swaggered out the door, the rest of the boys following him. Once outside they went whooping off up the hollow and over the hill. She wondered if there would be any boys in school this term! She wondered if there would be any school!

CHAPTER
❦ 10 ❦

THAT NIGHT SHE SAT IN HER SMALL CABIN with Lem and Hod and Gault and Wells and Jodie Simpson around her. All Pierces but Jodie, and he had married a Pierce.

"I'm goin' to tan that Rufe's hide till he cain't sit down fer a week," Wells said when she had finished her story. "He's jist been ahonin' fer trouble. He's gittin' too big fer his britches. I'm goin' to take him down a peg or two. Don't you weary yourself none, Miss Willie. He'll not lead off no gang o' boys agin soon!"

"No," Miss Willie said, "that's not the answer. Whipping the boys isn't going to help. I called you here just to tell you what has happened. I felt the boys took the law into their own hands, and I didn't think they should be allowed to get by with it. They have to learn to respect authority and to live under discipline.

91

Maybe I shouldn't have told them to bring written excuses, but I did, and I shall stand by it. They don't come back to school without them."

Lem and Hod had not yet spoken. Lem was stroking his long chin. "They ain't no doubt but what you done right, Miss Willie. Ifen you'd let 'em git by with it you might jist as well of packed yer things an' went. They wouldn't of never give you no peace. They's been more'n one teacher hounded outen Big Springs. But I dunno whether they'll ever bring them there excuses you want or not. That's what's wearyin' me."

Hod spoke then. "I think the trustees had better take united action on the whole matter. Then there won't be any doubt but that they're back of Miss Willie. Lem, you're the chairman. You call a meetin' at the schoolhouse for tomorrow night. The boys didn't count on this gettin' as big as it has, and they're goin' to be plumb scared of what they've started if we ring the parents in on it. But they've acted like little hoodlums down there long enough. They might as well learn right now Miss Willie don't stand alone."

Gault nodded his head in agreement. "Hod's right."

But Wells rocked back on his chair legs and twisted a forelock of hair. "I dunno," he said. "Believe I'd wait a day or two. See how many o' them excuses comes in tomorrer. Might be better to let the thing simmer down."

Miss Willie thought about it. "I believe Wells is right. Let's see what happens tomorrow before you take any action."

Hod and Lem and Gault shook their heads. She knew from the look on their faces that they doubted the outcome. "Well, I reckon a few days one way or the other ain't goin' to hurt," Gault said, "an' if she kin bring 'em to taw by herself, hit might be best."

When they left, Wells lingered. "Miss Willie, I shore hate this. Special since my Rufe was the cause of it. I wisht you'd let me git in after *him* anyways."

"No," Miss Willie answered. "I'm afraid you'll just make him hate me. Wells, he's a beautiful boy."

"Beauty is as beauty does, Miss Willie. He's a quare young'un. Never give me no special trouble, though. But he's allus roamed

92

the woods . . . him an' his dog. I ain't never understood the boy, but he's mostly been quiet-like an', like I said, not give to makin' trouble."

Miss Willie laid her hand on his arm. "Well, let's not worry too much about it. Maybe it will all blow over."

Wells put his hat on. "Hit will that. You'll see, Miss Willie. Jist don't give it e'er 'nother thought. Hit'll be all right."

He said good night and left her to her troubled thoughts. Her first day had ended disastrously. But the worst disaster was not the rebellion of the boys. The worst was that she had lost her grip in her anger and had reverted to pure schoolteacher type. She had let her sense of outraged pride make her become the autocrat . . . the disciplinarian . . . the typical unbending, un-yielding, unundersanding old-maid schoolteacher. Oh, she had spoken bravely of not wanting to be a dictator. But hadn't she been? Didn't she really want obedience . . . immediate, un-questioning obedience? Hadn't she cracked down, not only with her own authority, but with the authority of the trustees too? And even now wasn't she comforted by the knowledge that the trustees thought she had done right? Hadn't she fled to them, wanting them to pick up her lowered flags and fly them for her?

She twisted and turned in her bed, flaying herself with her own self-contempt, and driving herself into first one corner then the other. There had been so little excuse for what she had done! Just the excuse, she thought wryly, of what else could she have done! If she had controlled herself and had asked the boys to sit down and talk the matter over? If she had tried reasonably to get to the root of the matter? No. She knew better than that. The boys were trying to force her hand, and the only answer they would understand or respect was force.

If that's true — and she knew it was — then I wasn't so far wrong. Whatever I did that made them behave so, once it was done I have surely done the only thing I could do as a conse-quence! She felt better. Not good, yet. But better. She had no idea what she was going to do next. No plan would come. But she laid it away until tomorrow, making her mind quit seeking a lighted way, stilling her tired body and letting it sink deep into the mattress. A last chuckling thought raced through her mind before she drowsed off to sleep. Well, *veni, vidi,* but evidently not *vici!*

The next morning she was frankly nervous. Gault and Becky watched her as she tried to eat breakfast. Finally she pushed her plate aside. "I'm scared," she confessed.

Gault poured half his cup of coffee into a saucer and blew on it. "Got good reason to be," he said, sipping noisily. "Boys down at Big Springs is allus a handful fer e'er teacher we ever git. Allus has been that-a-way. Ever sincet I kin recollect. We was a handful, an' Hod's gang, they was, an' I reckon boys ginerally ever'-wheres is a trial to their teachers. Hit'll blow over, though. Don't know as I'd let it weary me too much. Jist go along with 'em. Don't believe I'd insist too hard on 'em asettin' diffrunt, though. Hit sort of goes agin the grain. Jist let 'em set where they're used to settin'. Let 'em come up to the front fer their classes like allus."

"Is that the way it's done? I intended to go to them for the classes."

"Hit does 'em good to git up an' stretch a little, an' move around."

"Gault," said Miss Willie, "tell me just exactly how the day should go? I think I need some help!"

The old man buttered a biscuit and took a big bite before he answered. "Well," he said, "I'll tell you how we allus done it, an' I reckon they ain't changed none sincet then. We marched in an' then we stood up an' sung 'America' or 'The Star-Spangled Banner,' or 'My Old Kentucky Home,' or somethin' ever'body knowed. Then we had the Lord's Prayer. Then we started off with readin'."

"How do you mean, started off with reading?"

"One class at a time come up front an' set on the benches in front o' the teacher's desk an' read to her. Mostly ever'body read one paragraph. That was all. Then we had spellin'. She jist give out the words, first to one then another. After recess we had arithmetic. That takened a longer spell. Then after dinner we had language an' history. An' then geography. They've got hygiene too now. But we never had none o' that."

94

Miss Willie took a deep breath. "And what about the first and second grades?"

"Oh, mostly the teacher jist called them up to her desk one at a time an' had 'em read to her. She jist kinder worked with them when she could. She never tried to have no class with 'em."

"And what did they do all the rest of the time?"

"I don't rightly know. Jist set there, I reckon. Drawed a little, mebbe. Sometimes when the weather was nice, she'd let 'em go outside a spell."

Miss Willie rose. She had a dazed look on her face. "I'll try," she said.

Miss Willie was early again that day and she deliberately stayed in the building until time to ring the bell. She thought she could hear boys' voices, but she made herself stay at her desk. When she stepped to the door, the bell in her hand, she glanced quickly around the yard, and then she sighed with relief. Apparently the boys had come back. The yard was full of them, and a vigorous game of baseball was going on. At the sound of the bell they came trooping toward the door, shoving and pushing and yelling, and lined up on their side of the steps. Once the lines formed, there was quiet. She stood still and watched them. Her eyes went down the line and took in each face, meeting the glance of each boy.

Rufe Pierce stepped out of line. "You want these here notes we got now, or after we git inside?"

"I'll take them now, please," she answered, meeting his challenge. Rufe moved forward and laid a folded bit of paper in her palm. His eyes met hers with a straight, deep look, a look that blazed at her, and she felt a long shuddering down her back. The look was full of hate.

One at a time the other boys brought their notes to her. Every boy in the line had his note. Every boy stepped out and laid it in her hand. Some were bold, as Rufe had been. Others were awkward and would not meet her eyes.

"Thank you," she said, and stepped back to the door. "Will someone beat the time, please."

"Hit's our time today," one of the girls said.

"All right. One of you older girls go ahead."

Inside, they filed to the places they had occupied the day before. Miss Willie laid the little stack of notes on her desk and turned to face the group. There was something queer about every boy being back in school today, with his note from his parents. But she wasn't going to ask any questions now. Whatever lay behind it, this wasn't the time to go looking a gift horse in the mouth! "Now," Miss Willie said, "we can just forget that whole episode. You may take your old seats if you like."

There was a moment of quiet, and Miss Willie looked at Rufe. There was an amazed look on his face. Miss Willie chuckled. We'll see who has won this first round, she said to herself.

She waited until the confusion of the shifting around had died away. "Now," she said, "we shall stand and sing 'America.'"

When the last note of the song had echoed through the room, she bowed her head and began the Lord's Prayer. One by one the clear young voices joined in. They stumbled when she automatically said "debts" instead of "trespasses," but recovered and went on to the end.

When they were seated again, she pushed her glasses up on her nose and cleared her throat. "We shall now have reading. Fourth grade, come forward, please."

Compromise? Her mind accused her. Of course. She lifted her chin and picked up a fourth reader. "Ewell Jones, will you read the first paragraph?"

CHAPTER
❦ 11 ❦

How's school going, Miss Willie?" Mary asked. It was a Sunday morning about two weeks after school had started. Miss Willie had slipped down to Mary's for a long talk. The burden of the air hung heavy over them and they sat quietly on the long screened porch, Miss Willie fanning herself occasionally with the bonnet she had borrowed from Becky. Hod was stretched out in a big chair, his feet propped up on the table nearby. Miss Willie laid the bonnet down and pleated its big back ruffles between her restless fingers.

"I don't know, Mary," she said slowly, "I just don't know. I got off to a bad start. There isn't any doubt about that. I ought to have found out how things were done here on the ridge. But it just didn't occur to me that even the children wouldn't be budged from the way things have always been done!"

"Now, Miss Willie, you're taking that entirely too seriously. It's all settled. The boys brought their excuses and came back, and you haven't had any more trouble, have you?"

"I still think there's something fishy about that. It isn't reasonable to suppose every last one of those boys went to their parents of their own accord and asked them to write an excuse for them. And the notes all sounded suspiciously alike. I asked Gault about it, but he wouldn't say a word. Said just to let well enough alone."

"That's just what I'd do too, if I was you," Hod said. He puffed a lazy smoke ring toward the ceiling. Miss Willie fanned industriously.

"I think somebody went to those parents," she said after a moment, looking at Hod intently; "somebody went to see every one of them after you all left my cabin that night and told them what had happened, and furthermore told them what to say in those notes. It couldn't have been you, could it?"

"It could have. But it wasn't."

"Then you admit somebody did."

"I don't admit nothin'. I just said it could have been me, but it wasn't."

"Well, I don't think Lem would have done it, and I know Gault didn't. Wells . . . of course! Rufe was the ringleader and he felt responsible. And he told me not to worry. Why, of course! That's just what happened! Now, look here, Hod . . ."

"*You* look here, Miss Willie. You're just guessin' at something. Forget it. Leave it lie. When you've stirred up one hornet's nest, it's just plain sense not to stir up any more. If Wells took the sting out of this one for you — and I'm not sayin' he did or he didn't — you better just be glad it don't sting no more, and forget it!"

Miss Willie looked at Mary, and caught the merest suggestion of a wink. Her angry retort died aborning. She pleated the ruffle and then fanned, and then went back to pleating the ruffle. "Well, that doesn't sting any more," she said finally, "but there are little things. You know all those tin cups I bought so that each child could have his own cup? They just disappeared last week. Every single one of them! Saturday I sent by Gault to get some more, and Monday they all disappeared. No one knows a thing about it, of course. When I ask, there's just a blank wall of silence. I don't know what to make of it, and I don't know what to do."

Hod spoke. "Who you think's doin' it?"

Miss Willie hesitated. "Hod, I'm afraid Rufe's at the bottom of this too."

Hod nodded. "That's what I think too. You'd better let Wells get in behind that young man."

Miss Willie shook her head. "No. I'll have to work it out myself. But I don't know what to do about the cups."

Hod shifted his feet and leaned forward. "Miss Willie, I went to that school when I was a kid, and I know how kids think down there. They're lined up against the teacher. They'll dare you every way they can, and as long as they can get by with it, they'll keep on daring. They're used to a teacher that lights into them with a hickory stick, and that's all they'll pay any attention to. Every time they get by with something they're gigglin' and snickerin' behind your back. They're bestin' the teacher, see? I tell you, there's only one thing they respect. Either you'll have to make up your mind to tan that little scamp yourself, or let Wells do it. He'll not give you any peace until you do."

Miss Willie pleated the ruffle of her bonnet. "I don't believe that," she said, finally.

"You'll see," Hod said flatly.

Mary eased herself in her chair. "I'm sorry, Miss Willie," she said gently. "I'm so sorry. I hate to see you troubled like this, and I didn't know how it would be or I would never have got you into it."

Miss Willie straightened her thin shoulders. "Now, Mary, don't you go feeling sorry about things. I'll lick this thing yet. I'll get it straightened out. You'll see. And don't you think for one minute I'm sorry to be here. This is just one small problem, and it'll take more than this to make me sorry I came. I've about decided to keep the cups locked in my cupboard and give them out myself at recess and noon, and stand there like a policeman while they're being used, and then gather them up and lock them up again when they've finished with them. I can't let Rufe get the best of me, and that's the only thing I can think of."

Hod laughed. "It'll be a lot of trouble, but I reckon it'll work. I still say the easiest way would be just to whale the tar out of that young man. That's something he'd understand and respect."

Miss Willie laughed too, but she still shook her head. "I'll try my way first."

A comfortable silence settled over them, and the noon sun rode hot overhead. A bottlefly buzzed lazily at the screen door, and Hod's dog snapped angrily at it.

"When you aimin' to have the school openin' party?" It was Hod who spoke.

"The opening party?" Miss Willie's voice lifted the question in amazement.

"Sure," he said lazily, "always open school with a big shindig."

Miss Willie collapsed against the back of her chair and she fanned feebly. "Oh, dear," she sighed.

"Miss Willie, you don't have to," Mary interrupted. "It's too much for you, just getting started and running into this trouble with the boys. Don't try it."

"Have they 'allus' done it, Hod?" Miss Willie wanted to know.

"Allus," he replied solemnly.

Miss Willie knocked her thumb against her chin. "That settles it," she said gloomily, "whatever has allus been done, I must do or die trying! What sort of party do they have?"

"Oh, usually a pie supper or spellin' bee. Or a box supper. Ridge folks always want to eat at their shindigs, but they don't mind bringin' their own food. Just announce at school when you're havin' the party, an' they'll all come."

Miss Willie looked at Mary and raised her eyebrows. Mary laughed. "We'll have a party, then," Miss Willie said. "When would be the best time?"

"About a week from Friday night," Hod put in. "That'd give 'em time to get ready for it."

"I thought you said it wouldn't be any trouble!"

99

"I did. And it won't. But folks'll have to have time to spread the word around and bake up their pies and such."

"It's so hot for a pie supper," Miss Willie objected.

"It's not ever too hot for a pie supper," Hod insisted.

"Why couldn't we have an ice-cream supper?"

"Take a powerful lot of ice cream. And folks would have to get ice from town. Now that'd be real trouble."

Miss Willie thought for a moment. "I could get several freezers already made. Would the men and boys be willing to pay for it . . . I mean, buy it like the pies?"

"Why, I reckon they would. They always buy the pies or boxes. Don't see there'd be much difference."

"They could draw for partners and buy the cream for them. And why couldn't we have a little program? Have some singing and let the young folks play games and have a speech or two," Miss Willie was getting enthusiastic. "I know — we could get Lem to make a speech, as chairman of the trustees . . ."

"And Miss Willie," Mary said, "as the new teacher of the school."

"No, no. That wouldn't be necessary."

"Oh, you'd have to say a few words anyhow," Hod said. "The teacher allus does."

"Here we go again," Miss Willie laughed. "Well, just a few. Just a welcome. Oh Mary, this may be fun! I'll get to meet all the parents! Mary, do you think we could find enough small tables and chairs so that people could sit around and be comfortable while they eat their ice cream? Maybe outside where it's cooler. Lanterns in the trees? Wouldn't that be pretty? Oh, we'll make this a really nice party!"

"We'll take the car one day, Miss Willie," Mary promised, "and scour the ridge for tables and chairs. And we'll get flowers to decorate. All the women will help."

Miss Willie went in the house to get pencil and paper to make a list. "I always forget something," she said as she went through the door.

Mary looked at Hod, and the corner of her mouth drew down. "You be sure and take your guitar that night," she warned, "and tell Wells to bring his!"

Hod let another smoke ring curl upward. "I'll remember," he promised.

Plans for the party went forward. Miss Willie announced the date at school and the news spread rapidly. A sparkling expectancy rose over the ridge. An ice-cream party! Well, I never!

"They ain't never been no ice-cream party fer the school openin' that I know of," Becky said.

"There's going to be one now," Miss Willie insisted. "And I want all your spoons and that little table, and all the flowers you can spare."

"Shore," Becky said, "we'll jist strip the yard. They ain't goin' to last long noways. With the heat an' all."

Mary brought the car, and for two or three days before the party she and Miss Willie drove over the ridge collecting tables, chairs, and spoons, marking them meticulously to avoid mixing them.

On Friday, Hod went to town and brought back with him the freezers of cream and a dozen rolls of white crepe paper. Miss Willie had dismissed school at noon, and she and Mary and Becky had been working all afternoon. The schoolhouse was gay with flowers. Late roses, gladioli, zinnias, and marigolds sprayed their brilliance around the walls, and over all honeysuckle drooped its sweet fragrance. The desks were moved back against the wall, and tables were set up in the yard. When Hod brought the crepe paper, the women set to work and soon had the tables covered with white squares, scalloped and crimped. Miss Willie gathered up the tin drinking cups and covered them with the white paper and set one full of flowers on each table.

"Doesn't it look pretty?" she asked.

"Hit shore does," Becky agreed. "How you aimin' to git enough light out here to see by?"

"Oh, we've got lanterns to hang in the trees," Mary said. "We borrowed all the lanterns on the ridge. How'd we happen to miss yours?"

Becky giggled. "More'n likely 'cause we don't have e'ern!"

Mary put her arm around Miss Willie. "You run on home now. You're all worn out. Lie down and rest a minute before you dress, and we'll come by for you early tonight."

When they had lighted the lanterns that night, the school yard looked unbelievably lovely. The dim, flickering lights swayed in the trees, casting long shadows over the white-covered tables with their bright spots of color. Miss Willie felt the familiarity of the place slipping away from her. This was not the school ground where the boys romped and ran and yelled, and the girls grouped themselves under the trees. This was a shadowed terrace, cool and softly lighted, where gracious people could walk and talk and sit quietly sipping their frosted drinks, and where muted music would presently flow gently over all.

Miss Willie pushed her glasses up and smoothed her dress. She had worn a thin white dress, belting it with a soft gold sash. Her fine brown hair was piled in an orderly mass on top of her head, but she had pushed a pearl-studded comb into the back of it, and had pinned one perfect yellow rose at the throat of her dress. She felt very splendid indeed! Her mouth crinkled. And for what reason should she want to be very splendid tonight? Her mind poked a ridiculing finger at her finery. She tossed her head impatiently. Must I examine every motive, she asked herself. Must there be a reason? Well, then, I should like to make as good an impression as possible on the parents of my children! Oh? Isn't it wonderful, then, that Wells Pierce is a parent? Oh, be quiet!

By dusky dark the crowd was gathering. Hod and Mary stood near Miss Willie, at the entrance of the room, greeting each newcomer and introducing him to her. Quietly and shyly they greeted her. Some of them she had already met at the all-day singing. Others she was meeting for the first time. They were all resplendent in their Sunday best, and awkward in their movements. "Pleased to meet you," they said. Or, "Glad to make yer acquaintance." Or, "Hit's a pleasure, ma'am." They shook hands gravely and then moved stiffly to the seats, which had been moved to line the walls. A respectful silence was observed.

Miss Willie looked at them sitting stiffly and grimly around the room. Oh, dear, she thought, why can't they move around and talk and laugh a little!

"It's time to start," Hod whispered, "ever'body's here that's comin'."

They moved forward to the chairs that had been set apart in

102

one end of the room. Lem joined them. It had been planned for him to make a short talk and introduce Miss Willie. Loosely and easily he stood before them.

"Folks," he said, "I ain't goin' to make no speech, although Miss Willie here has done ast me to. But you ain't wantin' to hear me. I'll jist say that we're proud you come, an' we want you all to have a good time. I'll jist say too that we got the best teacher this year we could of got. You all know who she is . . . Mary's aunt, Miss Willie Payne. She's been ateachin' school fer a good long time, an' she knows how's the best way to teach our young-'uns. Me an' the rest o' the trustees has got full confidence in her. We have done told her we'll do all in our power to uphold her, an' I'm repeatin' it here where you kin all hear it. We aim to do our part, accordin' to our lights. On account of we know she'll allus do her'n. As fur as we're concerned, whatever Miss Willie says in this here school goes. An' I want her to have her say-so right now."

The audience applauded when Lem walked over and brought Miss Willie to the center of the room. She felt confused for a moment. What could you say after an introduction like that? She had planned a little speech of welcome, but Lem had already done that. Funny. They had been coming to this schoolhouse for years. And yet she was their hostess tonight. She let her glance sweep around the room. There was Becky, primly proud and expectant. The teacher lived at her house. She had a right of ownership tonight. There was Gault, tall, lean, and ragged-headed. There was Hattie, Hod's mother, her starched apron fluting stiffly around her waist, her finely chiseled face profiled against the wall. There was Tom, Hod's father, lean like Gault but more stooped, honest face cleanly scrubbed. There were the Joneses, Ferdy with the gulping Adam's apple and Corinna with the newest baby asleep already in her lap. They were Ewell and Bewell and Sewell's parents. There was Old Man Clark and Mamie, and their brood cluttering around them. There were the Simpsons and the Taylors and the Jordans from over Bear Hollow way. There was even Matt Jasper, drooling spittle down his chin. But he was alone. She must talk to him tonight, and see why the children weren't in school.

103

Her eyes stopped finally on Wells Pierce, standing in the far corner of the room, his solid frame leaning easily against the wall. His clean blue shirt was open at the throat, and she saw how strongly his neck rose from his shoulders, and how wide and solid his shoulders were, straining under the shirt. He smiled at her when her eyes passed on over him. By his side stood Rufe, tawny and golden in the half-light, and near by sat Rose.

Oh, she had no welcome for these people! Rather, they should welcome her. She spread her hands slightly apart, appealingly. Well, say that, then. Say you want them to take you into their hearts and make you one with them. Say you have been lonely for too many years, and you want to be at home with them. Say what you hope and dream for this school. Say what you hope and dream for yourself and for them, here together. Say you want to walk the dark hills with them . . . let the streams of their lives flow through you, thread through you, quicken you. Say you want to walk under the moon and stars of Piney Ridge and bring them down to you . . . to fill yourself with them . . . you, who are empty. Say you want to fill the emptiness. Say it! She found Wells's eyes again.

She flung her hands wide and let them drop. Oh, no. Not yet. She stammered through a little speech, gaining poise as she went along. She hoped they could be friends. She wanted very much to have their help. If they ever wanted to suggest ways in which she could be more helpful, they were to tell her frankly. She would welcome such suggestions. She went on to talk of the school. Of the boys and girls who were her pupils. Of some of her hopes for them. She mentioned her own joy at being here, spoke gently of Mary and Hod, and ended with the reiterated hope that they might all be friends. She felt confused and foolish. She, who was usually so sure of herself!

When she had finished, she told them they had planned a few games, and she tried desperately to direct them in a silly guessing game, "Who am I?" Brightly she went among them, trying to enliven them, to draw them out. Their faces were wooden, and only a few were brave enough to speak out. Abandoning that, she went on to the next thing she had planned. Another mixer. But they wouldn't mix. How could you draw people into games who refused to be drawn? She tried two or three games, and her despair grew. Only Hod and Mary and Wells were responding. The party was dying of dullness. Did they always sit like sullen bumps on a log, she wondered.

"Let's sing awhile," she said brightly. She moved before them, her white dress glinting in the soft light. "Do you all know 'Flow Gently, Sweet Afton'? Let's start with that," and she led out bravely into the beautiful words. Mary's voice followed stoutly, and Hod's. Wells didn't know the words, but she saw that he was trying to follow her, and his deep voice lent power, even with its humming. No one else made any attempt to sing. Falteringly she came to the end of the first stanza, and the song died of its own weakness. Wildly she looked toward Mary and Hod. Hod was lifting his guitar from the corner. And then from the side of her eye she saw that Wells was coming forward with his guitar. Oh, yes! Let them take over! Let them stir some response from these lumps of clay! Let them resurrect this deadness, if they could!

Wells stepped easily to the front. "Miss Willie here has ast me an' Hod to he'p out with the singin'," he said, thrumming ragged chords from the guitar as he spoke. "C'mon, Hod, git yer chair over here. An' let's sing!"

The two guitars lifted their singing chords high, and the two men stormed into a gay, fast tune:

" 'She'll be comin' round the mountain, When she comes.
She'll be comin' round the mountain, When she comes.
She'll be comin' round the mountain,
She'll be comin' round the mountain,
She'll be comin' round the mountain, When she comes.' "

The rollicking stanzas went on: "She'll be drivin' six white horses, When she comes"; "Oh, we'll all go to meet her, When she comes"; "We will kill the old red rooster, . . . When she comes." And soon every hand was clapping, every foot was patting, and every voice was shouting the loud, lusty song. "And we'll all have chicken and dumplin' When she comes."

Miss Willie looked at Mary and lifted her hands helplessly. Ridge people knew what they liked! And you couldn't fool them with "Flow Gently, Sweet Afton."

The two men swung the crowd into "O Susanna! Oh, don't you

cry for me!" and from that into "Buffalo Gal." They kept them shouting and clapping and stamping their feet with the fast-running rhythms. And then Hod stood up and shouted at Ferdy Jones, "Ferdy, come up here"; and to the crowd: "Form sets for a singin' game! Ferdy, you call 'em!"

Wells threw his guitar to the floor and grabbed Miss Willie around the middle, swinging her into the center of the floor. Ferdy threw back his head and yelled, "Balance all!" and Hod pranced his fingers up the neck of his guitar and rocked his shoulders.

"First young lady all around town," Ferdy bawled, and Wells seized Miss Willie and swung her twice around. Her glasses slipped down her nose and she pushed at them with her free hand. Wells let her go and the next man on her right grabbed her and started swinging. She hung on and let her feet fly on the corners. Her breath was coming fast, and the perspiration was tickling her back.

"Swing on a corner with a step and a swing!" and the next man in line grabbed her. Her glasses were on the end of her nose now, and she felt them bounce as she hit the floor between swings. They hung on her chin a moment, and hung there balanced carelessly by the earpieces. She clutched them as Wells came around again, and slid them off to safety as she promenaded home. The knot of her hair had slipped crazily to one side and she was raining hairpins. Oh, let it go! The music was getting inside her, and she was finding her second wind.

"Swing and do-si-do. Promenade all. Take your partner and we'll all run away. Second young lady all around town. Swing on a corner with a step and a swing." Wells was swinging her now, prancing with a shuffling step down the line. She bent her knees and let her legs go loose. "Oh, swing on the corner and we'll all go home." When they passed Hod, she saw his hands furiously plucking the strings, his head thrown back and his mouth shouting the words. Ferdy Jones was bellowing over the music. "Swing on the corner . . . and balance to your places!"

"Git yer breath, now," Ferdy called. "Next 'un'll be 'Shoo Fly.'"

Miss Willie stood where Wells had released her, her breath heaving violently out of her chest.

"Hey, Miss Willie," Wells laughed between his own gasping breaths, "you kin shore swing a lively leg. Now wasn't that grand?"

Miss Willie nodded, unable to talk. A lively leg! Miss Willie Payne! Suddenly she was laughing . . . great gusts of laughter shaking her, and the tears were running down her cheeks. A lively leg!

Wells joined in with his great roar. "Now, wasn't that somethin'? Miss Willie, how you like this here clambake?"

"Wells," she said, still gasping, "I like this here clambake!"

But she wouldn't dance any more. She wanted, rather, to stand and look on. They were having so much fun now. This was what they wanted then. And she remembered the white-covered tables outside, with the glow of lanterns on them. Gracious people walking and talking while muted music flowed around them. No. Lusty people, shouting and stamping, while lusty music flowed through them and within them. Ridge people singing their own hill songs, dancing their own hill dances . . . ridge people, dark with the soil, dark with the hills. Born and bred in the deep darkness of the hills. Hills as old as time. People rooted in them, timeless as the hills. She felt a new sense of timelessness herself . . . one with the earth and the earth's people.

She noticed Rose dancing with a tall, dark boy. He hadn't been there at first. His hair was black like a crow's wing, and his face was sun-reddened mahogany. He had bold black eyes and flashing white teeth. There was the look of a pirate about him. A predatory, swaggering look. He was too daring, too handsome, and he held Rose too tightly when he swung her.

"Becky," Miss Willie asked, "who is that boy dancing with Rose?"

Becky turned to look. "Him? Why, that's Tay Clark. Old Man Clark's boy by his first woman."

"I haven't seen him around before."

"No. He don't live here on Piney no more. He up an' left out when his pa married Mamie. Some says he's stillin' over on Wanderin' Creek."

"Stillin'?"

"Moonshinin'. Makin' likker."

Miss Willie's eyes widened. "Why, do they still make liquor here in these hills? I thought since prohibition had been repealed there wouldn't be any need for making moonshine any more."

"Some likes hit best. An' anyways, Adair County's dry. Allus has been. An' hit's a fur piece over to Marion County to git a drink. They's allus some makes it nearabouts."

When the music ended, Miss Willie watched Rose slip out the door with Tay Clark. She saw his arm hold itself around her plump waist and wondered if Wells would like that. Surely not, if the boy was a lawbreaker. She turned around to find him. But Mary was at her side. "Miss Willie, we'd better serve the ice cream now. If you want them to choose partners, you'd better get started."

"No," Miss Willie answered, "just get Hod to tell them the ice cream will be served outside. We'll let them do as they please about eating. And, Mary, tell Hod not to say anything about paying for it. This party's on me."

In the darkness under the trees Tay Clark and Rose stood. No light filtered in this closed place, and trees sheltered deeply on all sides. Tay pulled the girl into his arms. He bent his head and let his mouth down upon her lifted one. "Rose, Rose," he said softly, pushing her head back and laughing a little, then bending to drink deeply of her mouth again.

"We cain't stay long, Tay," she warned, "somebody'll miss us."

"Not fer a minnit yit," he begged. "I don't git to see you hardly ever. Days is so long over there by myself. An' I git to thinkin' of you. Someday I'm goin' to run off with you!"

"Not yit," she said, letting her lips run lightly over his chin.

"Don't do that!" and he pulled sharply away.

She laughed and, stretching on her toes, locked her arms around his neck. He pulled her close. "Yer pa'd take his shotgun to me ifen he could see us like this," he growled.

"He ain't goin' to see us," she said.

"What's he got agin me?" Tay grumbled. "Ifen you'd let me, I'd tell him to his face we was aimin' to git married soon as we kin. Hit ain't no sin to want to git married."

108

"He ain't got nothin' agin you personal, I reckon. But he don't like what he's heared about you. Says you been a wild 'un all yer life. An' he wouldn't noways put up with that there stillin'."

"Cain't a man change hisself?"

"I doubt he'd think so."

They heard the sound of the people moving outside the building. "I got to go back now, Tay. They're comin' out to eat the ice cream. You go on around the schoolhouse, an' I'll go back the way we come."

"Wait," he held her a moment longer. "You goin' to school?"

"Yes."

"I'll come up the holler when I kin. Listen fer a owl. I'll hoot three times, an' then three more times. I'll be in the pine woods."

She listened intently. "I'll git away when I kin. Ifen I don't come soon, don't wait. Hit'll be because somethin's holdin' me. Now git around that buildin', quick!"

People were milling around the door as he dropped a last light kiss on her lips, and she slipped easily under his arm into the darkness.

The ice cream disappeared like magic. Miss Willie and Becky dipped it up as fast as they could, but there was always another dish held out for more. There was an easy flow of talk and laughter now, and a high, good-natured give-and-take of fun. Miss Willie, so tired she couldn't stand, sat behind the freezers, full of contentment. Hod and Wells had saved the party, but that was not important now. What was important was that folks were having a good time.

Then Hod came to her. "Miss Willie, I'd like to end this party with a song from Matt Jasper. He can really sing, an' I think folks would like it."

"Of course, Hod."

Hod brought Matt into the lantern light, where he stood before the crowd, gaunt, dirty, and fumbling, his head hanging and his eyes darting. He had made some attempt at cleaning himself up, for his hair had been cut and his face was clean-shaven. Miss Willie saw with surprise that his lean, thin face wasn't bad-looking. She had thought him hideous when she and Mary met him and Lutie down in the hollow that morning. Now she saw that the bones of his face were chiseled into sharp, fine contours, and that his weak, mobile mouth was pathetically young.

He wet his lips nervously a time or two. Then he cleared his throat and lifted his head. He fixed his eyes at some point beyond the heads of the people and opened his mouth. A sweet, clear voice rose soaring above them all. Clear and sweet and soft, it floated over them. He was singing an old spiritual: "And I, If I Be Lifted Up, Will Draw All Men Unto Me." "If I be lifted up" . . . Miss Willie's eyes stung. The truest tenor in these parts! Matt Jasper used to be a fine-looking man! The voice lifted and fell, like a sweet-blown bugle in the night, full, clean, and fine. "If I be lifted up"! For this transcendent moment Matt Jasper was lifted up. Lifted out of the dull, prideless clod that walked the hills by day, lifted and changed somehow into something clean and noble. For a moment, this shining present, he was a man.

The voice rose to the last high, unbearably sweet note and held it suspended, as fragile as a star, letting it linger and fade, gently and softly, until it whispered into nothingness in the trees. A sob rose in Miss Willie's throat. It was too much that this man whom you couldn't bear to look upon, whose touch you would shrink from, who was foul and diseased and unclean — it was too much that from out of *that* should come that pure, sweet voice. This ridge . . . these people! She would never understand them!

When that last high note had been lost in time, the people wiped their eyes and cried for more, more! But Matt shook his head and shambled out into the darkness. The pure look that had lighted his face while he was singing was washed away, and the old sly, furtive expression crept back as he slunk off. Miss Willie watched him, and her throat was knotted in an aching lump.

And then the party was over. The first folks to leave came by as she stood there, ice-cream dipper hanging limply in her hand. "Hit was a real good party, Miss Willie." "Hit was a heap o' fun." She heard that repeated dozens of times. "Hit was a good party. Hit was a plumb nice party."

At the last Hod and Mary and Wells were left with her. While the men took the tables and chairs inside, Mary and Miss Willie stacked the little paper plates and crumpled the white table covers. They made one huge trash heap and burned it, and piled the littered spoons in a basket for the next day's returning. Miss Willie's feet ached, and she felt hot and weary all over.

"We'll take you home," Mary said, when they had finished.

"I'll take her home," Wells said. "I've got the spring wagon. Hit'll save you all the trip up the ridge an' back."

"Yes, Mary," Miss Willie agreed, "you go on. You must be as tired and worn out as I am. Wells has to go right by my place anyhow."

Wells helped her into the wagon and she settled herself on the quilt which was folded on the seat. He crawled up beside her and clucked to the team.

When they came out from under the trees, the moon was riding high and a froth of stars was following in its wake. The night was full of sound, and the wraiths of mist were curling in the low places, shot through with moonlight. There was a ghostly stillness which the singing insects could not disturb. A stillness that is full of sound, but that belongs only in the country.

As the wagon jolted down the road, Wells's shoulder moved against her own, and Miss Willie felt a hand of peace laid across her weariness. This man was so good, so solid, so earthy. He was part of the ridge, absorbed into the soil, bound to it, tied and yet free. He gave off an earth feeling, a closeness to land and trees and streams and animals. He had not lost his essential bondage to the earth which gave him his full, free manhood. He was not wasted or emptied. His shoulder here, so broad and strong, rubbing through the thin stuff of her dress, was built for swinging an ax, or pushing a plow, or handling a team. Or, she was honest, for cushioning a woman's head. She drew a deep breath. And he turned to her, speaking for the first time.

"You're jist plumb wore out, ain't you? Jist frazzled down. This here party was jist too much fer you."

"I am tired," she confessed, "yes. But it's a good tiredness. Do you think they had a good time, Wells?"

"Why, shore!" He was astonished. "Didn't you see 'em prancin' around alaughin' an' asingin'? Why, they shore did have a good time!"

"That was because of you and Hod. The party was dying on its feet until you all stepped in. Wells, when am I goin to learn?"

"Miss Willie, hit'll take the rest o' yer life to learn the ways of the ridge. You have to be borned here to know 'em all, an' to fit ever' time. Ifen you stay here the rest o' yer life, you'll git easy-like with 'em, but they's things that'll allus puzzle you. But it don't matter, Miss Willie. Jist keep this in mind. They don't expect you to be like 'em in most things. They think yer quare, but that ain't goin' to keep 'em from likin' you, an' bein' proud yer their teacher. Hit won't keep 'em from buckin' you when what you want don't suit, neither. But I reckon they'd be a mite let down if you wasn't some quare. Hit gives 'em somethin' to talk about. As fur as tonight goes, they'd of had a good time if Hod an' me hadn't of stepped in. They'd a set around an' takened it all in, an' et the ice cream quiet-like, an' they'd a went home an' talked about how purty the schoolhouse looked, an' how purty Miss Willie looked in her white dress, an' how good the ice cream was. Hit was smart of you to give 'em somethin' diffrunt. They liked it. Ifen you'd jist had another pie supper an' spellin' bee like they allus have, they'd a enjoyed it, too, but hit wouldn't of been in keepin' with what they was expectin' from you. Me an' Hod jist thought we'd as well mix in a little of the old with the new to satisfy ever'body. But don't go thinkin' that was all of it. Hit was you, in yer purty little white dress, an' yer nice speech, an' the flowers, an' ice cream 'stead of pie, an' tables an' chairs, an' lanterns in the trees. Why, they'll brag about this school openin' party fer years!"

Hot tears pricked Miss Willie's eyes. "Thank you, Wells," she said. "Thank you. For everything."

But when she was drifting off to sleep she could remember only one thing he had said. "Hit was you in yer purty little white dress." He had noticed the dress then!

CHAPTER

❧ 12 ❧

August stole over Piney Ridge with its long sun-filled days, and its cool, sighing nights. Miss Willie walked the mile and a half to Big Springs, watching the changing fields. The corn was browning and the ears hung heavy on the stalks. Broom sedge along the way was losing its silky look and turning light and yellow. Goldenrod was heading up and sumac was beginning to redden.

The tobacco was bleaching in the sun, standing tall, crowned with the pale, amethyst, oleanderlike blooms. They looked so waxen and so creamy that she stopped by a field one day and gathered an armful for the schoolroom. The children laughed when they saw them on her desk in a tall urn. "Terbaccer blooms," they snickered. "Teacher's got a bouquet of terbaccer blooms!"

"Beauty is where you find it," Miss Willie insisted stanchly, "and if you're looking for it, you can find it anywhere, even in tobacco blooms!"

The nights were starlit and still. The cowbells in the pasture carried far over the hills, and the incessant drone of katydids and nightjars hummed out of the shadows and dark places. And always from the creeks and ponds came the bass growl of the frogs. To Miss Willie the night sounds formed the perfect accompaniment for drowsy contentment. Night after night when she lay on her old cherry bed under the window watching the moon and the stars circle the skies, these sounds lulled her to sleep. And she slept so deeply and awakened so refreshed! If the days took their toll of her strength, the nights filled and replenished her, giving her in the cool dawns a sense of power and grace. The spring of life was rewinding. She felt full of health and an inner sap which flowed through her joyously. She was well, she was busy, she was happy.

And she felt she was beginning to accomplish some things. Her little scheme about the drinking cups had worked. She felt a little guilty about that. It was another compromise. But at least the cups hadn't disappeared again, and however she had won the victory, it was still a victory. Things had quieted down at the school.

And she was beginning to get somewhere with her plan to make Gault have a well dug for Becky. She giggled as she thought of it. She hadn't even told Becky she was working on that. She had just started helping Becky bring up the night water. A time or two she had noticed Gault watching them. Once or twice she had dragged behind with her bucket so that Gault, coming to the house, had overtaken her. "Becky's back gets so tired," she had explained, "carrying water all that long way up the hill." Gault had not offered to carry the bucket, but she'd have him doing that next. Let him see how heavy that bucket was once, let him roll under that barbed-wire fence and carry two full buckets of water up that hill, and he'd start thinking about a well!

She jogged along in Hod's old car, keeping it in the ruts of the road, letting it nose along slowly. She had borrowed it to go calling. She wanted to know the parents of all her children, and she wanted to see for herself the homes they came from. Right now she was headed toward Wells's place. Not that a call there was necessary. She saw Wells frequently, but she admitted to more than a little curiosity about his home. Out of what had Rose and Rufe and Abby come? How did they make out, now, with Rose keeping the house? Mary said they did very well. But she wanted . . . what did she want? She just wanted to see Wells's home. She was compelled, somehow, to see where he lived, and how. Compelled to . . . to what? To be where he was? To stand familiarly where he slept and ate and worked? To look at the four walls that enclosed him daily?

The house stood off the main ridge road, on a high point in a long sweep of fields. A grove of trees surrounded it and shaded it from view until you were right up on it. Miss Willie drove the car up to the fence and got out. It was a big house, larger than most on the ridge, two stories in front with a T added in back. But it had a neglected look. The grass and weeds had overgrown the yard, and the fence sagged badly. The house had once been painted, but now the paint was scaling off, leaving dead and patchy places, like scabs on old sores. There were cardboards in the missing windowpanes across the front, and when she stepped up on the porch, a loose board gave treacherously under her. She felt a shock of sympathy and pity. A man alone had so little time for beauty.

When she called, Rose came to the door and pushed the sagging screen outward to let her in. "Why, hit's Miss Willie," she said. "Come in. Come in, ifen you kin git in. I wasn't expectin' nobody today an' the house ain't cleaned up or nothin'. Git you a chair, Miss Willie."

Miss Willie looked around the room. Rose was right. The floor was littered with odds and ends. In one corner was a bed, not yet made, and across from it stood an old bureau, its top cluttered with bottles, boxes, Rose's purse, an old hat of Wells's, and as much other stuff as could be gotten on it. The faded blue wallpaper had come loose in the corner over the bed and hung sagging and bellying in the draft that swept through the open door.

Hanging on the wall were several brightly colored calendars, and hooked up near the ceiling, by cords passed under their arms, were three dolls. Miss Willie remembered that here on the ridge little girls did not play with their best dolls. Only the old, ragged ones were to play with. The best ones were hung on the walls.

Over the fireplace was an enlarged and tinted photograph of a woman, hung at that precarious angle which was considered correct on the ridge. It was a gaudy, cheap piece of work, framed in a wide and ornate circle of gilt, and the glass bulged drunkenly over it. But neither the gaudy colors, nor the cheap ornate frame, nor the bulging glass could detract from the winsomeness of the brown-haired, brown-eyed woman laughing down from the wall. Her eyes crinkled at the corners and her mouth spread widely across her face. That's Matildy, thought Miss Willie. That's Wells's Matildy, who used to sit here before this fire and laugh with him, and hold her children close, and laugh with them. These four walls closed safe around them and their laughter, and held them tight. She looked around as if the walls had moved closer in. And then these four walls didn't hold them tight any longer. Wells, trying to hold the bits together. And the bits flying farther and farther apart. How empty Matildy's going had left

115

these four walls! A slow ache spread over Miss Willie, squeezing her and smothering her. How empty Matildy's going had left Wells!

She rose abruptly. "I'd like a drink, Rose," she said.

"Yessum," and Rose led the way into the kitchen. Rufe sat near the door, cleaning his gun. He looked up when they entered, but ducked his head when Miss Willie spoke and went on drawing the oiled rag through the gun barrel.

The flies swarmed through the unscreened windows and settled in a heavy cloud over the uncovered table. The dishes and the remainder of the breakfast food still sat there, greasy and sodden-looking. Miss Willie felt a tremor of nausea.

Rose took a bucket from the wash shelf and emptied its contents out the door. "I'll jist draw up a fresh pump," she said, shooing a chicken from the stoop as she went out.

Suddenly Miss Willie turned. "Rufe," she said, "why don't you keep the yard trimmed, and the fences mended? And why don't you fix the screens, and the windows? Your father has so much to do. He can't do everything. But you're a big, strong boy, and you could be such a help to him if you would. Instead of hunting and fishing all the time, why don't you try to be more thoughtful of your father?"

A closed, sullen look crept over the boy's face. "I he'p him," he said. "All I kin, an' all he wants." He snapped the bolt of the gun in place and stood it in the corner. Miss Willie spread her hands helplessly. And Rose sloshed water across the floor lifting the bucket to the shelf.

Miss Willie turned to her. "Rose, I'll help you do these dishes while I'm here."

"Miss Willie, they ain't no need o' that. I'll git to 'em sooner or later. They ain't no hurry."

"Oh, let's do them now. Two of us will make fast work of it."

"Yessum," and Rose put a kettle of water on to heat while Miss Willie set to work stacking the dishes.

"Do you always have flies this bad, Rose?"

"Yessum. The screens is bad, an' Pop don't git around to fixin' 'em, looks like. An' they jist swarm outside the door, what with the chickens flockin' around, an' ever'thing."

116

"Can't you pen the chickens up somewhere? They oughtn't to run loose in the yard. And, Rose, if you wouldn't throw water close to the house there wouldn't be so many flies. Or garbage and refuse. Take it away from the house, and empty all the water somewhere else. Those things draw flies, and you'll find there won't be so many if you take care."

Rufe snorted and went out the door, slamming it behind him. Miss Willie flushed, and heat poured up into her face and neck. "I don't mean to interfere, Rose," she went on, though, "but you'll have a home of your own someday, and you'll want it nice and clean, and if you don't learn now, it will be hard for you later on."

"Yessum."

Miss Willie had a hopeless feeling. Rose was so compliant, so soft-spoken, so agreeable. But she doubted if a word she had said meant a thing to her. O Wells, Wells! How truly empty had Matildy's going left this house!

When Miss Willie returned the car that night, she was tired and white-faced. She handed Hod the keys and sank into a chair, her knees trembling and her back aching. "Mary," she said, "I wouldn't believe what I have seen today, if I hadn't seen it with my own eyes!" She rested her elbows on the arms of the chair and put her hands over her face. "I have been in ten homes to-day, if you could call them homes. They are where people live, at any rate. Where the parents of those school children live! In not one have I seen the least comprehension of the necessity of sanitation, cleanliness, or even comfort! I can't quite believe even yet what I have seen!"

Mary laid her knitting aside. "I know, Miss Willie. I've tried to tell you."

Miss Willie shook her head. "You could never tell anyone what the actual circumstances are. They beggar telling. You have to see this sort of thing for yourself. Mary," and she sat up straight, "I stood on the porch at Mamie Clark's and watched her separate her milk. The flies were so thick they drowned in the milk as it poured from the separator, and Mamie reached in with her hand — her hand, mind you — and dipped them out, and went right on

117

separating!"

"And at the Joneses'," Miss Willie went on, "the baby was sick — 'summer complaint,' Corinna called it — and do you know what she was giving it? Soot water! Water, with soot from the chimney stirred in it! Said it was the best thing she knew for stopping summer complaint. And the poor little thing lay there, crying and fretting! She gave it a cold rind of bacon to gnaw on to hush it!"

Miss Willie's hand fretted nervously in her lap. "And at the Simpsons', Quilla is down with her stomach ulcers. 'Stummick trouble,' she called it. I asked her how long she'd had stomach trouble, and she said she didn't rightly know. All her life, nearly! She lay there and told me in the calmest sort of way how she had spit up blood this time. I asked her if she'd seen the doctor, and she laughed and said it wouldn't do any good. She'd been once, a long time ago, and he'd told her to stop eating soda bread and chunk meat and soup beans, but she said she didn't like the stuff he told her she could eat, so she'd just gone ahead eating like always!"

Miss Willie sat forward in her chair and pointed her finger. "Mary, half the people on this ridge have ulcerated stomachs! You can't think of a family but one or two have stomach trouble. And they go right on eating hot soda bread three times a day, fried chunk meat, boiled beans — greasy and soupy — and raw onions! They raise wonderful gardens and they don't like garden stuff! They get plenty of good, rich milk, but they separate their milk and sell the cream to the creamery, and drink coffee or skimmed milk! Fried meat! Fried apples! Fried potatoes! They only know one way to cook anything, and that's to fry it! Oh, I always thought people in the country had the best, the most wholesome food in the world! But not here, they don't! They literally eat themselves to death on their greasy, fried foods!"

In her agitation she got up and took to pacing around the room. She stopped in front of Mary and shook her finger again. "And do you know that in five of those ten homes — five of them, mind you, exactly half — there wasn't even a toilet! No outhouse of any sort! They use the barn! A whole family, eight or ten people, and they use the barn! And in three of those homes they carry water from a spring. There wasn't any well! I asked why they didn't have a well. It costs money to dig a well. 'Then,' I said, 'why don't you have a cistern? All it would take is a little energy to dig a hole, just a small amount of money to line it with cement and to trough the eaves of the house.' Drink rain water! They looked at me as though I'd lost my mind! They wouldn't think of such! I said they could keep it pure with chloride of lime, and they would know positively it was clean. Well, they knowed the spring water was clean. Why, it was so cold it hurt your teeth, and so clear you could see yourself in it! No matter, of course, that cows drink from it too! No matter that lizards and snakes and bugs crawl all around it, and maybe in it! No, the spring water was clean and pure! Oh, it's terrible! Terrible!" And Miss Willie sank back into her chair and shivered.

Mary moved restlessly. "Well, these are our people, Miss Willie, and that's the way they are."

"That's what's so hopeless about the whole thing," Miss Willie cried, "you've expressed it exactly! That's the way they are, and there's no changing them this side of heaven! That's the way they've 'allus' been! That's the way they're satisfied to be! How on earth can you help people who don't even know they need helping?" In a fury of frustration she flung her hands wide. "Never in my life have I been so angry, and never have I felt so completely helpless! It makes me furious that here in this country of ours, the wealthiest in the whole world, there are people living as these people on the ridge are living! But that's not the worst of it! The worst is their lethargy. Their not wanting anything better or different! They have no conception of what it is to live freely, and graciously, and healthily and cleanly! They make out, just like — " she paused — "I started to say just like their fathers had before them. But I believe these people have sunk farther into apathy. They don't have the initiative their fathers had. Their fathers and their grandfathers turned their minds to work and made them serve them. The women spun and wove and stitched and sewed. The men sawed and hewed and experimented. They had to. There was no alternative. But these people have lost all the things their fathers knew and have learned nothing new. They sell their healthy, wholesome living for the cheap things they can buy. They'd rather have sardines and bologna and bottled pop

119

from the huckster than their own good milk and eggs and garden stuff."

Her glasses slipped down her nose, and in her agitation she shoved furiously at them. The nosepiece snapped with a sharp, brittle sound. She snatched the broken glasses off and glared at them. "Now," she said in exasperation, "now, that's just the last straw! That's just the end of all I can stand today! I'm going home, Mary. I'm no fit company for anyone in the mood I'm in!"

She strode across the room, turning at the door to brandish the broken glasses at Mary. "But you wait and see! You wait! There's a way to wake these people up, and I'll find it! I'll think of something! And then I'll do it!"

And she stumped doggedly out of the door.

CHAPTER

❧ 13 ❧

Aᴜɢᴜꜱᴛ ɪɴ ᴛʜᴇ Pɪɴᴇʏ Rɪᴅɢᴇ country was also the time of revivals and great preachings. Big white tents mushroomed in the hollows and on the ridges, each ministering to a particular neighborhood. It mattered not what denomination sponsored the revival; the folks came, tanned and leathered by the summer sun, to hear the power of the Word. To shout and pray together, and to fall, abashed, confessing their sins at the mourners' bench.

Piney Ridge had its meeting too. Out of the flatlands beyond the hills came a traveling preacher with a tent. He set it up in Matt Jasper's field, about halfway down the ridge, at the corner where the roads crossed, and where the mailboxes were set. Gasoline lanterns gave a brilliant white light which filled the tent and spread out over the field, throwing long shadows across the clover and the bushes that edged the field.

The people came and filled the tent, and sat in the clover and crushed it so that its sweet, spicy smell mixed with the odor of sweat and tired, soured bodies. Night after night the people came, believing, with perhaps the last sure belief left in this sophisticated land of ours, in their sinfulness and in their need for redemption. Sin was real here on the ridge. There was none among these people who had not sinned. Who had not gossiped, or cursed, or drunk from the flowing jug, or dealt a hand from a deck of playing cards, or been tempted in the ways of the flesh. Sin rode hard upon their shoulders, and nightly they came and writhed under the lash of the preacher's words.

The sin that he laid upon them the hardest was that of the tobacco crop. It was a crop inspired by the devil! "Them that uses it," he shouted, "is doomed! Them that raises it is damned forever . . . forever and endurin' damned!"

But how else were they to feed the house full of young'uns that overran the doors and porches? How else clothe them against the winter's cold? Tobacco was hard money in their overalls pockets. There was no other crop to bring them cash. They fought and groveled and promised. But always they made another tobacco crop.

Miss Willie went one night with Mary and Hod and sat bewildered and confused on the back row. She felt as if she were witnessing a scene lifted straight from Dante's *Inferno*. These moaning, sobbing people were not her neighbors. They were actors upon a ghostly stage, with the dirty sides of the tent providing a slovenly backdrop, and the sputtering, spitting lanterns hissing a monotonous orchestral accompaniment. It was lurid, tawdry, and gross.

This was the crying out of a tortured people, of a burdened and sin-laden people, begging for deliverance. She saw neither dignity nor truth there. Only frenzy, and emotional fury, and chaos. She went no more, for it had saddened her inexplicably. She left it, impersonally, to itself.

But it didn't stay impersonal, for one night Mary told her sadly that Irma had professed during the revival. Irma was Hod's sister. Little Johnnie's mother.

"Well," Miss Willie said, "each of us must decide his religious beliefs for himself."

"If it were just for herself, we wouldn't be worried," Mary answered. "But this religion Irma has taken up believes in faith healing. They don't believe in having the doctor when you're sick. And Irma is the mother of a family. Suppose little Johnnie or the baby gets sick? Or she or John? This will affect all of them,

121

don't you see? We are terribly disturbed, Miss Willie. Hod just can't understand how Irma could have been so influenced by this faith."

Miss Willie rubbed her hand against the glossy arm of her chair. "It's just the ridge again, Mary. Just the lack of knowledge, experience, wider horizons. What else can you expect? Instead of arousing themselves to do something *now* about the drudgery and the sorrow and the sufferings of life in all its harsh reality here on the ridge, they go along apathetically, and find their release in some bright and shining state of life in heaven. Irma is the product of her environment, that's all."

"So was Hod."

"But Hod, my dear, is one in a thousand. And, say what you will, he got off the ridge long enough to look at it in perspective. He got away from it long enough to find himself. Had he never left the ridge, he might now be sunk in this same lethargy."

Mary found no answer to that. She turned restlessly to the piano, and her fingers sought comfort in a Chopin nocturne.

The big baptizing followed the revival. There were always twenty or thirty people who had been converted to be baptized. Some of them had been converted every summer, year after year, but during the long winter months they always fell from grace and had to be converted and baptized again the next summer. The time between revivals was too dragged out, and the Word was forgotten and the spirit became weak. So the people backslid and had to come under the Power again, and be dipped once more in the blood of the Lamb.

"Miss Willie," Becky asked that Sunday afternoon, "you goin' to the baptizin' with us?"

"I don't think so," Miss Willie said, shuddering away from another spectacle of rampant holiness.

Becky went on. "You better come go along. Hit's allus a sight to see."

"Do they preach and go on like they did at the revival?"

"Oh, no. The big preachin's over, an' the convertin's done. This is the bringin' in of the sheaves."

So Miss Willie decided to go. At least this was broad daylight, and the scene would lack the infernolike quality the glaring lan-

122

terns and the dark night outside had given to the meeting.

She dressed and went out to the back lot, crawled into the big wagon, and took her place in the hickory-bottomed chair Gault placed for her back of the wagon seat. They jolted down the road toward the pike and the Green River bottoms. The baptizing was to be held down below the bridge, where the water was shallow but where there were also pools deep enough for the immersions.

Miss Willie felt taut and she halfway wished she hadn't come. But, she argued with herself, I should know the *whole* life of the ridge. If this is part of it, I should know it. She couldn't say why the meeting had filled her with such revulsion. Perhaps it was because it had been so stark . . . so raw and so animal-like. She felt as if the people had stripped themselves before her, and she felt sore and ashamed when she thought of it. As if she had witnessed the most private and indecent baring of humanity's soul.

"Becky," she said, "did you know Irma professed the other night?"

"Yes," Becky answered tightly.

Gault slapped the reins against the backs of the horses. "Come up," he grunted.

"Don't you all go to these meetings?" Miss Willie went on. "I don't believe you went a single night."

"We don't hold with no sich," Gault said. "When hit's a reg'lar meetin', we go like the rest."

Miss Willie felt a sudden relief pour over her at Gault's words.

"What will Hattie and Tom think of Irma's being converted?" she asked.

"I'm thinkin' they'll not like it," Gault answered briefly. "We have allus been decent, God-fearin' people, abidin' by the Scriptures."

"The Scriptures says they shall speak with tongues," Becky murmured.

"Becky," Gault turned on her fiercely, "you ain't called on to interpret the Scriptures! I am the head of this house, an' I am beholden to speak what the Scriptures says as best I kin. Hit ain't fitten fer a woman to seek wisdom beyond what the head of the house has got. I have told you that before. Yore rebellious tongue frashes me, times."

123

Becky shriveled into herself and Miss Willie subsided. The head of the house had spoken!

When they came down off the ridge onto the graveled pike, they joined a procession of others going to the river. There were wagons and buggies and a few cars which pulled around the slower moving vehicles, raising immense clouds of dust which fogged down upon the road in an opaque veil. Miss Willie kept her handkerchief over her nose and fanned helplessly at the thick cloud which settled inevitably over her clean dress and made her hands and face feel gritty.

When they came to the bridge, they followed the others off the pike down into a beautiful green, parklike area under the trees. Many were already there, teams unhitched and tied to the backs of the wagons. And the crowd wandered up and down the riverbank, waiting.

The women who were to be baptized were gathered together under one tall tree. Young and old, big and little, they were dressed in white. Some of them had on long, flowing robes, evidently made from bed sheets, while others had on simple white dresses. Other women were going among them, kneeling and stooping and moving from one to the other.

"What are they doing?" Miss Willie wanted to know.

"They're aputtin' little rocks in their hems, to keep their dresses from floatin' on the water," Becky said.

"Oh."

The men to be baptized were gathered under another tree. Their clothing looked no different from every day. Except that their shirts seemed gay and colorful compared to the angel white of the women's robes. A man detached himself from the group, and, taking a long staff, waded solemnly out into the river.

At this point the stream was clear and emerald green. The white pebbles on its floor gleamed like crystal through the sparkling water, and the current eddied slowly around the man's trousers as he walked carefully into the water. He prodded with the staff before him, setting it down and then taking a step forward. He waded straight into the river until the water was waist deep, and then he turned toward a pool that was shaded by the overhanging branches of a willow tree. Here the water deepened

124

gradually. When he had reached a place where he stood chest deep, he stopped and, turning to the crowd on the bank, called to the preacher, "This here's about right."

The preacher, in a long, black, shapeless garment, waded in next. When he reached the man, he turned and raised his hand. Two men stepped to the side of the first of the women and supported her into the water. Slowly they made their way through the emerald current, stepping carefully over the stones and easing the woman's way. When she reached the preacher, he turned her toward the crowd, and at his raised hand a song was lifted into the air:

"'Shall we gather at the river? . . .
Yes, we'll gather at the river,
The beautiful, the beautiful river.'"

The rocks sewed into the hem of her garment weighted the woman's robe so that it hung wet and heavy on her. She was as white as her robe. The preacher's voice could not be heard above the song, but his mouth moved. Then he placed his hand over the woman's face and bent her back into the water until she was lost to sight. When he raised her up, she flung her arms over her head and started shouting, and the crowd on the bank shouted with her and started crying and weaving back and forth and singing.

"'Yes, we'll gather at the river, . . .
That flows from the throne of God!'"

This was the first of many. The two men brought the woman back to the edge of the stream, and she fell to the ground, moaning and crying. They took the next woman into the water, and she was trembling so that her robe quivered around her. Miss Willie saw that this was Irma, Hod's sister. Little Johnnie's mother. Little Johnnie, who drew blue jays with red and green and purple feathers, but who didn't know for sure whether hit was a blue jay because he was flyin' so fast!

Irma was quiet in the water, spent and subdued, and when she rose from the wet burial of her living flesh, she didn't shout and cry. Instead, her face was uplifted and transfigured. There was a radiance on it that glowed and shone. There was a look of muted joy and an illumination of some inner light shining through. She came to the shore and moved quickly through the shouting

125

women, as if they stood in her way. Miss Willie watched her go into the bushes to change her clothes. She shivered in the heat, and her own perspiration-damp clothes felt cold and clammy.

After the women came the men, and the afternoon waned before the baptizing was over. The river was muddied from the dragging feet, and the preacher dipped the gay shirts methodically now. The song had died away and the last man was immersed in a sudden stillness, so that the words of the preacher came across the water strong and clear: "In the name of the Father, the Son, and the Holy Ghost."

A finger of sunlight stole through the shadows and laid itself directly on the head of the man waiting quietly by the preacher's side. The scene was sharply etched before Miss Willie's eyes and there was a clean, fine dignity in the strong look of the man, and in the firm, loud words of the preacher.

"That's Irma's man," Becky whispered. "That's John Walton. Irma must of talked him into it too."

The man was bent backward and the water closed over him with scarcely a ripple. And then he was making his way, dripping and sodden, to the shore.

The people scattered to their wagons and buggies. There was a hurrying and a scurrying and a calling back and forth. Teams were hastily hitched up, and wagons turned onto the pike with a scattering sound of gravel thrown from under quick wheels. There was no friendly dallying for talk. It was getting late and the nightwork was still to be done. And the baptizing was over.

CHAPTER
❧ 14 ❧

AND THEN IT WAS SEPTEMBER and a feeling of fall was in the air. The days were still summery and lazy, but they were growing shorter. Now when school was out at four o'clock, the path through the hollow was darkened by the long shoulders of the ridge. The hillsides were taking on the look of an artist's palette, with the solid green background broken here and there by brilliant splashes of color. Some of the trees were hasty with their giving to autumn, abandoning themselves freely and easily, strutting early in their gorgeous colors. But the great oaks and the tall elms hesitated. A few leaves had mottled and veined into a dull reddish-yellow, but mostly they still clung stubbornly to their pristine, virginal green. It was as if they offered, grudgingly, one leaf at a time to the season, counting miserly their remaining hoard. As if they knew the splendid gold and scarlet garments so gaudily worn by the other trees were but a brief prelude to the inevitable and withering nudeness of the winter. In their wisdom they postponed the time when their black ribs would be stripped and exposed, frozen and shrunken. Winter was a long, long time.

Miss Willie picked her way down the ridge path one morning, thinking she must absorb all this color and beauty, for the time was so short now that she could walk. All too soon she would have to ride around the road. These few days in September were all that were left. She must breathe deep and let her eyes drink the full cup of the hills and the hollow and the creek. She must spread out and take in all the green and the gold and the red, a savings against the gray days ahead.

A noise in the bushes off to her right startled her. It was a rattling and scratching, as if some big animal was thrashing around, loosing pebbles and shuffling the dried leaves. She stopped. But quickly she decided it must be one of Hod's cows wandering off up the hillside, and she started on. She had taken a few steps when she felt fear crawling up her back, raising the hackles on her neck. A cold wind blew down her spine, freezing and paralyzing her. Her stomach was gripped by an iron hand, squeezed and knotted, and her legs felt limp and heavy. When her fear reached the border of panic, she whirled, her mind instinctively telling her to face the unknown danger.

And then she saw him. Matt Jasper was clawing through the bushes, a little back of her and to the right. He was staggering and reeling drunkenly, pulling himself along by the bushes. He fell to his knees and frantically crawled along on all fours, careless of the undergrowth which tore at his face. He pulled himself heavily to his feet and staggered a few steps toward her, and then fell and rolled to her feet. She screamed then. One high, rending scream which rose spiraling over the hill.

But Matt was clawing at her feet. "Don't let him git me. Don't let him git me. Please, Miss Willie, he's acomin' after me. He's acomin' up the trail down there. Hide me, Miss Willie. Hide me. Don't let him git me." He was plucking at her shoes, his face drawn and taut, his eyes fixed and staring. Foam had gathered in the corners of his mouth, and his teeth worked over his under-lip, gnawing it raggedly.

Miss Willie made herself stop shuddering, and she swallowed the tightness in her throat. "Who's coming, Matt? Who is it that's going to get you? This is just Miss Willie. There's no one else here."

"He's acomin' up the trail. I seen him down there in the holler. He's acomin' to git me. He's agoin' to take me to Danville to the 'sylum. I ain't agoin'! I ain't agoin'! Ain't nobody agoin' to put me in no 'sylum! I'll kill 'em! I'll kill 'em!" His voice rose shrilly, and then his body stiffened and his back arched high. He began to jerk and his head twisted on his neck. His mouth drew into a grimace, and the muscles of his face twitched and jerked in a chorea of tiny movements. His hands beat against the ground, and his feet pulled and twisted.

A spasm of nausea gripped Miss Willie, but she felt the weakness of relief surge through her. This was just an epileptic seizure and he was harmless now, at least. But what should she do? Run back to the house and tell Gault? Run down in the hollow and get Hod? Nerveless she stood there, and while she waited inde-cisively, she heard footsteps on the path. Fearfully she turned to meet this new threat. The path was full of evil this morning. All the beauty had fled.

The steps neared the big rock, and then a lusty voice broke into song: "Git along home, Cindy, git along home! Oh, git along home, Cindy, I'm goin' to leave you now!" So great was her re-lease from tension when Wells rounded the rock and came into view that Miss Willie sagged against a tree and let herself slide ignominiously to the ground. She dropped her face into her hands and let the tears flow, catching her breath in great, gasping sobs.

Wells took in the whole scene at a glance. Matt Jasper's inert form on the ground. Miss Willie's collapse. But he ran first to Miss Willie, dropping to his knees beside her and pulling at her

128

hands. "Miss Willie! Miss Willie! He never hurt you, did he?"

Miss Willie let her forehead sag forward and rest against that big, broad shoulder. Oh, it was so solid and safe! And his voice was so warm and comforting. The urgency of it filled her with security and safety. She shook her head and rubbed her nose against his shirt. "No," she sobbed, a hiccup catching her between words, "no, he didn't hurt me. He just scared me half to death!"

"Why, hit's jist old Matt Jasper, Miss Willie. He's harmless. He's sort of natural-like, but he wouldn't hurt a flea. Them fits of his'n is skeery, but they ain't dangerous. He allus comes outen 'em as mild as a baby. But he's not harmful. I thought fer a minnit mebbe he'd grabbed at you, or fell over you, or somethin'. You shore had me skeered!"

Miss Willie drew away and pulled herself up. She pushed at her glasses and straightened her hair and blew her nose. "I don't usually go to pieces like this," she apologized, "but he frightened me so!"

"Tell me what happened," Wells said, brushing the twigs and leaves off her dress.

"I was walking along, feeling awfully gay and happy, sort of dreaming, I guess. Thinking how pretty the hills looked and thinking it wouldn't be long until winter, when I heard a noise off to one side of the path. It startled me, but I thought it was just one of Hod's cows, and I started on. Then I just felt as if something terrible was right behind me. Something awful and repulsive. When I turned around, there he was, coming through the bushes, clawing and reeling and falling, and frothing at the mouth. And then he fell right at my feet. He kept saying: 'Don't let him git me. Don't let him git me.' And when I asked him who was trying to get him, he said it was a man from Danville coming to take him to the asylum. And he said he wouldn't go. He'd kill him first." Miss Willie's hands were picking at her handkerchief as she talked, and Wells reached out and stilled them between his own large palms. She wrenched at them and then let them lie quiet. "He said he saw the man down in the hollow."

"I reckon he seen me. I been down to Hod's to take his saw back. They wasn't nobody else in the holler as I know of. Hit

129

must of been me he seen." Wells wrinkled his forehead. "Wonder what's come over him to think ever'body's fixin' to send him to Danville. Jessie said he threatened him one day down at the store. Ain't nobody aimin' to send him off to the 'sylum. He's bright enough when he don't have them fits."

Miss Willie drew a long, shuddering breath. "Wells, I'm not so sure he's not dangerous. If he's got this fixation about being sent to Danville, and if he didn't recognize you and thought you had come after him . . . I think something ought to be done."

"Aw, shucks, Miss Willie. Ever'body here knows Matt Jasper. Knows he has fits an' is sort of quare. But he's harmless. He'll git over this spell o' thinkin' somebody's goin' to take him to Danville. But I'm real sorry he skeered you. Look, he's acomin' to, now." And Wells turned to the lank form lying in the path. He bent over it.

"Matt," he called. "Hey, Matt. C'mon, git up. You had a spell here an' might' nigh skeered Miss Willie to death. C'mon now. Git yerself up from there." He shook the limp shoulders and slapped the limber neck, rubbing his hands up and down Matt Jasper's back and over his face. "C'mon, now, boy."

Matt slowly sat up and rubbed at his mouth. He looked blearily at Wells and past him to Miss Willie. He shook his head and felt of the back of it. "Doggone," he said, twisting and craning his neck, "that'n shore was a good 'un."

Wells helped him to his feet. "You better git on home, now. Tell Lutie to give you somethin' to eat. You ain't got no business walkin' the ridge 'fore breakfast!"

Matt grinned sheepishly and ducked his head at Miss Willie. "I'm shore sorry I skeered you, ma'am. I cain't never tell when one o' these spells is comin' on, but I hate fer you to of seen it." He slapped his old hat against the leg of his overalls and pulled it down over his ragged hair. "Thank ye agin, Wells," he mumbled and started off up the path.

Miss Willie sighed as she watched him lurch up the trail, and shook her head. "He's not like the same person, is he?"

"Matt Jasper was as fine a boy as ever lived on this ridge," Wells said, "until he started havin' them fits. But his pa had fits, an' I reckon hit was jist in the blood. Old Man Clark's woman,

130

Mamie, is Matt's sister, an' she has 'em too. Now, you come on. I'll walk the rest of the way with you."

"Oh, no. You needn't do that, Wells. I'm all right now."

Wells grinned at her. "Well, you don't look it. Don't give me no bad time, now. C'mon, I'm goin' with you."

The mention of Old Man Clark reminded Miss Willie that she had meant to ask Wells about Rose and Tay Clark. But she found it hard to bring up. They walked in silence down the trail, Wells occasionally whistling little bits of the song he was singing as he came around the rock. Finally Miss Willie summoned her courage and blurted out, "Wells, does Rose go with Old Man Clark's son, Tay Clark?"

"Not that I know of. And she better hadn't," he answered grimly. "Why?"

"Oh, nothing. I just noticed her dancing with him at the party the other night, and wondered."

"Oh, them kids allus dance with ever'body. Hit don't mean a thing. I reckon he's tried to talk to Rose, but I told her not to have nothin' to do with him. He's allus been sort of wild. I'd hate fer Rose to git mixed up with him."

"Yes." Miss Willie found that she couldn't tell him she had seen Rose slip out into the darkness with Tay. Maybe it didn't mean anything, anyhow. Maybe Rose flirted a little with all the boys. And Tay had just been the handiest one that night. She couldn't run telling tales. There was just this uncomfortable feeling that there was something between those two. The boy's eyes had possessed the girl, and his arm had crooked too knowingly around her waist. But she had no right to trouble Wells, especially if the trouble was only in her own mind.

He left her at the schoolyard. "I'm agoin' to bring you a horse," he promised. "You cain't walk this fur much longer. Hit'll set in to rain 'fore long, an' after that winter'll be here. I got a good little mare you kin use this winter. Gentle as a baby, an' she rides easy. I'll bring her over next week."

"Can I buy her?"

Wells hushed her. "Nope. You cain't buy her. Come spring, I'll be needin' her. Jist count it part o' yer pay. I'm a trustee, remember?"

131

Miss Willie laughed. "You're awfully good to the teacher, Wells."

"Well, she's sort of easy to be good to. Ifen e'er person ever asts, you kin tell 'em I like the teacher a heap. Been studyin' about goin' back to school, jist so's I kin be around her more."

Miss Willie felt her face go hot, and she became very busy with her belt. "I've got some studying to do right now! Thank you for bringing me to school, though. And I'll take good care of . . . what's her name? The horse's, I mean?"

Wells's chuckle rippled between them. "That's who I thought you meant. Her name's Pet. The horse's, I mean."

Miss Willie giggled. "That's a nice name." She hesitated, then offered him her hand. "Well, good-by now."

She walked stiffly toward the schoolhouse, not looking back. Don't be a fool, Willie Payne, she scolded herself. At your age! Blushing like a schoolgirl! There's nothing so ridiculous as an old maid simpering around a man! Her head came up at that, and she sniffed. She had *not* been simpering, and why not blush? Goodness knows there had been precious few opportunities for her to blush when she was a girl, and none at all for the past sterile twenty-five years! Why not blush! It was good to have a man speak admiringly, even if it was only in fun! Come to think of it she had a lot of blushing to catch up on, and after all there was no one except herself to jeer at an old maid's vanity!

As she rounded the corner of the schoolhouse, a sidewise glance of her eye caught the shadow of a fleeting, shifting movement behind the tall elm. There was just time to see the vanishing outline of an overalled figure, topped by a tawny head. She frowned. Now what was Rufe doing at school so early?

In the two months since school had started Miss Willie had settled herself into its routine. She had organized and shaped a schedule, bending it as best she could around eight grades, and while she felt frustrated at many points, on the whole she thought she had made as much headway as could be expected. Hod and Gault had constantly emphasized, "Go slow." And she had contented herself with a few things in which she could take genuine

132

satisfaction. The bookshelves were being used now. Not to any great extent, true, but each day someone wandered over to the shelves and took down a book to explore, even tentatively, its hidden treasure. The first- and second-graders now had low tables and benches behind her desk, and she managed to give them greater freedom of movement than at first. By using the older girls to supervise them, they had more frequent playtimes outside. Rose had proved especially good with them. And from her own income Miss Willie had furnished extra books and colors and learning toys. From these smallest ones she reaped her greatest happiness.

In addition to the bookshelves for the older ones, she had set up a long table along the wall, which she called a science table. It was rapidly becoming loaded with specimens of rocks, birds' nests, various pressed and mounted flowers, ferns, leaves, and anything at all that took the eye of a boy or girl on the way to school. She had been amazed at the enthusiasm with which they had received the idea, and at the knowledge of their own land that they displayed. She had encouraged every interest, and several group projects had developed. The sixth grade, for instance, had worked two weeks on a project that began with a hornet's nest one of the boys had brought. The nest had been carefully cut apart and its cellular structure examined. The bookshelves had been resorted to for information, and the interest of the whole school was caught and fanned by the intensive research. Finally a notebook on the hornet was assembled, painstakingly illustrated by drawings and mounted specimens.

She could take pride in these things. They were good. But there were still the major questions of the short school term, the irregular attendance of many of the children, the open spring, and the primitive outhouses. And she could not close her eyes to the fact that she had made little or no headway there. But she reminded herself that there must be first the acorn and then the oak. Except for Rufe, who remained stubbornly aloof, she was winning the confidence and friendship of the school. And she hoped by the end of the term to be able to show the parents so much improvement that they would trust her judgment about the more important things to be done. At the end of the term she meant to make a report to the chairman and the trustees. And she meant to include in it some strong recommendations. But for the present she was satisfied.

The September day heightened to noon, and waned toward four o'clock. It was Friday, and, in accordance with the custom of the school, the last quarter of the day was given over to a program. This program consisted of stories, songs, recitations, and it was varied sometimes with a spelling match or with games in the yard. Today the little folks were excited because they were to do a dramatization of the story of Little Black Sambo.

Irma's little Johnnie, who was Sambo, was near apoplexy with his pent-up feeling of importance. His small earnest face was beet red, and his tongue licked nervously in and out of the empty space where his front teeth were gone. Miss Willie watched him fondly. He was such a sturdy little fellow. So independent and resourceful, and so alert. His mind was eager and quick, with a farseeing, visionary quality that made the distance between the real and the fanciful very short for him. His imagination soared lightly over whatever he did, touching his thoughts and his dreams with enchantment. Little Black Sambo was very real to him today.

The children were grouped to take their parts, and after much whispering and shuffling around and some giggling, they waited for the story to begin. Miss Willie turned to her book and read the opening lines.

Suddenly Johnnie cried: "Wait! Wait, Miss Willie! I have to get the tiger!" And he ran out the door before Miss Willie could stop him. She was puzzled, because redheaded little Sarie Simpson was supposed to be the tiger. Sarie stood now, her head drooping and her thumb in her mouth. "I was the tiger," she quavered.

"You're still the tiger," Miss Willie comforted. "When Johnnie comes back, we'll go on with the story."

And then Johnnie struggled through the door with his arms full of a strange, striped animal. And with him came an awful, penetrating odor! As he came down the aisle, the odor spread, growing stronger and more powerful with each step. Johnnie's face was screwed up in a knot, and his nose wrinkled away from the stench he was carrying. It dawned on the boys and girls and

134

Miss Willie simultaneously what the animal was, and as Miss Willie rose to her feet, there was an uproar from the pupils and the schoolroom emptied in a mad rush for the door. Johnnie and the skunk were shoved aside, and in the confusion Johnnie loosed his hold upon the animal and it fled to the farthest corner, still pouring out its dreadful, protective stink.

Miss Willie could hardly breathe, but she found Johnnie and led him outside. He was sick from his close proximity to the animal, and he reeked of the oily smell. Irma would have to scrub him with her strongest soap, Miss Willie thought, and his clothes would surely have to be burned! For that matter, every person in the school would have to be scoured and scrubbed, including herself! The children stood huddled in the schoolyard now, waiting for some word from her. They were fanning themselves, and pulling at their repulsive garments.

When Johnnie got through being sick, Miss Willie took him to the water tub and bathed his face. He was a wretched little chap! When finally he could talk between his sobs and his retching, he said mournfully: "He never smelt like that when Rufe give him to me! He never smelt atall, Miss Willie! An' he was so purty. Rufe said he'd make a awful good tiger on account of his stripe down his back. The pitchers in the book had stripes on the tiger, an' I was goin' to s'prise you!" He buried his face in Miss Willie's skirt.

She patted his head gently. "Never mind, dear. Never mind. It's all right." And then she disengaged his clutching fingers and walked over to the group of older pupils. She felt her anger rising within her until it boiled up and burned her face like fire.

"Where is Rufe?" she asked the group.

No one knew, and then Miss Willie remembered that she had not seen him since the afternoon recess. No. He wouldn't stay and risk contaminating himself! He would just turn it loose upon the whole school while he got safely away! What a dirty trick, just to take one more lick at her!

"Did anyone else have any part in this?" she asked.

"No, ma'am!" The answers were vehement, and accompanied with emphatic shakings of heads. She had no doubt they were truthful. No one, knowing what was to happen, would have

135

stayed around to see it. The penalty for that would have been too great. The smell saturating these boys and girls was proof enough that Rufe had perpetrated his trick alone.

"You may go home, then," she told them. "And I'm terribly sorry for all the trouble this is going to cause your folks. A harmless joke is fun for everyone, but a joke that causes trouble is no longer a joke. It's just plain meanness!"

"That Rufe Pierce," one of the girls scolded. "He'd ort to be whipped! Stinkin' up all our clothes like this! My mamma's shore not goin' to like it."

"This is my best dress," another one chimed in, "an' I'll bound the smell won't never come out!"

"Your mothers will know what to do with them, if anything *can* be done with them," Miss Willie said. "Now run along home."

When they had scattered, Miss Willie set out determinedly for Wells's house. The awful stink that went with her was settling into her skin and hair, and she wondered if she would ever be clean of it again. But this had to be settled with Mr. Rufe immediately!

At Wells's she stopped outside the gate and called. Wells came to the door and seeing her started down the path. "Come in," he shouted, "Come on in."

"I can't," Miss Willie answered, "I smell too bad. And don't come any closer. You'll get it all over you."

Wells stopped and looked queerly at her. Being downwind of her, he had just got a whiff of the odor she was carrying. He sniffed and wrinkled his nose. Then he laughed. "I declare, Miss Willie! Don't you know a polecat when you see one? I thought ever'body knowed what a skunk looked like!" He pinched his nose between his fingers. "Whew! You must of got hold of a powerful one!"

Miss Willie's lips firmed and she shot him a malevolent look. "I know very well what a skunk looks like, Wells Pierce. I haven't been playing with any polecat! It was forced on me very much against my will! On me and the whole schoolroom, as a matter of fact. Where is Rufe?"

Wells sobered quickly. "You ain't sayin' Rufe turned a skunk loose in the schoolhouse, are you, Miss Willie?"

136

"I'm saying just that," she snapped, "only it was worse. He played a mean, scurvy trick on little Johnnie . . ." She went on to tell the whole story.

When she had finished, Wells's face was flinty and set. "Miss Willie, I don't keer what you say, I'm goin' to take keer o' that young gentleman my way this time! This here business o' bein' a troublemaker has got to stop. They ain't but one way to handle a young'un that's gittin' outta hand. A good, stout strop laid acrost his backside'll make him think twicet afore he does any more meanness! An' I'm jist the one kin lay it on. I've had all this foolishment I'm goin' to put up with!"

"No," Miss Willie answered, "this is still between Rufe and me. Is he here?"

"No, he ain't here yit. He don't hardly git home from school till a little later. I reckon he's hidin' out somewheres, waitin' till time to come in."

"Oh. I wanted to talk to him myself." She thought for a moment. "I'll be by early in the morning. I'm going to take him to the schoolhouse and see that he scrubs that building from one end to the other. If you don't mind, that is."

"Mind! I'll go along an' see that he does it!"

"No, you'll not! Wells, I don't know why Rufe doesn't like me. Right from the start he has been set against me. It's hard for me to believe he could hold a grudge from that first day of school, and I don't understand what's wrong. He does well enough in his schoolwork, but he never says one word more than he has to. There's a reason for it, and something is building up inside him. And I hate to add fuel to the fire. But he can't keep on doing things like this."

"I don't know what's wrong, either, Miss Willie. Hit's been a sight o' trouble to me. An' I shore hate it a heap fer him to weary you like this. I'll do e'er thing you say."

"If I could just get at the root of it. If I could just once get close to him. But he won't let me. It's as if he held me in contempt. He will have nothing to do with me!"

They stood there, a short stretch of grass between them, Miss Willie's polecat smell eddying around them, one young, tawny-headed boy filling the moment with hurt. That he was by nature

137

a mean boy Miss Willie did not for one second believe. She had spent too many years with children to believe that. Something was troubling the boy. Something connected with herself. Something as yet nebulous and vague. And until it opened up of itself, she must simply go on with him, taking one thing at a time. If only the parents and the trustees didn't grow tired of this conflict between them!

When she reached home, Becky clucked sympathetically over her and helped her heat gallons of water with which to scrub her hair, her skin, and her clothes. They filled the tubs in the woodshed and Miss Willie laboriously rid herself of the horrible stench. When she finally stretched herself wearily on her bed, she thought cynically: This is the ridge for you! Start the day with a mad man, and end it with a polecat!

A silent boy accompanied Miss Willie to the schoolhouse the next morning. He was ready when she went by for him, armed with scrubbing brushes, soap, and buckets. He spoke pleasantly enough when she greeted him, and there was no trace of sulkiness on his face. There was no expression at all. It was as if he had deliberately wiped it clean of his thoughts and hooded his eyes before her.

He took up the load and walked with her, keeping his steps down to match hers, whistling occasionally, but otherwise making no sound. Miss Willie matched his silence with her own.

At the schoolhouse he filled the buckets and set to work. The smell was still strong and heavy. Miss Willie took the curtains down and washed them, and then she took the bright rugs outside, and laying them on the grass scrubbed them thoroughly with one of the stiff brushes. She left them there to dry and air. Then she joined Rufe inside and worked with grim determination by his side, scrubbing down the walls and scouring the desks and the floor. From time to time he emptied the buckets and refilled them with fresh water. But this was the only interruption to the steady swishing of the brushes.

When they finished, shortly after noon, Miss Willie's arms hung limp and nerveless, and her back ached with a throbbing pain.

But most of the smell was gone and the room was fresh and clean again. She laid the still-damp rugs back on the floor and gathered the curtains from the bushes where they had been drying, to take home with her to press.

With every muscle in her body begging for rest, she trudged back up the ridge with Rufe, the silence between them still deep. If he had felt any shame or remorse over his trick, he didn't show it. He had needed no direction in the work, and he had worked quickly and well. Miss Willie had no way of knowing what he thought about it.

At her gate she took the buckets from him and turned in. And then he broke the silence. "You needn't to of went," he said. "I'd a done it jist as good without you there."

She flung her head up and looked at him. His eyes were blazing at her and his face was red. How *was* it he always put her on the defensive? Her own eyes took fire and she threw her words at him angrily. "I didn't go to make sure you would do the work well! I went to help! But you must admit your behavior has not been such as to make me have any confidence in you!"

He appeared to be measuring her before he spoke. "That works both ways," he murmured.

Why, she wanted to cry out, why don't you have confidence in me? What have I done? Why don't you believe in me? I have done nothing to you! I have not wanted to hurt you! I only want to help! But she would not plead with this fourteen-year-old boy who stood half a head taller than she, making her feel small, defeated, frustrated. Helplessly she saw that the rift had only widened. "Well," she said, her voice betraying her weariness and hopelessness, "we got the work done, anyhow."

Rufe bent his head cavalierly. "Hit's been a pleasure, Miss Willie," and he turned on his heel and walked away, leaving her battling her tired tears.

And something inside her bled as her tears flowed. O Rufe, Rufe! She wanted to call to him, to run after him, and to hold his bright head close. She wanted to tell him how much she loved him. How dear he was to her. She looked hopelessly after him, watching his thin, awkward body stride down the road. And she thought how tonight he would take his dog and his gun and walk

139

the ridge and the hollow, restlessly knocking at some closed door which only his own heart sought with understanding.

How little we know of one another, she thought. How little we can commune with each other! We spend our lives together, coming and going and working and living together, and we never really get to know each other. What is deepest inside is hidden, and there is no way of crossing over. Of becoming even for one second that other person. Of feeling with his feelings, of thinking with his thoughts, of aching with his hurts. So complexly egoistic are we that we can never get outside ourselves. There is a veil around each one of us, which no other hand can draw aside. But some of us desperately need to rend that veil!

CHAPTER
❧ 15 ❧

A<small>S IF TROUBLE NEVER CAME SINGLY</small>, the next Monday afternoon Miss Willie came home to show Becky an itchy breaking out between her fingers and around her wrists. "I believe I've got a touch of poison ivy, Becky," she said. "Look here." And she spread her fingers and pointed to the whitish rash. "It's just about set me crazy today, itching. I couldn't let it alone, and I've kept scratching and clawing at it all day."

Becky pulled her to the door and looked closely at her hands. Then she laughed. "That ain't no poison ivy, Miss Willie. That's the pure old seven-year itch!"

"Itch!"

"Yes, ma'am! An', gentlemen, I mean to tell you hit's plumb troublesome to git rid of. You got a old pair o' gloves you don't mind spoilin'?"

"Why, yes. I can find a pair."

"Well, I'll make up a batch of sulphur an' lard, an' you'll have to spread it over yer hands ever' night, an' sleep with them gloves on. Worst is e'er thing you got has got to be washed an' scrubbed. E'er thing you've tetched is polluted, an' you'll jist take it agin as fast as you git rid of it. Hit shore is a plumb sight to git rid of."

Miss Willie collapsed on the side of the bed. The itch had been

140

something they talked about in whispers behind their hands when she was a child. Nice people didn't get it. It was a badge of poverty and dirt and shame. The kids from the other end of town were always having the itch, and you avoided them and kept even your skirts from contamination. Miss Willie spread her hands and looked at the white blisters, and disgust crept over her face. Things were piling up too fast! After the polecat, the itch! Now that was too much!

"How do you suppose I got it?" she asked.

"From some of them kids, of course! They's allus itch in a school. Cain't hardly ever git shet of it. An' I been aimin' to tell you to watch yer head, too!"

"My head!"

"Fer head lice. Might' nigh ever' year they's a regular go-round of them, an' they kin spread awful quick-like ifen jist one young'un has 'em."

Miss Willie's hand flew to her hair. Her scalp crinkled as if tiny legs were creeping over it already, thousands of tiny legs invading and infesting her skin, nesting and settling around the hair roots. The very thought sent shivers of horror over her.

Becky went to the kitchen and began to hunt around for the sack of dry sulphur. "Ifen you ever find one when yer a combin' yer hair," she called, "jist let me know, an' I'll go over yer head with coal oil an' a fine-toothed comb. They ain't nothin' better that I know of. Hit usual kills 'em right now. Sometimes hit takes two or three goin' overs, but that ain't common. Mebbe, though, you've heared of somethin' better yerself."

"No," Miss Willie said weakly, "no. I've not heard of anything better."

For a week she slept each night with the sulphur and lard mixture smeared on her hands. It smelled to high heaven, but Becky told her it would get rid of the itch. So she endured it. But not patiently. "I'm going to clean up that school," she vowed to Becky. "I'm going to get the itch and lice and everything else those children have got out of there! I'm going to see every blessed woman who's got a child in that school, and I'm going to have them meet here at my house next Saturday afternoon. There's no sense in that sort of thing. Just a little cleanliness and

141

patience will prevent such things! You just wait and see!"

She stormed through the week, her anger at her own infection sustaining her. Each night when she anointed her hands with the stinking mixture she boiled up again. "There's no sense in it," she muttered. "There's just no excuse for it! Just plain shiftlessness. Anybody can be clean, no matter how poor they are!"

So she rode the little mare all over the ridge after school those evenings. But she was canny with her invitations. "Better not say yer havin' a health meetin'," Becky cautioned. "Folks hereabouts don't take to meddlin' with such like. Jist say yer havin' a party." So Miss Willie said nothing about the itch. She merely invited the mothers to her cabin for a little party. "So we can all get to know each other," she urged.

One and all they accepted. "Hit's right nice of you to give us a party, Miss Willie," they said, and they all promised to come.

"Saturday afternoon at two o'clock," she said.

"Yes, ma'am. We'll be there."

All, that is, but Irma, Hod's sister. It was late in the afternoon when Miss Willie hitched the little horse to Irma's front fence. She had saved this call to the last because she looked forward to it so much. It had promised her a special reward since she had become so fond of Johnnie.

She looked around her curiously as she knotted the reins about a spike paling. Mary had told her how Irma and her husband, John Walton, had started out eight or ten years ago in the tenant house on his father's place, and how they had added a room every two or three years as they added children, until they had changed the tiny tenant house into a sizable home. It was a low, rambling place hugging close to the ground, and its gleaming white paint shone cleanly in the late evening sun. The mat of grass in the yard was neatly clipped, and the last of the summer flowers bloomed gaily around the porch's edge.

Irma herself came to the door. She was a beautiful woman in her late twenties, with red-gold hair crinkling back from her brown face. Her figure was softly rounded, neither thickened with the bearing of her children nor stooped from the burden of farm work. Her face broke into a smile and she spoke warmly. "Come in. Come in," she said. "I'm that pleased you've come.

Johnnie's spoke of you a heap."

Inside, the house was bright, airy, and fresh-smelling. Irma was a good housekeeper. Everything was scrubbed and neat, and the curtains and braided rugs were spotless. Like all the other homes on the ridge, it was sparsely furnished, but there was no feeling of emptiness. Rather, there was the feeling of space and uncluttered living.

They talked for a time of school, of Johnnie's progress, of Miss Willie's fondness for him, and Irma spoke proudly of his affection for "teacher." And then Irma wanted to know how Miss Willie was liking the ridge. "I've heared you've got a peart little cabin o' yer own," she said, "all fixed up over there at Becky's. Mary was tellin' me how you fixed it up."

"I like it," Miss Willie answered, "and I'm beginning to feel very much at home there. I brought a few of my own things with me, and it's nice to have them around me."

"Yes," Irma agreed, "hit's allus nice to have a body's own things. Makes you feel more settled. I'd like a heap to see it."

"I'd like for you to come," Miss Willie said. "As a matter of fact, I am having a little party for the school mothers Saturday afternoon. Couldn't you come, then?"

Irma's face shuttered immediately. She shook her head. "We don't hold with worldly things like that no more," she said. "I reckon you know me an' John has been converted, an' we don't go seekin' frolickin' like we useter."

Then Miss Willie explained. "This is not really a party, Irma. What I actually want to do is to get the women interested in organizing a sort of health club. Right now there is an epidemic of the itch in school, and the only way it can be checked is for everyone to co-operate. And there are other things the mothers should know about the general health of their children. This isn't a worldly frolic at all."

But Irma continued to shake her head. "We don't hold with no doctorin', neither."

"You don't believe in doctors and medicine?"

"No, ma'am. The Bible says to have faith in the Lord. Hit tells of the healin' of them that believed. Ifen you believe, you don't hold with no doctorin'."

143

"But what if some of the children get sick? Or you or John?"

"Hit would be the Lord's will. An' ifen hit was the Lord's will, we would be healed."

"But, Irma," Miss Willie protested, "the Lord intended for people to use the knowledge of science and medicine in healing disease! He meant for doctors to help people!"

Irma's face was blank. "The Scriptures says the Lord heals them that has the faith. Hit don't say nothin' about doctorin'. The Lord don't need no doctors to he'p him in his healin', Miss Willie. All he says is to believe on him. He'll do the healin'. Ifen hit's his will."

"But don't you think the Lord uses people to do his work in the world?"

Irma's head jerked quickly in denial. "No, ma'am," she said flatly. "The Lord, he don't need nothin' nor nobody to he'p him out. The Lord is powerful enough to move mountains. Hit's jist the conceit o' men to think the Lord needs e'er one of 'em." Her voice softened. "Don't the Scriptures tell of him ahealin' the lame an' the halt, the sick an' the bruised, an' settin' free them that was captive? Ifen you believe, Miss Willie, he sets you free. They ain't no bonds no more."

Miss Willie was silent. The sun had bedded down behind the hills and the last of the day was being drained from the sky. Across in the east the reflection was pink and pearly, and in the fading light Irma's face was strong and quiet. Her eyes looked past Miss Willie across a far-flung space, and they held an ageless peace in their brown depths. Miss Willie felt as if Irma had gone away and left her standing there, emptied, spent, and alone. Irma's spirit had winged its way to heavenly heights.

Miss Willie mounted the little mare and turned her toward home. She rode slowly down the road, her thoughts churning. She tried to sort them out and fix upon something solid. They were fringed by dismay, and a foregathering of anxiety and uneasiness. Like ragged edges, they surrounded something she could not get at. Their frayed threads kept her from the center. On the surface was her concern for the physical welfare of the little family. Inevitably Irma's faith would affect not only herself but her children as well.

But Miss Willie's uneasiness went deeper than that. Irma's confidence and strong faith had thrown her back upon herself. It had made her uncomfortable and defensive of her own faith. There! That was it! The core of her feeling was an uncertainty, a troubled sense of guilt. The fountain-spring of her own faith was challenged. She turned her thoughts this way and that, remembering Irma's words. He don't need nothin' nor nobody. Oughtn't a good Calvinist to agree that God needed nothing and no one to do his work? Wasn't one of the foundations of her own faith that cornerstone of God's all-powerful reign over his world? Yes, of course. But there was a difference in interpretation.

Unconsciously Miss Willie tipped her chin upward. A cultured, educated mind sustained a faith that was just as real as this hill woman's. It did not require that one be naïve and literal like Irma to have an honest and absolute faith. But here her mind doubled back around another thought. How absolute was her faith? How complete was the faith of anyone she knew? "Except ye become as a little child." Could one have an intellectual faith? Doesn't faith require that one give himself completely into the hand of God, simply and unquestioningly?

The little mare clopped a measured rhythm down the dusty road. And Miss Willie's thoughts threaded out to their fine ends. But could one do that in this day and age? I believe in the Lord God, she stated defiantly. And then, honestly she added, I believe also in Miss Willie. Wasn't that the amendment to all life nowadays? Thy will be done. But unless thy will is my will, my will be done. Wasn't that, too, the modern version of the Lord's Prayer?

Inexorably she forced herself to consider further. How many times she had heard her father say, "We are in God's hands." And as a child how comforting that had been to her! She fled swiftly back to her childhood, and remembered how her days had been surrounded with the secure, confident knowledge that all was well with her and her world. Nothing could go very far awry if you were in God's hands. She had had a child's conception of that broad palm holding up the world, and she had felt certain Texas was in the center of it, safely distant from the rounded edges where one might fall off. China was off there near the edge. And Africa. And India. When she had dedicated herself to missionary

145

service that day so long ago, she had felt not only the necessity to serve; she had also felt, she now acknowledged, a certain chilling thrill of fear. The same kind of thrill one had when one stepped across the line on a dare. It would be going so close to the edge of safety.

That child's conception, however, had given her life a security and a sure sense of fast foundations. It had stood firmly between her and fear, and had hedged her around with certainty. As Irma's faith was doing for her now. But somewhere along the line of maturing wisdom such childlike faith had been tempered with caution, and with what she was pleased to call common sense. Being in the hands of God had ceased to be the final security. That implicit trust was tinctured with the reality of everyday living, and somehow it got glossed over until it no longer had the same meaning. It bogged down in the necessity of becoming a responsible citizen of the world. And although this generation gave lip service to the phrase, wasn't it usually true that a man must be backed into a corner and brought to his knees before he could genuinely and humbly put himself into the hands of God? Until then wasn't he usually confident and sufficient unto himself? And was his faith not something faint and thin, seeping through Bach fugues and chorales along gilded organ pipes, strained piously through the muted prism of stained glass windows, hushed sanctimoniously by the thick, plushy depth of red carpets? Nebulous. Unreal. Distant. Having little to do with man himself, being reserved, like bonds in the bank, for a rainy day?

Miss Willie's soul was horrified at herself!

When the little mare halted in front of the back lot, Miss Willie eased herself down from the funny, awkward sidesaddle Wells had brought her, and led the horse through the gate. When Wells first brought her the horse and saddle, she had wondered where on earth he had found the thing. Not since her childhood had she seen a sidesaddle. She had laughed and poked fun at him.

"You wait an' see," he said. "You cain't be dressin' to ride astraddle ever'day. An' yer goin' to be aridin' this thing ever' day, don't fergit. This here sidesaddle'll take you, however yer dressed, an' hit'll rock along easy as one o' Becky's rockin' chairs."

And Wells's wisdom had been greater than her own. She

146

crawled up on Pet in whatever dress she might be wearing, and she now crooked her knee around the horn as easily and familiarly as if she had never ridden any other way.

At supper that night she told Becky about Irma. Gault was not at home, having gone to the county seat for court that day. He would be gone overnight, so Becky and Miss Willie were two women comfortably alone. Becky listened quietly as Miss Willie talked. "It worries me, Becky," Miss Willie finished her story.

Becky leaned her elbows on the table and braced her chin in her palms. Her eyes took on the same faraway look that Irma's had held. "I was raised in the faith, Miss Willie," she said. "Hit don't sound unnatural to me. I never knowed nothin' else till I married Gault, an' he forbid me to have e'er thing to do with 'em. Hit's a comfortin' way o' believin', an' I don't reckon they's a thing kin take its place to them that believes thataway. Hit's like leanin' on the everlastin' arms, knowin' they're goin' to uphold you. Hit's agivin' over to man the keer of the little things in this world, an' aleavin' to God the keer of all the big."

She stirred and moved the lamp to one side. "The way I see it, Miss Willie, is that ever'body is bound to believe accordin' to their lights. An' whatever is the most comfortin' an' satisfyin' to a body is the true faith fer him. I don't reckon nobody is enlightened to the whole truth. That would be puttin' too much on one pore, sinful human. But at the last I don't reckon the Lord's goin' to argy too much about the diffrunce in the way people has believed. Ifen I was him, I'd keer a heap more about how they follered what they believed. I don't hold with preachin' one thing an' doin' another. If they's one thing I cain't abide, it's a hypocrite. Ifen Irma holds with the faith, an' holds hard an' strong, then I'd say it ain't nobody's business but her'n!"

Becky rose and began stacking the dishes. Miss Willie scraped her own plate thoughtfully. Becky could speak very strongly when she chose. Evidently she had been a dutiful wife when Gault had commanded her to have nothing more to do with those of her own faith, but it was equally evident that the fire of that faith still burned steadily. Gault had not dampened it with his

147

Baptist theology or with his stern prohibition. Gault was the head of the house, and in all outward ways Becky obeyed him. But Gault could not control Becky's spiritual house, and Miss Willie was surprised at its wide rooms and high-spired roof.

As the dishes went through the strong, sudsy water under Becky's hands, and came to her own from the hot, clean rinsing kettle, Miss Willie remembered something Saint-Exupéry had written in *Wind, Sand and Stars* — something about whatever was right and good and fine for a man being *his* truth. She wiped a glass until it glistened in the yellow light. Odd to hear almost that same thought from the lips of this ridge woman. There was a fine vein of wisdom in Becky. It flashed to the surface only occasionally . . . as on the first night she was here, and again tonight. Wisdom threaded through with humor, and far back beyond the present, with sadness. Wisdom that took people for what they were, and let them alone to be themselves — hating only, as she had said tonight, the false in them. That was pretty fundamental when you got right down to it. That was the essence of love.

"You're a mighty good woman, Becky," Miss Willie said at last.

Becky lifted her hands from the soapy water, letting them drip on the floor. Her mouth quivered. "Don't say that," her voice rasped sharply. "Don't never say that, Miss Willie. I have been the blackest sinner of them all. Hit lives with me night an' day. The Lord ain't never forgive me fer what I done. Don't never say I'm a good woman." Careless of her wet hands, she hid her face in them, and her thin, humped shoulders shook.

"Why, Becky!" Miss Willie dropped her dish towel and hurried to throw her arm around the bent, scrawny back. "You've no right to say that. Why, your own faith tells you that the Lord forgives every sin. No matter what you've done, he doesn't hold it against you. Besides, you can't make me believe you're such a sinner as all that!"

Becky let her hands drop and braced them on the table. "You've got no idee," she said. "I've prayed fer a sign, but hit's never been give to me. He has turned his face from me. I've got no right to talk about e'er other soul bein' a hypocrite! Ifen the folks on this ridge knowed the truth about me, they wouldn't be seen aspeakin'

148

to me! An' if you knowed, you wouldn't stay e'er other night on this place!"

"Now, I don't know about the folks on the ridge, Becky," Miss Willie answered, "but as for me, there's nothing you could have done that would make me leave you, or that would change my feeling for you."

But Becky only shook her head. "You don't know," she said in a low voice. "You don't know." She dropped into a chair and wrapped her hands in her apron and rocked back and forth, misery creasing her face.

"Then suppose you tell me," Miss Willie said, pulling a chair up close.

Becky's voice when she began to speak was harsh and grating. "Oncet," she said, "oncet I was a purty young thing, gay-like and happy. You wouldn't believe it, I reckon."

"I would believe it," Miss Willie said.

"I lived on yon side the Gap with my pap an' stepma, an' I loved ever' bit o' livin'. Hit was purty where we lived — down in a holler between the hills, an' the woods come up in back o' the cabin right up to the door. In the spring the dogwood was lacy-like an' the redbuds was like little fires aburnin' the limbs. You could allus hear birds asingin', an' they was a little creek went runnin' free an' easy down the holler. Hit was a purty place, an' I was happy there. I growed up never knowin' nothin' but the hills an' the holler, never feelin' nothin' but love fer ever' livin' thing."

She paused and rocked her chair back on its legs. "They was a boy lived up on the ridge. Him an' me used to meet down by the creek when we got through in the fields. An' knowin' better, but lovin' him so good, I done wrong with him. Hit didn't seem a sin, he was so fair an' sweet. Hit jist seemed natural an' right. An' then his folks moved away — clean over to Casey County. I never faulted him none, an' I never knowed till he was gone I was in trouble. He aimed to write, an' he allus said he'd come git me soon as they was settled. An' I waited an' waited, but he never wrote. An' he never come. An' I knowed I had to do somethin'. I knowed my pap would turn me out when he caught on, an' the time was gittin' clost when he'd notice. So I jist left out one day. Hit was a bright mornin'. The sun was ashinin' down, warm an' soft-like.

149

But I turned my back on ever'thing I loved an' went away."

"O Becky, Becky!"

"I walked into the county seat, an' I got me a job cookin' fer a woman. An' I stayed until I had me enough money to git to Louisville. I didn't know what I was goin' to do there, but I knowed hit was a big enough place that I could hide away in it. I was awalkin' up an' down the streets, not knowin' where to turn, an' not havin' much money, when a woman stopped me an' started talkin' to me. She takened me home with her, an' I stayed with her until my baby was borned." Becky's voice was even, dry, toneless now. Her hands were restless under the apron, but the voice went on. "Hit was a little girl, an' sweet an' purty to look on. But the woman, she takened it away. I never seen it but oncet. She said it would be better if I never learned to love it. But I loved it from the start. She said she knowed some people would take it an' raise it like their own. Said they'd do fer it better'n I could. So I let her give it away. She wouldn't never tell me their names."

Miss Willie felt a twisting ache knot her stomach. She wanted to reach out and take one of the restless hands, but Becky was looking beyond her . . . back into the past. So this was why Becky wore black. This was the grief and the loss she still mourned. This was the sin she was still trying to atone.

Becky's shoulders bowed over her hands, and she rocked back and forth. "When I was well agin, the woman she said I owed her fer takin' me in an' takin' keer of me, an' I was bound to stay an' work fer her. I didn't keer, fer I didn't keer fer nothin'. Hit was like I was dead, an' jist my body awalkin' around. I stayed an' worked fer her a year, an' then we reckoned our accounts was even. She never rightly wanted me to leave. Said I was a good worker, but I was homesick, so I left out an' come home. Never told e'er soul what all had happened. Jist told my pa I'd been amakin' my own way in Louisville. He never ast no questions. So I jist come home an' takened up where I left off. Only somewheres I got a little girl I give away. An' the Lord ain't forgive me, fer he ain't never let me have no more."

Becky let her chair come to rest at last, and she stilled her hands. Her face took on a granite hardness, and it grayed around

150

the edges of her mouth. The lamp flickered as a small wind went searchingly across the room, and a curtain lifted and folded and dropped limply back against the wall. A white moth fluttered into the pool of light around the lamp, quivered ecstatically in the warmth of the chimney, and then plunged headlong into its fire, falling singed and blackened to the floor.

These things were embossed on Miss Willie's mind, standing forth in relief, graven and carved like the individual features of a statue. There were harsh edges to the room and the woman and the scene. Miss Willie's face was wet, and she had to speak past the tightness in her throat. "Becky," she said, "Becky, look at me."

Becky brought her eyes back from their gray memories and let them fix upon the present.

Miss Willie spoke softly, her voice steady and firm now. "Becky, listen to me. You're a good woman, Becky. You're a fine woman. One of the best I ever knew!"

The sharpness of Becky's face changed. It became diffused and softened, its seams folding gently together again. The dingy black dress burdened the bent shoulders limply. The lamplight washed over her quietly. Not until then did Becky's own tears flow. As if from some released spring within her they filled her eyes and streamed unheeded down her face. "You kin still say that?" she asked, "after me atellin' you? You kin still say that?"

"I can still say that, and I can mean it even more after what you've told me. You're not only a good woman, Becky; you're a brave one. Not one woman in a hundred could have rebuilt her life as you have done, and made a good wife and a good neighbor. That's what counts, Becky. Does Gault know this?"

"Oh, yes. I wouldn't of married him without."

"What did he say?"

"He said hit was over an' done with, an' best forgot. He ain't never named it agin sincet I told it to him."

"And Gault was right. And if Gault saw the goodness in you, don't you suppose the Lord sees it, too?"

"But he's left me barren an' without child! I've prayed an' prayed fer forgiveness, an' I thought hit would be a sign ifen he'd only give me a young'un agin. But he never did, an' now hit's too late."

151

"Becky, there could be a dozen reasons why you're childless! It's not because the Lord hasn't forgiven you."

"He don't trust me with a young'un is all I kin make of it. He give me one, an' I give it away. An' I reckon he never would trust me with no more."

"No, Becky, that's not the answer."

Becky stood and went back to the dishpan. She laughed quaveringly. "This here water's as cold as a wedge! But I feel better, atellin' you. I've not liked knowin' I was hidin' e'er thing from you."

"I'm glad you told me too, Becky. It makes me feel closer to you."

Becky's eyes were shining as she built up the fire to heat more water. "Hit takes a load offen me. Knowin' you know, an' don't fault me none. Hit makes me feel a heap better."

They had turned back to the dishes when they heard the sound of a car chugging down the road. They stopped their work to listen. Becky walked to the front door. "That's Hod's car," she said.

Miss Willie's heart jumped into her throat. "Hod's car!"

"Yes. Mary's time has come. He's agoin' after Hattie."

Miss Willie could feel her heartbeats pulsing in her wrists. For an exalted moment she knew the pulse of the universe was beating there too — the rhythm of tides and moons rising and waning, and winds blowing strongly, and rain drumming steadily. The rhythm of the earth turning around the sun, of corn greening and then ripening, of dayspring and nightfall, and of a woman's time come in the night. It was a rhythm of pain and ecstasy, mingled and blended until there was no knowing the beginning or the end of either. It was a rhythm that was timeless and spaceless — the rhythm of creation. Mary's time had come!

CHAPTER

❧ 16 ❧

Mary's baby was a boy. A lusty, strong-lunged child who barreled a fine, rounded chest up under his blankets and loudly voiced his opinion of this new world he was in.

"Mercy," Miss Willie said, coming into Mary's room the next morning, "has he got a pain?"

"Naw," Hod said, grinning. "He's just tryin' to make up his mind whether he wants to stay here with us or not. Mary bought everything she could think of for this baby, but she forgot one thing. She didn't get him a muffler! And if he keeps that up, he's goin' to need one!"

Mary looked tired, but amazingly recovered and beautiful. There was a shadow under her eyes of remembered pain, but already it was fading. "Isn't he wonderful?" she asked, stretching to see over the edge of his crib. "Did you ever see such a marvelous baby?"

"Well, if you'll both get back and let me see him, perhaps I can judge a little better," Miss Willie said, dryly. She elbowed Hod and squeezed past him.

Hod bowed deeply out of her way. "Make way for a lady!"

"Make way for a great-aunt," she snapped at him, and bent over the crib.

The baby had hushed, and was lying placidly blinking his deep blue eyes. He stared at Miss Willie unseeingly, with an ageless profundity, as if he had retreated into an ancient wisdom, some boundless space of eternal knowledge. His head was covered with a downy, yellow fuzz, which grew longer on the sides and curled back up over the tips of his tiny, perfectly shaped ears. Miss Willie touched it experimentally and sighed at its silky softness. His nose was a round little button fastened between his cheeks, which bulged fatly on either side. Miss Willie ran her finger down the side of his cheekbone, which ended in a chin that jutted strongly under his puckered mouth. The family mark was fissured deep in the flesh of this newest Pierce man. He had

153

a dimple sunk sweetly in his chin, like Hod, and like Wells.

"I'm glad he's got the dimple," Miss Willie said.

"He'll cuss it, come the day he starts shavin'," Hod answered casually.

"Just the same, I'm glad he's got it. He wouldn't be a Pierce without it. What are you going to name him?"

Mary laughed. "Ask his daddy!"

Hod stuck his tongue in his cheek and leaned his shoulder into the doorframe, scrubbing it roughly up and down. He examined his thumbnail minutely. "Well, I tell you," he said finally, "he's got a right smart name. We couldn't hardly leave anybody out, so we just sort of tacked 'em all onto him."

Miss Willie raised her eyebrows. "How many generations did you feel it necessary to include?"

Hod scratched his jaw, his hand rasping over his beard. "Just four. Miss Willie, meet young Jeems Dowell Thomas Hodges Pierce!"

Miss Willie and Mary exploded, and Hod joined in their laughter sheepishly. "But I reckon we'll call him Jeems."

"Why didn't you save one of the names for the next boy?" Miss Willie asked.

"Might not be boys," Hod drawled.

Mary yawned and stretched. She ran her hands down her sides luxuriously. "Golly," she sighed, "I feel like I could sleep a week!"

Hod strolled over to the baby's crib and looked down at him. "Ain't he a doodlebug, though? Look at that head, and look at those hands! Looks like a heavyweight already. Gentlemen, he's shore goin' to handle a plow right handy one of these days!"

Mary's eyes rested on Hod affectionately. "You're glad he's a boy, Hod?"

"Yes," he said simply. "A man likes his first to be a son."

Hod's heart spoke through his voice and implied the things his words left unsaid. That a man felt a need of the drawing out of himself into a man-child to come after him. That to become a whole man there must be this extension of himself, this division, and this passing on of his bones and flesh into the male succession. That this sonship was the continuing stream of life, threading simultaneously through their masculine veins, carrying forward forever the power of generation.

Further, Hod's voice was saying that one day this boy of his would walk the fields and the woods alongside him, shouldering a fishing pole or a gun, and he would talk with him of many things. They would walk the dark hills, the ridges and the hollows, under suns and moons and stars, and he would show him the growing things all around him and teach him how they grew. He would teach him to fish and shoot and hunt and swim, and they would explore together the mysteries of life. And one day he would curl his own great hand around the boy's small one, and curve it lovingly about the handle of a plow. "This is my beloved son," Hod's voice was saying. "My beloved son."

Miss Willie's eyes pricked and a feeling of tenderness welled up and poured over inside her. A man with his first-born son was a beautiful thing to see. She cleared her throat. "I'd better be going. Mary needs to rest, and I've got cookies to bake this afternoon for my party tomorrow. Becky's all in a dither over the party. And she doesn't think I can cook at all. She'll dog my steps from the cabinet to the stove, breathing down my neck and cautioning me every move I make." She rose and moved toward the door. "This is going to be a right smart crusade, Mary. I wish you could be there."

"Keep your flags flying, Miss Willie," Mary warned.

"I intend to! Big Springs School is going to be itch- and louse-free, come next Saturday, so help me! Ugh-h-h!" And she wiggled her hands distastefully in front of her. "That was the nastiest stuff Becky made me use! But it got rid of it! I'll come again, Mary."

"Miss Willie," Hod complained, "haven't you learned yet the proper way to take your leave on the ridge?"

"I forgot! You all better come go along!"

"Cain't," Hod drawled, "you better stay."

"Cain't, got to be goin'."

Hod's mouth quirked at the corner. "Get a little more drawl in it next time, Miss Willie, and bring it out through your nose a little stronger. We'll make a ridge runner out of you, yet."

Miss Willie giggled. "Maybe," she said. "Maybe," and she waved as she went out the door.

The party went nicely the next day. About twenty women from all over the ridge and the neighboring hollows came. There was Quilla Simpson and Corinna Jones, Mamie Clark and Lutie Jasper, all from right down the road on Piney Ridge itself. And there were the Harpers and the Taylors, and the Simmses from Coon Ridge. There were several Miss Willie didn't know at all, but word had been sent by the children. She was dismayed at first because they all brought their youngest children, and Mamie Clark brought all of hers. Becky sniffed when she saw them coming up the road. "Mamie's heared you was goin' to have somethin' to eat, an' she's figgerin' on fillin' up all them kids o' her'n, so's she won't have to cook tonight."

Miss Willie was doing rapid calculation. "Becky," she said distractedly, "I don't believe I made enough cookies."

"Oh, don't weary yerself," Becky said. "I knowed they'd all bring their young'uns. I made a batch yestiddy mornin' whilst you was down at Mary's. They's aplenty."

Miss Willie relaxed. "I don't know what I'd do without you, Becky."

The children were sent to play in the yard, and the women settled down to talk. The group was stiff at first, and Miss Willie caught them stealing sly looks around the cabin at her furniture, the pictures, the books, and the curtains and rugs. She knew they were fixing them in their minds to discuss them later. No doubt they would think all of them "quare." But since Wells's talk with her, she knew they expected her to be queer about some things, and would be disappointed if she weren't. They expected her to dress, act, and talk differently. And if they also expected her to know by some remote instinct the areas in which they assumed she would be like themselves, she must stumble across them alone and unaided. If she ran into the barriers their own long years of walking the earth as free people erected, she must pick herself up and go on, unhurt. The untrammeled hills had given these people a way of life which had its own pockets of pride and its own guarded sense of worth. An outsider must discover those for himself, or must go defeated. So inherent were these things that it was not so much a matter of the hill people being unwilling to explain and share them, as it was an inability to understand why

156

they would need explanation, and an unquestioning expectation that they would be shared. "Why, hit's allus been that way," they would say in amazement. And if you argued it wasn't that way outside the hills, they looked puzzled and remarked, "That goes plumb foolish!"

Under Miss Willie's friendly guidance the first awkward moments passed, and soon the group were talking freely of their homes, their families, the local gossip, the size of their cream checks, and the price for a pound of chunk meat. Miss Willie let this go on until someone mentioned casually an illness among her children. Then she craftily led the conversation around to the prevalence of itch in the school. There was a nodding of heads and a telling of favorite remedies and the scandalous agreement of what a nuisance it was to get rid of. When Miss Willie suggested that they all combine to make a unified fight against it immediately, they agreed without a murmur. "Hit shore would be a good thing," they said. "About the time you git yer own young'uns cured up, one asettin' alongside of 'em gits it, an' hit's all to do over agin."

When she mentioned making minute and concerted searches of heads, also, they received the suggestion favorably. She had supposed there would be some who would haughtily denounce the whole proposal. But evidently these were ancient complaints, to be taken in one's stride and without fuss and bother. It was also evident that they were common enemies, shared alike and without distinction by every family sooner or later. There was no other end of town here on the ridge. No one could conveniently draw aside her skirts here.

When Miss Willie poured hot tea for them in her thin china cups, they accepted it gingerly, handling the cups carefully and examining them cautiously. They sipped at the tea, patently meaning to do the right thing, but obviously not enjoying the unfamiliar drink.

"Hit'd go a sight better ifen they was a slug of moonshine in it," Mamie Clark opined.

"You hesh, Mamie," Becky scolded. "This here's fine Chiny tea Miss Willie's got, an' you'll not see its like ever agin!"

"Well, I ain't aimin' to fault her none," Mamie went on. "I jist

157

was sayin' hit'd go a heap better."

"We heared you the first time," said Becky, bitterly.

Lutie Jasper, whose mouth looked slack without its hump of snuff, twisted around in her chair to look at Mamie. "Is Tay astillin' over there on Wanderin' Creek yit?"

Mamie nodded and crunched a cooky between the yellow stumps of her front teeth. "He's adoin' right good over there," she said. "Runs off a batch ever' week. But he come over yestiddy. He's a talkin' to some girl hereabouts, I reckon. They was a big mess o' lipstick on his shirt collar. The old man was jokin' him about it, but he never let on who it was. He come up from the holler, though."

"Why, hit's Rose Pierce," Lutie said. "Me an' Matt's seen 'em time an' agin on the side of that hill down by the schoolhouse when we was sang diggin'."

Miss Willie was startled. "How could that be?" she asked Lutie. "Rose is in school every day. She hasn't missed a day since school started!"

Lutie shrugged her scrawny shoulders and drained her cup of the last drop of the tea. "Hit ain't none o' my put-in," she said, "but I seen what I seen, an' they's no mistakin' hit was Rose an' Tay."

The women eyed each other slyly, but there was no further comment. Tongues would lick over this later, and Miss Willie was troubled and puzzled. Rose was such a willing helper with the younger children, always ready to supervise their more frequent play times outside, always at school, rain or shine. How could she be meeting Tay, then? She shook her head and turned back to the talk idling around her.

Lutie was still talking. She hiccuped noisily. "That least 'un o' your'n is shore fleshenin' up, Mamie," she said. "He's jist afillin' out all over."

Mamie yawned. "Well, I don't know whether he is or ain't. Hit might jist be bloat. We had one oncet jist bloated up on us an' died. You cain't never tell."

Miss Willie's mouth went dry and she hastily swallowed a gulp of tea. Just as if she were talking of a hog, she thought. It was this callousness that made some of these people seem on the level of beasts to Miss Willie. If they had any finer perceptions and emotions, they were seldom evident. They worked, ate, slept, and raised young'uns, sunk in apathetic and dull acceptance of a sluggish and brutal existence. If they saw beyond those horizons, it was not apparent. Something like shame crept over Miss Willie every time she was around such people. Shame that anything human could be so porcine and brutish.

The party began to break up early because everyone had evening chores to do, and most of them had some distance to walk. They gathered around Miss Willie and said their good-by's. "Hit shore was a nice party," they said, over and over. "Hit was plumb thoughty of you to have it."

And thus Miss Willie's health class was organized. She pranced around the room after they had left, exulting mightily. "I told you so, Becky," she said. "I told you so!"

Becky, picking up napkins, emptying cups, straightening chairs, said nothing.

Miss Willie flung her arms up and reached on tiptoe to touch one of the old blackened beams across the ceiling. "It's a start," she said, her voice deepening with her pleasure. "That's all I wanted. Just a start with them. Just for them to trust me. Now, we can move along."

"Miss Willie, honey, don't count on it," and Becky poured the last drop of tea from the pot and drank it down. "They'll come, an' they'll drink yer tea, an' they'll listen. But they ain't likely to *do!*"

"All right, then, they'll listen! But they're going to listen every time I open my mouth! I'm not going to stop preaching against itch and lice and flies and skimmed milk and fried apples as long as I've got any voice left! If that's all they'll do, listen, then I'll see they have something to listen to!"

Becky's eyes twinkled. "I'll bound you will, at that!"

Miss Willie went to the door and looked off down the ridge where the trees bent and broke over the rim, disappearing down the hillside. A lavender haze smoked up from the hollow. There was a sea look to it, of far distances, as it filled up and lapped at the edges of the ridge. As if it stretched out to the horizon and beyond. Back of it the sun sliced thinly into the sky, striking through the haze with a light that was like golden sherry, a light that was so delicate and fragile that it looked as if it could be shattered with the finger of a touch.

Miss Willie's breath caught in her throat. There is so much beauty on this ridge, she thought. Every hour of the day, and every season of the year brings its own gift of loveliness. And it stretches one's body until the skin is taut and tense, and until it spills over and runs like liquid through all the senses. So much unbearable beauty. In the hills. And the people? A sadness ran through her filling her with exquisite pain. There *must* be beauty in the people too.

She turned back to help Becky, and her mind ran on to what Lutie had said of Rose and Tay Clark. "Why do you suppose," she said musingly, worrying her lower lip with her thumb, "why do you suppose it's Wells's children who worry me so much? Rufe, and now Rose. What must I do about Rose and Tay Clark?"

"Nothin'." Becky's voice was uncompromising.

"But Wells doesn't want Rose to go with Tay," Miss Willie protested.

"Miss Willie," Becky said, crumpling a napkin in her hand, "they ain't nothin' Wells nor nobody else kin do. Rose is sixteen year old. Ifen she's a mind to be seein' Tay Clark on the sly, an' ifen he's takened her fancy, she'll do it, come hell or high water! Wells jist as well to make up his mind to it, an' hit's none o' yore put-in. You'd best leave it alone."

"If she's slipping off from school to meet him, it's some of my put-in! Wells is going to a lot of trouble to keep her in school another year, and I'm not going to stand by and see her pull the wool over his eyes!"

Becky shrugged. "They's nothin' you kin do."

"I can tell Wells. I can do that!"

"Shore. You kin tell him. An' he kin bawl her out. An' all it'll do is make her an' Tay take keer a little better. Hit'd be a heap better if Wells'd jist come out in the open an' let him court her fair. Tay ain't sich a awful bad boy."

"How can you say that when he's running a still and everybody

160

knows it! It's a wonder to me someone doesn't turn him in!"

Becky whirled suddenly. "They's a thing you got to know, Miss Willie. We don't go turnin' in our own to the law on this ridge! Ifen the whole countryside knowed Tay was stillin', they wouldn't nobody do a sneakin' thing like that! Wells wouldn't hisself! An' you better not go gittin' no notions of yer own like that."

"My goodness, Becky, I'm not intending to turn him in!"

"You'd have to leave the ridge if you did! Jist mind yer own business, Miss Willie."

Miss Willie stiffened, and her temper huffed immediately. But at almost the same moment that questioning, reasonable part of her mind began to function. *Was* she examining these people with critical eyes, weighing them in scales balanced by other standards and other values? Was she assuming that those other standards and values were absolute? Were there, then, relative areas of right and wrong? On the ridge, evidently there were. Tay Clark was stilling, breaking the law. But on the ridge the law cut across a man's freedom. Freedom to do what he would with the corn he raised or bought. Freedom to earn his living in a familiar pattern. It was the law that was wrong to these people, and they took their own way of keeping it. If a man wanted to make moonshine, he hid a still back in a hollow, and all the ridge threw a protecting guard across his path. It was a man's right to make likker if he wanted to. It was the law's duty to find it out if it could. No one sat in judgment on the man who made moonshine. No one sat in judgment on the revenue officer who did his duty. Each was doing right as he saw it. But the ridge folks were on the side of the moonshiner. Inevitably their flag was raised on the side of freedom as they saw it.

Becky turned to Miss Willie as she stood brooding by the fireplace. She laid a timid hand on her arm. "Don't be ill with me, Miss Willie. Hit's jist that yer so right down ignorant about some things."

Miss Willie patted the roughened hand and smiled wryly. "I know, Becky. I know. And I'm beginning to think I'll always be right down ignorant about some things. The way people on this ridge think is something I don't think I'll ever understand." She shook her head. "But thank you for trying to help. I don't know

161

what I'd do without you."

She kicked absently at the little rocker by the fireside and set it moving to and fro. And then, as if coming to some decision and putting it behind her, she turned and vigorously attacked the remaining disorder. "Come on, let's get through with this. Wells and I are going down to see young Jeems Dowell Thomas Hodges Pierce tonight!"

CHAPTER

❦ 17 ❦

COON RIDGE LAY ABOUT HALFWAY between the Piney Ridge convolutions and the pass in the hills called the Gap. It was deeply ribbed with lapping folds and it speared the mother ridge sharply at its joining. Back in one of its deepest wrinkles, Wandering Creek slipped from the hillside in a pure freshet, icy cold from the spring that gave it birth, and crystal clear. It twisted and turned down the hill, gullying a course between rocks and boulders, and, after it reached the hollow, scratching a channel in the loamy soil. In one place it doubled back upon itself in a deep, rounding curve, pressing upon the hill a peninsula almost entirely surrounded by the stream.

It was here in this hugging curve that Tay Clark had hidden his still. And it was an almost perfect place for it. The trees were thick on both sides of the creek, and beneath them the underbrush filled in with a heavy growth which hid the flat arm of land completely. In the circle of trees there was a clearing, sandy, shaded, and protected. The still was in the clearing.

Back of it, jammed hard against the hill, was a shack, which he had thrown up out of rough, weather-beaten lumber. There were no doors or windows, but a burlap sack hung across an opening in front. Sheer rock rose behind it. Inside the shack Tay had a cot and an old chest of drawers. And he kept his sugar, cornmeal, bottles, and other supplies stacked in one corner out of the weather. This was the only home Tay Clark had.

Tay took a pride in his likker. He often said you couldn't beat good, clean Kentucky corn and Kentucky limestone water to make moonshine. The way he made it, he'd stack it up agin bourbon any day in the week. And they was plenty that liked it a heap better. Men that had a strong taste for their likker. And these Kentucky hill men would not have been able to translate the Celtic phrase "usquebaugh," or even the Latin parallel, "aqua vitae." They would not have known what the first old monks meant when they spoke of their fermented juices as "aqua de vite." But, gentlemen, they would have agreed that in any language Kentucky moonshine was truly the water of life!

On a crackly, frosty dawn early in October, two men stood by the fire in the furnace, hunched close to its warmth in the new chill of the day. The air was so light and so thin that the first cautious rays of the sun splintered it and shattered it into fragments which smoked and rose in curling wisps over the winding stream. A silver rime plated the ground and sheathed the trees and bushes. It was cold for the first week in October.

Tay stood with his hands in his pockets, shivering and yawning. "You takened yer time gittin' here this mornin', Matt," he grumbled. "Hit's broad daylight already. They's aplenty to do today."

Matt Jasper worked his chunk of tobacco around his mouth from one cheek to the other, and spat a hissing stream of juice into the fire. A week's stubble of beard blackened his jaws, and his chin dripped where his mouth had overflowed. "I cain't allus git away so early," he complained. "Lutie don't like to stir so soon these cold mornin's. An' a man's got to have his breakfast 'fore he kin git out to do e'er thing. I git here quick as I kin."

Tay yawned again and stretched, rumpling his black hair sleepily. He stood tall and loose in his joints, easy on his feet. There was a careless grace about every movement he made, and when he reached his arms up over his head, the gray work shirt tightened across his shoulders. He was flat and narrow-hipped, and his leanness boned up beneath the stretch of his blue denim pants. Tay Clark was a handsome lad.

"Criminy, it's cold!" he shivered. "Git a pot o' creek water an' put it on," he told Matt, "an' the coffee's in the shack. I'm goin'

163

to wash up."

He strode to the creek and doused his head under, yelling with the cold. But he splashed his face and neck and wetted down his hair before he went sprinting back to the fire. "Come winter, I'd like to hole up like a bear," he grumbled, wiping his face on his shirt tail.

Matt had put the sooty granite coffeepot on to boil, and stood turning his hands before the fire. "What you aimin' to do today, Tay?" he asked.

"Mash down a batch, an' I reckon you kin bottle yesterday's run. I'm aimin' to git away from here about ten o'clock."

Matt snickered. "You goin' hootin' agin?"

Tay looked at him darkly. "What you know about me hootin'?"

"Oh, I know." Matt threw a handful of coffee into the pot and stirred it down. "Me an' Lutie's seen you over at the schoolhouse. We was sang diggin' over there, an' we heared a old hoot owl, a whooin' soft-like. I knowed hit wasn't natural, so we sneaked around an' peeked. We seen Rose Pierce come to that there grove. The kids was all aplayin' an' amakin' a noise, but I reckon she was listenin' fer them owl signs."

"E'er other person seen us that you know of?"

"Not that I know of."

"Well, keep yer trap shet. Wells, he don't like me, an' Rose don't want him knowin' she's atalkin' to me."

"You aimin' to marry Rose?"

"That's fer me to say. Hit ain't none o' yore put-in. You jist keep yer trap shet, like I say. An' don't go sang diggin' round the schoolhouse no more. How about that coffee?"

"Hit'll do. Mought be a little on the weak side, but hit'll do." He poured a tin cup full and handed it to Tay. "Tay, kin I have me jist a little bottle today? I'll not tetch it till I git through workin'."

Tay gulped a mouthful of the scalding coffee. "I reckon," he said. "But if you git drunk 'fore yer through, you'll not work e'er nother day fer me. Hit costs cash money to make this here stuff, an' I ain't aimin' to have a batch ruint."

"I'll be keerful," promised Matt, and he settled himself against a log to drink his coffee.

That afternoon a blustery, cold wind blew up, and the rain squalled fretfully against the schoolhouse roof. Although it had stopped by the time the afternoon recess was due, Miss Willie decided that it was too cold and raw for the children to be out a full half hour, so she sent them out for a brief ten-minute run. "It's dark and gray," she explained, "and it's turning colder. We'll dismiss an hour earlier today instead of taking recess."

They were hardly settled in their seats again when Rose's hand waved apologetically. Her face was demure, and she slid her question upward toward Miss Willie from downcast eyes. When Miss Willie raised her eyebrows in surprise, Rose reddened, but she nodded her head vigorously. Miss Willie shrugged her permission, and the girl slipped quietly outside.

Just as she reached the door, an owl hooted softly. It was hardly more than the echo of a sound, but in the quietness of the schoolroom it sounded low and insistent, with a quality of urgency. Something about it penetrated Miss Willie's consciousness, and her head came up sharply. What made her look at Rufe she didn't know, but when her glance fell on the boy, there was a listening look on his face, a foxlike, animal look of interpreting some message. His head was turned toward the door, bent just a little, and he threw a sly, cornerwise look at her, and then jerked his head back, his eyes blazing.

Suddenly Miss Willie moved quickly and quietly to the door. She opened it slightly, and through the crack she could plainly see Rose running toward the grove. She closed the door and stood leaning against it for a moment. So. The owl was Rose's signal to come to the grove. And it was so common a sound in the woods that only listening ears could hear it. And it was timed for a recess period, of course, or one of the play times of the younger children, when Rose would be outside. The noise of the playground would mute it except for Rose, who must always be waiting to hear it. And it was only an accident that it had come today during a quiet time. And it was only an accident that she had somehow caught it herself. They were very clever, Rose and Tay. And Rufe, knowing too, had never given it away. Not until today. How stupid she had been not to realize that their scheme would be so simple!

165

Outside, Rose ran swiftly to the grove. Tay stepped from behind a tree and caught her hard in his arms, lifting her and swinging her off the ground. He closed his mouth eagerly over hers and held it for a long time. He ran his hands over the girl's shoulders, slipping them down to her waist, then he bent to her mouth again. "Glory!" he muttered when he raised his head again.

Rose pulled loose and held him off. "I cain't stay," she said quickly, "they ain't no recess today on account o' the rain an' cold, an' I had to make like I had to go outside to git away when you called. But I'll have to git right back. She'll suspicion somethin' if I don't."

"Hit's allus like this," Tay growled, pulling her close again. "Sneakin' over here two, three times a week, hidin' around, waitin' to see you ten or fifteen minnits at a time! They ain't none of this to my likin'."

"Well, it ain't to mine, neither. But I don't know of e'er thing we kin do!"

"We kin git married!"

"Not till school's out."

"What diffrunce does it make?"

"Hit makes a heap. Pa wanted me to go through the eighth grade. He fixed it so's I could go this year, an' I ain't aimin' to quit till I'm through. Hit ain't so long."

"Have it yer own way," Tay laughed.

"Have it Pa's way, you mean," Rose said. She turned in his arms restlessly, but she tarried a moment longer. "Tay, what you reckon it'll be like? Bein' married, I mean. Hit's goin' to be powerful quare."

Tay bent her fingers back and then crushed the small brown hand in his own. "Hit's goin' to be powerful good to me! Us bein' married. One thing, cain't nobody fault us none, oncet we're married an' I'm workin' regular."

"You goin' to quit stillin' like you promised?"

"I'm aimin' to quit. I done told you that, an' I aim to keep my word. I wouldn't foller stillin' now, except I don't know no other way to git the money fer us to git a start."

"I ain't so shore," Rose laughed, hugging him hard. "Yer kinder venturesome. An' I've wondered some ifen you jist don't like to go agin the law."

"You've no call to say that," the boy protested. "I been sort of wild in my time, but I promised I'd quit all that when we was married, an' I'm aimin' to keep my word. You ain't got e'er reason to doubt me."

"I'll not doubt you, never," Rose whispered, "but I don't reckon it'd make much diffrunce noways. A girl hadn't ort to love a boy so good, ifen she wants peace o' mind."

Tay stopped her words with his mouth. "You shet up," he said when he lifted his head. "How much peace o' mind you reckon I got? I spend all my time athinkin' about you," he said, shaking her gently and rubbing her face with his rough cheek. "Nights over there on that lonesome crick I dream about you, an' think of how it'll be when we kin be together. When I sit by the fire, I kin see yer face in it, an' seems like the crick water is a mumblin' yer name whilst it is runnin' over the stones. I don't do nothin' but think of you!"

"An' make moonshine," Rose teased.

"An' make moonshine," he agreed, laughing.

"I got to go now."

"Wait."

"No. Leave me go."

"Git along, then. I'll be back a Thursday."

"I'll be listenin'," she promised and slid out of his arms. By the time she reached the edge of the grove, he had faded noiselessly into the depths of the thick-grown trees and was lost to sight.

When she sidled back into her seat, Miss Willie raised her eyes and looked at her long and steadily. "I want to see you for a moment when school is out, Rose," she said.

She knows, Rose thought. She's caught on! But her heart was strangely light. It didn't really matter. They'd find another place and another way to meet. Tay could think of somethin'. Tay wouldn't never let 'em be parted. Ifen she jist don't tell Pa, she thought. That's all that wearies me. She darted a look at Rufe and he drooped one eye cautiously. Yes, she shore knows. "Yessum," she answered Miss Willie, meekly.

When the others had left and there were only the two of them sitting in the schoolroom, Miss Willie asked Rose to come to her

167

desk. "Rose," she said, speaking slowly and carefully, "I think you've been meeting Tay Clark in the grove ever since school started. I don't like to say this, but I must. What happens on the school ground is partly my business, and you can't go on meeting him here. Your father thinks you are in school when you're here, and in good faith he is making a real sacrifice so that you can have this last year of school. He doesn't like Tay, and he doesn't want you to go with him. That much of the affair is between you and him. But when you use the school ground for a meeting place, it becomes my affair too. And it can't go on."

Rose's eyes were on the floor while Miss Willie was talking. When she ceased, the girl lifted her head and looked straight at Miss Willie. "I'll not meet him here no more," she said softly.

Miss Willie picked up a ruler and laid it with a pile of pencils under her hand. "I wish you and your father could get this straightened out. But, as I said, that's between you and him. I only wanted to say you couldn't go on meeting Tay here."

"Pa jist don't know Tay," Rose said unexpectedly, her voice warm and full. "All he's got agin him is that he's Old Man Clark's boy, an' he's been kinder wild-like. An' the stillin'. Pa don't hold with stillin'. I don't neither, but Tay ain't goin' to foller it allus."

Miss Willie tapped the ruler gently against the desk. Oddly enough, now that they were talking, she felt a sudden sympathy for the girl. Tay was a handsome lad — there was no denying that. And most of the boys on the ridge went through a more or less wild time. No doubt Wells himself had sown a few wild oats before settling down. Maybe, if Wells would let them see each other openly, the affair would wear itself out. Or maybe the boy could be influenced. One thing was sure — a hidden flame always smoldered dangerously. Maybe she should talk to Wells after all. He was touchy about this subject, but she had got to know him pretty well. And maybe a woman's hand was needed in the matter.

But she said nothing to Rose except: "Well, that's all. If you and Tay meet here any more, I'll have to tell your father."

"Yessum," Rose said, turning toward the door. "I've done said we won't meet here no more. I'll keep my word."

She ain't goin' to tell Pa, Rose was thinking. That's the main

168

thing. We kin find another place. We don't need her old grove. But she ain't goin' to tell Pa, leastways. We've jist got to be more keerful. Tay'll have to think of somethin'.

A short distance from the schoolhouse Rufe was waiting for her. When she came up to him, he spoke. "She caught on?"

Rose nodded. "She wanted me to promise I wouldn't meet him in the grove no more."

"You promise?"

The girl's laugh rang out. "Shore I done so. Hit don't make no diffrunce. I was skeered plumb to death, though. I thought shorely she'd say she was goin' to tell Pa. Hit would of been natural to her. But she said ifen we seen each other at the school-house e'er 'nother time she'd tell him. I told her quick-like we wouldn't do that no more. I reckon she knowed, though, I wasn't givin' my word not to talk to him no more. She acted kinder sad-like."

"I figgered she'd caught on," Rufe said. "He give that owl agin jist as you was leavin', an' it come all over the room plain as day. She give me a look an' then went scootin' to the door. I figgered you hadn't got time to git clean to the grove yit, an' she seen you. She never said nothin', though. Jist closed the door an' stood there alookin' at the floor."

"She never takened on much. Jist what I said. I'm jist glad she ain't aimin' to tell Pa. Course he'll have to know soon or late, but we ain't aimin' to git married till school's out, an' that's some time, yit. Reckon what Pa'll do when I'm gone? Git Aunt Manthy to take Abby too, an' you an' him batch?"

"Oh, we'll git along I reckon."

Rose giggled. "Pa'll mebbe give you a new ma one o' these days."

"He'd better not!"

"He's been alookin' right sweet at Miss Willie, an' atakin' her around right smart. How'd you like her fer a ma?"

Rufe spat and snarled, twisting his mouth to one side. "Her! That mealymouthed, pussyfooted, dried-up little old maid! Ifen I was a man an' couldn't git better'n her, I'd do without!"

Rose was thoughtful. "I don't know, Rufe. She's got real nice ways, an' they's times, when she gits all het up about somethin', when her face reddens up an' her eyes sparkles an' she's almost purty. An' you kin say what you like, she loves kids as good as anybody I ever seen. She'd do fer the least uns like they was her own. But I don't reckon she'd have Pa."

"He ain't good enough fer her, huh?"

"He ain't her kind is all. Reckon she's used to perfessors an' sich. Pa's good, but he ain't real educated. An' hit's bound to be quare fer her here on the ridge. I kinder like her, though."

"Well, I don't! Hit was a sorry day when she come here, nosin' around, tellin' ever'body do this an' do that! The sooner she leaves out, the better I'll like it! I ain't got no use fer her at all!"

"You're jist jealous," Rose teased. "You're afraid Pa *will* like her!"

"I ain't!" Rufe denied fiercely. "I jist don't like her, that's all!"

"All right, then, you ain't," Rose said. They were nearing the pasture fence just around the bend from home. "You go on an' git the cows up, an' let's git the work done up. I got a heap to do tonight."

Rufe whistled off key and ducked between the wires of the fence, his yellow head scraping the wire. "You're goin' to pull them curls o' your'n out by the roots one o' these days," Rose warned. "But I'd ruther see you do that than tear a hole in yer britches."

Rufe wrinkled his nose at her and streaked across the field. Rose watched him a moment and then hurried on to the house.

That night Miss Willie sent Gault over to get Wells.

"You aimin' to tell him?" Becky asked.

"No," Miss Willie said. "I told Rose I'd have to tell him if she met Tay at the schoolhouse any more. I suppose that's a sort of promise not to tell this time. I just want to talk to him . . . see if I can't get him to let them go together openly. He's driving them to meet secretly the way it is. Maybe if he'd let them alone, the whole affair would wear itself out."

Becky shrugged. "I've my doubts."

"Well, I feel like I've got to talk to Wells about it, anyhow."

She felt very unsure of herself, timid about interfering with

170

his family affairs. But she kept remembering the wild, handsome grace of Tay, and the still look on Rose's face when she spoke of him. Admit, she told herself, that Wells knows more about this boy than I do. Admit he knows Rose better than I do. Admit that Rose is too young to make a wise choice — too young to be making any choice at all. But here on the ridge the sap rose early in slender green trees, and who was to say that slender green trees couldn't root themselves firmly and bend and sway before the wind without breaking? Who was to know whether the cup of this girl's love was for this man or that? And who was to say whether its measure should be full and running over before it was tipped to the lips of any man, or drained before it had filled? Who but Rose could know how full it was? Who but Rose could hear the high, wild notes of love that bugled in her ears, could feel the beat of her heart send the blood surging wave after wave through her body, could see with sure eyes down the long, twisted trail of tomorrow? Shouldn't she have a fair chance to listen to her heart? Or to deny it, if she must?

You fool! Miss Willie admonished herself. What do you know about love? Love between a man and woman, that is. Dream a fine dream about bugle notes in the air, blood coursing thickly through the veins, visions of tomorrow! What do you know about it? Dream it . . . and call it by its right name! She rubbed her thin hands together and shrank them against her chest. I know enough, her heart whispered, to know what I've missed! Dream or not, I know when I'm empty! She flung her hands wide. Is it Rose or Miss Willie that's dreaming? Is it Rose or Miss Willie that hears that wild bugling? Is it Tay's voice that calls, or Wells's? She stood before her mirror and watched the slow blood creep up into her face. Fool, she accused. Thou fool!

When Wells sat before her fire later, a cup of coffee cooling on the table at his elbow, she felt fluttery and nervous. He sat in her rocker, his stocky body filling it and his broad shoulders spanning the back. How like him, she thought, to sit there, still, solid, motionless, rocklike in his strength! His face was clean-shaven, smooth and faintly pink beneath its deep tan. There was a fresh smell of soap about him — soap mixed with the clean smell of his clothes, wind- and sun-dried after their washing. He lighted his pipe and leaned his head against the tall back of the rocker, and the smoke curled lazily between them, veiling his face. The smell of his pipe blended with the other smells, and they became whole, the essence of maleness. And his presence overflowed the chair and filled the room, and washed over into Miss Willie until she was faint with its compelling insistence. She reached out a hand to steady herself and jingled the spoon on her saucer in her tremor.

"This shore is nice," Wells said, kicking a foot against the floor and setting the rocker in motion. "This here's purty an' homey. Them curtains o' your'n, the rugs, an' all. You shore did make you a purty little home outen this old log cabin. Hit takes a woman ever' time to figger things out."

"I like it," Miss Willie said. The coffee was hot, and as she sipped it, she steadied. It felt warm and heavy in her stomach. A log snapped in the fire, cracking sharply in the silence and sending a shower of sparks out onto the hearth. Wells leaned forward to juggle the log with the poker.

"I like chestnut wood," he said. "Hit burns mighty purty, but hit makes a heap o' noise doin' it. Sounds like them little firecrackers agoin' off."

"Yes."

When he had fixed the log to suit him, Miss Willie put her cup and saucer down. "I suppose you're wondering why I sent for you," she said.

Wells looked at her quizzically and grinned. "I ain't so curious," he said. "Whatever hit was, I'm powerful beholden to it fer givin' me a chancet to come an' see you."

Miss Willie felt her face heat. "It's about Rose," she blurted out.

Wells sighed and set his own cup and saucer on the table. "Well, I knowed in reason you had somethin' on yer mind, an' I reckoned it'd be about one o' them young'uns o' mine. I was afeared it was Rufe agin."

Miss Willie shook her head.

"What's Rose been up to?" he asked after a time, when Miss Willie said nothing further.

She had been searching for the right words, hoping to find some tactful way of barging into his personal affairs, and wishing

172

she had never started the whole thing. She shook her head again. "It's not that. It's just . . . Wells, do you think it's best for you to forbid her seeing Tay? Don't you think maybe if you'd let them go together openly, they would eventually tire of each other? Are you sure you aren't driving them together this way?"

The urgency in her voice turned his face sober. She looked at him anxiously to see if he resented her questions. But his face only reflected a seriousness and earnestness that paid tribute to her and her opinions. She breathed easier.

He cupped his hands about his updrawn knee. "No," he said slowly, "no; I ain't a bit shore but what I'm doin' jist what you say. I ain't so blind but what I know they're a meetin' sly-like. That's jist what I knowed they'd do."

"Well, then, why don't you let them go together?"

"Hit's like this, Miss Willie. Here on the ridge we do things different, I reckon. But ifen a girl's folks don't make no fuss about her talkin' to a boy, hit's jist the same as givin' 'em leave to stand up before the preacher. An' I cain't in conscience give my consent to her marryin' Tay Clark. That's jist what it would be if I give 'em leave to talk. I look fer 'em to up an' git married one o' these days. But leastways, if they do, hit'll not be on my conscience that I give her over to sich as him. Folks cain't fault me none about that."

Miss Willie studied. "Would you rather have the good opinion of the people on the ridge, then, than to lose their respect trying to help your daughter?" Her voice was dry.

"Hit ain't jist thataway, Miss Willie," he explained patiently. "Hit's all mixed up, an' I ain't shore I kin explain it so's you kin understand, you bein' new to the ridge. You see, Miss Willie, Tay an' Rose knows where they stand. Rose, she wouldn't understand if I tried to tell her she could talk to Tay but couldn't marry him. Hit would jist tangle her up like. She wouldn't make no sense o' me givin' her leave to talk to him, an' not givin' her leave to marry him. But this way hit's all open an' clear. Her an' Tay, an' folks all over, knows I don't give my leave. Ever'body knows they're meetin', an' likely they'll up an' git married. But I've took my stand, an' I'm bound to stay by it. Folks expect it, an' Rose an' Tay expects it. Hit would go agin the grain all round if I

173

didn't, now. A man's called on to take his stand on some things, an' he cain't noways go agin the grain an' call hisself a man. I couldn't never sleep nights ifen I was to out an' out give my leave to Rose marryin' sich as Tay Clark."

"But suppose she marries him anyhow?" Miss Willie's voice raised sharply. "You just said that more than likely she will! What happens then? You'll just lose your daughter, that's what!"

Wells's look was puzzled. "Why, no, Miss Willie. Ifen they git married, hit's done an' over . . . water over the dam. Likely they'll jist move in with me, an' Rose'll jist go on akeepin' house fer us like allus. Hit'll jist be Tay amovin' in with us."

"You mean you'll object until they're actually married and then it won't make any difference?"

"I reckon that's about the size of it. A man's called on to take his stand. But if his young'uns don't bide by it, hit's outta his hands. Ifen Rose an' Tay gits married, he'll be in the family then, an' nothin' to do about it. You don't turn on yer family."

Miss Willie closed her eyes, and her hand made a futile brushing gesture across her face as if to brush a cobweb away. And that's exactly what she felt she was trying to understand. The cobweb of ridge ways. The fine distinction that only ridge people could possibly fathom! It was beyond her!

She stood and picked up the empty cups. "Well, then," she said, "I've just butted in where I had no business again. Forgive me."

Wells looked up at her and smiled wistfully. "That ain't a word I like, Miss Willie. They's no call fer one human bein' to forgive e'er 'nother one. I don't rightly know that they's e'er one of us good enough fer that. Hit's like a body was settin' hisself up over the other. Hit ain't a thing e'er one of us ort to feel, seein' as we're all liable to the same mistakes. An' besides, Miss Willie, I'm catchin' on to you. You was jist doin' what you thought was yer bounden duty. I kin jist see you mullin' it over in yer mind, adecidin' you was called on to have a talk with me. Ifen you don't take keer, Miss Willie, folks is goin' to be sayin' you an' me is talkin' instead o' the young'uns!"

Miss Willie let her breath out sharply. "Don't be silly!"

"Hit ain't so silly, Miss Willie. Me, I kind of take to the notion!"

174

Miss Willie's eyes brimmed and cooled suddenly with tears. "Well, now," she said brightly, "let's talk about something else. Tell me, is it all right for the school to have a Christmas tree and a program, or is that something that isn't done on the ridge?"

The rest of the evening passed swiftly, but when Wells finally left, Miss Willie lay long awake remembering his bulk in her little old rocker, his laugh ringing around the rafters, his pipe smoke wreathing his brown face. The deep tones of his voice lingered in her ears: "Hit ain't so silly, Miss Willie. Me, I kind of take to the notion!"

She snuggled under her blankets and watched the last of the fire settle itself down for the night. It glowed softly and with a red sheen, and her own happiness and contentment glowed within her. I kind of take to the notion too, Wells! She took a deep breath. But, not too fast, she warned herself. Not too fast.

CHAPTER
❧ 18 ❧

NOVEMBER CAME IN ROARING on the high-winded tail of a sleet storm. The last leaf was driven before the gale, and the bones of the trees rattled in their nakedness. The ridge was stripped, and it reared its scrawny spine against the slashing knives patiently and with stony endurance.

"Hit's goin' to be a hard winter," people told Miss Willie as she stepped the little mare carefully down the icy road. "Winter of 1918 set in jist like this. Had twenty-two snows that winter, an' oncet we never seen the ground fer two months on end."

By Thanksgiving the prophecy was well on the way to coming to pass. Twice the earth had been blanketed with snow, and the earliest hard freeze ever known in the country had locked the little creeks and their tributaries into stillness. The surface of the earth shivered and tensed and hardened itself into plated armor. The little mare's feet rang when she stepped now, as if she were walking on sheet metal, and they struck sparks that hissed in the frozen air.

The houses were haunched against the ground, huddled and

175

low, their shoulders humped up against the wind and the pelting snow. Smoke from the hearths rose slowly, loath to leave the fire, and it hung in wreaths around the sooty stones of the chimneys, hugging the warmth one last time before ascending into the icy air.

Miss Willie had Thanksgiving dinner with Mary and Hod. Afterward they sat, stuffed and sleepy, before the fire. The sleet hissed softly against the windowpanes, and outside the black-boned trees iced themselves with glassy plate. Miss Willie was knitting an afghan for the baby, but her fingers plied the needles automatically. She lifted her eyes from time to time to glance smilingly at Hod, who sat in his big armchair, his son cradled in the curve of his arm and his pipe dangling from one corner of his mouth. Mary wandered over to the piano and let her fingers drift into soft, improvised chords, which resolved themselves finally into the sweet minor notes of a song.

"What is that?" Miss Willie asked after a time.

"It's an old English melody. The words are a Christmas song: 'What Child is this, who, laid to rest, on Mary's lap is sleeping?'" She continued playing, sometimes singing the words, sometimes humming. "I don't remember all of it," she said. "It's been a long time since I thought of this song. My primaries used to sing it during the Christmas season."

"It's beautiful." Miss Willie counted stitches and turned. "And that reminds me. Could you spare some time to help me with the Christmas program at school?"

Mary's hands dropped from the piano. "I guess so. If Hod's mother can stay with the baby. What kind of program are you going to have?"

"Wells says it's customary to have a tree the last Friday night before the holidays. And I thought it would be nice to have a sort of pageant. Maybe have someone read the Christmas story from Luke, and dramatize it with some simple scene, and use the Christmas songs as much as possible. That's where I want you to help, Mary. Children's voices are so beautiful when they're properly trained, and I'd like the people to hear some real singing for a change!"

Mary laughed. "No 'do, re, mi,' is that it?"

"That's it. That song you were just singing would be nice, wouldn't it?"

"Beautiful. High, soft, and minor. And it isn't too difficult. I think we could manage something pretty good."

"Wells is going to get a big cedar tree, and we thought we'd put it up in the corner of the room at the back, and after the program we'd give all the children bags of candy and nuts, and an orange maybe. What do you think of that? I've got so I'm scared to make a move without asking Wells or Becky or someone if it'll go 'agin the grain' here on the ridge. But Wells told me the Christmas tree and program would be all right."

Hod laughed. "I reckon you've had to learn the hard way, all right."

"I certainly have," Miss Willie sniffed.

"The whole thing sounds lovely, Miss Willie," Mary said.

"I thought maybe we could dramatize the manger scene, and let the shepherds come, and the Wise Men bringing gifts. We could use a big doll for the child. I'd like for Johnnie to be Joseph." Miss Willie pinched her lower lip as she thought. "I wish we had some way of lighting it. It would be so much more effective with spots on the scene."

"I wonder," Mary said—"I wonder if you can still get those little boxes of magnesium powder we used to use for tableaux when I was a little girl. Where did we use to get them, anyhow?"

Miss Willie clapped her hands. "Why, Mary, that's the very thing! We got them from a school supply house! There surely is still some demand for that sort of thing. I'll start trying to locate some at once!"

Mary laughed. "I never could keep from jumping when the powder first flared up. I knew it was harmless, but as many of Mamma's tableaux as I was in, I always had to steel myself against jumping when that first bright light flared up. And I remember how it smoked."

"Yes, but it does make an effective scene. That was a real inspiration, Mary. We'll have some sort of curtains, and Hod and Wells can stand in the wings and light the powder at the right time. Red on one side, and green on the other, I think."

Hod shifted the baby. "Hey, look! He's tryin' to sit up!"

177

Mary looked at Miss Willie. "He can't wait until the baby sits alone, and tries to walk and talk! He'll have him following a plow by the time he's a year old!"

"Well, it seems like he's takin' a long time bein' a baby," Hod complained. "I wanna know what he's thinkin' about when he rolls his eyes around and puckers his mouth at me! He gets such a doggoned faraway look on his face, I'd like to know where he's gone!"

"Pooh," Miss Willie said loftily, "more than likely he's trying to make up his mind what sort of person he's drawn for a father. The way you go on with him sometimes I'll bet he thinks he's out of luck!"

"That's all right, son," Hod confided to the baby. "Don't you pay any attention to 'em. That's just woman talk, an' you'll be hearin' it all your life. Just let it go in one ear and out the other. That's the way I do. You and me, we're menfolks, and one of these days we'll have some good old man talk."

Mary chuckled. "Well, you better let me have a little woman talk with him right now, and give him something to eat!" She rose and went across the room to lean over the man and baby, and lifted the child high in her arms. "You may be menfolks, little fellow," she said, shaking him gently, "but all your life the womenfolks are going to be mighty important to you. How would you get your milk right now, huh? And who would teach you when you start to school, huh? And who's going to marry you someday, and raise your young'uns for you, huh? Don't you let your daddy belittle the womenfolks to you!"

Hod's laugh echoed round the room. "I haven't got a chance," he said to Miss Willie. He stood and pushed his chair back with his heel and strode to the fireplace. He poked a log into place and put another one on top. Then, turning, he leaned his elbow on the mantel and looked fondly at the two of them as Mary bent over the baby. Funny, he thought, how the sight of your wife holding your son made you feel so much of a man! It poured through you and washed out everything but the cleanness of pure manhood, made you taller and straighter. It made you grow clear up to the stars, somehow. Made you ache and at the same time healed the aching; stripped you down, and at the same time

178

wrapped you around with the mantle of fatherhood. Drained you and emptied you, and at the same time filled you full. This business of living. Of being a man and a woman, and of having a son! There's nothing like it in the world, he thought. Nothing to compare with it!

The afternoon light was waning when Miss Willie dropped her knitting in the bag by her side. "It's growing late," she said, "and I'd better be going. Hod, will you saddle Pet for me?"

"Just take the night, Miss Willie," Hod suggested.

"No, I'd better go home. Becky and Gault might worry. Besides, Wells is coming over for supper with us."

"Ah, *there's* the reason," Hod gibed, and Miss Willie's face turned rosy. "She must brave sleet and storm, for Lord Randall is comin' courtin' tonight!"

"Hush up!" Miss Willie said. "I don't want that kind of talk to get spread over the ridge. And the best way to start it is to tease about it."

Hod bowed with exaggerated politeness. "Just as you say, Miss Willie. Just as you say, but," he continued softly, "I'll bet a plugged nickel it's done started in yore heart!"

"Hod," Mary warned, and he left the room chuckling.

Miss Willie looked slantwise at Mary and fumbled with her hat. "Wells has been a big help to me," she said, "and of course he comes pretty often. After all, he's one of the trustees, and then too I've had quite a problem with Rufe and Rose."

"Why, of course, Miss Willie," Mary said quietly. "Hod's just teasing."

Miss Willie went to the window to watch for Hod and the little mare. She stood there fingering the shade pull and doodling on the moist windowpane. Mary pinged one note over and over on the piano. Miss Willie squared her shoulders suddenly. "I like him, though," she admitted, her voice loud in the quiet room. "I don't mind everybody knowing I like him . . . a lot."

"We all like Wells," Mary said. "He's a grand person. Next to Hod, I think he's the finest man I ever knew."

Miss Willie's mouth trembled into a smile. "Well, not being married to Hod, I can't say that I put him first."

Mary crossed the room to lay her arm around her aunt's thin

179

shoulders. "Be careful, Miss Willie. Be careful, and make sure. There's an awful lot to be considered."

Miss Willie nodded and reached to kiss Mary's cheek. "That's what troubles me. Oh, pshaw!" and she shook herself vigorously. "Christmas is coming, and we're going to have a lovely pageant, and everything is fine! I am simply going to enjoy myself these next few weeks, and refuse to be troubled about a thing. I'll pick up my troubles after the first of the year. Right now I want to sing and be happy and gay!"

"Is that the way he makes you feel?"

Miss Willie giggled like a child. "That's exactly the way he makes me feel! Young and light and carefree! He makes me feel important and needed. And he makes me feel beautiful and womanly and feminine. And it's a good feeling, Mary. Especially when you're a dried-up, musty old maid!"

"Miss Willie," Mary said softly, "I'll put my plugged nickel right alongside Hod's!"

Wrinkling her nose, Miss Willie picked up her knitting bag. "There's Hod." She opened the door and the wind blew her next words across the room. "You wouldn't lose your nickel, Mary."

Excitement rippled over the ridge as children went home from school and told the news. Miss Willie was goin' to have a Christmas program . . . they was goin' to be a play thing, somethin' she called a pageant . . . an' a Christmas tree with candy an' stuff fer ever'body! "An', Ma, I got to have a costume. I'm goin' to be a shepherd, an' I've got to have a costume. Miss Willie said she'd ride over here an' tell you what to fix."

Miss Willie rode from one end of the ridge to the other, helping mothers devise simple costumes. Burlap sacking for the shepherds, and sheets draped with bits of bright colors for the Wise Men. Hod and Wells made the beards out of lambs' wool, and the boys made the shepherds' crooks from rugged, knotty hickory limbs.

All the ingenuity of women long accustomed to making do with what they had came to the front. And at school the children were busy practicing. Those who did not have part in the pageant

180

were in the choir, and, sensing their desire to be costumed also, Miss Willie suggested that sheets or table covers could be draped over them for choir robes.

Mary came for several days to help with the songs, but once the children learned them, Miss Willie could manage alone. "Softly," she cautioned them over and over again. "Softly."

She had asked Rufe to read the story.

"No, ma'am," he said.

"But Rufe you have such a nice voice, and you read so well," she pleaded.

"No, ma'am," he said. There was no sullenness in his voice. Just an immovable stubbornness.

She was hurt and disappointed, but her pride would not allow her to press the matter further. She had envisioned Rufe in the part, his golden head shining tall in the lamplight, his full young voice reading the beautiful lines. He would have been perfect. But she hid her disappointment and gave the part to one of the Jones triplets, Sewell. She coached him carefully, and he quickly learned the detail of the dramatization: when to wait for the pantomime, when to pick up the story again, when to pause for a song, and when to resume. But his reading was flat and uninspired, and she sighed over his meticulous monotone. Rufe would have made the lines come alive. He would have made the pageant live and move. But . . . no matter. Corinna and Ferdy would bask in sunny pride over Sewell's reading, and doubtless no one else on the ridge would find anything amiss with it.

Now it was less than a week until the program, and the boys and girls were working feverishly on the decorations for the room and the tree. The green and red paper chains grew by yards and were draped in gaudy festoons from the ceiling. Strings of popcorn and cranberries were ready for the tree, and as the week wore on, the children brought armfuls of cedar and pine boughs to place in the windows and around the room. At night Becky and Miss Willie, and sometimes Gault and Wells, sacked candy and nuts for the tree.

The day of the program there was no attempt to have school. Wells brought the tree and the oldest boys put it up. In happy confusion it was decorated. The manger was set up on a platform

181

and strewn with hay, and the curtains, made from sheets, were strung on tight wires across the platform. Wells and Hod came to help and set the pans to hold the tableau lights. One last rehearsal of the pageant was held, and Miss Willie explained the tableau. "Don't be afraid," she told the children. "It will flare up and make a bright light, but that's just what we want. That will be the tableau. Don't move. Just stay in your places and hold your poses, and when the lights die down, Wells and Hod will pull the curtains. Don't move until then."

Everything was ready. The tree in the corner was tall and green, giving off a spicy, pungent smell of cedar. Its boughs were hung with the popcorn and cranberries, and the red and green paper chains. Tinsel stars sparkled here and there, and the bags of candy and nuts, and the bright round oranges weighted down even the tips of the branches. It was a beautiful Christmas tree.

The people gathered early. By deep dark the school ground was crowded with teams and wagons. It was a warm, friendly crowd, laughing and calling out to one another as they saw the tree and the gay room. It was a congregation of neighbors coming to see their children perform, and to share the ancient tradition of a festive tree. Small shepherds and Wise Men bustled importantly up and down the aisles until Miss Willie herded them behind the curtains, and finally sent them filing to the back of the room to await their cues.

At a signal, Sewell started the reading, and Hod and Wells slowly parted the curtains. Miss Willie settled back with a sigh. Johnnie and Sarie were in their places by the manger, and the large doll rested comfortably in the straw. The choir took up the story with the song of the shepherds, and the first shepherd came forward somewhat sheepishly, hitching at his burlap tunic, but carefully and slowly as he had been taught. The star over the manger swung tipsily and revolved endlessly on its length of wire, but it shone brightly just the same.

Then the choir sang the song of the Wise Men, and the first of the Wise Men, splendid in purple and gold, strode haughtily down the aisle, kneeling properly before the manger to present his gift.

The scene moved flawlessly on. Sewell never faltered in his

reading. The choir of young voices came in at exactly the right moments, their voices blending softly and sweetly in the old songs. The young actors moved through the pageant with familiar ease and practice. Miss Willie let her hands relax in her lap. There remained now only the tableau. All the actors were on the stage, the choir was softly chanting "Silent Night," and Miss Willie nodded to Hod, who was peeking through a fold of the curtain. There was the flare of matches from either side backstage, and then the full glory of the red and green lights burned up. As they reached their most brilliant light, there were two sudden, sharp explosions of sound, filling the room and reverberating from the ceiling.

There was a stunned silence, and then, "Hit's a *explosion!*" someone cried, and instantly the audience was on its feet screaming and milling senselessly. There was a panic-stricken rush for the door, and a rush toward the stage by terrified parents to rescue their children. Frightened, the children broke and ran, crying and stumbling about in their costumes. Smoke from the sulphur and magnesium mixtures was filling the room with a heavy pall.

"Fire!" someone shouted. "Fire! Clear the room. Hit's a fire!"

Miss Willie had been paralyzed at first. She could only think that somehow the powder had been defective and had actually blown up! The crowd jostled her and shoved her aside, and she was pushed gradually against the wall. A complete sense of disaster overcame her, and she thought futilely that she ought to get up on one of these benches and shout and make herself heard and bring some sort of order out of the confusion.

Then she noticed that Hod and Wells were jerking at the curtains, and then Wells stood before the group. He cupped his hands over his mouth and bellowed at the crowd. "Set down, you fools! They ain't no fire, an' that wasn't no explosion! Set down, I'm a tellin' you!"

When the stentorian voice roared out above them the people turned. "Set down," he bellowed again. "Set down!"

The rush toward the door stopped. A few sat down on the back seats and others followed their example, sliding hesitantly onto the benches.

"I'll be back in a minnit," Wells yelled, and he started lunging through the crowd toward the door. "Ever'body jist set down an' wait fer me."

He disappeared through the door. There was an uncertain milling around of people, and the burr of sharp talk rose around the room. Hod appeared from behind the curtains with the pans in which the tableau mixture had been burned. He held them up for the crowd to see. "You can see for yourselves," he said, "there wasn't any explosion. There wasn't any fire. This is just a harmless mixture of magnesium and sulphur. When it's lighted, it flares up brightly and burns for a few seconds, and then it dies down again. There's no way it could possibly explode!"

There was a disturbance in the back of the room, and Wells pushed his way through the crowd, dragging Rufe by one arm and marching Tay Clark ahead of him. Tay walked carelessly and nonchalantly, his hands in his pockets, a malicious grin on his face. At the front of the room Wells halted them.

"Here's yer explosion," he said. "Long as you fellers been huntin' these ridges an' hollers, I'm ashamed you don't know a shotgun when you hear it! This smart-alec young'un of mine, an' Tay Clark here, thought it'd be fun to play a dirty trick on ever'-body. Skeer the daylights outen 'em, an' start 'em trompin' one another down to git outta here. An' that's jist what they done! I knowed as soon as I heared it, it was a gun." Bitterly he went on. "I ain't claimin' no excuses fer my boy. But I aim to see he don't fergit this. As fer Tay, mebbe he'd better say fer hisself."

Tay shrugged his shoulders. "Aw, we never meant no harm. Hit was jist a trick." His grin widened. "You all shore did look funny stampedin' around in here. You ort to of seen yerselves!"

"An' you ort to be ashamed o' yerself! Playin' a fool trick like that, growed man that you are! Somebody might of got hurt!"

Tay laughed and ran his hand over his black hair. "Well, I tell you," he said, "I reckon I been samplin' my own goods a little too much. Hit jist seemed like a good idee all at oncet. Don't hold it agin Rufe too hard. Hit was mostly my idee."

"I'll hold it agin him," Wells promised. "I'll hold it agin his backside when I git him home! An' right now that's where he's a goin'."

Miss Willie had not taken her eyes off Rufe during the entire

184

scene. When his father turned him loose, he had straightened himself and stood tall before the crowd, looking over their heads into space. By not so much as one troubled look had he given any notice that he heard anything Wells said. The winter was bleaching his summer tan, but the golden wash over his face and hair was still there. There was a still look of endurance on the face now. A withdrawn look, as if he had pulled himself in tight. It would be better, Miss Willie thought, if he were insolent, like Tay. If he would flaunt his contempt, openly.

For she was certain that once again Rufe had found a way to show his enmity for her. She felt her breath tighten in her throat. Why did this boy hate her so? What had she done, or what had she failed to do? She felt as if a fog had closed in around her, blanking out familiar landmarks. There was nothing she could hold to . . . nothing she could see, except the misty currents of dislike that eddied between her and this tawny-headed boy.

"Now git on home," Wells was saying. "You cain't stay fer the tree, nor fer nothin' else. Git yerself home. But wait up. I'll tend to you when I git there."

Miss Willie stood up. "No, Wells," she found herself saying, "no, don't make him go home. Let him stay for the tree." She started toward the front of the room

Rufe looked at her then. Directly. Steadily. "I wouldn't keer to stay," he said.

Miss Willie stopped where she stood. Her teeth caught her underlip and it quivered slightly. She felt as if he had struck her. But the years of her pride rose within her, and she made her voice steady as she answered him. "Just as you like, Rufe," she said.

And he walked past her without again looking at her.

When the door closed behind him, there was a rumbling of talk through the room. Some of the men looked at each other and laughed sheepishly. The women were complaining in undertones, and there was an occasional shrill whisper against such goings on. "Ifen he was mine, I'd take a strop to him, an' I reckon that's jist what Wells'll do too."

There was a virtuous gathering of their own children to their sides, and Miss Willie felt as if Rufe had been outlawed. Bleakly, she heard Wells telling Tay he had better get going too, and in her alienated misery she watched him swagger down the aisle. At the door he waved to Rose, holding the door open so that a gust of wind made the lamps flicker.

"Shet the door," somebody yelled, and he laughed and banged the door behind him. Miss Willie wondered if the reason he had thought of this trick lay in her own refusal to let him and Rose meet on the school ground. Wearily she shrugged the thought away. No matter now. She had done what she must.

When Tay had left, the tension eased and people started laughing and joking together, jeering at each other. "Gault, I seen you jump two foot when that there gun went off," Tom said, poking Gault in the ribs.

Gault laughed. "Hit shore skeered me outen ten years' growth," he admitted.

"I never jumped," Tom bragged.

"No, you was too busy makin' fer the door," Hattie accused dryly.

There was a shout of laughter, and then Hod was calling for quiet. "Let's have the tree, now," he shouted. "Ever'body turn around and face the tree, an' Miss Willie'll give out the presents!"

Miss Willie made her way to the foot of the tree, and Hod crawled up on a ladder to hand down the sacks and oranges. Remembering her joy in planning this night, Miss Willie was shaken by its dreary ending. A chill of shivering fled through her, and she steadied herself against the ladder. And then the bright, expectant faces of the children focused before her, and she thought, Why, the evening hasn't been spoiled for them! She looked around the room, and in the soft lamplight the faces of the people were friendly and warm. It hasn't been spoiled for them, either, she thought. Just for me. Me . . . and Wells. And maybe Rufe.

She drew herself up and handed the first two sacks of candy and nuts and the first two oranges to Sarie Simpson and Johnnie. They beamed at her, and Sarie ducked her red head shyly. Johnnie's round face broke into a toothless grin.

"What do you say, Johnnie?" Irma prompted.

"Thank you, ma'am," Johnnie said importantly.

186

"You're quite welcome, Johnnie," and Miss Willie tousled his hair fondly.

The next sack she handed to Lutie Jasper. "Fer me?" Lutie questioned. "I thought it was jist fer the kids."

"For everyone," Miss Willie answered. "Christmas gift for everyone!"

"Christmas gift! Christmas gift!" the voices shouted around the room. High up on the ladder Hod started singing "Jingle Bells," and soon everyone had joined in.

When the tree had been divested of the last sack and the last orange, people began to leave. "Hit was a nice program, Miss Willie," they said. And: "Don't you feel bad about yer lights. Hit come right at the last, an' never spoilt a thing."

It was Ferdy Jones who mentioned the choir. "The kids sung real good, Miss Willie. Hit's a pity, though, they never sung out good an' loud. Reckon they was too skeered."

Miss Willie was too tired to reply. It didn't matter anyhow.

But, tired as she was, she tossed sleeplessly on her bed later. I could fight a grown man, she thought. I would know how to go to him and have it out in the open. But Rufe's stony and implacable barrier of enmity thwarted her in the way a tangled skein of yarn baffles one. If only you could find one loose end! It would take patience to ravel the knots, but they could be managed and eventually they would come smooth, if only you could find the starting place! She had tried. Goodness knows, she had tried. She had tried to interest him in reading, but he wouldn't even take the books home. She had tried to interest him in the science table, suggesting he collect things on his wanderings through the woods. She had said: "Rufe, you know the woods so well. Why don't you look for things when you're out with Jupe, and bring them for us to see? Indian spikes, unusual flowers, insects or small animals. You could add a lot to the table." He had only looked off through the window and shaken his head.

Restlessly she turned and wrinkled the smooth sheets, until finally in exasperation she rose and straightened the bed. Crawling back beneath the blankets, she rationalized. School's nearly over now. Maybe it will work itself out this summer. Maybe by the time the next term starts I'll find the answer. Maybe the Lord will pass a miracle, she jeered at herself! Well, go to sleep now, she commanded her tired mind. You're not called on to settle everything tonight.

CHAPTER

❧ 19 ❧

School closed the middle of January, earlier than expected. The weather was so bad after Christmas that attendance dropped to a mere fraction of the enrollment. Only those children living near the schoolhouse could brave the deep snows and the bitter cold. The trustees decided to close two weeks early.

Miss Willie worked hard over a written report she wanted to make to the trustees. She dwelt at length upon the things that had been accomplished, pointing them out with pride. And then she concluded by summing up the things that were still wrong, and with her own frank suggestions as to how to right them. She wrote in her bold, schoolteacherish hand: "The school term is much too short, but as yet I see no way to deal with that problem. The children must come such long distances, over such bad roads, that at present it is physically impossible for them to attend when the harsh weather of winter sets in. We need improved roads, so that a car can travel the year round. Perhaps the trustees could lead in a fight to get the county to do some work on the roads."

Then she went on to point out: "I must protest against the open spring from which the drinking water comes. In its present condition it is dangerous. An epidemic of almost any kind could easily start, since the water from the spring flows for some distance in an open channel. It may be fouled by cattle and other animals, and even by people. I strongly urge you to cement the spring in an enclosed box, and to pipe the water to the school-house. The cost of this would be small in comparison to the satisfaction in the security offered the children.

"The open toilets are another thing that should be corrected. New buildings are needed, and modern chemical disposal units should be installed. In their present condition they constitute a health hazard of the gravest sort, to say nothing of being ex-

188

tremely offensive to the eye. Education," she went on to say, "is not simply a matter of learning from books. Children learn from their total environment. Ugly buildings, offensive sanitation units, careless health habits are teaching them things just as surely as the textbooks in arithmetic and geography. They are teaching them that, although their hygiene books stress sanitation, no one takes it seriously. They are teaching them that, although 'teacher' talks about beauty and encourages them to develop an appreciation of it, the unbeautiful things within a stone's throw of them are ignored.

"We have accomplished much this school term. We can take pride in many things we have done. But I appeal to you as the trustees, and more important, as fathers, to consider seriously these things I have called to your attention, and to act upon them before the beginning of the next term."

There, she thought, when she had finished, now that's said. They can't sit back smugly and pat themselves on the back and say: "Miss Willie shore done a good job this year. Best school we've ever had." That report's got something in it that ought to make them stir their stumps!

But she was glad she didn't have to report some other things in which she had fallen short. The health class had had to be abandoned when the weather began to break, and she had to admit to herself it was just as well. As Becky had prophesied, the women had come and had drunk her tea and eaten her cookies, and listened. For she had been as good as her word and she had preached and preached. Diet, sanitation, health, cleanliness — she hadn't left anything untouched. And the women listened docilely, nodded their heads in agreement, and said, "Yes, ma'am," to everything she asked them to do. But the children's lunch buckets continued to hold cold biscuits and fat meat, the children continued to come to school with the itch, with colds, and even with whooping cough.

And she winced every time she remembered that neither had she got very far with Becky's well! When she thought of that, even yet, it made her face go hot with chagrin. Gault had neatly circumscribed her on that! As long as she lived she would never forget the morning he had gathered up his tools and some slabs

189

of old lumber. "Well," he had announced to her and Becky, "reckon I'll make that thar gate Becky's been awantin'. Hit was bad enough long as hit was jist her arollin' under that bob-war fence, but ifen they's goin' to be two of you arollin' I won't never see no peace."

And he had had the audacious nerve to cut a gate in the barbed-wire fence across the path to the spring, so that she and Becky could carry water without rolling under the fence! She could have sworn there was a ghastly twinkle in his eyes when he did it too!

She copied the report and mailed it to Lem as the chairman of the trustees. And then for several weeks she waited for him to reply. She expected him to call a meeting of the trustees to hear the report read, and she thought he might ask her to be present to discuss the details of her suggestions.

But the time went by and nothing happened. At first she was not restless. The weather was bad, and she thought Lem was waiting for a break in the cold. She spent the days quietly, either reading and studying by her own fireside or up at Becky's, helping her. The long winter months which forced the ridge folks inside gave Becky her best opportunity for plaiting and sewing her rag rugs, and for stitching the infinitesimal pieces of quilt tops together. Hour after long hour passed with Becky on one side of the fire and Miss Willie on the other.

"Yer right handy with a needle," she told Miss Willie one day. "Yore stitches is littler than mine. Seems like I cain't see so good no more."

"You ought to have your eyes examined," Miss Willie said, bending over to select another color from the basket. "You probably need glasses."

"Doubtless I do," Becky agreed. "I told Gault if he'd give me the next calf, they was two things I'd like to do with the money. Git me a pair o' glasses, an' git me a wrist watch. I've allus wanted one o' them little wrist watches."

Miss Willie was silent. She knew better than to suggest that maybe Gault would give her the next calf, or even that maybe he would get her the glasses and wrist watch. Gault would do exactly what he pleased about it, as befitted the head of the house. And

190

Becky would not want him to do differently. She knew that too now. Becky had been as proud as punch of the new gate in the barbed-wire fence! So Miss Willie kept quiet.

After a time she asked, "What is this pattern we're working on now?"

"This here's the Double Weddin' Ring," Becky said. "Wait till we git it all together, an' you'll see. The rings all lap over an' makes the purtiest pattern! Hit's one of my favorites. Some folks makes it all one color, but I like to mix 'em up. Hit's brighter thataway."

"I like it better mixed up too."

Becky rose and went into the kitchen, returning with the granite coffeepot, which she set in the ashes at the front of the fire. "Reckon a mite o' coffee'd go purty good, wouldn't it?"

"It would," Miss Willie said, without looking up. Then, "Becky," she asked, after the coffee had been poured, "why do you suppose Lem hasn't said anything about my report? It's been nearly a month since I sent it to him, and I haven't heard a word from him. Has he said anything to Gault about it?"

Becky eyed her quizzically, and then shook her head. "Not that I've heared of."

"Well, I think it's very queer he doesn't do something about it."

Becky poured her coffee into the saucer and blew on it meditatively. Then she sipped carefully. "Miss Willie, he ain't goin' to do nothin' about that report o' your'n. Hit'd surprise me if he's read it. Likely he jist looked at it an' laid it away, aimin' to git around to it one day. An' if he's read it, I doubt he'd do one thing about it. Things jist moves slow here. You'd ort to of learnt that by now. You'll jist have to take yer satisfaction from knowin' you've done what was right, an' hope you started a idee in somebody's head. Mebbe five, ten years from now somethin' will come of it."

Miss Willie laid her sewing down. She shoved her chair back and, getting up, started pacing back and forth in front of the fire. "Isn't there anything else I can do about it?"

"Well, you kin write you out enough reports to go clean around the trustees, an' that's about all. But if ever'one of 'em has it, leastways they'll know what you had to say. I reckon Hod an'

191

Wells would be fur e'er thing you said, but they ain't the whole shootin' match. Send Old Man Simpson one, an' Gault. Gault, he'll go along with you as fur as he kin, but he kin be powerful mule-headed when he wants to be. But don't look fer too much from it. Like I said, about the best you kin do is git a idee started, an' hope it ketches on."

Miss Willie pushed her glasses up furiously. "Oh, this ridge!" she muttered grimly. "I'd like to take the heads of these stubborn people and knock them together. Maybe I could knock some sense into them. I never saw people so set in their ways! They won't listen to anybody! If it's 'allus' been done one way, it's 'allus' got to be done that way! That spring's got to be cemented. There'll be an epidemic of dysentery or typhoid one of these days, just as sure as anything. It's just got to be fixed!" And in her agitation Miss Willie pounded one fist into the other. "It's just got to be fixed!"

She stopped and pinched her lower lip, thinking. "I know," she said so suddenly that Becky jumped. "I know what I'll do. I'll just have it fixed with my own money. That's one of their excuses. They never have the money. If it's fixed and doesn't cost them anything, they can't object."

Becky raised her eyebrows and stuck her tongue in her cheek. "I wouldn't do that if I was you, Miss Willie."

"And why not, for goodness' sake?"

"Hit's allus best to let folks do fer theirselves. You jist keep on atalkin'. Jist keep on apoundin' it in. But don't take the bit 'twixt yer teeth an' run off with it. Let 'em work around to it their own way when the time's ripe."

Miss Willie sat down and picked up her sewing again. She sighed heavily. "I suppose you're right. You usually are. But it needs doing so badly, and they may take four or five years! If they could just see what a menace it is!"

"Time passes, Miss Willie. Hit comes an' hit goes. You're all frashed about this now, but jist remember that there spring's been givin' drinkin' water fer the Big Springs School fer more years that you been livin'. I don't know as any great harm has come from it yit."

"That attitude is just what I mean! All of you say the same

thing! How do you know how many cases of typhoid fever could be traced to that spring? Didn't you tell me that Gault and Tom and Lem all had typhoid when they were little? And hasn't nearly every other family on the ridge had a case of typhoid at one time or another? How do you know where they got it? How do you know?" Miss Willie's glasses slipped down her nose again.

Becky laughed. "You needn't preach at me, Miss Willie! I'd like to see you git that spring boxed in, bad as you would. I'm jist tryin' to tell you not to kick over the milk bucket 'fore you git through milkin'."

Restlessly, Miss Willie got to her feet again and walked to the window. She pushed the curtains aside and peered out.

"Is it fairin' up?" Becky asked.

"I think so. The wind's dying down too, I believe."

"Hit'll be clear, come night."

"Becky," Miss Willie called suddenly, "Becky, here comes Wells!"

"Reckon where he's goin' this time o' day? Is he afoot?"

"No, he's riding Pet." She went to the door and flung it open. A biting wind blew through the room, scattering the fire and making Becky jump.

"Land sakes, Miss Willie, wait'll he gits here 'fore you open the door!"

"He's here. Hello, there," she called. "Come on in!"

Wells came in, stamping his feet noisily and slapping his gloves free of his hands. "Howdy," he called, and the room shook with his voice. "Howdy, there, Becky!"

"Git yerself inside," Becky answered dryly, "an' shet the door! Freeze a body plumb to death!"

"Nice warm welcome a feller gits when he comes to this house!" Wells laughed.

"Hit'd be a sight warmer if Miss Willie didn't blow the fire all over the hearth lettin' you in!"

"Quit grumbling, Becky," Miss Willie said. "Wells, how about a cup of coffee?"

"Jist the thing," Wells answered, letting his chunky frame down on the floor by the fireplace, propping his back against the warm stones and stretching his legs out in front of him. "Jist the thing."

Miss Willie handed him the coffee and sat near him on the small stool. "You haven't been over in quite a while. What brings you today?"

Wells set his cup down on the floor beside him and took his pipe out of his pocket. He took his time about filling it, tamping the tobacco down carefully and flinging the shreds in the palm of his hand into the fire. He peeled a splinter from a log on the pile near him and lighted it from the fire, carried it to the bowl of his pipe, and drew slowly until the pipe was going. He puffed a time or two. "Why, I thought you all might like to know Rose an' Tay got married yesterday," he said finally.

Miss Willie looked at him in amazement. He had said it so casually. "Married?" she repeated, as if not comprehending.

"Yep. I been lookin' fer it, like I told you last winter. An' I take it kindly Rose went on an' ended up the school term before she done it. Hit wouldn't of surprised me none if she hadn't of, but I reckon she figgered she'd ort to do that much like I wanted, at least."

"Reckon they went in to the county seat," Becky put in.

Wells nodded. "They come in about suppertime last night. Said they'd jist got spliced. Hit's all legal. I seen the papers."

"Well, Rose could of done worse," Becky said, never missing a stitch. "Leastways she's married now, an' you'll not have no more wearyin' to do over her."

"I'm relieved hit's done," Wells agreed. The two, understanding each other perfectly, spoke comfortably together. "Long as they was jist atalkin' I never knowed. I couldn't rightly give her over to Tay Clark, an' I was allus afeared he was jist foolin' her. Hit would of gone hard if he'd a done wrong by her."

Becky nodded. "Hit's best. Likely he'll settle down now an' make her a good man."

"That's what I'm hopin'. If he'll give over stillin', I kin use him on the place. They's plenty o' work fer two growed men. Rufe is too spare yit to do a man's work. Tay kin be a big he'p if he will."

"Are they going to live with you?" Miss Willie asked.

"Fer the time bein'," Wells answered. "He's got a little money saved up, an' they allowed they'd like to build 'em a place o' their

194

own soon. But they's no hurry about it. They's room an' aplenty fer 'em there."

He drank the last of his coffee, knocked out his pipe on the hearthstone, and pulled himself up. "I got to be gittin' on. Jist thought I'd stop by an' pass the news along. You all come an' see 'em now."

"We'll come," Becky promised. "Tell Rose we'll git around."

Wells started to the door and then he stopped suddenly. "By golly, I was about to fergit! Miss Willie, how'd you like to go possum-huntin' tonight? Me an' Hod's goin', an' Mary said if you'd go, she would. They kin git Hattie to come take the night an' stay with the boy. Hit looks like it'll be a good night. Wind's clearin' up the clouds, an' hit'll be cold an' moony."

"You tell Mary I'd love to go!" Miss Willie said. "I'll just jump at the chance to go! I've been indoors too long lately. A little more and I'd be house-crazy!"

"You'll freeze yer front teeth out, goin' out sich a night," Becky grumbled. "An' at yore age!"

"What's wrong with her age?" Wells wanted to know. "She kin outwalk an' outlast e'er person on this ridge, I'll bound ye. An' we won't let her freeze. Gits too cold we kin allus build up a fire."

"Sure!" and Miss Willie's chin went up. At her age! Becky talked like she had one foot in the grave! She'd possum hunt right along with the best of them. Becky would just see!

When the door closed behind Wells, Miss Willie stood at the window watching him mount the little mare and ride off down the ridge. "He didn't seem at all upset about Rose, did he?" she said finally.

"Nothin' to be upset about," Becky said. "Hit's like he said. Hit's a relief to him that it's over an' done with. You never acted very surprised yerself!"

"Oh, he told me about it some time ago. Remember that night I asked Gault to tell him to come over? You remember I wanted him to let them go together openly. He explained it to me that night. And he said then that he expected them to marry sooner or later. So I wasn't surprised. But I *was* a little surprised at him. He acted almost like he was pleased about it."

"Why, shore. He don't like Tay so good. But cain't nobody he'p

195

bein' pleased when young'uns gits married. Hit's sich a happy time fer 'em. Hit would be a pore makeshift of a human that'd begrudge 'em their rightful happiness. They ain't no lovelier sight in the world than two young'uns like that that's jist got spliced. Hit's jist like they owned the moon an' the stars an' the sun fer a time. Course, later on when the babies starts comin' an' the goin' gits hard, hit ain't so easy, an' they got to settle down. But a new wedded pair is the apple o' the Lord's eye."

"I must try to think of something to give Rose," Miss Willie said.

"I'm aimin' to give her this here Double Weddin' Ring quilt. I had it in mind all the time," and Becky looked sweetly and intimately across the room at Miss Willie. "Hit'll be right nice, won't it?"

It was good dark when Wells came by for Miss Willie and they set off down the road toward the hollow. It was a cold night, tingly with frost. The stars glittered with a frozen pallor, scarcely blinking in their remoteness. Underfoot, the ground was as hard as iron, and their footsteps rang bell-like against it. Miss Willie saw her breath puffing warmly from her mouth, a thin veil of vapor before her. She felt snug in her heavy wraps, small and isolated from the cold and the night, and Wells's bulk was very heavy and solid beside her.

They talked very little, both feeling the night and the starry skies and the insulation of the dark. Miss Willie tried to remember when she had known this snug, wrapped-in-the-dark feeling before. Long ago, she knew it was. Back, back down the years. When she was a child. Yes. Yes, now she remembered. She had gone with her father, alone, to evening service. He had carried a lantern against the night, and, bundled warmly, she had followed in his huge footsteps, feeling safe and secluded and secure against the dark and the cold. She remembered the exalted feeling of being alone with him, just the two of them at the center of warmth and light. Darkness held at bay out on the fringe of the lantern glow.

Instead of a lantern, Wells carried a flashlight, but the feeling

196

was just the same. Only the two of them, at the heart and core of space, the night held off, and the two of them safe and warm. She dropped behind and tried to stretch her short legs to Wells's long strides, placing her feet carefully in his big footsteps. This was the way it was that night with her father. A little girl, safely following a big man, who held all darkness away from her; who stood between her and the night, and all things unknown and fearful.

Miss Willie stopped abruptly. All things unknown and fearful! A big man who stood between! Broad shoulders, sturdy body, strong arms and legs. Between her and the night. Between her and . . . insecurity? Loneliness? Lovelessness? For heaven's sake, she cried at herself. *Must* you go psychological about everything? Must you go back to beginnings and analyze every feeling? This is a possum hunt. This is Wells Pierce. And this is Piney Ridge. Come down to earth, Willie Payne!

"What you doin', Miss Willie?" Wells called back, and she realized that he was a hundred yards ahead of her. She giggled. If she didn't watch out, the big man wasn't going to be standing between her and the night very long!

"I'm coming," she called. "I got to thinking."

"Well, upon my word an' honor! You better wait an' do yer thinkin' in front o' yer fire some night. You got to keep movin' out in the cold like this!"

"I'm coming," she repeated, and caught up with him.

The walk to Hod's place didn't take long, and soon he and Mary were with them. "Where'd you reckon to go, Wells?" Hod asked.

"Head o' the holler, I thought," Wells answered. "Hit used to be a good place."

"Good as any," Hod said, and turned his dogs loose.

With an excited barking, the dogs struck up the hollow, and the four of them followed. The night, the cold, the dark, and the hunt were exhilarating to both Mary and Miss Willie, and their mood struck sparks from each other so that they were giggling and laughing like a pair of schoolgirls. They stumbled along and lagged and bumped into things in the darkness. Until finally Hod turned and said sternly: "Now you girls got to keep up. We don't

197

want to miss a possum because you all are lost somewhere behind. And we can't wait for you, once the dogs strike a trail. It's every man for himself then, and you'll have to keep up, and you'll have to be quiet."

Rebuked, they were subdued and they bent themselves to keeping up. Up and up the hollow they went and the ground got rougher and rougher. As the hollow pinched in, the trail was lost, and they broke through underbrush, vines, dried canes, and rank, matted growth at every step. The men set a fast pace, crossing the creek and climbing the straight, steep sides of the far ridge when the dogs ran out of the hollow. No one offered to help either Mary or Miss Willie. And they had to work desperately to stay up.

The hillside was so steep that they climbed, literally, a ladder of rocks and ledges. Miss Willie scrambled and fell and grabbed at whatever handhold she could find, her chest heaving and her heavy coat smothering her and weighing her down. She wished now she had worn only a windbreaker, like Wells. Branches and brambles clawed at her face, and her short legs ached as she pulled them up the steep climb. She stumbled over stones and logs, and she slipped and slid on the slippery leaves underfoot. She was determined to keep up, though. When she looked at Mary, she saw that she was having just as hard a time, puffing and panting just as much, slipping and sliding just as often. She hoped the men would wait up when they got to the top of the ridge!

The hill was interminable, and she lay flat getting her breath when Wells finally gave her a hand over the last ledge. Well, she was up. At whatever cost! And then the dogs tore down that awful hill again and off across the creek to the far side. Suddenly they gave tongue and the night was full of their sharp, excited yelps. Yip-yip-yip, came from the bottom of the hollow, and yip-yip-yip it went on up the other hillside!

"Trail!" yelled Hod, and plunged over the rim of the ridge.

"Trail!" yelled Wells, and followed on Hod's heels.

"Trail!" sung out Mary, and she disappeared in the night.

Miss Willie crawled over to a tree and pulled herself up. She knew she couldn't get down that hill again, across the creek, and

198

up another hill. It was physically impossible to do it. The human body, hers at least, was built to stand just so much, and it had stood it! It would never take her through what lay ahead!

But they had gone off and left her! She couldn't stay here in the dark and the cold alone! She had to follow! Well, she thought, recklessly, you can die only once, and she might as well do it trying. So, "Trail!" she echoed feebly, and then she simply sat down on her backside and let nature take its course!

She passed Mary and Wells and Hod somewhere along the way as she went slipping and slithering down, and she remembered the horrified look on Mary's face in the faint glow of Wells's flashlight as she flew by.

"Hit's Miss Willie!" Wells shouted.

"She'll be killed!" Mary screamed.

She tried to call out that she was all right, but just then she brought up against a tree with such a solid thump that all the breath was knocked out of her. She lay motionless, wondering if all her bones were broken, while she struggled for breath. When she could move, she felt of herself gingerly. She seemed to be all in one piece. By golly, she was down that dratted hill, and she was still alive!

And then the others were crowding around her, talking all at once, and Mary was crying.

"Oh, for goodness' sake," Miss Willie said sharply. "I'm all right. I just wasn't going to try to walk down that hill!"

Wells took in a big lungful of air and let it out explosively. He looked at Hod, and suddenly the two men started laughing. They laughed and they laughed, bent over double, tears streaming from their eyes, slapping each other on the back, until they were weak and gasping, and leaning against each other.

"I don't see anything funny about it," Miss Willie said testily, and she indignantly replaced the glasses which she had been holding clutched tightly in one hand. Mary had sunk weakly to the ground and laid her head against her knees. Her shoulders were shaking too.

Miss Willie eased herself up, limped a step or two, brushed off the leaves and twigs, and: "Come on. Let's go possum-hunting," she said.

"You'll do, Miss Willie," Wells said, his voice still shaky with laughter. "You'll shore do!"

"Listen!" Hod's voice was sharp.

The short yips of the dogs had changed now to a deep, long bay — a mellow, bell tone — which echoed through the hollow and came back off the hills. "They've treed!"

And once again the chase was on. Across the creek and up the hill. And then there was the possum, high in a tree, sullen in the beams of light from the flashlight.

"We'll have to shake him out," said Wells, and he started skinning up the tree. Now that she could stand still and get her breath, Miss Willie was crawling with excitement. She watched Wells inch up on the possum and shake the limb until its hold was loose and it fell sprawling to the ground. At once the dogs were upon it.

"Hold it, Duke," Hod called, and the dog stiffened with the neck of the possum between his teeth. "It's a nice, big, fat one," Hod yelled, and expertly he slipped it into the big burlap sack he had brought along. "Good dog," he said, patting the dog's head. "Good dog."

But already the dogs were restless, and when Wells was on the ground again, Hod turned them loose. "One up an' two to go," Wells said. "We allus git three."

In her ignorance Miss Willie had thought this was all. They'd caught a possum, hadn't they? Two to go! She stiffened her spine. O Becky, Becky, how right you were! At my age I should be home by the fire knitting!

But she set her teeth and she stayed with it, and along toward midnight sometime she saw the third possum sacked. The dogs were weary, Hod and Wells were weary, and Miss Willie and Mary were practically crawling when they turned homeward. And there was all that long way to walk yet!

Hod and Mary were in front, and Hod had his arm around Mary, helping her. A cold, lonely moon had risen over the gaunt trees and hung frozen in the sky. Miss Willie stumbled. Wells held her and gently drew her hand through his arm. Arm in arm they walked, then, and the heat from his warm, stocky body crept up Miss Willie's arm and through her veins, coursing vitally through the living streams of her body. It warmed her clear to her toes.

"How'd you like the possum hunt?" Wells asked finally.

Miss Willie leaned her forehead tiredly against his shoulder. "I liked it. But, Wells, I got awfully tired!"

Wells chuckled low in his throat. "So did I, Miss Willie. Just between you an' me, so did I. We better leave this possum-huntin' to the young'uns, I reckon. Yore little rockin' chair an' the fireside's a heap more in keepin' with us!"

Miss Willie lifted her face and saw a star blink twice. She laughed softly. And then a scud of clouds thinned over the moon and left a shredding trail of mist behind.

CHAPTER
❦ 20 ❦

It came on to snow the last of February. There was no sun that morning. Only a pale thinning of the gray overcast in the east. The sky came down flat to the edges of the ridge, thick and smoky and opaque. Trees and houses were anonymous in the murkiness, losing their sharpness and their solid lines. The level stretches of pastures and fields reflected the smokiness of the day and took on the dull look of a gray, calm sea, changeless, monotonous, endless. The cattle herded together in the low places, still and wise, hunched against an unborn wind. Head to rump they stood, as if building a barrier. There was a waiting feeling in the air.

Just before noon the first flakes fell. Big, wet, woolly patches of white which covered the ground within thirty minutes. Then a wind blew out of the north, moaning low around the eaves, whistling shrilly down the chimneys, squeezing and shaking old timbers, and whining like a fine wire around the corners. Before it, the harassed snow whirled giddily, driven in a crazy, mad swirl to seek a resting place.

Half a day the wind blew, and then as if some giant had been amusing himself puffing his stormy breath at the ridge and had tired of his fun and gone away, a great calm fell, so quietly and silently that the absence of motion and sound was like a great noise itself. But the snow continued to fall.

Early in the storm, when the first wind came screeching across the rim of the ridge, Gault had gone down to Miss Willie's cabin. "Hit's comin' on to storm," he told her, "an' from the looks of it, hit's goin' to be a good 'un. You better bring some things an' come on up to the house."

Miss Willie peered out the window. "I've got plenty of wood, Gault," she said. "I'll be all right here."

Gault shook his head. "Hit might be you couldn't git to the house to eat, Miss Willie. You better do like I say."

So Miss Willie packed a bag with a change of clothes, several books, her knitting, and went back to the house with him.

The slow hours passed. Outside the storm wind blew and the snow pelted against the windows. The room, with its blazing fire on the hearth, was shut in, imprisoned by the gray blanket outside. Becky hunched over her quilt pieces and Miss Willie knitted and read. Gault slept most of the day away, rising when the room darkened to see about the animals at the barn. He wrapped himself in a heavy coat, tied a scarf over his ears, and pulled his old cap down securely over it.

"Gault, how can you find the barn in this drift?" Miss Willie asked.

"I'll foller the fence to the barn lot," he answered, pulling on his gloves, "an' it's jist a piece from there. I'll make it all right. Leastways, I got to try. The animals has got to be fed."

When he opened the back door, the snow swirled high through the room, the door swinging crazily on its hinges until he could catch it. It took all his strength to pull it closed behind him.

"Gentlemen! This here's a real blizzard," Becky shouted to Miss Willie from the kitchen. She was sweeping up the loose blown snow and she stopped to peer anxiously out the window. Miss Willie joined her.

"You think he'll make it?" she wanted to know.

"Oh, shore," Becky said, putting the broom back in the corner. "He'll foller the fence like he said."

Becky built up the fire in the cook stove and set about making bread for supper. Miss Willie set the table and put out the butter, preserves, and milk.

"How long do you think it'll keep this up?" she asked.

"Hit'll die down durin' the night, likely," Becky answered, her hands working the biscuit dough.

"It looked pretty deep out there already."

Becky nodded. "Oh, hit's liable to be a good two foot 'fore it gits through."

Gault came in just as the biscuits were browned. He shook his head as he stamped the snow from his boots and shed his big coat. "Hit's shore a storm," he said, unwrapping the scarf from his head. "That there wind like to blew me clean offen the ridge! All I could do to hold onto the fence. But ever'thing's fine at the barn. Cows is in, an' the horse. I got 'em down a right smart bit o' hay. They'll do all right now."

Miss Willie felt an elemental satisfaction in all this. The storm keening against the small house. The four walls snugged in around the fire. A man keeping his responsibility for his animals. A woman making a hot meal in the lamplight. This was meeting nature head on, asking no quarter, bedding down to endure. This was man close to nature, with nothing to hold it at bay. No steam-heated rooms, no storm-sashed windows, no deep-comforted warmth. No tempering of the wind. Just man and woman, with the storm howling at their heels, tiny and alone, but neither helpless nor afraid. This country made tough, fibrous men and women, she thought. And she felt a heady sense of being spectator to a living drama.

Then the wind died down, and the snow came straight down, heavy, thick, and full of substance. All night it fell, and the next day. Late in the evening of the second day a timid sun blinked down at the shimmering earth, and then ducked behind its gray curtain again. It snowed for another hour or so, but that night a full moon cleared the sky and rode a high promise for fair weather toward the dawn.

On the morning of the third day the world glistened under a heavy fall of snow. It lay unbroken, save for Gault's trail to the barn, widening and softening the ridge top, stretching out beautifully pure from one horizon to the other. The crystalline surface glittered in the sunlight, sparkling like a jeweled blanket. The trees bore heavy crowns of white, and the fence rows marched like ghosts across the fields.

Miss Willie looked down the road. No track had yet marred its smooth whiteness, which glinted like cake icing in the sun. Down the ridge a wisp of smoke curled up over the trees. Old Man Clark's folks were making breakfast then. Up the ridge another wisp of smoke curled. Hattie and Tom were up too. Miss Willie wondered if Hod and Mary were all right, and then she looked far down the road, knowing she could not see, but looking for smoke from Wells's house.

"I can see smoke from the Clarks', Becky," she called out to the kitchen, "and from Hattie's place too. I guess everyone's all right. But I wish I knew how Hod and Mary made out."

"Don't weary yerself, Miss Willie," Becky called back. "Hod's a old hand here on the ridge. He kin read the weather as good as Gault. He made ready fer this. We'll shore be housebound fer two, three days, though."

After breakfast Miss Willie bundled up and took a shovel to help Gault clear a path to her cabin. She felt invigorated and childishly happy to be outside again after the long time indoors. She took deep breaths of the cold, clean air and swung her shovel energetically, throwing snow in tall mounds on either side of the path. In a short time she was puffing and blowing like a porpoise. Her shovel moved slower and slower until Gault laughed and said, "Better rest yerself a mite, Miss Willie."

She leaned on the shovel and pushed her glasses up on her nose. "I guess I'm out of condition," she admitted.

"This here's hard work," Gault said, going on with his shoveling. The path was two feet wide, and Gault's side was clean and sharp. His shovel bit into the solid white wall precisely and took out a huge square with each lift. Miss Willie eyed her side. It was chewed and hacked, with here a deep cave in the wall and there a fat bulge. She giggled. "As a snow shoveler I'd never qualify as an expert."

"Yer doin' fine," Gault assured her. "Hit don't matter none how you git it out. Gittin' it out's the main thing."

The sound of bells — gay, jingling bells — came from down the road. Gault slanted his head to listen and Miss Willie turned toward the road. And then they saw a team plodding heavily

204

through the thick piled snow on the road.

"Who in the world . . ." Miss Willie wondered.

"Well, I'll be dad-blamed!" Gault laughed. "Ifen that there Wells ain't put runners on his old buggy! Well, I swear! Hit takes Wells ever' time to think o' things!"

Down the road came the team, bells jingling from their harness with each step, and cutting through the drift behind them was Wells in the old buggy. It was slow going, heavy going, but they made progress. He waved to them and pulled up in front of the house.

"Howdy," he called, "Miss Willie, c'mon an' take a ride with me!"

"Where you goin' in that there rig?" Gault yelled.

"Nowhere special. I figgered Miss Willie'd like to see if Mary an' the baby was all right."

"When didja make them there runners?"

"Oh, I smoothed 'em out durin' the storm. Couldn't do nothin' else. You wanta go, Miss Willie?"

"Why, shore," Miss Willie laughed. "Gault, you tell Becky where I am."

Wells gave her a hand and she crawled into the buggy. He tucked the blanket around her and she felt a rich warmness at her feet.

"Did you bring a stove along too?" she asked.

Wells grinned. "I jist het up a big rock. Figgered it'd keep you warm till we got there. Hit's purty cold."

He pulled the team into the road again, and they set off down the ridge. Miss Willie settled herself under the blanket comfortably. "Wells, this is fun! How did you happen to think of it?"

"Nothin' much else to think of, an' like I said, I knowed you'd be frettin' to git down to Mary's soon as the storm was over. An' then, I allus did like to git out after a snow with a sled. Don't git many deep snows like this'n, an' I thought it'd be right nice. Hit'll be a heap better when it's melted some an' hardened over. Runners'll go smoother then."

"This is nice the way it is. And the bells sound so merry and gay!"

"I figgered you'd like them too." Wells stuck his tongue in his

205

cheek. "I'm atryin' ever' way I kin to please you."

Miss Willie felt her neck heating and the flush rising to her face. But she looked at him bravely. "Have you been taking lessons in pleasing ladies from Tay lately?"

Wells's great laugh shook the buggy. "I'll have you know, Miss Willie, I don't need e'er nother man to give me no lessons in how to please a lady!"

"I wouldn't think so, either," Miss Willie agreed softly. "You do right well on your own."

"Thank you, ma'am," and he bent over in a mock bow.

"How silly we are!" Miss Willie giggled. "Tell me. How are Rose and Tay?"

"Snug as two bugs in a rug! Jist as happy as if they had good sense! Rose, she has a fit ever' time she opens a present, an' the folks is shore doin' right by 'em too. Never seen so many nice things. Becky, she sent over a quilt, an' Hod an' Mary, they sent 'em a set o' chairs Hod made. An' Hattie give 'em a box o' canned stuff. They're gittin' set up right off."

"That reminds me. I want to give them something, but I don't quite know what. I wondered if Rose would like one of the pictures I have packed away. I have several very good ones. Do you think she would like something like that?"

Wells nodded. "I know in reason she would. She'd think a heap of it, comin' from you."

"Well, as we go home, I'll get it and you can take it to her."

The runners hissed through the snow and the old buggy ran smoothly. It was hard to believe that this was the road so eaten and rutted that usually you had to hold on to keep from being bounced out.

"Wells," Miss Willie said after a while, "do you think Tay will quit making moonshine now that he and Rose are married?"

"Hit's hard to tell, Miss Willie. I'm hopin' he will. I'm a givin' him ever' chancet to work on the place, an' I'll split even with him on the crops if he'll work right. I'm afeared stillin's in his blood, though. Hit's a easy way to make big money, an', besides, Tay's allus been a wild one, adrinkin' an' aplayin' cards, an' arunnin' with a crowd over at the Gap. Come clost to trouble a time or two. But seems like he's powerful in love. Only thing is, when the

206

new wears off he's liable to go back to his old ways. Cain't tell yit, though, an' it ain't fair to say."

Miss Willie sighed and leaned back against the seat. "I do hope he settles down now and makes Rose a good husband. Rose is a good girl. I do so want her to be happy."

"You an' me both, Miss Willie. Rose *is* a good girl — a heap like her ma — an' I'd not like to see her wearyin' over him."

Miss Willie was quiet a moment. Then: "Wells, tell me about Matildy. I noticed her picture one day when I was over there."

Wells pulled a rein through his hand and straightened it before answering. "Ifen you takened note of her picture, Miss Willie, you seen how she was. Ifen you could of knowed her in the flesh, you would of said the same."

"How did she look, Wells? Was she tall or short? Fair or dark? Plump or slender? If it's none of my business, tell me. But I've wanted to know."

"I don't mind tellin' you. She was short. Little bit of a thing, allus plump as a partridge, an' mostly you'd say fat, I reckon, along towards the last. She had brown hair, curled up sweet-like at the ends . . . big, brown eyes, sort of crinkly-like at the corners. Allus alaughin'. Nothin' never frashed Matildy fer long. She'd git fretted over the young'uns, times, but soon's they was straightened out, she was alaughin' an' ajokin' agin. Some thought she done too much of it. But I allus liked her fer it. I'm turned the same way, an' hit makes fer easy livin'. We was first cousins, I reckon you know. Some thought we ortent to of got married, but I never held with that. An' Matildy, she never did, either. We growed up here on the ridge together, an' never had no thought from the time we was little but what we'd git married someday. Hit worked out fine too."

Miss Willie's hands were gripped tight under the blanket. "I wish I could have known her, Wells. I know she must have been a wonderful person. And I know you must miss her an awful lot."

Wells's eyes were on the road ahead of the horses. "Hit was hard at first. Hit was like havin' part o' yerself gone. Seemed to me like I never would git used to her not bein' there. An' it was bad fer the kids. Rose, she stepped in an' done the best she could, but Matildy had allus done ever'thing an' Rose hadn't

207

never carried the full load. But she done good. Rufe, he takened it awful hard. He thought a heap of his ma. The night she went, he takened his gun an' the dog an' went off in the woods, an' never come home till after the funeral. An' he's never named her agin to this day."

Tears pricked Miss Willie's eyes. "That's mostly what's wrong with him, then."

"I allowed so too. But he's got no call to keep on bein' so wearisome. Boy or man, he's got to learn to take trouble as it comes. You cain't side-step trouble. Hit comes to all. I made allowances fer him fer a while, but I been wearied about him. He'd ort to of pulled hisself outen it by now. But don't seem like nobody kin git next to him. Ifen he keeps up thisaway, he'll end up in some real trouble time he's growed!"

"I wish he'd be friends with me. I don't know why he doesn't like me, but it seems as if he hates me sometimes."

Wells laughed. "He's jealous, fer one thing."

"Jealous!"

"Well, I don't reckon he's figgered it out. But he feels it jist the same."

"How could he be jealous of me?"

"He ain't. He's jealous of me. He knows I think a heap of you."

"O Wells!"

Wells called to the horses, and when they had stopped, he squared around on the seat. "Listen, Miss Willie. I've told you how it was with Matildy an' me. I wouldn't try to tell you it'll ever be jist like that agin fer me, with nobody else. They's jist one time when yer young an' lighthearted an' yer girl is young an' sweet alongside of you. But they's another time when yer settled an' knowledgeable, an' the fire, mebbe it don't blaze so high, but it burns mighty steady-like. Hit ain't that bright, new blaze, but it's a warm burnin' jist the same. An' they's ways mebbe it's a heap more satisfyin'. I wouldn't never ast no woman to take Matildy's place. I wouldn't want no woman to. But, Miss Willie, I'd like to ast you to take yer own place alongside of me. Yer own rightful, proud place."

"Wells, what are you saying?"

"I'm a-astin' you to marry me, Miss Willie."

208

A thin, high note bugled through the air and sang sweetly in Miss Willie's ears. It pierced her with its exulting song and lifted her heart, filling and stretching it until she thought she must burst. Her throat was tight with the feeling of it and the fullness of it. And the singing made her dizzy and she closed her eyes, swaying gently to still music.

Wells's arms went hard around her, and before her eyes flew open, his lips had laid themselves against her own, warm against the coldness of her mouth, warm and soft, but firmly insistent. Not for twenty-five years had a man's mouth been pressed against her own! And never before in love. Only the light kisses of youth had come her way. Lightly given and lightly received. Never before this hungry warmth, this seeking firmness, this taking from her the source of her strength! She felt as if this man pulled from her the last drop of her coursing blood, and left her drained and sapped.

When she could no longer stand it, she pulled her head back from him and pushed her hands against his chest. Even her hands trembled at the touch of that solid chest. "Don't, Wells," she murmured, hiding her face against his shoulder.

Wells gathered her hands in his own and bent over her again, "Miss Willie," he said softly, "Miss Willie, don't say no."

She let him have her mouth again, savoring the wine of his maleness, the faint odor of shaving soap on his face, blended with the smell of tobacco on his breath. She let herself drink up the feeling of his strong, hard mouth, the feeling of his thick shoulders under her hands, the feeling of his heart beating against her own. She gave herself over completely for one long moment to the transcendent joy of being joined with him. She let her hands slide around to cup his face, feeling it clean-shaven, but with the roughness of his beard just underneath. The eternal symbol of the full-grown man! She wondered fleetingly at it, and at the thrill that went through her fingers. And then she pushed him away again. "Not any more, Wells," she protested. "No more. I'll have to think. You'll have to let me think."

Wells laughed triumphantly and he gathered up the reins. "All right, Miss Willie. Think all you like. But don't fergit what you jist felt! That was a growed man tellin' you he loved you!"

Miss Willie pressed her hands against her hot face. Where had the cold gone! A moment before she had felt the quivers of chill down her spine, and her face had been frozen. Her mouth had been numb. Now there were needles of fire pricking her lips, and her cheeks were burning!

"How long you want to think, Miss Willie?"

"Oh, I don't know, Wells. I don't know." And she repeated that trite expression, "This is so sudden!"

Wells pulled his pipe out of his pocket. He handed the reins to Miss Willie. "Here, you drive while I git my pipe to goin'."

When he had it lighted, he took the reins again. "You mean to say you never expected nothin' like this?"

"I don't know. I really don't know what I thought or felt or anything, Wells. Should I have? I thought you were awfully nice to me, and I have liked you so much. Oh, I haven't let myself think about it! I'm forty-five years old, Wells! I'm past the time when a woman thinks of love and marriage!"

"I'm forty-five years old too, Miss Willie. An' I shore ain't past the time when I think of love an' marriage! An' I'd say it was high time you was givin' it some thought. What you got to think about, anyhow? Didn't you feel like you loved me a minnit ago?"

Miss Willie wouldn't meet his look, but when he persisted, "Didn't you?" she answered bravely. "Yes, I felt it. But there's more to it than that!"

"What more?"

"Oh, a lot!" How could she tell him? The ridge, and everything. How did she know she wanted to live here the rest of her life? And Wells himself — overalled most of his days, happy to follow a plow, butchering every rule of grammar, crude, uncouth in many ways. Kind? Yes. Good. Heartwarmingly good. But there was so much difference in them. How could she tell him that? She couldn't. She could only repeat, "There's a lot more to it than feeling."

Wells pulled on his pipe and sent a cloud of smoke over their heads. "Well, I reckon yer right at that. I've give it some thought, though. I ain't to say well off, but they's aplenty, the way we live here on the ridge. You've seen the house. Hit ain't nothin' extry, but it could be made right nice. An' they's allus a good livin' off

210

the place. I'd ort to tell you they's close to two thousand dollars in the bank at the county seat. A woman *had* ort to think o' them things."

"But I wasn't thinking of them, Wells," Miss Willie said. He didn't know, then, of her own income. But it didn't matter. "I wouldn't worry about material things. Oh, it's all mixed up. Just let me think about it for a while."

Wells shifted his pipe to the other side of his mouth and slapped the reins on the fat backs of the team. Miss Willie was trembling, and the cold seeped through her, sending a ripple of chills down her back. She shivered. Wells reached over to pull the blanket closer around her. "Yer gittin' cold, ain't you?" he asked.

She nodded, biting her lips. Suddenly she wanted to cry. She wanted nothing so much as to burrow her head against Wells's shoulder and weep and weep. She wanted to cry away all the problems and have him hold her close and tell her everything was all right. She wanted him to make her feel safe again, like a child. You can't cry things away, she told herself sternly. You have to face them.

"What about Rufe?" she asked, after a while, and in spite of herself her voice quavered.

"Well, what about him?"

"He wouldn't like for us to be married."

"He'd jist have to git used to it. He'd be all right in time."

Miss Willie shook her head. "And what about Rose and Tay?"

"Oh, me an' Tay'd build them a little place. They's room aplenty. They want their own place, anyways."

They rode silently for a time. Then Wells slanted his eyes at her and grinned. "Ain't you goin' to ast me what about Abby? An' Veeny?"

Miss Willie smiled at him. "I wouldn't worry about Abby. And your sister has Veeny. Abby and I would get along fine."

"You an' the others'd git along fine too. Rose, she'd like it straight off, I'll bound. An' Rufe wouldn't be no worse off than he is now. In my opinion, he'd be a heap better off, oncet he got used to the idee. If you got to make up yer mind on account o' my kids, don't go decidin' what they like 'fore you know. Fur as I kin see, the main thing is if yer goin' to let them make *you* unhappy."

They were coming up in front of Hod's place, and Miss Willie fidgeted with her scarf and her gloves. She pushed her glasses up and patted her hair, loosening the scarf tied over it and retying it. Wells chuckled. "You reckon Hod an' Mary kin see that there kiss smack in the middle of yer mouth?"

"They can see a whole lot more than you think they can, Wells Pierce!" Miss Willie bristled. "And don't you say one word about this until we decide something. You hear!"

"I hear. Cross my heart, I'll not say e'er word. When you reckon we'll decide?"

"Oh, let me alone, Wells! You know what I mean. And don't you go taking anything for granted, either!"

Wells grinned. "I'll not. Say, that there's John Walton's team hitched in the back there. What you reckon he's doin' over here? Must be somethin's happened to Irma or one o' the kids to git him out in this here snow!"

He pulled the team up by the gate and got down and tied them. Wading back to the buggy, he said: "You better let me carry you to the porch. Hit's deeper along here where it's drifted."

"I've got on galoshes," Miss Willie protested. "I can walk. Just help me down."

Wells lifted her to the ground, where she sank in the soft snow to her knees. "I thought you had on galoshes," he heckled.

"I have!"

"Powerful lot o' good they're doin' you, buried down there! Here," and he bent in front of her. "I ain't carried nobody piggyback sincet the kids was little. Yore size is jist about right."

Before she knew what he was doing, his arms swept under her knees and she was lifted to his broad back. "Here we go," he shouted. "Hey, Hod! Open the door!"

Stumbling, half falling, through the deep, soft snow, he plunged toward the porch. Mary opened the door, surveyed them with a startled glance, and then started laughing. "Hod, come here," she called back into the house. "Look who's coming!"

Hod appeared in the door. "Hey, Wells," he yelled, "what you got there? A bag of beans?"

"Nope. Jist Miss Willie!"

Miss Willie was giggling. She waved at Hod and Mary and called out: "Miss Willie Payne, on her personal and private puddle jumper! Gangway, you two! I can't stop him!"

Laughing, they tumbled through the door, and Wells eased Miss Willie onto the couch. He was puffing and snorting. "By golly," he said, "you weigh a heap more'n I thought you did. You ain't as much of a lightweight as I'd guess!"

"Nobody asked you to carry me," Miss Willie huffed.

"Well, it was a sight better'n wadin'. Howdy, John."

John Walton was standing in front of the fireplace. He had laughed with them when they tumbled through the door, but almost immediately a strained look had come over his face. "Howdy, Wells," he answered.

"What brung you out in all this snow?"

"I come over to git Hod," John said, his troubled eyes seeking Hod and Mary on the other side of the room. "Johnnie's sick. He's bad sick, an' I cain't git Irma to let me git the doctor. I thought mebbe Hod could talk her into it."

"Fer the land's sake! Why don't she want you to git the doctor?" Wells's voice was brittle with astonishment.

Hod was lighting a cigarette, and he threw the match into the fireplace viciously. "It's that fool religion she's taken up with! Don't you remember she was baptized last summer?"

"Hush, Hod," Mary's voice was soft, and she put out a hand to still him.

"Well, what am I supposed to do — stand by and say nothing while the kid dies? From what John tells he's got pneumonia, or nearabouts, anyhow."

"Oh, no!" Miss Willie said, her hand coming up to cover her mouth. She leaned hard against the back of the couch.

Wells rubbed his jaw. "I'd plumb fergot that," he said. "Wasn't you baptized too?"

John nodded. "Irma wanted it. An' I didn't keer one way or another. But I ain't got the faith like her. I cain't jist set there an' look at the pore little feller an' pray like she kin. I want to git a doctor, quick. But she won't hear to it. Says a doctor won't do him no good. Says the Lord'll cure him, ifen it's his will."

Hod was on his feet again. "Well, I'm goin' to help the Lord's

213

will out a little! Come on, John. We'll go get the doctor. You're the kid's pa, and you've got as much right as Irma to have a say about this."

"Don't you think you'd better talk to Irma first, Hod?" Mary asked.

"No. It wouldn't do any good to talk to her. We'll get the doctor. Wells, you take Mary and Miss Willie over to Irma's, and Mary, you tell Irma we've gone to the Gap and we're bringing the doctor back with us. Tell her any way you like, but tell her that the doctor is coming, and he'll look at little Johnnie when we get there with him!"

"John, is this what you want Hod to do?" Mary asked, going over and laying her hand on John's arm.

John studied the toe of his boot, and then he raised his head and looked at Mary. "I reckon it is, Mary. I hate to go agin Irma, but I cain't stand it no longer. Ifen he died, it'd be on my conscience the rest of my days."

"Well, let's get goin'," Hod said, bundling into his heavy coat. John reached for his coat, and the two men went out the door.

Mary turned to Miss Willie and Wells. "I can't take the baby out in this cold," she said. "I didn't think of that."

Quickly Miss Willie spoke. "I'll stay with the baby. You go with Wells."

Within a few minutes Mary was ready, and Miss Willie stood at the window and watched her and Wells drive off down the road. All the gladness had gone from the day. There was this cold fact staring them in the face. Johnnie was ill, desperately ill, and there was a chasm between his father and mother. This day, whatever its outcome, would leave scars on both of them. Scars that might never be healed. Irma's faith stood on one side of the chasm, and John's fears stood on the other side. Between them was a deep and dark divide.

And then Miss Willie thought of Johnnie, remembering him that first day of school showing her the bird he had drawn and telling her in his slow, exact voice that he thought it was a blue jay. Remembering him the day Rufe had given him the skunk to use for the tiger in the play, remembering how his round little face had screwed up as he carried the smelling animal into the

214

schoolroom. Remembering what a stanch little Joseph he had
made in the Christmas pageant. And remembering, Miss Willie
found her prayers joining with Irma's: "Let him be all right, Lord.
Let Johnnie be all right!"

The hours went by and night came. Miss Willie found wood
piled on the back porch and she brought in plenty for the night.
She fixed herself something to eat, fed the baby, and put him to
bed. And then she sat alone before the fire. There was no sound,
either in the house or outside. A log burned through occasionally,
and fell with a chunking sound into the ashes, sending sparks
flying up the chimney. She kept the fire going and kept a lonely
vigil with her thoughts. They would not leave the bedside of
Johnnie. Finally she lay down on the couch, pulling the bright
afghan Mary kept folded there over her, and along toward morning she slept.

She was awakened a few hours later when Mary and Hod and
Wells returned. Sitting upright, and startled, she searched their
grave faces for news. Wells shook his head at her. "He's mighty
sick," he said.

Mary sank into a chair and covered her face with her hands.
"It's horrible," she whispered, "it's horrible!"

"Did you get the doctor?" Miss Willie asked Hod.

He nodded. "We got him. He's still there. Said he'd stay till
the worst was over."

"Who's there with Irma now?"

"Ma. We stopped an' got her as we came back with the doctor."

"How did Irma take it — the doctor, I mean."

"Quiet. She just stood to one side and let us in, and then she
never went near Johnnie's room again all night. She was on her
knees in the next room, and you could hear her prayin' sometimes.
I don't know what's come over her. Irma used to be such a com-
monsense girl." He flung his coat over a chair and dropped to the
couch. He leaned his head back and closed his eyes.

Mary rose and went toward the kitchen. "I'll fix some breakfast.
Was the baby good?"

"He was fine. There's not been a sound out of him all night.
215

Mary, I want to go over there. Do you think it would hurt anything?"

Mary stopped at the kitchen door. "I don't see any reason why you shouldn't go if you want to," she said. "There's nothing you can do, of course. Hod's mother is helping the doctor. But if you want to go, go ahead."

Miss Willie turned to Wells. "I know you're worn-out, but will you take me before you go home?"

"Why, shore," Wells said, "there'll be little enough rest e'er one of us'll git till they's a change one way or another. I ain't aimin' to go home."

"Eat some breakfast first," Mary called from the kitchen.

After they had eaten breakfast, Wells drove the long miles through the snow again. John let them in. He shook his head when they asked if there was any change.

"Where's Irma?" Miss Willie asked.

"In there," and he motioned with his head toward the back room.

Irma was sitting quietly in a chair, looking out the window across the wide, white fields. She looked up when Miss Willie entered the room, and a brief smile flitted across her face. "Hit's good of you to come," she said.

Miss Willie choked. "O Irma. I've been thinking of you all night. And of Johnnie. And I've been praying that he will be all right."

"He's all right, Miss Willie. Johnnie's all right. He's in the Lord's hands."

"Yes," Miss Willie murmured.

There was a look of absolute peace on Irma's face. A calm look of certainty and assurance. Miss Willie's eyes went blind with tears, and she stumbled from the room. What if he dies, she thought. She is so sure. So certain. What will happen to her if he dies!

Wells lay down on the couch and slept, telling Miss Willie to call him if he were needed. The morning wore itself out. Hod came back, and at noon Miss Willie set food on the table. She

216

roused Wells and they all tried to eat.

Late in the afternoon, just as the sun laid its last brilliant band of gold across the ridge, Johnnie died. He had not been conscious all day, and as the fever rose he had weakened, struggling with decreasing strength against the virulent infection that had him in its grip.

It was John who went back to tell Irma. The others sat stunned, and sunk in the depression of fatigue and grief, by the fire.

As the doctor was leaving, Irma and John came into the room. Irma stood tall and straight, and although John was beside her, she seemed to stand alone. Her face was as quiet and as calm as it had been in the back room.

"I'd like to thank you all fer what you've done," she said. "Fer comin' an' helpin' the ways you thought best. John done what he had to, I reckon. I don't fault him none fer that. An' you," she turned to the doctor, "hit was good of you to come out in the cold an' the weather, although I wouldn't of troubled you. Hit was unneedful." She turned back to the others. "But now I'd like you to go."

Hod kicked at a log on the fire. "All yer prayin' for the Lord to save him didn't do no good, did it?"

Miss Willie saw Irma's lips moving, but when she turned to Hod her voice was level and quiet. "Hod, I never prayed fer the Lord to save Johnnie. I prayed fer the Lord's will to be done, an' I prayed fer him to give me strength to abide by it."

She turned quickly to the others and flung her hands out in a motion of appeal. "I want you to go, now. All of you. An' leave me with my own!"

And then she turned and went into the room where Johnnie lay, closing the door gently behind her.

CHAPTER
❧ 21 ❧

THE REST OF THE WINTER CREPT BY, softly, whitely, slipping the days through the week like a kitten making sly tracks in the snow. Little Johnnie was buried and the snow covered him over, leaving no new-mounded scar to stand raw and hurt against the earth. But there were hearts that bore deep, bleeding scars.

There was Hod, whose hurt was as bitter as gall in his mouth. He could not and he would not understand Irma's attitude. Not that he continued to quarrel with her about it. But he brooded over it and had no patience with it. There had always been a warm friendliness between him and his sister. Now there was a rift in the warmth.

There was Mary who yearned over Irma and the emptiness she must now be feeling, and who looked at her own healthy, round-cheeked boy shudderingly, remembering how swiftly Johnnie's life had been snuffed out. And she clutched small Jeems tightly and fearfully.

There were Hattie and Tom, who had buried eight of their own eleven. Hattie, more than most, would know what it had cost Irma to lay little Johnnie in the winter ground. She had laid so many of her own there.

And then there was Irma herself. Whatever peace her new-found faith brought her, it could not keep her from listening for Johnnie's quick, running footsteps through the house, for his high, sweet voice calling through the rooms, for his rumpled curls so soft under her palm, and for his chubby, skinned knees so often needing washing. Faith might comfort, thought Miss Willie, but it couldn't rub out all the memories, and it couldn't fill up all the emptiness.

And there was John, who must put away now the dream of his son growing tall alongside of him. Who must forget the things he had planned to teach him, and the hours he had hoped to spend with him. Who must tide over the loneliness of the future years, which had loomed so full and so content with a man-child to stand beside him. There was John, who must also remember that he had gone against the wife of his young years in trying to save his boy, and who must go through the days knowing he had doubted, and would always doubt, her faith. Knowing there was this road he could not walk with her, although he had tried. Knowing there would always be this wall between them, and that again and again it would build itself up and divide them.

And then there was Miss Willie, who had her own special grief and bewilderment. That first day of school Johnnie had walked into her heart and part of it had belonged to him ever since. It was almost more than she could bear to think of his bright, blue look, lifted so quickly and so lovingly to her voice, forever gone, closed off, shut out. To remember his grubby little fist closed tightly around a crayon, his tongue between the gaps in his teeth, trying so stubbornly to make his birds and his trees and his houses fit the proportions of the paper. To remember his voice, serious and sweet, in the Christmas story, and its breathy catch when his mother had reminded him, "What do you say, Johnnie?" when Miss Willie had handed him his orange and candy. "Thank you," and it had been like a song. The gift had been so overwhelming!

But besides her grief over the child and her sense of personal loss, Miss Willie was troubled by a growing feeling of strangeness. She felt bewildered and confused. Little by little she had lost her first feeling of strangeness on the ridge. She had not, it is true, presumed even to herself that she understood these people and their ways. And she admitted honestly that she had done very little of what she had set out to do. But she had lately felt as if she had settled into a place of her own among them. Mary and Hod, Becky and Gault, and, most of all, Wells had sustained and strengthened her. She felt safe and secure in their friendly affection.

But as the days blew cold and icy, she felt alien again, as if they had withdrawn from her. Hod was so moody and silent, and Mary was so wrapped up in the baby. Not that they weren't kind to her. They were. But she realized too suddenly that she was not at the core of their lives at all. They were complete without her. She was only on the fringe of the circle. They loved her, but it was not the glowing flame of the love that bound them together. And that was right, she scolded herself. That was as it should be! But even its rightness didn't make it any the less cheerless.

And Becky too had grown remote. As if she herself had lost another child. The winter bound them in the house together, but the warmth of the days before Johnnie's death had gone, to be replaced by a chilled and shrunken companionship. Becky shriveled into a thin, warped little shadow, hands eternally busy, but

219

silent and broody on her side of the fireplace. Miss Willie knew that because Becky had grown up in the same faith, she had banded herself with Irma against the outspoken censure of Hod, the silent criticism of Hattie and Tom, and her own lack of sympathy for the belief. She knew that Becky had slipped a portion of the guilt that they all were placing on Irma's shoulders to her own. And because Miss Willie was on the other side, with those who did not understand and keep the beautiful comfort of the faith, Becky had, forsooth, to draw away from her.

And the cold and the snow and the ice kept Wells from coming. Not entirely. Occasionally he rode by for an hour or so beside the fire. But he did not try to recapture the mood of that day. Only once did he refer to what had passed between them. "You been thinkin'?" he asked her.

She had shaken her head mutely, and he had let her alone. That day she had been been particularly restless, poking the fire, wandering around the room, pulling at the window curtains. This Kentucky winter was so different from the ones she had known in Texas. The days were so brief and so dark. The sun so seldom shone, and there was a damp rawness in the air which chilled her to the bone. She longed for the sun again. These gray, dreary days on the ridge beat her down into herself until she felt caged and imprisoned, and the low-ceilinged rooms stifled her.

Wells sat stolidly by the hearth popping corn, and in a sudden, angry despair she had resented his bigness and his calmness. Marry this solid, hulking man? This broad, heavy-shouldered creature who walked with a lumbering stride and whose hands were calloused and hard and rough? This ignorant, insensitive person who butchered the most common rules of grammar every time he opened his mouth? Marry him, and spend the rest of her life feeling the house shake every time he walked awkwardly across the floor! Having his horny hands touch her! Listening to his illiterate language day in and day out! Marry him? She had been crazy to think of it for one small second!

"If the winter would just pass," she said wearily, leaning her head against the frosty windowpane. "The days are so short and we are so closed in! The sun doesn't shine for weeks and weeks, and the mornings are dark and the evenings are dark! We *live* in darkness, like moles crawling around!"

"Hit is wearisome," Wells had answered. "Along about this time of year, hit gits awful tiresome. Seems like time has jist stood still. But hit'll pass. Hit allus does. Spring'll come before you know it."

"Oh, go away," Miss Willie had muttered, fretfully. "Go on home!"

She couldn't stand his everlasting "hits" and "alluses" another minute! "Leave me alone, Wells," she cried, "go on home, and don't come back for a long time. Just leave me alone."

He had wrapped his big, ugly Mackinaw around him and gone. And perversely she had wanted him back at once! He needn't have taken her so literally! What was the matter with her anyway? Why had she taken her restlessness out on him! He was good and kind and didn't deserve to be the victim of her nervous tongue. She was turning into a regular shrew! But he was gone, now. Maybe, she thought, he understands a woman pretty well. Matildy must have lashed out at him sometimes too. Maybe he knew that during times like this a woman couldn't abide a man's big and comfortable ways. Maybe he guessed they only frashed her more. There, she slapped her hands together in exasperation! She was getting to where she talked like the ridge too!

Somehow the time passed and March went by. When Miss Willie turned the big calendar on Becky's kitchen wall to April, she felt her heart lift. It was cold yet, and the buds on the trees were hard, frozen little knots. But the promise of spring was at hand. Just another week or two and the hard, frozen little knots would unfold and leaf out greenly. Just a little while and the whole ridge would be soft and lazy with the sun. Flowers would bloom. Birds would sing. And up and down the ridge people would come out into the open again. Men would work the fields and women would sit in their yards, and there would be laughter and lightness once more. Miss Willie felt a singing in her veins and she wanted to shout for gladness. The winter was almost over.

Becky stood in the kitchen door and sniffed the air. "Hit ain't fur off," she said, turning, and she smiled with her old, friendly smile at Miss Willie. "Spring's nigh. I kin smell it on south wind. We'll be havin' poke sallet agin you turn that calendar leaf oncet more."

Like a forgiven child, Miss Willie felt a high moment of exaltation. She seized Becky's hands and danced her around the room. "Spring is here! Spring is here!" she chanted, and Becky lifted her skirts and cut a fancy step or two.

Gault's footsteps on the porch sent her flying to the stove. "Don't you be tellin'," she warned Miss Willie.

"I'll not," promised Miss Willie, but the song danced on through her body and made her feet light the rest of the day. Spring was here and Becky was her friend again.

Three weeks later the ridge was a bright, clean world, fresh and shining and newborn green. The maples were almost fully leafed out, and the hickory and beech were slowly unfolding their own tender leaves. Redbud was blushing on the hillsides and dogwood was opening shy, white buds. Pastures were greening and tobacco plants were pushing at the white canvas covers over their beds. Plows were being tried in garden patches, and women washed and starched their bonnets against the heat of the coming sun.

Miss Willie threw a light jacket around her shoulders after dinner one day. "I'm going to see if I can find some violets in that woodsy place down the road," she told Becky.

Becky laid a clean cloth over the food on the table. "Hit was allus a good place," she said, "likely you'll find you a nice bunch."

Miss Willie followed the road down past the old, abandoned church. She held her head high and breathed in deeply the spiced, tangy air. The sun fell warm and bright on her head and shoulders, and the earth was springy beneath her feet. The sun, she exulted. The sun! No wonder ancient men worshiped the sun. It's the center and the hope and the promise of life! Just let the sun shine, Lord, she pleaded, and I can do all things!

Miss Willie stretched widely and laughed. She felt strong and invincible. This was going to be a good school year, she promised herself. She would set herself to all the old problems, and she would somehow, someway, make things move! She would even resolve that old hurt of Rufe!

She gathered her violets in the quiet, wooded place. A double handful, enough for Becky too. And then she crawled through the fence and wandered idly up the road, just looking and soaking up the sun and being glad spring was here. A wagon jounced slowly around the bend back of her and she stepped aside to let it pass. It drew up beside her.

"Where you goin', Miss Willie?" It was Wells, with Rufe on the narrow seat beside him.

She held up the violets. "Been flower-pickin'. Where you goin'?"

"Got to go down to the holler an' git a load o' cook wood. Winter's run us kinder short. Come go along."

"I won't be in the way?" she asked eagerly. The afternoon stretched long ahead, and it would be fun to rumble along with Wells in his old wagon.

"Why, shore not!" he said, and reached down his hand to give her a lift over the wagon wheel. "Rufe, you git in the back." But as Miss Willie clambered up, Rufe disappeared over the tailboard.

Out of the corner of his eye Wells saw him and turned to call: "Rufe! Rufe, you git back here. Rufe, you hear me?"

But Rufe was already in the edge of the woods. Miss Willie sank to the wagon seat and looked at Wells. "He's run away because of me, hasn't he?"

Wells was watching the woods. He set his jaw. "I'm shore goin' to have to lay onto that boy. They ain't no call fer him to act like that. I cain't make him out. Seems like they's jist a streak o' meanness comes out in him e'er time he gits clost to you. Don't mind, Miss Willie. Don't pay him no mind."

Miss Willie laid her violets sadly on the floor of the wagon. "I do mind," she said. "I do mind a lot. But there doesn't seem to be anything I can do about it. Unless I give up and leave the ridge." She laughed, and the laugh broke midway.

"Now, Miss Willie," Wells said quickly, "don't you go talkin' like that. Hit'll all work out some day. Jist don't go givin' up thataway."

Miss Willie shook her head ruefully, and then determinedly she straightened her shoulders. No use letting the boy spoil the afternoon. "Let me drive, Wells," she said. "Let me see if I can."

Wells handed over the lines. "Shore you kin! Jist keep a easy hand on the lines. Don't tighten up. Steady, but easy, an' the team'll never know the difference."

Miss Willie settled her glasses firmly and stiffened her elbows to her sides. Steady but easy! And the team nodded their heads on down the road, the wagon swaying and bumping along behind them.

Down in the hollow Wells took the reins again and pulled the mules off the road onto a dim track in the woods. "Got some hickory already cut over here a piece," he explained.

When they came to the pile of wood, Miss Willie crawled down and helped load it into the wagon. It felt good to be reaching and bending and lifting and swinging. She missed the wagon occasionally, but Wells laughed and didn't seem to mind. They worked easily and slowly together in a companionable silence. Wells *was* a good companion. He didn't talk too much, and you didn't need to make conversation with him. The silences that fell between them weren't awkward. They were natural and easy, and if they stretched out for an hour at a time, they still filled the space between them. It ought to be that way with a man and a woman, Miss Willie thought, heaving a heavy stick. The silences should be as full as the talk.

Wells straightened up suddenly and stood listening. Miss Willie held the stick in her hand to listen too. They heard the murmur of voices coming down the track. And in a moment Matt Jasper slid between the trees, followed closely by a big, heavy-set man whom Miss Willie didn't know. Miss Willie looked at Wells, but he was watching the two men, a frown puzzling his forehead. They stood quietly, the trees hanging a heavy screen over them, and the men went on down the track, never glancing in their direction. When they had gone, Wells still looked after them.

"Who was that with Matt?" Miss Willie wanted to know.

Wells shook his head. "Don't know. Never seen him before. Looked like a city feller to me." He shrugged his shoulders and went back to his loading.

When they had finished, he eased down on the ground against a tree. "Let's rest a mite 'fore we start back," he said, and he rolled a cigarette and cupped a match to it.

Miss Willie perched on a down log nearby. Wells puffed a few smoke rings. "Miss Willie, I'm might' nigh shore Tay's astillin' agin."

"Oh, no, Wells!"

He nodded his head. "Ever' sign's apointin' that way. He's takened to goin' off ever' few days, an' he's slacked up on work around the place. Oh, he done right well fer a spell. I had hopes he wouldn't turn to it no more. But the winter got him twitchy, an' he commenced aramblin' off 'fore the thaw set in. He makes out like he's workin' over at the sawmill. But I've my doubts about that. Worst is, Rose is expectin'."

Miss Willie studied her feet, and noticed absently that she had scuffed the toe of one of her shoes. Funny, she thought, how you'll notice a thing like that at a time when you're hunting for something to say. What *was* there to say? Wells had known, if Rose hadn't, that you couldn't change a boy like Tay Clark. You couldn't take a boy who had never learned to yield to any control but his own wild will and expect marriage to control him. There wasn't even any justice in expecting it.

A pity for Rose stole over Miss Willie. A girl was always so certain her love would be enough. So certain that no matter what a man was before, marriage would give him the last ultimate contentment. Would fill him and satisfy him forever. For her, it sufficed. She built her life around her heart and could not believe so wondrous a thing as their deep and secret knowledge would not also fill him to overflowing. And her love was a trap, stretching her body to bring forth new life as often as the man, roaming free, returned to her side. Poor Rose.

Miss Willie lifted her head. "I'm sorry, Wells." There was nothing else to say.

Wells threw his cigarette away and pulled himself up. "Time we was goin', I reckon," he said, and he helped Miss Willie over the wheel. He pulled the team back into the track and Miss Willie felt his shoulder slump heavily against hers. He shouldn't have to be so fretted over his children, she thought. He needs Matildy. He needs you! But she slid her mind away from that thought, and pushed it from her. The mules settled into the climb up the ridge and Wells slapped the reins against them. "Come up, Beck," he called. "Come up, Sal."

The wagon swayed and Miss Willie slipped her arm through his. "Don't worry too much, Wells," she said. "After all, they're married, and it's their life to live. You can't face life for your children. There always comes a time when they must do it for themselves."

Wells smiled at her. "Thanks fer he'pin' me load the wood, Miss Willie."

"Thanks for letting me," she answered. She picked up her violets from the floor of the wagon. They had drooped a little. But, she thought, they'd freshen up when she put them in water.

CHAPTER
❧ 22 ❧

Mᴀʏ ʙʀᴏᴜɢʜᴛ ᴡᴀʀᴍᴇʀ ᴅᴀʏs and tobacco-setting time. Miss Willie was learning that the seasons on Piney Ridge were counted around tobacco. Along about March she and Becky had gone with Gault over into the far woods and had there watched him stake off his plant bed. "Why don't you put your tobacco bed closer to the house, Gault?" she had asked.

"You want to grow yer seedlin's in new ground," he had answered. He lined off a long, narrow, oblong piece of ground, framed it with sapling logs, and then piled brush on it and slowly burned the brush to ashes. These he mulched with the soil; then he sowed the seed. Becky sowed her tomato, pepper, and cabbage seed around the edges. Last of all he stretched the fine, sheer tobacco canvas across the frame and tacked it securely.

"Now what?" Miss Willie wanted to know.

"Now hit grows. Come May, we pull them seedlin's an' set 'em out."

Now it was May, and the fields had been plowed, harrowed, and fertilized. Miss Willie put on her wide straw hat and went out to help. Gault had gathered a tubful of the young, pale-green plants, and he told Miss Willie to fill her basket and walk ahead down the rows, dropping a plant every eighteen inches. Gault came along behind her with a sharpened stick and bored the holes, pouring a small amount of water in each one. Becky came last, crawling on her hands and knees, sticking the plants in the holes, and firming the ground around them.

Miss Willie and Becky changed jobs occasionally, and after one row of setting the plants, Miss Willie's knees were raw, her fingers sore, and her back kinked into a tight knot. "There must be an easier way of setting tobacco," she said.

"They is," Becky answered. "Down in the bottoms on them big farms they got a contraption drops the plants, waters 'em, an' firms the dirt around 'em. But hit costs a sight o' money. Ain't nobody on the ridge kin spend fer sich as that."

Miss Willie laid the flat of her hand against her aching back and crawled on to the next plant. She was remembering that someone had written a book about tobacco-growing, and had called it green hell! He was right! The whole long process was tedious, torturous work. After this stuff was planted, it would have to be plowed and hoed. Then when it had grown enough, it would have to be topped, and, after that, suckered. Finally it must be cut and speared onto sticks and hung in the tobacco barn to dry. When it had cured sufficiently, the dried leaves would have to be stripped from the stalks and bound into hands, and finally, along about the middle of December, it must be hauled to market and sold. It took a whole year to make a tobacco crop. But since the Government had taken over control of growth, it brought a fair price.

"I kin remember," Becky said, "when yer terbaccer never brought enough on the market to pay yer haul bill. Ten cents a pound fer prime burley! Now, hit allus brings a right good price. Forty or fifty cents a pound."

"How much will you make off this acre?" Miss Willie asked.

"Last year Gault takened in might' nigh a thousand dollars offen it. But that's the best hit's ever done. Hit was mighty good terbaccer, an' you cain't expect to hit ever' year like that. But we'd ort anyways to git seven, eight hundred dollars."

And that was the cash for the year. A thousand dollars. But Miss Willie wondered if Gault and Becky used even half of that!

She fell into bed that night certain her back was broken. But she was out the next day, stiff and sore, determined to finish the job! It took them a week, for the ground was hard and dry. "If it would jist come a season," Becky moaned.

"What's a season?" Miss Willie asked.

"A good, hard rain. Hit'd soften up the ground an' we wouldn't have to water the plants none. We could jist fly."

But the rain held off. Wells came by one day and helped, but he had two acres of his own to set and couldn't spare them much time. "I'd like to borry yer help," he joked with Gault.

Gault eyed Miss Willie dubiously. "Don't know as she'd last out," he said finally.

Miss Willie crippled over to a stump and rested against it. "Wells, does being a farmer's wife mean she has to do things like this all the time?"

"Miss Willie," Wells said, "e'er time you want to take me up on that there proposition I made you, you kin rest easy hit won't include no field work!"

Miss Willie inclined in a mock curtsy. "That takes a load off my mind, I assure you."

"Offen yer back, you mean, don't you?" And Wells raised his brows and squinted at her provokingly.

Miss Willie went back to her tobacco-setting. "Don't think I won't remind you of that, if I ever need to!"

"Ifen you ever need to, you'll not have to remind me," his answer shot back.

"What in tarnation them two atalkin' about?" Gault fretted to Becky, offering his cut plug.

Becky cut herself a chew and put it in her mouth. When she spat, she said, "They're courtin'."

Gault humphed and gouged his tobacco stick a little deeper. "Quare courtin'," he said.

Almost before she knew it another school term was starting. This year Miss Willie was on familiar ground. The faces before her were known to her now, and the habits of each child were an old story. She looked around her the first day, missing the old eighth grade. Pearly and Bill and Rose. Ah, Rose. Last year a schoolgirl. This year a bride and an expectant mother. Time didn't stand still for young folks. But then time hadn't stood still for her, either. She had come a long way since this time last year.

Rufe moved up to the seventh grade now, his beautiful golden head a little browner than last year, a little less boyish. Sylvie Clark, tanned by the summer, but still elfin and nymphlike with her silvery curls, moved up with him. There was no need this year to separate the classes. There was no discussion of seats. There was just the familiar routine, known to them all.

There were five new faces in the first reader and Miss Willie looked at them lovingly. I shall always love the little ones best, she thought. Standing before them, with their expectant look fixed upon her, she wondered why. Because they are so young, so fresh, so trusting and lovable. Children grow out of that lovableness very soon, she thought. Or is it, her mind pursued the thought, because they are so malleable! You've been a teacher long enough to like the malleable ones!

Aware suddenly that the group was watching her patiently and waiting for her to speak, she shrugged the thought away. "The short seats down front are for the little ones," she said, "let them come forward, please." And the pattern was smooth and the year was begun.

Swiftly it moved through July and August and into the first cool fall days of September. Miss Willie walked to school with a joyous energy running through her. The sumac had turned scarlet, and the first maple leaves were yellowing in the brittle sunlight. Goldenrod was tawny in the fence rows, and ironweed had a shaggy, purple crown. Corn was in the shock and great, golden pumpkins were piled around its edges. Late apples glinted red on limbs fast becoming bare, and the katydids sawed at their incessant question slower and slower. It was a time of sharp, cold mornings, warm, winy noons, and hazy, purple evenings. There was a feeling of gathering in, of making ready, of harvesting, and of snugging down before the cold.

And it was in this beautiful golden time that the thing Miss

Willie had feared from the first came about.

It was Wells's own Abby who came down first with typhoid fever. She was not at school one day. Other children might stay at home on the slightest pretext, but Wells's children were always there. Rain or shine, cold or hot, unless they were really ill, Wells saw that they came to school.

"Is Abby ill, Rufe?" Miss Willie asked.

"Yessum."

So when school was out that afternoon, Miss Willie went by to see her. She found Abby listless and feverish, although she was dressed and languidly up and about.

"Have you had the doctor?" Miss Willie asked Rose.

Rose shook her head. "Not yit. Pa said if she wasn't no better tomorrer, he'd take her in to see him."

"Where is your father?"

"Out shockin' corn."

"I'm going out there to see him, then."

Rufe was helping Wells. When they saw Miss Willie coming across the field, they stopped and Wells flung an arm up in greeting. "Hi, Miss Willie!"

"Wells," she said without preliminary, "I don't think you'd better wait until tomorrow to have the doctor with Abby. Children take too many things with a slight fever and that listless, languid look. She may be coming down with something serious. If I were you, I'd have the doctor this evening."

Wells looked surprised. "Why, I never thought but she was jist a little puny. Mebbe she eat somethin' didn't agree with her. She ain't complained to amount to nothin'."

"Maybe not, but that doesn't mean she might not be seriously ill. I'd feel a whole lot better about her if you'd have the doctor immediately."

Not even to Wells was she going to say what she feared. What she had feared ever since she saw that open spring at the schoolhouse, and even now she prayed that Wells might be right. That Abby was just upset from something she'd eaten, or maybe she was coming down with a cold. But she felt a scared, cold queasiness in the pit of her stomach, and she had to know one way or the other as soon as possible.

230

Rufe skipped a stone across the field and watched the two sullenly. Wells scrubbed his hands down the side of his overalls. "Well, reckon if you feel thataway about it, I'll git ready an' go fer the doctor. I aimed to take her tomorrer ifen she wasn't no better."

Miss Willie picked up a dried corn leaf and rustled it between her fingers. "She should be in bed, Wells. I know it's hard on Rose to take care of her just now, but until we know what's wrong it would be safer to keep her quiet."

Rufe sniffed. "Aw, she's just eat too many apples. Ain't nothin' wrong with her."

Miss Willie gave him a bleak look. "That's for the doctor to say, Rufe."

"Yeah," Wells agreed. "Hit's best we find out."

And he and Miss Willie started back across the field. Rufe picked up an ear of corn and slammed it against the ground. There she was agin! Buttin' in! Tellin' folks what to do! Wrappin' Pa around her little finger! Reckon Pa'd ort to know what was best fer his own kid! But e'er time that old maid come around poppin' off, looked like Pa was jist ready to do whatever she said. He kicked at the pile of corn lying ready to shock. Hit'd be the gladdest day of his life ifen she'd jist up an' leave this here ridge! Wasn't nobody had e'er peace o' mind sincet she'd come!

When the doctor had finished examining Abby that night, he told them: "It may be malaria, but I strongly suspect typhoid. Can't tell until I hear from the laboratory on these blood tests. Where do you get your water?"

"Deep bored well," Wells answered.

"Let me see it."

And Wells took the doctor out to the well. When they came back he shook his head. "Should be all right. No drainage or seepage from the outhouses and barns."

Miss Willie took her courage in her hand. "Doctor, I think possibly it's the spring at the school. It's an open spring, and I've been afraid of something like this ever since I came here to teach."

The doctor pounced on her words. "Open spring! My Lord, I thought they'd all been condemned! How many children in that school?"

Miss Willie quivered. "Forty," she managed to say.

The doctor stared at her. "Haven't you got any better sense than to expose forty children to that sort of thing? What are you a teacher for?"

Wells stood up suddenly. "Now, here," he said, "don't go blamin' her! She's been tryin' ever sincet she come to git the trustees to do somethin' about that there spring! She's preached about it night an' day. Hit ain't her fault!"

The doctor turned on his heel. "All she had to do was report it to the county health board," and his voice was dry. "Open spring! I didn't know there was one left in the county!"

"Then you don't know much about this county!" Miss Willie snapped, smarting from his barbed tongue.

The doctor merely looked at her. "You'll have to close the school. I'll report the spring and tests of the water will be made. In the meantime, be sure to report any other cases of illness. Every child in that school will be suspect for several weeks. I'll let you know about these blood tests. Keep her in bed," he cautioned Rose, "and I'll probably be back day after tomorrow."

Miss Willie's heart had stopped when he said she should have reported the spring to the county authorities. The one simple, sure procedure she should have taken had never occurred to her! Bitterly she watched the doctor put his thermometer back in its case, stick it in his vest pocket, and then bend to close his bag. Of course she should have reported it to the county! Not only was it the simplest way of getting the spring either condemned or improved, but it was the authoritative, the organized way of doing it! Why hadn't she thought of it? *Why!*

She'd been too busy trying to do something about it herself, that's why! Miss Willie Payne, who saw what needed to be done, and did something about it! She reviled herself, and felt sick at the thought of all the children who might now have to pay for her thoughtlessness. She turned abruptly toward the window to hide the tears that burned her eyes. She felt old and worn and bruised. Again she had floundered and done the wrong thing. Was there

232

no end to the things she had done wrong here on the ridge? Was there no way of learning? She was a teacher, but she couldn't teach herself!

When the doctor had left, Wells looked helplessly across the room at Miss Willie. "I reckon you was right," he ventured finally.

Miss Willie looked at him. Like all men in the presence of illness, he looked big and awkward and helpless. His face had that worn, blank look of confusion and frustrated strength. She went toward him, touched and moved by his awkwardness. She laid her hand on his shoulder. "We'll just have to do the best we can, now, Wells. I'll dismiss school tomorrow, and then I'll come help Rose."

He reached up and enclosed her small hand in his own two big paws and he laid his forehead against it. "Yer good," he said, "yer good not to condemn me. Hit was as much my fault as e'er other one. I'd ort to of made 'em listen to you. Hit's like the hand o' the Lord strikin' back at me, Abby bein' the one to take down thisaway."

"Don't, Wells," Miss Willie said, rubbing the black, wiry hair with her free hand. "The Lord doesn't strike back at people. It's more my fault than anyone's, if we are to start condemning. But that does no good now. We'll just do the best we can. They have new ways of treating typhoid these days. It's not as serious as it used to be. Let's not get discouraged about Abby yet."

Wells freed Miss Willie and stood up. "I jist pray they ain't no more takes it. I'll feel the burden of 'em all till we know."

And so will I, Miss Willie thought. And so will I.

It was typhoid, and within the week three other children came down with it. One of the Jones triplets, Ewell; a Simpson child; and Sylvie Clark. Sylvie, the elfin, the moonlight nymph! Something clutched at Miss Willie when she thought of that pure, crystalline beauty lying fouled in the squalor of the Clark home. To her Sylvie had been like a lily, stemming slenderly and splendidly up out of the mud of her roots. But now she was brought down among them.

With school closed, Miss Willie shuttled back and forth to the homes of the sick ones. She threw herself into a frenzied doing of the actual chores of the home . . . cooking, washing dishes, mopping floors. And when there was nothing else for her to do, she sat quietly by a sick child, reading to him or talking to him, feeding him and tending him. She found a sort of surcease of guilt in driving herself thus. She left her own cabin early in the morning, and she rarely returned to it before dark.

Becky and Mary both remonstrated. "You'll make yourself sick, Miss Willie," they scolded.

"No, I'll not," she answered. "I'll not be sick. But I *have* to do what I can. Surely you can see that!"

And they let her alone then.

The Jones boy and the Simpson child were never very ill, and shortly they were well on the way to recovery. Abby too responded surprisingly well to treatment. She had looked frail and thin, but there was a core of strength in her slight body which reacted well. But Sylvie was dangerously ill from the start. She didn't react to any of the injections or to any other treatment given her, and she lay day after day, her small, slender body burning itself up. The doctor looked grave when he spoke to Miss Willie about her. "There are too many things wrong," he said. "She's undernourished, and her heart's bad."

As soon as the others were out of danger, Miss Willie devoted herself to Sylvie. As long as she lived, she would never forget her first visit there. When she stepped inside, the foul, fetid air struck against her like something solid, closing her in and smothering her. Even this early in the fall, the heating stove was up and a hot fire was going. Every window was shut tight, and the doors were closed.

There were three beds in the room, huddled into corners. They were ancient, decrepit iron bedsteads, leaning crazily in all directions, and Miss Willie wondered what held them up. The mattresses were very thin and lumpy. She saw that there were no sheets and that the ragged, torn quilts were crusted with dirt and grime. Sylvie lay upon the bed nearest the door, her hair uncombed and matted about her face, her eyes listless and heavy, and her cheeks flushed with fever. Her single garment was a princess slip, made of flour sacking, gray with unwashed age, and

234

crumpled from the child's tossing.

The floors were littered with dirty clothes, scraps of food, parts of the cream separator, bucket lids, and other odds and ends the smallest children had been playing with. It was hardly possible to take one step without wading through things, or without kicking them out of the way.

Miss Willie picked her way through the litter toward Sylvie's bed, and out of the corner of her eye she caught a movement along the wall. She stopped. A line of bugs was streaming up and down the window facing. An infinite variety of bugs, some of them large, some of them small. Roaches, silver fish, ants, and the flat bodied chinch bugs. In fascinated horror she watched them, and then she saw another stream of them over by the door. And another by the kitchen door. They were everywhere, infesting the whole place, a steady river of bugs going and coming up the walls. Her stomach squeezed, but she made herself lift a garment off the only chair in the room to sit down. From under it dozens of bugs scuttled off in every direction. What shall I do, she thought frantically. What can I possibly do?

She shivered as though the bugs were already crawling on her own flesh, and then, to her utter horror, she watched Sylvie, on the sour and soiled bed, brush languidly at two that were inching up her arm! Miss Willie froze stiff, and the skin on her own arms prickled into quivering bumps. At the same time, however, something in her snapped into action. There was just one thing to do. She must get Sylvie clean and comfortable if she had to kill every bug in the house with her own hands. She turned to Mamie with quick determination. "I'm going home," she said, "but I'll be back in a few minutes."

She made two trips, carrying clean sheets, two of her own blankets, nightgowns, soap and cleanser, and half a gallon of fly spray. She told Mamie to put buckets of water on to heat. She wrapped a towel around her head, tied one of Becky's clean aprons around her waist and set to work with murderous intent. She moved Sylvie into the next room, and then she swept and mopped and scrubbed. She took down the beds and scoured them, and she made Mamie put them up in the other rooms. "No one should sleep in this room with Sylvie," she said.

"But, Miss Willie, hit's the only room with a stove. We'll freeze come a cold night, off in that plunder room!" Mamie said.

"You'll just have to pile covers on, then," Miss Willie said, shortly. "Sylvie has to have peace and quiet, and keep the other children out of here!"

Mamie was frightened enough to obey, and she even fell to work helping Miss Willie. They put Sylvie's bed back up and Miss Willie spread it with clean, fresh-smelling sheets and the soft woolen blankets from her own blanket chest. They had a sweet, piney odor. Then she brought Sylvie in, bathed her, and slipped a white, lavender-scented nightgown over her head.

Sylvie slid her hands down over the smooth material in a caressing movement, and then she fingered the narrow blue satin ribbon at the neck. "Hit's so purty," she said softly, "hit's so purty, and soft." Then she laid her fair hair back on the pillow and rubbed her cheek against the pillow slip. "Ever'thing smells so good," and she sighed and drifted off to sleep.

Miss Willie fought a daily battle thus for Sylvie's comfort and care. The bugs crept in from the other rooms and she harried Mamie into giving them a semblance of cleaning. Mamie grumbled, but she did what she was told as best she could. Her idea of cleaning never reached Miss Willie's conception of it, but she got rid of most of the litter and surface dirt, and Miss Willie herself kept the whole house sprayed.

She also made Mamie keep out half a gallon of whole milk each day for Sylvie, and keep the freshest eggs for her. "We cain't git along without the cream checks," Mamie said, "an' the egg money. Hit's what I use to buy meat an' beans with."

"Drink the milk and eat the eggs yourself," Miss Willie snapped, "and quit buying that greasy fat meat and so many beans. You'll be a lot healthier!"

"Don't none of us like milk an' eggs," Mamie sulked.

Miss Willie faced her. "You can do as you like about the rest of the family," she said, "but Sylvie has got to have good, whole milk, and plenty of it, and lots of eggs. Do you want to kill the child?"

"No, ma'am."

"Then do as I say!"

So Mamie strained out half a gallon of fresh milk each day for Sylvie, kept half a dozen eggs for her, and Miss Willie made her good, rich eggnogs, custards, and milk toast. She had Becky make soups and broths, and every hour or so during the day she poured nourishing food down Sylvie. Valiantly she fought against all the odds, a shrew and a termagant when the way was balked, pitting her own energy and strength against the slothfulness and sloven-liness of Mamie, against the fever, against the malnutrition which had sapped Sylvie's body of recuperative power, against even the murmuring and protesting heart in the child's shallow chest. She fought grimly and she would not give up.

And she won. The day came when the doctor stood by Sylvie's bed and smiled across it at Miss Willie. "She's going to make it," he said, "she's all right, now. But she owes her life to you."

Miss Willie's knees gave way under her and she pulled a chair up under them. She'd won. She felt her hands quivering strangely, and she wanted to lay her head down on the bed and cry and cry. She was so tired! But she'd won! Ah, no. Sylvie didn't owe her anything. She had owed Sylvie her life. Sylvie and those other children. Thank God the debt hadn't been any greater than four out of the forty! And thank God the toll exacted hadn't been extreme for any one of them! They were all recovering. None of them had died. She had been let off lightly, after all.

CHAPTER
❧ 23 ❧

A SUDDEN COLD SPELL CAME on a late October morning. A Saturday it was. There was a whippy wind scudding across the face of the earth, sending leaves skittering through the air, piling them in heaps in the furrows and ruts, and mounding them against the sides of low banks. It tore at them and heckled them and battered them into the ground. It was a wild kind of day, with clouds swelling at each other and racing wildly around the sky. It was a lowering day, full of frowns and growls.

At the still, Tay worked swiftly bottling his likker that morning, hurrying so that he might finish and make his deliveries early. He cursed the wind as he worked, tugging his old hat tighter on his head, eying the storm clouds to decide whether or not he must take his work inside the shack. But he kept on at the bench outside.

Matt Jasper corked the bottles and set them in rows against the wall of the shack. Occasionally he clinked a bottle against another, and the full gurgling tinkle made Tay raise his head. "Don't break e'er one of them," he warned. "I've got ever' drop of this sold, an' I ain't aimin' to lose a penny on this run."

"I'm bein' keerful as I kin," Matt said. There was a changeless futility about him which made it impossible for him to work effectively. He moved frantically, his hands flying like those of a scarecrow flapping in a cornfield, but he seldom found the right-sized cork for a bottle the first time. He made a dozen impotent motions to complete one operation, so that Tay constantly grumbled at him under his breath. "Dodderin' fool," he growled at him, "they ain't nothin' you kin do right!"

Matt's mouth worked tremblingly. "I'm atryin' to keep up, Tay."

"Git me some more bottles there in the shack," Tay ordered.

Matt shambled through the opening in the front of the shack, and Tay straightened his tired back as he waited. The fumes of the likker hung heavy over the bench, and his eyes stung. He closed them and rubbed them with the back of one hand. In that single moment Tay's fate closed in on him, for when he opened his eyes, it was to see a man with a gun advancing over the clearing. He whirled to leap quickly for the shack, but the man's voice stopped him: "You're covered, Clark. Stop where you are."

From the corner of his eye Tay saw that another man was advancing from the left. He turned his head slightly and saw another one coming from the right, and as he looked, two more broke cover in front of him. He eased his feet on the ground and hitched his pants higher on his hips.

His mind gnawed on the hinges of this trap like a frantic animal gnawing his own foot off to find release. It surged and clawed and ran desperately down corridors of escape. His own gun was under his shirt. But they'd take it, likely. He saw no way out. Five men coming at him with guns made a barrier he could not climb.

238

In that moment of surrender his thoughts went to Rose, and his heart wept and its tears were bitter salt. Rose, Rose! Her name was like a dirge in his ears, and the remembered warmth of her mouth died cold on his own tightened lips. But he slitted his eyes and shuttered his face, blanking it of all expression, and when he turned to face the first man, his features might have been chiseled from stone. "Hit takened aplenty of you," he commented grimly.

"Never mind how many of us it takes," the man said. "The point is we've got you." He called to another man. "There's another one in the shack. Get him."

A man stepped from the circle and pulled aside the burlap curtain. He dropped the curtain behind him, but emerged shortly. "Ain't nobody in there," he said.

"I saw him go in there myself not two minutes ago. He must be in there."

"Well, see for yourself. There ain't nobody in there now."

Tay laughed a short snort through his nose. "He's got away. You wouldn't be thinkin' they was jist one way in an' outen that shack, would you?"

The man motioned for two more men to enter the shack. "Search it," he said. "Get whatever you need to take with you, Clark. We'll be going to town."

Tay reached for his coat hanging on the lower limb of a tree and shrugged into it. "How'd you find this place?" he asked.

"Oh, it wasn't hard," answered the man, motioning Tay toward the creek. "There's always folks that'll talk."

Tay looked at him straight and hard. "They ain't nobody on this here ridge that'd knowingly talk to the law. Ifen e'er body on this ridge told, hit wasn't intentional. You got it outen somebody unknowin'."

"Somebody like your partner there?"

Tay's lips firmed. He might have known! Stupid, dull-witted old Matt! He'd been a fool to let him hang around here! That's what he got for feeling sorry for him and letting him make a little extra money! He'd been a fool!

"Move on, Clark," the man said. The two men came out of the shack. They joined the procession heading toward the creek.

"There's a hole in the back wall of the shack," they reported,

239

"Got an old chest rolled in front of it to hide it. It comes out behind that big rock there on the side of the hill. The other one probably ducked the minute he heard us."

"We'll get him," said the leader. "We know who he is. We can pick him up any time."

"He ain't got nothin' to do with this," Tay said. "He jist works fer me oncet in a while. Jist he'ps out some. He don't know nothin' about this business. An' besides he's natural an' simple. He wouldn't even know what you was gittin' him fer."

"We'll take care of that," the man answered. "There's a car down the hollow. Keep moving. Casey, you and Martin break up that still! Don't leave a whole piece. Bust the bottles and see that there's no likker left either. Bring one bottle along for evidence. And don't go samplin' it!"

Tay laughed. "Hit's right good stuff, boys. Good corn meal an' pure spring water. You couldn't ask fer no better moonshine! Hit's might' nigh as good as bourbon!"

He felt a sudden exaltation. They weren't going to search him. A great contempt for them flowed over him. Muddlers! Fools! Didn't they know about a shoulder holster? But he had his gun. He'd have a chance now.

They splashed through the creek and headed down the hollow. Tay looked back once as he heard the ring of an ax on the metal drum. The man had started wrecking the still. "That was a plumb good still," he murmured. "Hit's a shame to bust it up."

When Matt Jasper had heard the voices outside the shack, he had known instantly what was happening. Tay had told him that no one else knew the exact location of the still. There was always the possibility that someone out hunting, sang digging, or herb-gathering would stumble over it. But that was not too serious. They would be ridge people, with the ridge loyalty to their own. Nearly everyone knew that he had located a still on Wandering Creek, and most could guess that it would be somewhere back in the convolutions of Coon Ridge. "Hit's jist better," Tay had said, "fer as few to know as kin. Ifen they don't know, they ain't likely to give it away."

Tay had further warned him that raids came quietly and swiftly. There would be no warning of the presence of officers. They would be lucky if there was the rattle of a loose stone, or the spatter of creek water as a foot slipped, to give them time to move. And then Tay had showed him the hole in the wall of the shack and had added: "Ifen the law ever comes, an' yer caught in here, likely you kin git away. Make a try fer it, leastways. An' you kin be shore I'll do the same. In this business hit's ever' man fer hisself. Ifen we're ever caught, strike out on yer own. Don't think none of what'll happen to me. Fer one thing's shore, I'll not be thinkin' none of you, neither. Git out with a whole hide, if you kin."

So when Matt heard the strange voices outside, he dropped quickly to his knees before the old chest, and pulled it gently away from the hole. There was no indecision in his movement. Tay had told him to get away if he could. He eased his thin body through the hole, coming out behind the big rock pressed against the hill. From here he could peer around and see that all the men were preoccupied with Tay. He noted their guns and their encircling movement. Only a second did he pause, and then he began to climb up the steep wall, screened first by the rock, and then by the thick growth of bushes. He crawled along flat against the ground, inching his way gently, hoisting himself gradually by pulling from one bush to another. Silently and smoothly he ascended the hill, and, for all his crawling along, he moved rapidly up the steep slope.

He did not stop until he reached the rounded cap of the hill, far above the clearing and the still. Here on this gentler level, out of sight and hearing of the men below, he allowed himself to stop and ease his breath. This far Matt Jasper's mind had functioned normally, reacting to fear in the same way as any other man's would have done, needled and frightened, and pushed by the necessity of reaching safety, but at the same time keeping its balance and sanity, not yielding to panic.

When he stopped to breathe on the easy slant of the hilltop, however, this changed. The sound of a single shot reached him, immediately followed by a fusillade of shots and a chorus of yells. It was then that panic overtook him, and his timid mind began

241

to chase itself, circling madly round and round. That man . . . that man, down there. He'd had on a blue coat. That 'un that come around all time fer a while, he had on a blue coat too. The guards at Danville wore blue coats, he'd heared. Danville. The asylum. Blue coats. Guards. One thought caught the tail of the other and they surged and pressed in on him, until he lifted his hands and pounded them on his head to make them quit. Blue coat . . . blue coat . . . blue coat! Round and round they went. Men and blue coats and bars over windows and Danville, and more men and blue coats, and Danville again. And him inside the bars. They wasn't lookin' fer Tay. They was lookin' fer him!

His breath came harshly, tearing out of his chest, ripping at his throat, and he tore his shirt collar open and gasped the air in great, rasping sobs. The pupils of his eyes dilated and fixed themselves unseeingly on space. His nostrils flared and whitened, and the drooling spittle frothed at the corners of his mouth. His hands clenched and the fingers worked convulsively. The muscles of his face twitched in an uncontrollable dance of tiny movements.

At the height of the spasm, when rigidity usually came, his rabbity mind caught hold of another thought. "Somebody turned me in. Somebody told 'em I was crazy! Somebody . . . somebody . . ."

And then a cunning idea occurred to him. "I know who done it," he whispered slyly. "She's been lookin' funny at me fer a long time. She done it. She turned me in to the law. She told 'em I was crazy!"

His eyes drooped and softened and shuttered over the dilated pupils, and the drooling mouth relaxed and curved gently at the corners, sweetly, like a child's. Every tense muscle in the body of the man, which a moment before had been screaming in spasmodic seizure, eased into looseness. His shoulders sagged down and rounded and his arms hung limp by his sides. His head lolled to one side and a vacuous grin stretched his mouth. He studied a bird hopping on the ground in front of him, giggling nervously. He hiccuped, and swallowed noisily. The purposes of his mind were forming, now.

As they steadied, his fingers fumbled at the buttons of his shirt, and when the last final necessity of thought was reached,

242

he jerked upright and snapped his body tense again. "I'll fix her," he said. "I'll fix her good. I'll fix her so's she cain't never turn me in agin. That's what I'll do."

And he set off at a dog trot over the hill. Thus did Matt Jasper's tormented mind flee its last moorings and slip unrestrained into madness.

CHAPTER

❧ 24 ❧

LATE THAT SATURDAY MORNING Miss Willie and Becky walked to the mailboxes, and Becky took along a basket of quilt scraps for Lutie Jasper. "The pore thing is allus needin' new covers," she said.

The wind whipped at them and they felt a winter bite in its teeth as they bent into it. Miss Willie was glad she had worn her knitted cap and gloves. Her finger tips were cold as it was, and she dug them deep in her pockets. "Such a day!" she yelled at Becky, the words torn from her mouth and sent flying swiftly with the wind. "I never saw such a wind!"

Becky's scrawny shoulders were hunched against the cold. "Hit is a flyaway day, ain't it? Wouldn't wonder if it ain't acomin' on to snow."

When they came up to the Jasper house, a small smoke was tailing out the chimney of the lean-to. "Reckon Lutie's startin' dinner," Becky said.

They called from the front gate, and when there was no answer, they let themselves in and went up on the porch. "They couldn't possibly hear us in this wind," Miss Willie said.

The door was closed, but Becky pushed it open, calling at the same time: "Lutie? You home, Lutie?"

It was then that they saw Lutie lying in the middle of the floor in the dreadful pool of her own blood, her head bashed in and horribly mutilated, even her body cut and slashed almost beyond recognition. Life had long since drained out of such gaping wounds, and she lay hacked and distorted, like a butchered animal.

Miss Willie stood frozen and paralyzed just inside the door,

243

unable to move or to take her eyes from the body, and as horror seeped through her, her own blood slowly congealed in her veins. Her heart pumped painfully hard, and in the region of her stomach an iron fist closed tightly, sending a sudden, stabbing thrust of pain down her legs. She swayed and clutched at Becky, and whimpered like a child having a bad dream.

Becky stood, shaking, her free hand holding her quivering mouth. "Lord God above," she whispered. "A fiend from hell must of been here! Who could have done sich a thing!"

Her quilt scraps dropped to the floor at her feet, scattering an incongruously bright patchwork of color across the gray floor. One small square floated delicately into a scarlet pool, and Miss Willie felt a queer compulsion to pick it up. It will be wet, she thought. I must get it, *now*. It will be ruined. She knew her mind was working slowly, refusing to face this horror. It felt as thick and hardened as the fingers on her hands, as numb and jelled.

But it hit upon one thought. "Matt," she said, and to her surprise her voice moaned out of her throat like a sobbing wind. "It was Matt! I told Wells. Oh, I told him that man was dangerous! Why didn't he listen to me? Why didn't I make him listen!"

"Sh-h-h," Becky whispered, and Miss Willie's eyes followed Becky's look.

As if in answer to his name, Matt Jasper slid through the kitchen door. Like a spectral shadow, he inched through it, sidewise, and then he crabbed along the wall, making no noise as he slipped into the room. Even in that mad moment which Miss Willie was sure would be her last, she had time to wonder briefly where Matt Jasper had found the costume he had on, and why he had it on. For over his grimy, filthy overalls he had put on a gorgeously regal, purple-satin princess slip. It hung from his thin shoulders in loose folds, and its heavy lace gathered about his knees. It was spattered and bloodstained, but as he leaned loosely against the wall he touched it lovingly, smoothing its shiny richness over his hips with a caressing hand. He crooned over it and whimpered a small song in his throat, nodding his head on its limp neck, patting the purple folds and preening himself carefully. His eyes were shuttered and his mouth drooped childishly. The corners curved softly into a smile, and little crying, whimpering songs whispered across the room. In the other hand he still held the ax. It hung lazily, swinging gently as he swayed back and forth against the wall.

He began to hum, and then in a quavering voice he started singing. " 'And I, if I be lifted up . . .' " The voice was small and thready at first, but then it strengthened, and the pure sweetness of it rang out and filled the room. " 'If I be lifted up . . . will draw all men unto me!' "

Miss Willie leaned against the wall, and sobs shook her and the tears poured down her face. Dear Lord! Dear Lord! It's too late! It's too late for Matt Jasper to be lifted up! It's too late!

" 'And I, if I be lifted up . . .' " the song went on. Suddenly Becky moved toward the man. Miss Willie put out her hand, but Becky brushed it aside. "Matt," she said, her voice loud and strong. "Matt, you better give me that ax. You cain't sing so good holdin' onto it thataway. You better give it to me."

Matt drew back and clutched the ax. The song stopped and he eyed Becky slyly. His face widened into a grinning mask, and then a terrified look crept over it. "Hit was the wind an' storm," he whispered, his eyes going past Becky to the door, and filling with terror. "Hit was a powerful wind an' storm. Hit come. Hit come all at oncet, an' hit takened me up on high. I was lifted up! Hit takened me up, an' hit blowed an' blowed! The lightnin' an' the thunder squalled. The lightnin' an' thunder kept asquallin'. The lightnin' went streakedy, strikedy, an' the thunder went baw, baw, yanny, yanny. That's what it kept sayin'. An' I was lifted up! Clean up above the world. Up over the trees an' the fields an' the houses. Clean up above the world! Baw, baw, yanny, yanny. Baw, baw, yanny, yanny! The lightnin' went streakedy, strikedy, an' the thunder went baw, baw, yanny, yanny!

"An' I had my ax in my hand, an' hit was powerful heavy. But I didn't dast let go, fer had I done so, hit would of split the world in two! The wind an' the rain an' the storm kept awhirlin' an' aturnin', an' my arm got heavy an' tired. But I helt on. An' the lightnin' an' thunder kept asquallin'. Baw, baw, yanny, yanny. An' I had to let go! I had to! I couldn't noways hold onto the ax no longer. Hit was too heavy. An' it hit pore Lutie! See! See, where it hit pore Lutie an' busted her head wide open! The Lord

245

told me not to let go. But I couldn't noways hold onto it no longer. Hit was too heavy. Too heavy. An' hit went baw, baw, yanny, yanny, an' I couldn't noways he'p it." The eyes drooped and the head dropped and Matt Jasper sagged against the wall.

Becky reached him then. "Here, Matt. I'll hold the ax for you. I'll not drop it. I'll hold onto it, tight."

Before his eyes closed, Matt looked once more at her. "You shore you kin hold onto it? You shore? Hit wouldn't noways do to drop it no more. Hit would certain split the world in two this time."

Becky's hand closed around the ax handle and she slid it out of his unfolding hand. "I'll not drop it, Matt. I'll promise I'll hold onto it tight."

He sighed briefly and slid into a grotesque huddle on the floor.

Becky turned. Her face was ashen, but her voice was steady. "Let's git them young'uns, now."

Miss Willie hunched over. "I can't, Becky. I think I'm going to be sick."

Becky took her by the shoulder and shook her hard. "No, you ain't! You ain't goin' to be sick! They ain't time fer you to be sick! I don't know whether he's asleep or dead, but we got to git them kids an' git out. You kin be sick when we git away from here!"

Miss Willie's teeth chattered, but she clenched them and took a deep breath. "All right," and she found that she could make her legs support her, and that she could swallow her nausea.

The children were huddled on a bed in the next room, the covers drawn around them. They were frightened, but, except for a sobbing whimpering from one of the smallest ones, they were quiet. The oldest girl held the baby hugged against her, and when Becky took it, Miss Willie saw that it was asleep. There was a strange unreality in the fact that even a baby could have slept through all that had happened here! And Miss Willie fought off a hysterical desire to laugh. Sleep! She would never sleep again!

Becky hurried the children into wraps and hustled them out the other door. She didn't want them to see Lutie in the next room. Miss Willie followed with the baby.

"Hit don't seem right," Becky said, when they were down the

road, "hit don't seem right to leave her thataway. But I've heared you shouldn't ort to tetch a body that's been kilt. Hit's the law, I reckon. But it don't noways seem decent."

Miss Willie shuddered. "No. You mustn't touch anything."

Becky took the baby, and it stirred in its wrappings and mewled plaintively. She patted it tenderly and bent over it. "Pore little thing," she murmured, "pore little motherless thing." She wrapped its shawl tighter against the wind, and as the two women and three children moved slowly down the road, there was a shining look on her face.

CHAPTER
❧ 25 ❧

THE NEWS THAT MATT JASPER HAD RUN AMUCK and killed Lutie traveled swiftly over the ridge, and Wells had gone immediately to do his part in whatever must be done. He told Rose not to look for him back before morning. Likely he'd be kept all night.

Heavy and awkward, within four weeks of being brought to bed, Rose moved through the afternoon, wishing for Tay and watching the road. She was restless and fretful, without knowing why. Why don't Tay come home, she wondered. Ever sincet he'd takened to goin' off two, three days a week, she'd been uneasy about him. Not that she mistrusted him. He was makin' right good money sawin' them ties over at the sawmill. But she wisht he'd come on home now. Hit give a body the creeps, knowin' Lutie was alyin' over there. Ifen Tay was here, she wouldn't noways feel so quare.

She'd start supper early. If she kept busy, the time'd pass quicker. She picked over a basket of late beans and put them on to cook. Then she went out and hacked up a little cook wood. She stirred about, doing first one small chore then another, and the sun slipped lower behind the ridge, the air chilling behind it.

When she heard a horse out front she ran, flinging the door wide, eager to feel Tay's arms about her, and to hear his comforting voice. But it was Wells, heavy and tired and sober-faced. She turned back to the house and he followed her. "I thought you was

Tay," she said, listlessly.

Wells laid his hands on her shoulders. "Honey, you got to be a brave girl."

Rose slipped out from under his hands, and she faced him, her face suddenly white. "Somethin's happened to Tay! Somethin's bad happened to him! I know. Tell me!"

The white stillness of her face frightened Wells. "Rose, set down, honey. Jist set down an' try to be calm."

"Tell me! Jist tell me an' be done with it!"

And then he had told her, as kindly as possible. But no kindness could gloss over the brutal fact. Tay was dead, riddled by bullets from the officers' guns. "He'd been astillin' agin," Wells told her. "I don't reckon you knowed that. But I suspicioned it away last spring. An' the law, they tracked him down. Way they tell it is, they takened him without no trouble. He was bottlin' up a run. He acted like he was peaceable enough, an' they could see he never had no gun ashowin'. They was five of 'em, an' they never figgered he'd give 'em no trouble. Said they was takin' him to the car when he whirled, quick-like, drawed a gun outen his shirt, an' started firin'. He never fired but one shot before they got him."

"Where is he?" The words were short, sharp, explosive.

"They takened him to the county seat. To the mortuary over there."

Rose ripped her apron off and caught up her old brown coat from behind the door. "Let's go," she said.

"Rose," Wells begged. "Honey, let me go. I'll bring him home to you. They ain't no call fer you to see him over there."

Rose turned on him swiftly. "You think I'll let e'er other hands tetch him to do fer him but mine? He's mine! You hear? Cold or warm, he's mine! I'll fetch him home, an' I'll do what's to be done fer him. Let's go, I said."

Dully, Wells followed her outside and went to the barn to hitch the mules to the wagon. He thought to pile a load of sweet straw in the wagon bed, to soften the ride home for the lifeless body. He had not overly liked the boy. But that was not important now. The boy was dead, and his girl was stricken and grieving. His own grief rose instantly to walk beside her.

248

So Tay Clark was brought home, and that Saturday night three bodies lay corpses on the ridge. For Matt Jasper was dead too, when they found him huddled against the wall, wrapped splendidly about by his royal purple princess slip.

Gault and Hod and Tom went to sit up with the Jaspers. Wells and Rose kept lonely vigil over Tay.

The tragedy stunned the ridge. Nothing like it had ever happened there before. There was always death on the ridge. Every family knew its stalking footsteps at the door. Men had been mangled in the sawmills, or shot when out hunting, or drowned while swimming in the river. The various forms death took were not new on the ridge. But this violent purging of life dazed them and stupefied them. People walked on tiptoe and talked in whispers as if the ghost of Matt Jasper might still be lingering near. No one had dreamed he could ever really do harm. He was just Matt Jasper, who had fits, and who had wandered like a lean, lank shadow among them, drooling his tobacco spittle and upon occasion lifting his sweet voice to the hills. There had been kindliness in their attitude, and indifference. There had been tolerance and pity, and a kind of shaming ridicule. But now they clustered together and remembered his disintegration. His fear of being taken to Danville. His conviction someone was coming after him. His haunted, terror-stricken days, when he ran away and lived in the woods, avoiding everyone. Two by two they put things together.

They even tried to understand the purple petticoat. "Matt give it to Lutie one Christmas," they said, "a long time ago. She wouldn't never wear it. Said he'd ort to of spent the money on somethin' to eat, instead o' wastin' it on foolishment!"

It was known, too, that Matt had been helping Tay over at the still. And it was also known, now, that Matt's careless tongue had prattled all his knowledge of the still, proudly, to an officer away last spring. They'd taken their time, folks said. Had made sure of their man, and then had moved in relentlessly. "The wages of sin is death"! Sagely the men and women of the ridge nodded their heads. You could mock the Lord jist so long in yer wrongdoin'. But hit would ketch up with you, jist the same. "The wages of sin is death"!

Over at Becky's house Lutie Jasper's baby thrived, sleeping and eating and fattening under Becky's loving care, neither knowing nor caring whence it had come or where it was going. Becky moved its cradle and the few poor clothes Lutie had provided it to her home after the funerals. So far as the ridge knew, there was no one to take the baby except Mamie Clark, and she had her hands full with her own young'uns and the rest of Lutie's. No one disputed Becky's right to the baby. No one else wanted it. They reckoned if she wanted the pore little thing, she could have it. After all, she was the one that found it and takened it first.

Only Miss Willie argued with her about it. "Becky," she said one morning when Becky was bathing the baby, her face alight with love and her hands gentle on the tiny form. "Becky, have you thought how much grief there may be ahead for you in this child? Remember that her father was an epileptic who went insane, and that her mother was little better. How do you know this baby won't grow up and have fits like her father?"

"I don't," answered Becky, wrapping a towel about the baby. "I don't know but what she'll have fits, or mebbe go crazy like Matt. But," she said, holding the baby close, "is that e'er reason why she ortent to have a home, an' have a ma, an' have somebody to love her an' keer for her? What are you goin' to do with little 'uns like this? Throw 'em in the crick?"

She lifted the baby to her shoulder, patting its round little backside softly. "No, Miss Willie. This here's my baby. The Lord sent her to me. I ain't athinkin' he made pore old Matt go crazy an' kill Lutie so's I could have me a baby. I ain't a thinkin' that atall. But he aimed fer me to find this little 'un. He led me, plain as day, so's I'd find her, an' he aimed fer me to have her an' to raise her up. He'll take keer of the fits an' the craziness. But they ain't nothin' goin' to stop me from lovin' her an' makin' her my own."

Becky laughed. "You know what I'm goin' to name her, Miss Willie? I'm goin' to call her Hannah, after my own little 'un. An' Gault says we'll git papers on her, so's she'll be a Pierce right an' true! Hannah Pierce! Ain't that a purty name?"

CHAPTER

❧ 26 ❧

Miss Willie came down sick about a week after the funerals. Belatedly the hard work she had done during the time the children had typhoid, and the shock she had suffered at finding Lutie and seeing Matt, told on her, and she lay abed, listless, feverish, and spiritless.

Becky sent for Mary, and in a panic Mary made Hod go for the doctor. He could find nothing seriously wrong. "She's just worn out," he told Mary. "All this has been too much for her. Let her rest. Feed her and try to interest her in something else."

So Mary had packed her up and moved her home with her. "I want you where I can look after you," she had told the protesting Miss Willie. "I can't be running up here every day. Not with young Jeems just at the age to get into everything. And besides Becky has her hands full with her own baby. You come on and don't say another word."

The days at Mary's were slow-moving and peaceful. Miss Willie slept long, restful hours; ate, at first sparingly then more heartily; and sat before the fire while Mary played for her, knitting, sewing, playing with the baby. Young Jeems took up many of the hours. He was beginning to walk now, and his eager pattering feet took him exploring in every nook and cranny of the house. He was a fat, healthy, boisterous youngster, and he bestowed his favors upon Miss Willie as impartially as upon his mother.

Miss Willie loved him, but she felt only languidly interested in him. Everything seemed too much effort to her. She was too worn and too bruised. Nothing was worth doing any more. And suddenly Texas seemed very dear to her. She began to think with longing of its wide, flat spaces, of its far horizons, and of its deep, deep skies. If she could just go home again! If she could just get away from the ridge! Maybe then she would purge some of this horror from her mind, and some of this languor from her body.

The sense of failure rode hard upon her shoulders. She brooded over it, and she found a whipping boy for her own sense of guilt

251

in the ridge. It wasn't for her, after all. It was a monstrously inhuman place. Ugly, uncouth, bestial. It was a place where she could no longer dwell. She must put it behind her. Such thoughts kept running through her mind. And she lived in a deeply despondent and depressed mood most of the days.

On one of the worst days Wells came to see her. Jeems was playing piggie with his bare, pink toes on Miss Willie's lap when Wells came in. He promptly transferred his affection to Wells, and when he sat down across the hearth, Jeems crawled down from Miss Willie's lap and padded across to clutch at Wells's knee. Wells took him up. "We'll be havin' a fine lad like this at our house soon, I reckon. Rose's time is due."

Miss Willie's hands fretted together. Wells brought it all back with him. The ridge and the trouble. The ugliness and the failure. She noticed that his face was seamed with tiredness and his eyes were dull and apathetic. Why did he have to come? Why did she have to think about any of it again? Why couldn't the ridge stay up there where it belonged and let her alone? Why did she ever come to this awful place, anyhow?

She paced across to the piano and ripped her finger down the keys. "How is Rose?" she asked grudgingly, finally.

"She's takened it awful hard," he said. "I reckon she's about as well as could be expected, but I look fer her to have a hard time birthin' the baby. Seems like she don't keer about it none at all. Don't never name it, or act like hit's even comin'."

Miss Willie's hands flew to her face. "I don't blame her!" she cried. "I don't blame her! I wouldn't want it either! Why bring another child onto this awful ridge! Oh, I don't blame her!"

Wells rose quickly and crossed the room to lay a broad arm about her shoulder. "Why, Miss Willie," he said, softly reproachful, "you don't mean that. You're jist upset!"

Miss Willie shook his arm off. "I do mean it! I do! What has Rose's child, or any other for that matter, got to look forward to in this horrible place? What has *she* got to look forward to? I do mean it! And I'd feel just like she does, in her place."

Wells patted her arm awkwardly. "Now, Miss Willie," he soothed, "now, Miss Willie. I tell you! Let's you an' me go fer a little walk. Hit's not too cold out today. Git yer coat an' let's jist walk up the holler a ways. Hit'd do you good."

Miss Willie snubbed her tears and mopped at her eyes with her small handkerchief. "Here, take mine," Wells said, offering her his own huge square of white, "hit's man-size an'll do some good."

Miss Willie took it, but it smelled strongly of harsh soap and she shuddered away from it. "No, I'll get something," she said, thrusting it back into his hand, and she went into her room, leaving him looking at the unused handkerchief.

I don't want to go walking, she thought listlessly. The very idea of walking with Wells made her tired. She wished he would go away. She didn't want anything but to be let alone. To be let alone and to forget everything that was ugly and tragic and ignorant and dirty. Everything that was foul and diseased and coarse and uncouth. Oh, everything that was the ridge. The fields, the hills, the streams, the school, the children, and most of all, the people! The heavy, plodding, animal people! Forget it! Forget it! But she got her coat and went with him. She hadn't the heart not to. He tried so hard to please her and to help her. It would be so rude not to go.

They walked up toward the head of the hollow into the clean wind which swept down off the hills. Wells walked awkwardly, lumberingly, by her side, silent, as if he knew she would rather not talk. Miss Willie ducked her head against the wind and braced into it. It cut through her coat and she shivered. She had been a fool to come! She was going to freeze, and it would do no good.

When they came to the edge of the woods, the trees screened them from the wind and it was warmer. They walked into the woods a way, and Wells found a down tree. "Would you want to set down a spell?" he asked.

"We might as well," Miss Willie said wearily.

They still found nothing to say, and Wells picked up a pronged stick and dug absently in the dirt with it. A dog nosed around the end of the log and sniffed at his feet. "Why, there's Rufe's old Jupe dog," he said. He turned to look around. "Rufe must be somewheres clost by. Diggin' sang, likely."

Miss Willie eyed the dog disinterestedly, and after a moment it wheeled and made off in the woods again.

253

Miss Willie pulled at a loose piece of bark on the log. Suddenly it came free and she flung it down. Rising abruptly, she stood in front of Wells, ramming her hands deep in her pockets. "Wells," she said, "I'm going back to Texas."

When he lifted his head, startled, she went on swiftly: "Oh, not right now. I'll finish out the school term. If I'm able," she added ironically. A rasping file of irritation fretted out to the ends of her fingers, and she made them into fists in the pockets. "There's no use my staying on. You must see that! There's nothing here for me to do! There's nothing here for anyone to do! The people won't listen to me. They don't want to learn anything. And I've not got half a chance with the children if their parents won't help me. It's no use struggling any longer."

Wells prodded with his stick. "Surely you can see," Miss Willie went on, "you can see how it is. Nothing will ever be different on this ridge. Folks will always go right on doing things the same old way. They don't want to do any different. They're your folks, Wells, but they're not mine, and I've got to say it. They live so poorly, and they're content that way. Most of them are dirty, uncouth, don't-care people. They live and they die without even the common decencies of life. Patched-up old houses, patched-up old barns, patched-up old fields! Flies, dirt, disease! Water from springs and old wells! Never a balanced meal in the whole of their lives! And you can't get them to do any different! You could bear all of it, if they'd just try! But you can't even get them to eat wholesome food if they had it! They wouldn't like! And here on this horrible ridge, if folks don't like, that's all the excuse they need not to do a thing!"

Miss Willie's hands trembled, and the quiver ran on down into her knees. Her voice was shaking too. "I'm going home! That's all. I shouldn't have come. But I had to learn the hard way that there are some kinds of people you can't help at all! I thought all people could be helped. I came to help! But not ridge folks! You can't help ridge folks! They won't let you! So I'm going home. Back where I belong. Back where if a man is crazy something is done about it, and he isn't left free to kill his wife! Back where people have the doctor with a sick child! Back where there is decency and cleanliness and comfort in living. Back where you can

254

hear beautiful music, and not this everlasting whang-whang of hillbilly quartets and guitars! Back where there is some graciousness to life . . . some culture . . . some . . . some . . ."

Suddenly Rufe was with them, coming around the end of the log, his hand on the dog's head. He stepped over his father's feet and came straight up to Miss Willie, his head flung back and his eyes blazing, his face set and hard. He came so near that involuntarily Miss Willie stepped back. And then he stopped and his chin jutted forward. "Back where they's some easy livin', ain't that what you mean, Miss Willie?" he said, and his young voice was brittle and thin with contempt. "Back where you won't have nothin' hard, like we do on the ridge. Back where you flip a thing on the wall an' yer lights come on. Back where you turn a faucet an' the water runs out. Where yer bed is soft an' springy an' they's rugs under yer feet. Where you turn a little gadget an' yer fire's lit. No coal oil lamps, no drawin' water, no bare floors, an' no choppin' kindlin' ever' night. Back where things is easy an' soft, an' they's nothin' to turn yer stummick, like Lutie Jasper alayin' in her own blood!"

A sudden wind blew down off the hills, cold and chill. It caught Miss Willie's shoulders and ran down her spine and set her to shaking and shivering. She hunched against it and set her teeth to keep them from chattering. Her mouth was trembling and she covered it with a hand.

Wells jumped at the boy, laying rough hands on his shoulders "Rufe!" he thundered, "yer fergittin' yerself!"

The boy broke loose and hit out at the man with his free hand. "No, I ain't!" he said, "I ain't fergittin' myself! Hit's her that's fergot herself!"

"Let him alone, Wells," Miss Willie said between her teeth. "Let him say what he's got to say."

The wind ruffled the boy's hair as he squared away before Miss Willie again. "Don't they never have no murders back in Texas?" he asked. "Don't they? Don't they never have pore people that's dirty an' ignorant an' hungry? I reckon ever'thing's clean an' sweet an' pure-like back in Texas! I reckon they ain't no dirt nor craziness nor moonshinin', like they is here on the ridge! Nor no flies nor no dishwater throwed out the back door nor no window-

255

panes out!" He pointed his finger at her to emphasize his words. "You know they is. You know good an' well they is! They's meanness an' dirtiness an' poreness an' craziness ever'wheres! You've jist shet yer eyes to it all yer life! You've lived nice an' easy an' never looked at the nastiness! Hit was there, though, all the time. Only thing is, up here on the ridge you cain't shet yer eyes. You got to look at it. Hit's there, an' hit's right in front of you. You cain't turn away. Hit's too clost to you. Hit's yer own folks, likely! But you don't like the sight of it, do you? You want things clean, an' easy, an' nice! You don't want none o' the mess of livin', do you?"

The words fell like hard little pellets on Miss Willie's ears. She closed her eyes, but the brittle young voice kept on and on. Make him stop, she prayed, make him stop!

"You come up here on the ridge like you was God hisself, tellin' ever'body do this an' do that! Handin' out what you knowed so high an' mighty! Like nobody but you ever knowed e'er thing in the world! Nosin' around into ever'body's kitchen, squawkin' over dishwater an' flies an' sich! Turnin' up yer nose at folks 'cause they wasn't as clean as you! Thinkin' you was better than folks! What did you think ridge folks was? Pigs? Ridge folks is folks jist like ever'body else. They got feelin's. They got rights. They got a right to live their own way! An' as fer you thinkin' you could he'p 'em! How could you he'p 'em? What have you got to he'p 'em with? They need he'p, same as all folks does. Ain't nobody kin git along 'thout he'p, times. But they ain't no way you kin he'p 'em none. You was right about that! They git along together here, an' they he'p one another. That's their way of doin', an' they don't need none of yore puttin' in, neither!"

The boy was sobbing now, his anger running out into tears, and he hiccuped between words. His shoulders shook, and even in this moment of despair Miss Willie felt a deep tenderness for him, and wanted to lay her arms about him and comfort him. His hurt was so deep.

"I reckon Pa'll whup me when he gits me home fer talkin' like this," he went on, and the words came wildly, "but even my pa, even my own pa you think yer better than! You won't marry him 'cause he don't talk right, an' he wears overalls, an' he plays a gittar! But he's a heap sight better'n you are! I kin tell you that right now. He's good, an' he never hurt nobody in his life, an' he don't think he's better'n other folks. But you wouldn't think none of that! He's ridge folks, an' ridge folks is jist mud under yore feet! Well, all I got to say is, Go on back to Texas! Go on back! Go back where you belong, an' leave us alone!"

He flung himself around and ran toward the woods. Miss Willie saw him swiping his eyes on his coat sleeve as he ran. The dog was close on his heels. "My son! My son!" her heart cried, and the salt of her tears was bitter on her mouth.

Wells stood beside her, too stunned to speak or to move. Miss Willie touched him gently. "Go with him, Wells," she said softly, "go with him. And don't scold him."

Wells hesitated.

"I'll be all right," she promised. "Go with Rufe, and stay with him tonight. Stay close to him, so he'll know you're there."

When they had gone, Miss Willie started walking again. She took little note of where she was going, following the creek aimlessly. She did not feel the wind or notice the cold. Hands deep in her pockets, head bent, she plowed up the hollow. The sun struck warm against her face, and without thinking she turned toward it. There was no peace for her until this thing was settled within her. The boy's words had been like a sword piercing her heart. They had knifed deep and drawn blood. But they had forced her to her knees. Humbly now she sought the truth. With relentless honesty she compelled her mind to look upon herself and to face reality. She must search herself, discover her motives, find her utmost integrity and courage. She must learn, now, what manner of person was Miss Willie Payne.

You want an easy way of living, the young voice had accused. You want things soft and nice. You don't want it hard. That's not fair, Rufe. And it's not entirely true. I haven't had it too easy this year. And I haven't missed the easy ways of life outside too much. I've built my own fires and done my own washing, and carried water from the spring. And I haven't minded too much. It's only human to want life to be as gentle as possible. I'd like the comforts, but that's not what I've missed the most, nor minded doing without.

But you don't want none of the mess of living, he had said. And she winced from that. No. No, I didn't want it, she admitted. The ugliness, the dirt, the disease, the ignorance . . . the mess! I drew my skirts aside from that, she confessed. I didn't want to touch it. I didn't want any part of it. I didn't want to look on it. Back in Texas? You were right, Rufe. It's there too. But it was over on the other side of the tracks from me, and I never went over there! I didn't have to look at it. "But here on the ridge," the young voice had said relentlessly, "here on the ridge you've got to look at it. It's too close to you! It's your own folks, likely." Your own folks! But she had told Wells, "They're not mine!" She had denied them!

"Come up here like you were God himself, telling folks to do this and to do that!" But she hadn't meant to! She had only wanted to help! Surely it was right, when you had superior knowledge and experience — ah, there it was! Superior! Omnipotent! Like God himself. The only knowing one! Hadn't she, even in her most gracious moments of sharing her knowledge, felt superior? Hadn't she always in her heart felt herself better than these people? Hadn't she always patronized them?

Remembering her first days on the ridge and her missionary zeal, she took her thoughts down another trail. Were all zealots, then — all those who, convinced of their own rightfulness and eager to convert — were they all guilty of the same patronizing? Could you honestly set out to help people without believing yourself better than they? Didn't you first have to believe in yourself and in the righteousness of your convictions? And believing thus, didn't you then set out to convert people to your way of thinking? Your way of doing things? Your way of life? Didn't you set out to convince them that *you* knew better than *they* what was good for them? You, from your heights would reach down and help them up from the lower levels!

She had come to the ridge thinking: These poor people! They need help so badly. They need me, Miss Willie Payne, so badly. She had been horrified and shocked at conditions, and she had gone about preaching and lecturing. She had known the right way to do all things, and she had never hesitated to say so. She had pitied these people and patronized them. And what people of pride ever wanted pity or patronage!

But she had tried so earnestly to help them! She *had* tried. The wrong way, maybe. But she had tried everything! Everything? Now her heart told her. Everything . . . but love! She remembered crying out to Mary: "Where can you start? Where can you start?" You start with the people . . . and you start with love for the people! "The gift without the giver is bare"! And she had never given herself! Her time, her energy, her knowledge. But not herself! She winced from that thought, but she faced it in all its bitter gall. She had never loved them! Not even when she had fought so hard for Sylvie Clark? She pleaded for that time. Not even then? Relentlessly her mind closed down the hope. Not even then. She had fought so bitterly because she had been at fault. She had failed, and she would not let her failure be absolute. She had had to be certain that Miss Willie Payne did not pay the ultimate price for her failure.

Love was the way. And lovelessness had been her greatest sin. Out of a dim, long memory Miss Willie remembered a text of her father's. "Take my yoke . . . and I will make it easy." The words came back to her now, and repeated themselves over and over. "Take my yoke." "Take my yoke." That most perfect One had lived "together" with the people. What did He mean by His yoke? "Take my yoke . . . and I will make it easy." Could He have meant — was it possible His yoke had been living and working with people who never understood Him? Common, ordinary, ignorant people, who wouldn't listen and who wouldn't change? People who didn't want anything better than they had? People who were dirty, diseased, and foul sometimes, and who were clean and noble and fine other times? People who loved and hated, fought and made peace, witnessed against their neighbors and then stood by them? Could He have meant living with them and loving them just as they were, unchanged and unchanging?

Like the eastern sun flooding the sky with light, Miss Willie understood in a flashing, transfiguring moment what it meant. It meant to live *together* . . . under the yoke, together! Not one standing above, reaching down to pull the others up! Not one

259

saying, "I must help these people"! It meant, instead, the banding and linking of people, one to another, in love and pity and yearning. It meant saying, "*My* people"; not, "*These* people." It meant getting under the yoke alongside of people, one with them, pulling the load with them. Not standing aside telling them how to pull! It meant grieving with them, and sorrowing with them, and laboring with them, and laughing with them, and, most of all, it meant loving with them. "Take my yoke"! *He* had been yoked with the people. He had meant, then, live with them where they are. Love them as they are. Take the yoke, and lift it. All lift together!

This was so precious a thought that Miss Willie clung to it tightly, treading softly, lest it vanish before she had made it completely hers. It was so fragile. So perfect. So true. "Take my yoke." Take the yoke of the ridge. Get down where the people lived. Live there with them. Don't reach down. Get down yourself. Then lift up! Ah, there was the pearl at the heart of the thing! But could she do it?

As if meeting a challenge, her step quickened. She could try. She could try, and the way was clear! Over there at Wells's house there was a man, lonely and heartsick, who needed a wife. There was a girl, beset with trouble, who needed a friend. There was a boy, rebellious and frustrated, who needed a mother. Wife, friend, mother. It mattered not what you named it. All of them needed love. Not Miss Willie Payne. They could get along without her. But they would die for lack of love. And *she* would die for lack of love. She needed them! Husband, friend, son. Desperately she needed them!

She saw with surprise that it was dusky dark, and when she lifted her eyes, the first stars were stabbing the cobalt sky. She turned and quickly started home. She would be late and Mary would be worried. She felt as if wings had been added to her feet, so lightly and so swiftly did they go. This warm glow won't last always, she warned herself, chuckling. You know yourself too well for that. You'll be taking on a mighty big job, and there'll be hard days in store. You'll get frashed with Wells, you know you will! Times he gets to sitting there in front of the fire like a bump on a log, you'll feel like bashing him over the head with something just to make him stir! And Rose is lazy and shiftless, and there'll be the new baby soon. At your age that baby will set you screaming sometimes. And there's Rufe. You're starting out with him set against you! You're walking right into a hornet's nest with him! It would be a lot easier to go on back to Texas and finish out your life quietly and peacefully — you know it would!

She grinned in the dark wryly. Ideals are fine . . . fine and fancy. Take my yoke! But it was going to drag mighty heavy sometimes, just the same. Go back to Texas and dry up like a piece of withered moss! Go back to Texas! Not in a hundred years!

CHAPTER
❧ 27 ❧

THEY WERE MARRIED ALMOST IMMEDIATELY, in Mary's big living room, standing before the fireplace. Wells was still bewildered by Miss Willie's sudden decision. He told Hod over and over again that day: "I jist cain't believe it! Hit don't jist seem true!" But his face wrinkled into beaming smiles as the people began to come, and he pumped the men's hands and seated the ladies joyfully.

Miss Willie had said at first: "Just a quiet wedding, Wells. Just home folks."

Wells had laughed until his shoulders shook. "That'll be ever'-body on the ridge, then, won't it, Hod? They ain't nobody but home folks lives around here."

And Miss Willie, knowing it was so, and further knowing how disappointed Wells would be, gave in. So the folks from all about, the hills and the hollows, came to see them married. Becky and Gault and small Hannah. Hattie and Tom and Sarah. Irma and John and little Sue. The Simpsons, the Clarks, the Sandersons, the Joneses. From all over they came. Rose was there, dispirited, big, untidy. Rufe was not.

This would have troubled Miss Willie once. But the time was past for that. She had thought she must win the boy to her before she even considered marrying his father. Now, all thought of winning him to her was gone. She was only concerned with giving him something he had long been needing. A home, and a mother,

261

and love. Whether he knew it or not, that's what he had been seeking . . . in those long hours in the woods, in those bitter quarrels with her, in the deep hurt of his anger. He might never be won to her. She had to take that chance. But, however Rufe felt toward her, he could not help taking in some of the good that would come out of a clean home, good meals, loving-kindness, and the happiness she hoped would prevail.

The folks crowded into Mary's living room and sat or stood during the simple ceremony. Miss Willie, in a soft green wool dress, greeted them all and then went to stand beside Wells and give herself over to his keeping. She felt a solemn sense of dedication then. A new kind of dedication, and when she heard Wells's deep voice in the first response she felt a thrill of pride. This man, with his big human heart, with his work-roughened hands, with his friendly, kindly smile, loved her. And she loved him. That was all the dedication any woman needed. To love!

And then it was her own time to answer and she found her voice coming out strong and true. She felt no fear trembling through her. No sense of strangeness. Instead, there was only an infinite peacefulness, as if she had been waiting all her life for this moment.

After the ceremony there was much merrymaking. It was a noon wedding, and Mary and Miss Willie and Hattie and Becky had worked long and hard over the food. It was no delicate wedding breakfast that they served. It was ham and chicken and beans and salads and pies and cakes! It was a big meal for a lot of people! And it was Wells's hearty voice that yelled, "Come an' git it!"

The table was long, and they crowded around it, and there was music and laughter and singing and the inevitable friendly, teasing jokes. Wells was in his element, at the center of his friends and kinfolks, dispensing hospitality, proud of Miss Willie, and proud of his place beside her. She had dreaded this part of the day, but she found that after all it had a folksy, homey feeling that drew her into its heart. She wasn't just Miss Willie now. She was Pierce kinfolks!

When it was over, and the last good-by said, she and Wells crawled into his old wagon, he clucked at the mules, and they

262

went away from Mary's home to Miss Willie's new one. Both she and Wells thought a wedding trip would be silly. There was too much to be done at home. And besides they couldn't leave Rose at such a time.

Miracles didn't start happening when Miss Willie married Wells Pierce. That winter was just as hard as she had thought it would be. At times it was even harder. But at the bedrock of Miss Willie's nature was a fund of good common sense, and while she felt she had a new and sweeter understanding of her role here on the ridge, she didn't let it make her abandon habits she felt were of intrinsic worth. She was prepared to make adjustments in this new relationship she was entering, but she did not once make the mistake of believing she must make them all. If she had a new humility along with her new understanding, she did not allow it to become Uriah Heepish. Instead, she made it a proud humility which expected the family to do their own part along with her. She knew herself too well to suppose that she could give over the habits of a lifetime of cleanliness, orderliness, neatness, and she did not feel it incumbent upon her to do so. She felt that love could include those things, and should.

So she set about making the old house clean and comfortable. It was a big job. Wells painted the outside, with Rufe's sullen help, and they tidied up the yards and mended the fences. Inside, Miss Willie scrubbed and scoured. She and Wells ripped off all the old wallpaper, and between them they made a fair job of putting on new. Wells leveled the sagging floors and Miss Willie painted them and waxed them, and then she strowed dozens of Becky's braided rugs around the rooms. New panes were put in the windows, and they were washed to a state of gleaming spotlessness. Then fresh curtains were hung in every room.

Miss Willie sold her Texas home and had her furniture shipped to the ridge. When it came, she distributed it around the roomy old house, and when she finished, she found she had a lovely, gracious home. It was a farm home, geared to the comfort and convenience of a farm life, but that did not detract from its beauty or its graciousness.

263

Wells and the children had not used but three rooms of the ten that rambled sprawling everywhere. But Miss Willie took them over and made them all habitable. She gave Rose a room for herself and the baby, and she delighted Abby's little-girl soul with a small room done in candy-pink-and-white sweetness. She also told Rufe to choose a room for himself. He was startled at the thought of a room of his own, and at first paid no attention to the suggestion. Miss Willie let it ride a few days and then, firmly, she said to him: "Rufe, you are going to have a room of your own, whether you select it or not. It would be better if you choose the one you want, and fix it up to suit yourself."

"You mean I kin fix it up any way I like?"

"Of course."

Then he became enthusiastic about it, and Wells took him to town to choose his own curtains, rugs, and furniture. He used remarkably good sense in arranging his room too. He wanted one of the narrow bunk beds, and an Indian rug on the floor. He built shelves all around the walls, and put his collection of rocks, shells, and arrowheads on them. He made a rack for his gun, and he even brought in one day a huge, dry hornet's nest. "Reckon you wouldn't let me have this in my room, would you?" he asked Miss Willie.

"Has it any hornets in it?"

"Naw. Cain't you tell it's dry?"

Miss Willie had laughed. "I don't know much about things like that, Rufe. But if it's safe, why, of course you can have it in your room."

Miss Willie didn't consciously assume any policy in working with Rufe. She was much too busy. She simply included him in all the plans that were made, in all the work that was done, in all the fun that was had. He was aloof and sullen sometimes, but she paid no attention to those moods, going right on, instead, including him. She made no issue of discipline with him. She implied that he would want to do whatever she asked of him. He didn't always, of course. But at least there was no open rebellion.

At first he was suspicious of her. Resentful. She had expected that and she ignored it. But when he saw that she didn't tattle to Wells, that she wasn't constantly heckling him, he relaxed a little. Grudgingly, and then more willingly, he let down in the home. Miss Willie had put all her faith into the belief that what Rufe needed was the order, the discipline, the security of love, and she was right. In spite of himself he reacted to it. He wouldn't have admitted it, but he liked the clean, shining house, the regular, well-cooked meals, the feeling of something to be done each day, the bustling energy Miss Willie brought to the whole family. He didn't mean to, but he soaked it up and it softened him.

Miss Willie never made any deliberate approaches to him. He was the son of the house — the dear son, she never failed to let him know — and as such he had his own rights and privileges. She never stepped over the door into his room, and if he stayed in it a great deal, she never asked him why. Neither did she question him about his wanderings in the woods. Nor were they curtailed, except as he was needed about the place.

One day he brought home three squirrels, killed and neatly dressed. "I thought mebbe these'd be good fer breakfast," he said, offering them.

Miss Willie didn't like small, killed things. But she suspected this was the first of Rufe's sharing with her. "They sure will," she said, taking them and salting them down until morning.

He frequently brought home small game after that. Thus he brought what had belonged to him in solitude into the home which was slowly enfolding him.

At Christmas Miss Willie asked him to find a tree for them. "Aw, what you want a tree fer?" he had asked sulkily. "We ain't never had none before."

"We're going to have one this year," she had replied firmly. "Will you get it for us, or shall I have your father get it?"

"I'll get it," and he had put on his cap and coat and gone out. He may have gone unwillingly, but she noticed it was a beautiful, full, green tree, perfectly rounded. And he had set it up, straight and level. He hadn't taken any part in decorating it, but he got up Christmas morning and came down for the opening of the presents. And when he saw the new gun for him, his eyes had glowed.

And he loved Rose's baby. The baby had come just ten days

after Wells and Miss Willie were married. A beautiful girl child, looking so much like Tay that Rose had wept bitterly upon seeing it. But when the child was actually form and flesh, and she could hold it in her arms, Rose had lost her careless unconcern for it, and had cuddled and held it tenderly. She called the baby Taysie.

Rufe would spend long hours with her, caring for her so that Rose might be free to help Miss Willie. And when Miss Willie passed through the room and saw the young face, washed so clean by his love for the baby, so tender and so raptly attentive, she knew that Rufe, even without his knowledge, was safe among them.

Yes, it was a hard winter, and a long one. There were times when Miss Willie went to bed so tired that every bone in her body ached, every muscle was sore, every nerve quivering. Times when the baby was so tiny and colicky and got them all up in the night when she wanted to cry in frustration. Times when Wells's mood didn't match her own, and she wondered if two people so completely different in temperament could ever make a good marriage. Times when Rufe's sullenness hacked away at her and she wanted to take him by the shoulders and shake him hard. Times when Rose's shiftlessness made her want to take the broom and sweep everything that belonged to the girl outside. Sometimes she flared up and the whole family skittered before her temper. But nearly always she controlled it, or got outside and walked or worked it off.

Little by little they settled into a family, with a routine of chores and work to be done in common. Cows to be milked, meals to be cooked, dishes to be washed, the baby to be bathed and tended, the house to be kept clean, stock to be cared for, the tobacco bed to be burned, fences to mend, a new barn to build. They had a community of interests and each had his part in them. It can never be true that people who live together don't have anything in common, Miss Willie thought. They have *everything* in common!

Neither did miracles begin to happen in Miss Willie's relationships with the people of the ridge. Mamie Clark went right on straining her milk with the flies swarming around her. Quilla Simpson nursed her ulcers in contempt of the doctors, and Corinna Jones kept on adding a new baby to her household each year. But Miss Willie found that when she quit trying so hard, when she quit preaching and lecturing, when she quit being so critical, she could find much that was good in each of them. Mamie, for all her slovenliness and do-lessness, was a loyal and good neighbor. She came when the baby was born, and she took over the chores and the hardest work. Not until Rose was up and about again did she stop coming every day. There was something worthy and good in each of them, and Miss Willie began to feel an encircling bond stretched around her. No one had to bear his burdens alone here on the ridge. There was a grieving, suffering, helping hand extended in time of sorrow. A glad, rejoicing, sharing hand in time of joy. She began to know intimately what it meant to live "together."

Miss Willie found she could let her neighbors alone, but there were some things about which she remained adamant. The school and the improvements were one. When she and Wells were married, she had not gone back to the schoolroom. On the ridge a wife and mother had no time to work out, even if a husband were willing, and few were. A woman's place was in the home. As a matter of fact, life revolved around her and a home was helpless without her. But Miss Willie went, as sternly and defiantly as ever, before the trustees and demanded new outhouses and better roads and a school bus. There was this difference. She was no longer Miss Willie, the teacher. She was Miss Willie, Wells Pierce's woman, with children of her own in the school. She said *our* children, now. She was one of them, and could lift up with them.

Partly because of the typhoid scare, but mostly because they would listen to one of their own, a few things were done, and Miss Willie had faith that in time the rest would be done. It made a big difference, being Wells Pierce's woman!

So the winter passed and another spring came around and Miss Willie sat in the back yard under the apple tree, sweet with

267

blossom. The day was washed with warmth, and the sun laid a golden bar across the baby's head. She lay stretched across Miss Willie's lap, reaching for the shadowy leaves swinging overhead. Miss Willie hitched her chair a little farther in the shade. The baby grabbed her finger and held it tight. Miss Willie laughed at her and shifted her to her shoulder. Wells would soon be coming in from the field, and it was time to be starting supper. But she lingered yet a while in the April evening.

Rose came to the door and called, "You want I should lay the the supper fire?"

Miss Willie called back, "If you will, please, Rose."

Rufe and his dog came around the corner of the house and dropped onto the grass nearby.

"Come take the baby, Rufe," Miss Willie said. "I must cook supper."

He settled the baby on his arm and she turned toward the house. From the nearby beech grove came suddenly the high, sweet, soaring song of an early thrush. Like a golden stream, its liquid purity drenched the apple-blossomed air, the fragrance and the sound blending to a breathlessly perfect whole, becoming inseparable in an unbearably fragile and sweet moment. Miss Willie stopped, and her hand went to her throat which ached with bird song. "Listen, Rufe," she said softly. "Listen! The first thrush!"

The boy's head had been tilted toward the bird. At her words his face turned slowly toward Miss Willie. There was an unbelieving look on it, and then it was swept by such joy and gladness that it blazed with glory! "Miss Willie!" he said, and the tawny, golden head of Taranto stood before her again. "Miss Willie! Kin you hear the birds sing too?"